THE
LONG
FORM

Library of Congress Control Number: 2022952246
ISBN paper: 978-1-948980-21-0
ISBN ebook: 978-1-948980-22-7

Art on cover by Orra White Hitchcock
Strata near Valenciennes, France, 1828–1840
22 x 69 cm., Pen and ink on linen
Archives & Special Collections at Amherst College

The publisher wishes to thank Ally Findley and Stephen Mortland.

Design and composition by Danielle Dutton
Printed on permanent, durable, acid-free recycled paper in the United States of America

Dorothy, a publishing project books are distributed to the trade by New York Review Books

Dorothy, a publishing project | St. Louis, MO
DOROTHYPROJECT.COM

THE
LONG
FORM

Kate
Briggs

Dorothy, a publishing project

"My problem: how to pass . . . from a short, fragmented form ('notes')
to a long, continuous form (typically called 'the novel')."
—Roland Barthes, 1978, tr. Kate Briggs (2011; 2023)

"To be sure, prosaic creativity generally proceeds slowly, begins in narrow spheres, and is hardly noticeable. For that reason we do not see it,
and think that innovation must come from somewhere else."
—Gary Saul Morson & Caryl Emerson, *Mikhail Bakhtin: Creation of a
Prosaics* (1990)

CONTENTS

FIRST THING

GUESSING AND MOVEMENT IN THE LIVING ROOM

The beginning of each new project was always a continuation. For the time being, it was the basic but not obvious project of sleep.

A co-project: involving Helen and her baby, starting out from where they were first thing in the morning, carrying forward the experience of their long and wakeful, interactive night.

Helen: tall in proportion to the room, her hair hanging heavily, heating her neck.

The baby: wide-open, shifting and lively in her arms.

Spread out over the floor was a playmat: a thick square divided into four distinct sections.

Its colours were a bit faded. From the sun, from the heavy rounds it must have done in someone else's washing machine. Its spaces looked touched, well-mouthed; its closer textures more or less exhaustively pre-explored.

Even so, like the light show enclosed in a moulded plastic star, the all-in-ones they'd received handed-down, along with the mat, in a large-format bag-for-life, to Helen and the baby, it was all new.

Weirdly, relentlessly, startlingly new.

Underfoot, the mat made the thin carpet soft.

Already, it changed the whole inhabitation of the room.

SLEEP

One of the mat's zones looked agricultural: satin crops of different shades of green furrowed with dark-brown artificial fur.

Helen wanted to rest her head in that patched field. She was tired.

We could sleep there, she thought.

She looked down. The baby's head was a weighted sphere, warm and solid in the crook of her arm, the rest of her fidgety and light.

The baby lifted her chin, gazed back up.

Helen loosened the idea from her own head and offered it out: smiling and nodding with it. Floating it, like a proposition, to the baby.

She let the baby's gaze range, intently, around the edges of her face.

Then, on second thoughts, tugged her idea back in: actually, *I* decide.

She looked up, away, and restated this firmly to herself: I decide.

And *I* say we lie there and go to sleep.

The task of kneeling without support: squatting, then kneeling. It was a bit unsteady, ungainly, doing this, with a baby in her arms.

Carefully, she set the baby down in the field portion of the mat.

The baby arched her back, kicked her heels, sensitive to the change of surface: this sudden flatness underneath her; the way it seemed to give in.

Helen lay herself down, too, stretching out her frame to its full extent, then turning towards her, drawing in close.

The smells of the field mixed with the deep and different body-smells of the baby.

The field smelled like lemons.

Like something else: a chemical note.

It was yielding, comfortable: a duvet, almost. But ridged and bumped here and there with plastic parts and scratchy parts, on the floor.

She nudged her nose against the baby's shoulder. She pulled her knees all the way up until they touched the small heels of the baby's feet, making her body into a protective container wall.

The baby twisted her hands, twitched her legs. She opened and closed her mouth. Something above her, at an angle, caught – it captivated – her attention.

Helen lay her head on her elbow, exhaled. Her breath blew a warm breeze across the baby's face.

She changed her mind, shifted: rested her cheek in the cupped palm of her left hand.

She whispered sleep well to the baby and closed her eyes.

Slowly, one by one, she gave her limbs permission to relax.

Then, in the next moment, she was back up to standing again, her head bopping the rim of the ceiling lamp, setting it swinging, releasing a great puff of dust into the air, the baby high in her arms, because for her part the baby – feeling too loose, too unbounded and far too infinite on the mat – preferred to be held.

In one holding position and then another.

Always with a slight bounce to the hold.

THE EARLY MORNING

The night they'd had.

The playmat.

Their pressing project.

It would all have to be reconsidered.

HELEN STARTED AGAIN

The mat was a big square.

Spread out over the floor, it made a path around itself. A narrow walkway of carpet tracking the edges of the small front room.

It was a garden. Say it was a garden.

A squashy formal garden to be turned around, not napped in, or trodded over.

Within the square, zones: the field scaled down to a patchy bit of lawn. The bed to one side of it grew fabric flowers. Glinting among them: the small rounds of scratched, card-backed mirrors.

Helen was tired. It had felt good to curl up on the floor. Now she decided – new decisions displacing recent decisions, her ever-adjustable resolutions – that around-about it, indirectly, she would walk, sway, hold.

Motion the baby to sleep.

The third section of the mat grew lift-the-flaps, zig zags, and other dotty patterns.

Its fourth, plainest-looking bed grew sounds (deep pockets of un-expected underground sound).

INDOOR WALKING

A slow start. In recent weeks, she'd learned that there was no point in hurrying this.

So let there be no hurry.

Moving at a regular, bouncing pace. Lifting one bare foot on the rising beat. Setting it down on the falling beat as the other began to lift. Marking one time-gap, another time-gap. These timeworn measures – they spoke of rhythm, body-balance and complicated coordination. The path was made from ridged, hard-wearing carpet. It hugged the wall all the short way to the window.

Already, a rest-stop.

Helen stopped here, shifting her own weight as a way of bouncing the baby, looking out at the street through a clear space above the mountains. (Overnight, condensation made a mountain-scape on the glass.)

Here was the teenager from a few doors down: head bowed, earphones in, mooching off to school. What time was it, exactly?

She looked down at the baby.

The baby was wide-awake.

Sleep time.

In the tree outside, offsetting the sounds of cars starting, she could hear insistently, irregularly: a bird singing.

For the moment, just one.

One solitary, hard-peeping bird.

ALTERNATING

Swapping out a run of high, light, tip-toed steps for a sequence of longer, flatter, heavier steps, she followed the path to the desk at an angle to the window. A cut of plywood resting on trestles. Helen had g-clamped the plastic end of a mobile to the far edge of it; positioning it in such a way so that it could reach out, arc, and suspend its open structure over the baby's chair – which, turning the corner presented by the mat, was now directly in their path.

She stepped over it.

It was two, three paces to the hard arm of the sofa.

Then round the corner, along the sofa's edge, past the big plant and it was out – out of the volume of the living room and into the narrower, darker shadows of the hall.

Stop here again, and rest.

It was very short: their one turn about the mat, the duration of their indoor walk. Helen stood in the hallway, her mouth open against the baby's hard head, breathing in her fine dark hair, taking this on board.

Then it was back on the path to the window.

Hello street.

Still parked cars; powerful peeping bird.

Streetlight and tall, new-leafed tree.

On the desk was a lamp, its matted vegetable base and big paper shade. Above it: some bookshelves. Helen adjusted her hold, hitching the baby a bit higher up, cupping the back of her head with the hollow

of her hand. The lamp: together they peered down into it, checking in from above on the blue-grey bulb. Was it lonely?

Yes? No?

What a question. We don't know.

One of the books on the shelf had been turned outwards. Propped in this way deliberately, to make its cover face the room. Black against white, cut out and high-contrast: stimulating for the baby. Helen really liked it. It was a picture of a man lying on the ground: his wide back, his knees bent, the weight of his large upper body resting on his elbow. The creases in his clothes picked out in white, showing where his limbs folded. From the slope of his shoulders, the size of his ears, it was clear that he was not a young man.

He was studying.

There was foliage sprouting to one side of him: the branches of a shrub with prickly, sharp-pointed leaves. There was no grass depicted but, as Helen saw it, he was clearly studying something: a flower, or a creature. She imagined a snail feeling its way forwards, stickily, in the grass.

A loose time-scene: it spoke of calm and concentration.

Perched – one on his bald head, the other on his bended knee, their wings open to flap but seeming not to disturb his involvement, more participating in it, almost contributing to it – were two ducks.

Or were they hens?

Helen shifted the baby downwards into a chest-to-chest position.

Moorhens?

The baby bumped her brow, gently, against Helen's collar bone.

One moorhen and a woodcut – a linocut? – duck.

Onwards.

CHEST-TO-CHEST

This is a good position, she'd read: the baby can't see your face but she can hear your heart.

    Their walk had a slow tempo.

    It was a measured project, an even-sided square.

But every now and then it could quicken: high-stepping over the bouncy chair and jigging past the sofa.

Pausing again, resting to look anew at the big plant: its will-to-reach sideways, outwards, upwards, at strange, unexpected angles; noting how the dust was thickening on its split leaves, wondering whether this might be keeping it from breathing, in its plant-like way – and then it was out, crossing the threshold of the living room to re-join the shadows, the things on hooks, big coat, bright fluorescent hat, tightly wrapped umbrella, and bashed trainers of the dim narrow hall.

LIKE THIS

Helen walking a baby; her baby.

Telling herself that she was showing her things, introducing her to the world in this early domestic configuration; in these small, small doses.

Distributing emphasis and attention. Feeling tired and hopeful. That she would succeed in wearing the baby out with the different aspects of their shared living room.

The mat, a central sound-, colour-, pattern- and texture-garden, not to be trodden on.

The lamp and the desk and, attached to it, reaching out and away from it: the mobile. Its shapes dancing lightly in low open space.

The window.

Look at the mountains on the room-side of the glass.

Beyond them the tree, the cars, the houses and flats immediately across the street; all elements of the further-world, the immense more-of-the-world outside.

The baby gazing widely, loosely: getting drawn outward and feeling moved by a shift in her visual field; being intermittently faced with the closeness of Helen's big jumper: a sudden darkening; a louder heartbeat, too close, itchy and a bit too hot.

Tolerating this alternation, more or less.

AT THE SAME TIME

Helen walking herself. Helen showing herself things.

Helen introducing herself as if for the first time to the details of the room as way of seeing through this project: her own logic, enthusiasm; her private rationale and sense of broader purpose to doing what, if it were not for the baby, she'd have no cause to be doing.

Getting into this on a Tuesday morning, the start of an ordinary working day.

Walking around and around a playmat for the sake of getting someone else to sleep, also for the sake and the prospect of her own stretch of rest. This being the calmest indoor-way she could come up with, in the moment, of getting them both there.

It was a co-project, a complex interaction where, on both sides, the *it's all for you* – this sense of an action so clearly being undertaken for the priority-sake of *you* – was being ever-offset, resisted or supported by the counter-force of a *me*.

Not only you. But, in this case, Helen. Bringing her own style to it: the pace of her own needs, longings, interests, and imaginings.

Another square round.

The mat garden. Stuffed green around the edges: a hedge to contain its mix of pattern and colour.

Don't step on it.

Helen taking care not to step on it.

These superstitions, unlikely sorts of bargains she'd started to strike. Making regular deals with the universe, all the biggest forces: keeping to the path. I'll keep to the path, she said, privately. But in return: (please) let the baby sleep a good, long sleep.

ARTICLES

Testing the possibilities:

"A" baby: sounding non-specific, inaccurate when there was this evident weight and present, moving energy – this world-gazer, taking it all in gravely, with gravity – reaching in her arms.

"Her" baby spoke of attachment, beholden-ness, and protection. All orders of relation that Helen wanted and felt. But also of ownership, and something like command. Like a command of the situation, as if she'd had a chance to assess the nature of this new person, her character, her scope – and could claim to have some measure of who they were to each other, as well as a measure of herself.

"The" baby said: this person here, in her vulnerability, in her emergence – and not anyone else. It said "the only baby" in this setting, like "the only sofa in the living room," or "this particular tree." Of all the possible newcomers, of all the local species, *this one* growing outdoors, within sight of the window – what was it?

The kind that stretches its bark, breaking it into patches. Mottled black, brown, white and grey. Helen waited for the name, which surfaced and sank, to rise up and present itself again: a sycamore tree.

WALKING ON AND AROUND

The plant with its rangy shapes, its thicker stems supported by canes (long ago, Helen had tied them in with odd bits of string).

The small, skirted sofa.

On the trestle desk, a laptop and Helen's plugged in, lit up, charging phone.

The baby making muttering noises, starting to twist inward, growing fretful and harder to hold. Helen aware that she was pushing it: stretching out a path and a process that could only ever go on for so long, sharing their greetings around the room.

What had they snubbed – failed to acknowledge?

Look! A postcard from Rebba, tacked to and making an abstraction in the wall.

Again, the concentrated scene.

Black and white: the striking pleasure of contrast. A cut-out posture, speaking of study and calm interest, set facing outward, to share its gentle mood with the room.

Helen was conscious of her left breast aching, now singing out its proximity to the baby's face.

The book was a course of lectures delivered by the philosopher John Dewey in the 1930s. On the cover, the AS EXPERIENCE parts of its title – Helen noticed this now – were printed in the same wet, new-growth green as the leaves on the tree outside and one of the satins in the mat.

They bounced past the sofa.

Hall, shadows. Shoes.
Energy dip.

The best thing, though, was the window.
Coming back to the window.
Close, residential street.

Hello glass.
Touch it – I know, I know. I'll touch it for you.
It's wet.
It's wet because it's colder outside.
All the cars that were going to leave will have left by now.
The mountains have changed shape. We can wipe them.

Hear how it's quiet. It's quieter now and already a bit later.

Take your time, our time, to listen to the bird.
The one bird, repeating itself.

Register the increase. Morning: how already the room feels a bit fuller with light.

Then off again and around. Taking direction from the squareness of the mat on the floor. Using its shape for their own purposes. The dust from the ceiling lamp travelling with them through the air, dispersing, having not yet decided where to settle in the room.

Until at last the moment came when their shared capacities for movement and interest were exhausted. Opened then tested to the limit of being fully exhausted and – judging it – Helen moved to sit down. Tentatively, she parsed the room for a landing site. There was

a good spot on the floor. Near the sofa, close to the baby's chair. To reach it she cut diagonally across the garden. She trod over the lawn and the fabric flowerbeds, crushing them both underfoot. Her big bare feet took light away from the mirrors. Sitting herself down, the baby in her arms, she rucked up one soft corner, flipping it over, making the separated zones clump and touch. It didn't matter. The mat could be a cloister garth for a while: a temporary imaginative structure to get organized by and move around.

Now it could collapse.

SOUNDING AND LANDING
IN THE LIVING ROOM

SLEEP

With her one free hand Helen lifted her jumper together with the thin layer of her t-shirt, made darker in patches from milk. She bunched both under her armpit, releasing one solid breast from her bra. The baby, who'd been fretting, grew frantic. She knew what this sweet smell was – she knew it forcefully. But Helen's heavy jumper and then her t-shirt fell over her face and she started to cry. For a few long, fraught moments, Helen, the baby, their clothing, fought and failed, manoeuvred and failed to attach themselves together, until, in exasperation, Helen stripped off her top layers and dumped them, damply, on the sofa behind her. Against warm skin, the baby at last achieved her strong, airtight connection. And so Helen started the countdown. Counting down quickly, internally, from *five*,

four,

three,

two

stalling at *two*.

Now

one –

the moment when her milk released.

She did this because it was a distraction from the pain that could still detonate in the depths of her breast at the beginning of each feed (rarely, but always unexpectedly, and for that reason hard to prepare

for): sending sharp stars coursing down the inner channel of her arm into the palm of her hand then back up to her breast and from there to her brain. Also, because it felt silly, and a bit childish: to *dock* the baby against herself as if she were the smaller of two space ships. Then, because childishness felt like an act of private resistance, a way of pushing back against the colossal size and pressure of a sudden recent thought: of all the available positions she might go on to occupy, dynamically, tentatively, in her lifetime, she would no longer be – that is, if anyone ever is, she, Helen, would no longer solely or straightforwardly be – the child.

She fed the baby. A channel opened. The baby fed from her.
Like this.
Like this.

The initial sharp and short, rapid tugs giving way to an easier, calmer feeding rhythm. The tension leaving their bodies. Helen could feel her hard left breast soften, the baby, her baby, loosen and relax.

With her legs stretched out across the recent garden, her torso and her head adrift in some notion of outer space, she fed the baby.
In silence and then with a low hum.

She felt her back tugging down at the fabric she'd bought to disguise the sofa. When the bright blue throw she'd bought from the market managed to cover the sofa completely, the living room, the narrow kitchen, the bedroom, the bathroom, the hall, all four rooms and interim spaces of the flat felt like hers – like theirs. When the fabric slipped, as it often did, partly because the sofa was made from something coated and slippery, not really like textile at all, partly because the piece was not quite large enough, exposing the loud pattern

beneath it – blocky with red and black, white and grey – she remembered all over again that it all belonged – not the lamp or the books or the mat, nor the baby's chair – but her own big bed, the cooker, washing machine, the fridge, the rooms and the base components of the new home-life she was inventing for them both – to the short and sturdy, clipped-haired, clipped-toned woman who lived upstairs.

She fed the baby – creating, then maintaining the conditions for the baby to feed from her.

Like this.

Humming in and out of pop tunes, bolshier club anthems, making the *oots oots oots* sound in the back of her throat of beats heard at a distance, through a tiled wall or swinging door. Catching herself doing this, wondering at it for a moment. Then starting again more purposively with a lullaby. Letting that lull through her for a while. Until it, too, changed, merging in and out of the chorus parts of long-forgotten school-assembly hymns.

She shifted position, crossed her legs.

The support for her back was the base of the sofa. She leaned into it, and let her chin rest in her neck. She swallowed. With her head bowed, she closed her eyes. Tiredness fell down. It made a sinkage in her corner of the carpet and into it, partially, she sank. She could sleep now. She could very easily just simply fall asleep.

But there was a small draft making the long hairs among the freckles on her arms stand on end. There was the weight and tug of the baby still feeding in her arms. Together they held something inside of her taut, keeping her awake.

She fed her baby until the baby's eyelids began to droop, the strength of the gum-seal weakened, and her mouth eventually disengaged.

—

Then sat for a bit longer, humming on. Dipping the baby now and then, in memory of the bounce. Looking, on occasion, up out of the window.

The street so quiet. Quieter than anywhere she'd ever lived.

It had rained in the night.

From where she was sitting, through the mist and blur of condensation, she could make out the bark mottling the middle portion of the tree.

She worked her way up to a kneeling position.

To the sprung chair: with the baby in her arms, she walked the tiny distance on her knees.

Spacing them out.

Her mind now intent on spacing the spaces between her hums and bounces out.

The baby sighed; a whisper of outbreath tickled her arm.

Leaning over the chair, the back of the baby's head throbbing in her palm, she lowered. Thinking, as she had thought pretty much every time she'd done or attempted this over the past few weeks: so *this* is what "gingerly" means.

Caution.

Cautiousness.

A set of performatively delicate steps: taking elaborate care not to hurt anyone, including oneself, not to disturb anyone, including oneself.

She lowered the baby ever-deeper through unresisting – wide-open – space.

And through time: through stretching and unchecked, open-ended time.

—

Still bouncing her but now in ever deeper and wider arcs, each one a little bit lower and deeper than the last.

Still humming, intermittently, to the tempo, the rest and dip, of the bounce.

The origin of this was prehistorical:

When the length of a day was so much shorter, the carpet under-foot foamed high, deep green then mulched dry and brown with broken forest ferns, she would have bounced like this – surely she would have hummed and bounced like this? Making a contact call, singing:

I'm here.

I'm still here.

The baby's breath synched in and out of time with the measures in the room: Helen's own slower breathing, her heartbeat, the slow turn of the mobile and, outside, the stop-start, discontinuous peeping of the one earnest bird.

I'm here.

The mat, which had been kicked away, made a colourful hump in the near distance.

She landed.

Landing the baby in the proxy hands of the hot-pink recliner chair.

The chair that she had tipped back into relax-position, into it's-okay, it's-alright, you-can-sleep-here position.

I'm still here.

She maintained contact. Staying for one further prolonged moment still in touch with the baby. Skin-to-skin. Skin-to-the brushed cotton of a newborn all-in-one suit. Her inclined body, her hands, slightly sweaty, all extending the share of heat.

She crouched like this, one further breath, one further beat, holding still, her body a curve over the baby's, taking shelter under the dancing cover of the mobile – its laminated canopy of bobbing and gapped black-and-white shapes.

Here I am.
   The baby was drifting.

And you know what?
   I'm here.

She was pulling. They both were. Pulling deeply and widely in opposite directions. Helen pulling herself away, delighted to rediscover her hands, her arms, eager for this stretch of temporary separation.

Here I am.

Helen sat back on her heels. She rolled her shoulders and began to twist a bit of elastic off her wrist.

I'm still here –
   Now that her hands were free, she would use it to put up her hair.

And you know what?
   In that moment: a doorbell.

WELL?

Well! (The exclamation a means of starting a new phrase. Marking a pause. Or expressing a range of emotions: surprise overtaken by reflexive anger; not yet resignation, something like the furious opposite of relief.)

At first it was just the shock of sudden noise. A short event of intervention. But then it rang again, very decisively, like a buzzer on a quiz show:
Someone knows the answer!

Who? Hold on:

To what?

The doorbell.

Someone was outside. Pressing to call her out. Or to bring something in.

The baby jerked. She seemed to be grasping at something: at presentness, at Helen, at return.

The bell buzzed again.
The finger outside was pressing it hard – and releasing.
Then pressing it longer and harder – and releasing.
The baby's body twitched, her eyelids flickered open, flickered closed.
And now, unbelievably: her drifting-sleeping, separated baby was awake.

—

Helen shook her head.

She felt a heat rising in her spine.

The bell, its effects. They were all inside her body.

Fucker, she said, under her breath.

The heat from her spine spread to beat in her armpits; now it was pumping out colour in her cheeks.

The bell rang again. *Fucker.*

She said it louder, with more force. In her voicing the word meant you're kidding me. It meant *tell the universe it must be fucking kidding me.*

The bell. It wanted her to respond to its summons.

She knew this.

She considered the clothes she'd dumped on the sofa. She was half in, half out of her bra. But maybe the problem was. Maybe the point was:

she couldn't.

She looked at the baby. But the baby was fine. Her expression read as interested. As purposeful and engaged. She was already taking seriously the fact of being newly wide awake, from the laid-back position of her bouncy recliner chair.

So alright. ALRIGHT!

She could.

She would.

She scrambled to her feet, pulling t-shirt, jumper back on. She broke out into a large step, a great march to power her out of the living room and down the short distance of the hall. A furious chanting march:

Fucker

You fucker –
You *fucking* fucker –

She pulled the door open.
   The rush of cold air made her face feel hotter.
   She couldn't look at the person standing there.
   She couldn't greet him.
   He was holding something out.
   She wanted to hit – not him, but the doorframe, maybe, or herself.

She snatched the offering – a cardboard pouch – from his hands, her movements all theatrically oversized.

She let the door slam.
   Good, she thought.
   Good.
   Why not?
   Let it slam directly in his face.

For the problem.
   What was the problem?
   As in: her problem? She turned the question on herself.

The hall smelled like rainy days. Like her own coat and the insoles of her shoes, mixing with the past: the distant, layered living of different groups of people.

It was only the future.
   A doorbell, buzzed at a reasonable early-start time in the morning, and already it had changed the course, the whole future of their day.

It thwarted, parted, and redirected the morning. For now: *either* the whole recent sequence would have to be performed again. Only this time faster, and abbreviated, with the chances far smaller and fading of landing the baby settled and asleep in her chair:

the holding,

the walking, to the window, and the bulb in the lamp.

The square path.

The walk to the plant and can it breathe and judging it – no, not yet.

The eyelids and the lowering (gingerly, gingerly).

The crouching, prehistorically, and the landing, the crouching and the landing . . . Performing each of these actions all over again until, once more, in their different ways, and carried forward by their different motivations, they both arrived at the point of finally, *finally*, letting one another go: Helen letting the baby go, putting her down, exactly as the books instructed, clipping her an arm's reach away into her sprung chair; the baby letting Helen go; the baby releasing Helen, if only temporarily, from the nervous constancy of her own attention.

Or, the baby would stay awake.

She would simply stay awake now – for however long it might take for them both to live through another cycle of interest and hunger and drowsy-into-sleepiness. Only this time, Helen knew, her patience would in all likelihood be thinner. Because her hair was still down, loose and hot, it was more likely to fall heavily: flopping all over the baby's face, irritating them both. And because her sense of her capacities was now smaller, she was likely to go faster, to race through what had a chance of working only if it were paced – and the baby would catch her mood, quickening, agitating along with her own impatience and agitation, responding in kind. So while it might

be true – in fact, Helen knew it to be true; she had been learning this, and relearning it each day – that these cycles of waking and sleeping had a sort of looping pattern, meaning that whatever occasions for sleep were missed could be counted on coming round again, eventually – it was also, likewise, and even more powerfully the case that *how* these durations and intervals were lived out by the two of them through any given moment of the given day depended on this: on some boy-man *not* jogging up the steps in his bright breezy sweat-shirt, his soft easy joggers. On some unthinking finger, working to the tempo of its own unimagined urgencies, *not* pushing hard into the doorbell the very second the baby had been put down and released into sleep. On the loud buzzing of the bell *not* just sounding once, and letting it go,

    or twice and letting it go,

    but – pushing – pushing at it and pushing again –

    to the point of BASHING through the door not like a finger but a GREAT FOOT intent on KICKING at her time, the small bucket of gathered time she'd been collecting for herself as she'd progressed through the different levels of the morning, you

    FUCKER.

An elderly woman bumped her caddie along the pavement outside. Somewhere farther down the street a car door slammed. Each morning, the slow-paced woman would pull her shopping trolley with effort, then pause to scatter bread for the pigeons by the bench on the corner. On her daily trip to the shops; the same bench. It was also where the teenagers gathered after school.

Helen felt like crying. She felt like – sorry.

The anger she'd marched heavily to the door in – it fell from her shoulders like a costume, like a cloak.

Sorry, she said, though not sure for what. (For swearing, for shouting. For getting upset; for upsetting someone else.)

The feeling to cry – it gathered. It smarted. It passed.

Sorry, she said, willing the message out through the letter-box, so it might catch up with the young delivery man, lay a quiet hand on his arm.

Sorry: a habit-word. Also, a renewal-word. A spell for getting it together, starting again.

It was alright.
    The pouch she'd received held a book. A long book. A volume so thick because it was so long; unfit to fit through the letterbox.

Helen knew this because she'd ordered it. She'd even been waiting for it. Pacing back and forth to the window, hoping that it would be delivered that day. Specifically, a novel. Old, second-hand, but new to her. An interesting object to spend time with.

Helen went back into the living room.
    Her baby was healthy. And look – she wasn't crying.

It was all alright.
    The big plant was dusty but clearly still alive and there was light falling in from the window.

Her new-old novel had arrived.

It meant a different place to put her attention.

She had capacities. She did.

She would make a cup of tea.

Who knows but why not imagine that it (their day, and the future) had every chance – since both Helen and the baby had been born with most of life's chances – of being okay?

She would try feeding the baby again, eat something, and make a cup of tea.

Once more, she adjusted her sense of the morning.

It was remarkable to her – exhilarating and exhausting – how many times this could happen: how many adjustments a person could make, mining deep for a new seam of resources, despairing, altogether, of their existence, then finding them unexpectedly in the air, like the moon unsought at lunchtime. She counted on this. Sometimes, she worried over how far she depended on it: on having her resources handed back to her by the baby, replenished by some unexpected gesture or new expression of the baby's, or by something else, a message from Rebba on her phone. The strange colours of the river in the park; a duck with its bum in the air, or its weird grey-rubber feet, unexpectedly lifting her mood. Because what if they stopped? These offerings, offering themselves.

Or what if she stopped? Whatever this was, this capacity, an inner availability, to be changed and moved by them.

Helen returned to her spot on the carpet.

The novel she'd ordered was *The History of Tom Jones, A Foundling* by Henry Fielding.

First published in 1749.

Second-hand, it cost her one pound & thirty-two pence plus postage and packaging. Three days later, it was here – bringing in its different energy. Its humour and its ideas. Its love stories. Its own household arrangements. Of all the novels, this one.

said the red words, boldly. Now pulling away, now rounding the street corner, printed large down the side of a bright yellow van.

Hello baby, Helen said, turning her face to look directly at the baby in the chair. Her huge face, looming in.

Hey babe, she said, to amuse herself. Because who, really, says that to a baby?

Hey, she said it once, smiling, seeking eye-contact.

Hey, she said it again. Only this time more gently, breathing it out slowly (I greet you).

Then, touching at the different parts of the mobile, one after the other, setting each element of the composition moving, getting the whole delicate thing going, relating and offsetting, and making a sound pattern between them in the air:

hey

hey

hey

This is our situation.

ROSE

The baby, meanwhile, with her presence and her incipience, her actions and reactions, her own forms of experience, stared intently at Helen's forehead.

The baby's name was Rose.

THE MOBILE

SUSPENDED ABOVE ROSE'S EASY CHAIR

It nudged and slightly shuddered.
> It pressed. It lifted.
> Restless, it was never completely still.

Thrumming beneath it, for Rose it was like this. The mobile like her sensing of the world: it was near and juddery, gapped with negative space, edgy and alive. More or less monochrome. Patched with greys, bright pieces and looms of darker, heated shadow.

It was like this: schematic, suspended; held in readiness.
> Offering itself in one shaky arrangement, then another.
> In one close presentation.
> Then another.

The shapes it suspended were simple, very elemental. Sometimes they were layered, nested or split. One long afternoon, a week or so before Rose was born, Helen had sat largely on the floor, assembling them from a kit she'd ordered online.
> A round figure, with no corners or edges: a CIRCLE.
> A plane figure, rational and even-angled: a SQUARE.
> Two sharp TRIANGLES, positioned head to toe.
> DOTS! A sample of unevenly spaced dots.
> WAVES: a cross-section of undulations.

It was important that each shape offset the others, that each one be positioned at an appropriate distance from the others. For the whole thing to hover – hold itself out in space and counter-balance – it mattered that not one of its parts be given more weight.

She'd done this – with threading, with fiddly little knots, with clear fishing line.

She'd clamped the shoulder of its supporting arm to her desk.

And now, independently –

It moved.

It turned. It jogged.

With even the slightest current of air – a door opening, a person breathing near it, just heat – it could quiver, lift, and change direction.

It rotated.

It kept itself at a tolerable, tactful reserve.

Though sometimes, without warning, it encroached. For Rose, it could seem to rush at her, hemming down and packing her in. Her set-up in the sprung chair under the mobile: it was formidable, at times, how much Rose could hate it. How a gentle turning scene – a place of contrast, of involvement – could stress her, bewilder and oppress her.

For now, though, she studied it: the lilting canopy of overhead shapes.

Her focus lifted towards the circle: a big bright eye.

It broke loose from the circle.

It carried back to the undulation in the direction of the great light-source of the window. She felt the movement as a change in her insides, which were interacting with the room.

For Rose was a mass and a void, too.

She was pointed and gapped, full and empty, twisting and suspended, spacey and closed.

She was DOTS.

She was still, holding to her proportions. Now suddenly outsized.

She was a retreating ebb, now an un-gathered but gathering, persistent flow.

She kicked her legs.

Like this – sensationally, kinetically – the world hung all around her.

It took shape. It changed shape.

It beckoned to her with its light and shadow and with the stretches and points of her interest she turned towards it.

Phasing through calmed then bored, agitated then enlivened, stressed then distressed, her sensational life-force wholly uncontained by the space she could take up in a room, the crook of an arm, the dimensions of her tiny cotton suit, Rose flexed the space-time around her.

It flexed back.

She kicked out a leg to meet the world and she *vibrated* it.

Alongside her, Helen tore at the seam in the cardboard, weighed a novel in her hands.

The radiator beneath the window lifted its background hum to a slightly higher key: its way of announcing that the water running through it – like the package-sorting, like the freelance bodies who were at that moment delivering packages door to door by the van, like all the other networked, outdoor-to-indoor connective systems – was plumbed in, plugged in and working; now working harder.

The bird outside in the tree stopped its peeping.

Or, it continued, very likely. But in the remit of another window, a room inhabited by other people, a bit further down the street, somewhere else.

AN ENVIRONMENT WITH ITS OWN SUGGESTIONS

I'll start this maybe later, Helen said to herself, feeling all of a sudden a bit daunted by the reading choice she'd made. But she'd opened her novel without really intending to and her eyes had fallen on a paragraph. Here was the description of a house. All novels describe housing, living conditions, forms of human shelter, and the house on the page presented in 1749 as newly built. A big, roomy house – the word it used was "commodious." Set on a hill in the English countryside. Against a hill, "but nearer to the bottom than the top of it, so as to be sheltered from the northeast by a grove of old oaks, which rose above it in a gradual ascent of near half a mile." Low enough not to be overly exposed, "and yet high enough to enjoy a most charming prospect of the valley beneath." Protected, but with a wide-open view – Helen gave the whole passage her attention and the setting unfolded the way she felt it. It spread itself out like a cloth. A topography of distinct zones, each one embroidered with its own small details. High above the house, there were firs, rocks, and a waterfall. It tumbled to her mind's ear first as noise, then as a movement, a vague sense of white force foaming over blue, then a clear falling "over the broken and mossy stones." Now it flattened and slowed – "running off in a pebbly channel" before rounding the house to join in with the deeper waters of a large, glistening lake. It was the centrepiece of the view from every window in the front: a lake, filling "the centre of a beautiful plain, embellished with groups of beeches and elms and fed with sheep." The feeling, broadly, was of space: plenty of space, revealing itself over plenty of time. Sheep grazing. Old groves and groups of younger trees. But now it extended further. Out of the lake "issued a river" – tugging the view into its own beyond, meandering on "through an amazing variety of meadows and woods" for several miles, all the way out to the blue line of the horizon, and eventually emptying "itself into the sea."

Space, time: *extension* in all directions – though to the right the fabric bunched. Here was a smaller, shallower valley, "adorned with several villages." Clusters of smaller houses, poorer houses, gathered around the towers of an old, ruined abbey. Look to the left, though, and here once again was spread. It was more land belonging to the house; spread checked and marked by variety: "a very fine park, composed of very unequal ground, and agreeably varied with all the diversity that hills, lawns, woods, and water . . . could give."

The season: spring. It was the middle of May.

The time: first thing in the morning, the dawn of a new day.

Possibility, potentiality: the opening of a territory, large enough to present as basically open-ended, though in real terms somewhat delimited. To the South, by the thin blue arm of the sea. To the East, by "a ridge of wild mountains, the tops of which were above the clouds."

Now, a narrowing, a foregrounding: here was a figure in motion. It is Mr Allworthy, the owner-occupant of the house, a man *replete* with benevolence, pacing back and forth on the terrace, as the sun rises.

Helen read on.

She felt rather than saw the gait of an older person walking. She responded in her lungs to the description of the dawn: the pink lighting, illuminating in touches first the outer edges, then the central portion of the scene. But now, oddly, there was a turn. A jolt: a pinch or snag in the steady rolling out of the telling:

"Reader, take care."

It was the narrator speaking, switching unexpectedly from description to an informal direct address: "I have unadvisedly led thee to the top of a hill."

Not the geographical one, where the spring-source of the waterfall gushed forth between dark rocks, but a figurative hill as high as Mr Allworthy's exaggerated goodness.

The problem, as he saw it: I have led you up here. But now, "how to get thee down without breaking thy neck I do not well know."

From such open elevation, how to get things – like this possible person, this whole narrative project – down and grounded? That is, operating on a closer, more human scale?

The narrator, turning the matter over: Honestly? "I do not well know."

Other than together. "Let us e'en venture to slide down together."

Reader, my neck is your neck. The ambition: to see if it might be possible to do this, achieve this (the project of narration), without either one of us getting hurt.

And now – what's that? A bell's ringing.

Listen: Mr Allworthy is being summoned down to breakfast. Perhaps that will do it: locate us all in the common need to eat.

The narrator: clearly, "I must attend." An obligation (where I go, you go) he frames as an invitation to the Reader: "Come along."

Helen received it. She re-voiced it in her head, in the silent voice of her own private reading, and it was as if she were somehow inviting herself.

"If you please, I . . . shall be glad of your company."

HELEN LOOKED OVER AT ROSE

She looked at the walls. She took a new measure of the size of the room, the wet shapes on the window, the nearness of the street.

Their situation: it was supported and sustained by the fact of accommodation. (Thank you, Nisha; thank you, social connections; thank you, Nisha's husband's mother, who owned the flat and lived upstairs.) As well as, relatedly, by an income – a proportion of it paid out as maternity leave – to cover the rent.

At the same time, it's a living situation continually (re)produced and in a fundamental sense defined by their condition of intensive and continuous mutual address.

Their common addressivity; their common responsivity. Two people, facing each other: occupying, for what to Helen felt would be an incalculable time to come, the position of first responder (the other's most immediate, first because always-on-the-scene, addressee).

Is this what you mean?

This was Helen asking Rose.

I put it to you: with the action I am carrying out now, lifting you up, setting you down, keeping you warm, leaving you temporarily alone (*strapping you in* to your bouncy chair while I storm off to answer the door) – have I understood what you mean?

Is this what you need?

Is this what it – all of it – is, what aliveness feels like, and means?

This was Rose asking Helen, venturing back, responding in her own startling manner to what had been proposed or suggested – Helen asking: Are you hungry? Are you tired? Are you happy? Are you "good"?

(A "good" baby, she was learning, each day adding a new, unexpected definition to the ordinary words in her vocabulary: so, this is what "good" means. This is what they mean by it: predictable and easy-to-read. Settled. Pick-up-able and, importantly, put-down-able. A new person born already aligned with or at least willing to fall in without resistance to the adult rhythms, presenting within the expected range of not excessive, but reasonable and meetable needs.)

Rose, who had no speaking voice yet, only mutterings and cries, soft air-shapes and the syllable starts of possible sounds – responding to this. Or, more likely, to something else: some deep, powerful pang, the directive of a more ancient, unknowable intuition.

Rose, for whom there was no fundamental separation, only shared situation, sensation and extension between Helen, her environment, and the opening of herself.

I know, I know.

We don't know.

Is this how to do it – is this the way we are finding to do it?

Co-living? In *this* form?

Two possible people: one habituated to maintaining the edges of her body, the other like an open field.

All the time *conscious* of each other.

The one listening out for and receptive to the other: taking inspiration from the other.

Here's an idea, Helen would say to Rose.

Here's an idea, Rose would offer out to Helen, or appear to: with a gesture. The opening of her mouth. With the way, when hungry, or sleepy, she'd abruptly turn her head to one side. An idea that Helen would receive, sometimes as a clear visual cue to her brain, more

often as a strange inner feeling she'd attempt to identify in order to translate into action, handing it back. Let's do this.

It's important right now, very urgently in this moment, that we do this.

And they'd do it and their activity would produce new ideas, setting them off in the directions of something new.

It was a structural situation: a dynamic composed of two distinct vantage points, one here and one over there, or very close. Two different, situated positions, as well as the relation they were producing between them; each participant taking their own invested part in a dialogue that neither one of them could quite remember, now, having begun.

Helen and Rose: reaching for and connecting with the other, from their places in the room.

Managing to, very successfully, sometimes.

In proximity and immediacy, and effortless exchange. On the ball: asking-met-with-instant-answering. Action synched to a form of wonderful inter-comprehension that could happen anytime, at any moment, out of the blue: mid-morning, in the darkest middle of the night.

Also, missing each other.

Groping in the other's general direction across great distances and differences. Registering that you're there and I'm here. But I don't know what the question was. And in any case, this is not the answer. Throwing out only beside-the-point, inadequate responses: lobbing them in panic, in the grip of colossal resistance, refusals, tensions, and intolerable delays.

Rose's attention caught on a shape in the mobile that Helen couldn't see. Her body shook at it. Involuntarily, she kicked.

The hollow tubing of the sprung chair received the vigor of her kicks and bounded her back in reply.

Well, this works.

This was Helen speaking to herself, but also to the sprung chair and its position beneath the mobile; in relation to it, the comfortable arrangement of her own body alongside Rose. Surprised by this since a sleep had been skipped. But here they were: occupied; their attentions channelled in different directions, tired but floating in it; feeling unexpectedly content.

This works for now.

But for how long? And will it work – this fragile composition we've made: can it be remade and relied on to work the same way later, or tomorrow?

It was the setting for an improvised daily practice with all the workings laid bare.

A sentimental situation. In the sense that the oldest and the most powerful feelings were in play. Possibly in an exaggerated fashion; an overblown, slightly sticky, sweet-smelling fashion. But why not "sentimental" also in the sense that poet Friedrich Schiller ascribed to it? As one of two distinct attitudes towards writing and the world (towards writing the world). On the one hand: "naivety." The direct reporting of experience. Telling it. On the other: "sentimentality," a mode which draws on and makes explicit the poet's relationship to the materials, to the situation, to the experiencing of experience: "sentimental" on his terms meaning situated and self-aware; self-conscious, self-commentating. Thinking about it.

ENTER SELF-CONSCIOUSNESS

It was, for Helen, a situation so new, for which (like anyone doing anything without instruction for the very first time) she was so practically under-prepared that it couldn't help but produce a high degree of self-consciousness.

Is this how you do it?

This was Helen asking herself. But also her own mother, who lived a three-hour drive away. Nisha, her colleague. Her team leader. Nisha, with her three big healthy kids, all well past the baby-stages. Her generous bags of hand-me-down things.

Then more widely, more wildly: addressing the people she followed online; the competent parents she'd seen in action in the park, at the supermarket. (Who taught them?)

It was a situation of temporary measures and open guesses, negotiating with a weight of expectations, established behaviours and all the received information.

Is this "me" doing it?

Feeling watched, like the world was watching her, albeit somewhat generally, with a powerful will-to-judgement but limited detailed interest. Watching her as if from the other side of a perimeter fence, as if there were such things as fences, or boundaries, capable of sealing one sphere permanently off from all the others, as if to ensure that nothing of her situation ever reached out, reached through, and pertained to matters apart from itself.

Feeling overheard. Worrying almost constantly about this.

Are we bothering you? This was a question that Helen regularly addressed to the flat upstairs: measuring the volume of Rose's crying,

her own slams of frustration, how often, at what times in the night, how quickly, she could manage to quieten and calm them both down. Sending her questions up through the ceiling to touch at the under-soles of the landlady's indoor shoes, the French grasses plaited and coiled to make the espadrilles she'd seen her wear on her wooden floors, turquoise canvas making coverings for her toes.

Are we bothering you and is it – will it be – consequential?

Will you let us pay you (for the right to) to stay/live on?

Although, I'd like it to be otherwise – this was Helen musing to herself: I'd be very curious to know what it might be like to experience all this a bit more "naively." As in just doing, just action. Just getting on with it. Without too much thinking. Without overthinking it (without thinking from this split position of both in it and somewhere to one side or above it). If it were possible, that sounds (like it would be) really good.

It was a very common, very ordinary situation that had some degree of specificity but was not enclosed. A situation in indirect, sometimes direct, supportive or adversarial conversation with other situations and, with them, other practices, other bodies of knowledge, as well as the other objects, the other forces that gave shape to and conditioned their surrounds:

The lamp that Helen lifted from the desk in the evenings, plugging its three fingers into the wall nearer the sofa. Better than the ceiling light, it made a soft low circle for them both to calm down in.

The sofa whose under-pattern Helen didn't like. She hated it.

The book of philosophy on the shelf, set facing the room, the figure on the cover with his back to them, engaging closely with his own concerns. But even so: sharing out its mood, its big, provoking ideas.

Its insistence on "the *continuity* of esthetic experience with normal processes of living"; its arguments and vocabulary.

It was actually Rebba's book.

She'd bought it. She read it a few years ago as a student. She'd talked about it in her own way at the time – the parts she'd read of it.

Woah, listen to this, she'd said once, suddenly in the afternoon, calling out to Helen from the wicker armchair of the different flat which, until recently, they'd shared.

Lecture One, Chapter One: "The Live Creature."

Her voice enthused, her animation catching:

What a title! "The *Live Creature*."

Rose jerked, her arms lifting abruptly into the air as if to express sudden agreement: she was a live creature – a live and lively creature, emphatically.

Helen was, too.

Two live creatures of the same human species, unequal in power and agency, living together (inter-generationally) for almost six weeks now: inheriting a template, a loose set of directives as to what they were supposed to make happen *with* and *for* each other, actions that they both knew, in their different ways, with their own styles of intelligence, they had no choice but to find some means of achieving together (feeding, sleeping, carrying life on). But, within that general framework, Helen felt this keenly: basically making it up.

Two beginners, tasked with figuring out their own unique form of social relation, privacy opening onto privacy, in the close arrangement of their respective solitudes. Drawing on and making use of the

available resources. The ones Helen sought out, like the thick baby-care book she borrowed from the library. Like the novel she'd just bought in. Others which, more contingently, pressed or fell in. Here was someone else's idea, released from another context. Could we use it? Will it help? Phrasings of ideas entering their lives through the channels of the internet, by way of the weather (what else happened to be in the air?), and informing them: like the tree standing outside, like the sky-pinking morning sun.

Rose craned her head forwards, let it fall back. The shapes danced. She jogged and curved the world towards her from her position in the chair.

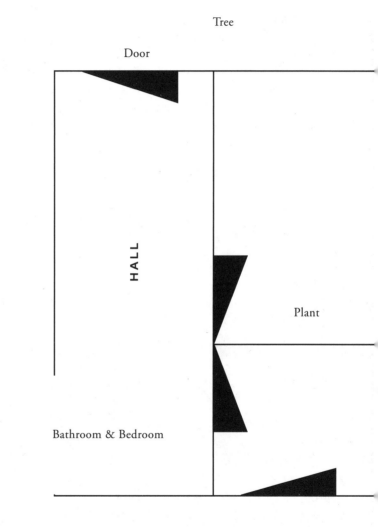

Tree

Door

HALL

Plant

Bathroom & Bedroom

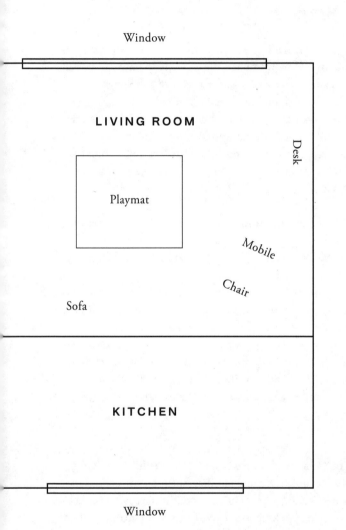

Window

LIVING ROOM

Playmat

Desk

Mobile

Chair

Sofa

KITCHEN

Window

Garden

LECTURE ONE: "THE LIVE CREATURE"

For John Dewey, it (life, in all its forms) starts like this. With a start of sensitivity, a rhythm of involvement – the capacity to have the spread and flow of one's attention *caught*. At least temporarily; on occasion, held. Already, he claimed, before there is ART, whether "in" or "as" a specialized form of EXPERIENCE, there are – there have always been – "events and scenes" standing out. Or, hollowing out: making formal settings, space-time compositions generative of their own local effects and sometimes they're catching, distracting, painful, or beautiful. Such as?

His example: "a fire engine." Rushing by.

A fire engine built of colour, plus acceleration, inseparable from its siren and rise of urgency. An unsought interruption. Unsought but bringing in with it an inrush of hot-cold concerns: What's wrong and where? Death? Danger? Loss? Whose? Questions that, like the engine, present as aggressive, primary, and loud. But soon (already) the fire engine is turning a corner. The siren recedes. It's out of earshot. Wherever the emergency is, whatever it was, it's somewhere else now. A relief: it was only ever a matter for someone else. The aspect of the experience was punctual and now it's over, dissipated and overtaken by the succeeding traffic because, look – the fire engine has gone.

Or, a building site.

The different example is of a building site: the slower, more phased scenes of "great machines excavating the earth." There's nothing, nothing of note: only the same familiar portion of street or land. Then, one day there's a hole. Another day and it is massive: a thing to be gaped at through an opening in a fence. It has scooped out another

perspective on the very foundations that the roads and the shops, the schools and the homes are built on, exposing the underground pipes and wire networks: earth, lots of sand. Showing how hidden creatures were also living there all along.

These examples are public, collective, at some level spectacular. Dynamically, "they hold the crowd." For different durations, they catch and manage the attention – producing temporary publics in the horseshoe shapes of small gatherings or crowds. But in addition, on Dewey's list of interesting ordinary involvements, there is an involvement of a different order. Presenting as more private, apparently calmer, and yet at the same time more actively, consequentially, and durationally involved: "the delight a housewife takes in tending her houseplants."

Can houseplants die of old age? Helen had looked this up once, typing it into her phone. The answer she found (among all responses her question prompted, the answer that she chose to read and believe) was a loose and general "no." Some species can live on, on and on, for as long as there's someone around to water them – to bear them in mind, not altogether forget about them. Who actually does this matters less, at least to the plants, than the spaced continuity of the tending gestures (the same article told of a woman bequeathing her plants and their maintenance to someone else, and how they lived on), the habit of working-with what the plant, in the right setting, and with a bit of assistance, most deeply wants to do. In the way this example was phrased, the emphasis was on the *activity* of this, the *ongoingness* of this – not the rare single event. It located aesthetic pleasure in "co-creating the conditions" for what might, one day, in a given season of the year, produce the bright visual pleasure of a brand-new leaf, or

an unexpected flower – an arrangement of shadows thrown by stems and leaves against a wall. Compared to the short-lived high-stakes drama of a fire engine, this one clearly presented as quieter and longer, comparatively lower key.

Though one day, when Helen was heavily pregnant and only recently moved in, she came back from a walk to the shops to find her big Monstera plant prostrate on the carpet. There it was, lying unnaturally, two of its largest leaves bent the wrong way, another snapped completely, exposing a wet line of broken cells, the whole live being surrounded by clods of dry earth.

Like it had been mugged.

This was how it had looked to her, coming in, happening upon the violence of the scene. This was how she described it to Rebba: as though, taking advantage of her absence, someone had broken into the flat and mugged the plant of its . . . *verticality*.

When in fact, she'd worked out afterwards, it had simply fallen over. Reaching, seeking the light. Risking a new posture, it must have lost its balance and fallen over. It must have grown.

BATTERIES

Over Rose, things were stalling. Now re-starting.

Here, again, was the presentation of a circle.

Helen would call it a bright full moon.

It held still.

Rose lifted an arm in its direction. She frowned, her expression charged with intention. Her chair rocked and bounced.

Very slowly, the moon angled. Now it thinned.

There was a slow pulling turn. The room tilted with it, sensitive to the planetary power of its drag . . .

Helen's thoughts lifted outwards, passing through the window pane to touch on the bark of the tree. They went part-way down the street in the direction of Rebba, who still lived in what had been their shared flat on the other side of the park. They hesitated on the corner. Now pulled back indoors to land on Nisha's big shopper bag. Also in that mix of hand-me-downs: the pale yellow star. Moulded from plastic with a little projector inside it. Two double-A batteries and it would play eighteen lullabies, make a small cinema on the ceiling, and help, Nisha had said. Helen would be able to go into the next room, and do things – do whatever. Whatever she needed to do. Meanwhile, the play of light and shadow could be entrusted to keep Rose company, even to make her feel drowsy, and to very slowly, very simply put her to sleep. The star powered by new batteries would work: sending ions back and forth, back and forth, it would do some of the work for her, she said. Like a dream, Nisha had said, insisting, in response to Helen's raised eyebrows. It *will* work. She'd promised: trust me. By which she meant: believe me.

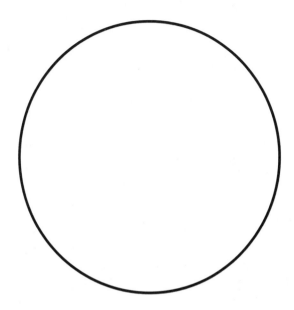

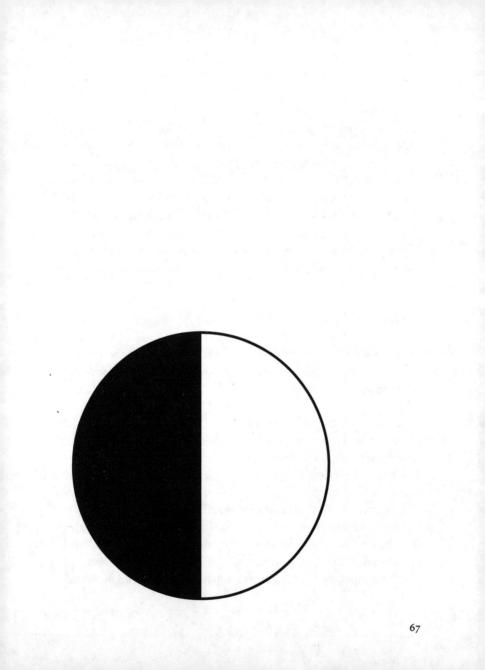

The person who accompanied her name was short and fine. Fine as in fine-boned, fine-featured, her fine hair shaved close to her fine-looking head. Fine as in the weather: clear, bright – basically energizing. Fine as in not just alright and tolerable, not merely "adequate." But, from the night they met aged twenty and twenty, stamping in the long cold queue to get into a hot club, their breath visible in lung-formed clouds, someone Helen admired and found excellent. As in, the finest – really very-very good. The contrast in height meant that when they walked side by side, for instance along a busy street, they were obliged either to keep looking up or keep inclining down if they wanted to talk. Which they did, all the time, willingly. It was just one of many adjustments they made to accommodate one another. Reciprocal adaptations. Rebba would hook her arm into Helen's and Helen would lower her own arm slightly farther than was comfortable and they'd enjoy walking about like this, feeling linked, looking unmatched, uneven – an odd pair. They were different: they each had friendships with people the other didn't like. Helen with Nisha and their colleagues she'd sometimes go drinking with. Sitting for hours around a pub table, diagramming recent alterations in the power-dynamics of the office, speculating on strategies as to how to rebalance things, shore them up, move them back or otherwise – conversations that Helen found important because she was impacted and implicated but that Rebba had no patience for. At the end of a day alone in her studio, Rebba would go for runs. Cladding her swift, light body in polythene and neon and exhaustively circuiting the park before sprinting back home to change and head to her shift at the bar. Helen hated running. But what was good was being around each other. They had a knack, somehow, for each other's happiness. The planes of Rebba's

face were sharp like her questions, which were almost always incisive and real. With them, she marked out a space for conversation that Helen, who was someone who thought as she talked, who worked her feelings and her ideas out through the gradual, interruptive production of talk (even if only with herself), could actually enter into, exist and move around in, without nervousness. Without fear. They never spoke *over* each other. It was not Rebba's habit to issue an invitation to respond, to ask a question, and this way open a door that Helen, in good faith, would begin making her way towards, preparing herself to step through, only to find it slammed closed, and a different one all of a sudden opened somewhere else. Other people did this, Helen noticed, regularly; pretty much all the time. As if talking were a game of here, speak to this, *here*. No, actually, *not* there,

over here, speak to this:
                    cutting across her – are you stupid?
Why are you still over there?

                                        Here! speak to this.
Or better don't move: just stay still and listen. In relation to my discourse, just stay still and submit.

It was bewildering, and frustrating.

With Rebba, though, it was different. She had this trick of snapping her fingers, or tapping a palm against a closed fist as she considered her English words, taking the time to reach for and very often find exactly the right phrasing for whatever it was, precisely, she wanted to ask – and Helen felt like she was being counted in. Enjoined to join her. She'd walk in the direction of the door and find like a blessing that the door-frame was remarkably solid and propped all the way open. She'd pass through it. And in that wide new room, over

the top of the rhythm Rebba had set for her, she'd talk: she'd respond, improvise, range all around. She'd go even outside, lift stones and look under them, put her hands in the grass, discover things. Meanwhile, Rebba would pull at some thread in the hem of her t-shirt, or rub at the soft roughness of her fine head, first the wrong way, then the right way – and she'd listen. There was never any sense of a time limit. There was no sense of a hurry. She'd wait, in the quiet place of her own interest. Then, in time, she'd respond. She'd take her turn, take over, take on whatever Helen had said, even the most inarticulate, casually ventured thing, and take it seriously. In her own more measured, carefully weighted manner, she'd add to it. Rotate it. Or fold it in half. Then return it to Helen in a new shape and lit differently. By the colours of the landscapes and the lore of her own experience, her different childhood. The rush of cold rivers over rocks and outdoor air. Weighted differently: by the thoughts she was having about her own work. They would pass time together like this: in long conversation, in short conversation, in total silence. Looking at the sky out the high window of the flat they used to share, in the early evenings, watching clouds form and pull apart. Then put on their music very loudly and cook or muck, leap, dance about. Helen thinking: I am bored of this track.

I'll shuffle the playlist now;

I will add cinnamon to this pot of made-up dish we're making – why not?

There are days when I am anxious, nothing holds steady, when everything presents as basically broken –

Hey, let's crack open a beer.

Rebba thinking: come on, let's skip this track.

Why not put in some cinnamon – would that be weird?

I know, I know. I feel this too: unsteadiness. A sliding feeling. The ice thinning – what did you say? Let's "crack open" a beer.

Let's crack open something, break the mould and ground a new form of life together. Because sometimes, across languages, across difference, they had the same thoughts. They sounded almost exactly the same. They could each predict and confirm exactly what the other was thinking – while also leaving the space for one of them, every now and then, to take the other completely by surprise:

I didn't know you liked that?!

I didn't know you thought that?!

I didn't know that you could *do* that?! Seriously?! Since when?

I had no idea.

What is the word for this protected, commodious existence with someone you really like? Friendship? Other people could come round, and they'd love them a bit. A lot. They'd offer the company of their warm bodies out in generous measures. They'd throw parties. Good parties and dismal parties in the flat they shared: four flights up, above a dry-cleaners, also a newsagent. The unventilated bathroom *mucid* with damp. Rebba had found the word, proposed it and delighted in it. Rebba, who on one of the first weekends had gone into every cupboard, pushed into the spaces under their beds. She'd flattened herself on the floor, eye-level with the skirting boards, systematically plugging every gap and crevice with wire wool then aluminium foil to keep out the mice. And it had worked: the corners, angles, edges of their living-space were outlined in silver; under certain lights, it could make the whole floorplan glitter. But the best of times, Helen reflected, were the spaces in between: just the two of them doing not a lot together in the long intervals before and after the potencies of other people, before and after the other parts of life happened. Rebba being quiet in the sagging armchair, its base threatening to fall out. Helen somewhere close by in the kitchen talking or trying to lie comfortably on their old sofa. Throwing out an arm

towards her, churning the air as she picked through and offered out a range of her mostly unconnected thoughts. It was a sustaining living situation made possible by cheap rent, small attentions, good health, and genuine mutual interest; also, knowing when to give each other a break. When to turn the volume down on the intensity, alleviate it, and pull away. Rebba asking nothing of her, less even than usual. Leaving Helen to it when she needed to be left completely alone, to withdraw from every pressure, every tugging form of social interaction and abruptly retreat, day-dreaming into her own room. Helen, sensing when quietness was getting tugged down from somewhere deeper into sullenness, into sadness, commanding Rebba to go out: OUT! Out into the outdoors to run somewhere really-really fast. To loop around it and then run to the gym. Climb the fake wall, scrabble up the steep rock-face made from chicken wire, made from fibreglass, scale it in her head as if it were truly a mountain then swing down and sprint back.

It was a home they'd made – for some years, going on through most of their twenties: it was a home they had each made a pact to invent and continue together.

It was not nothing: home-making; coming up with their own energetic co-inhabitation of a large, unpromising space. It felt like the basis of everything.

It was incredible, truly. Marvellous, like a fairy tale, how rarely they got on each other's nerves.

Over the years, Helen had tried to express this: that she was happy. That living with Rebba made her feel part of life. Into it, embracing of the best aspects of it and – in an everyday way, just happy.

How to say it? She began her sentence.

She was borrowing her line from a song she liked on the radio.

She was singing, though she was a poor singer. She began. It would be a declaration. Also a statement of simple fact. She sang: "When I'm with you:—"

She had Rebba's attention. Rebba, seated at the table in their old kitchen, silver foil glinting around the skirting boards, her eyes widened in amusement.

She was patiently waiting for her to finish. Or to start. Her face asked: Yes? Well?

But the song was one whose chorus started then stopped. It set out on the track of a full sentence, then abruptly pulled back. It seemed to need to do this. As if the full expression of its sentiment depended on this *almost*: on getting to the brink of saying it, and waiting there. Then, as if it were a swing, drawing back – the whole thing needed a bit more momentum.

Following its pattern, Helen spoke the up-and-down start of the sentence again:

                        you

            I'm

                with

   When

Kinetically, now, she was inside the wait. The brink: it was a space-pause, made trembly with anticipation. Helen used it to nod her head meaningfully, maintaining eye-contact all the while.

She laughed. She flapped her hands in the delay and made a few strutting moves like a big bird around the table.

Rebba laughed back. She waited and encouraged.

They both held still.

The lyric, the sentiment, had gathered enough tracked-back power. Now it could do what it wanted: swing forward, seeking and finding its release. Helen opened her chest and sang out

ma-gic.

(Long high note then a short low note, both of them out of tune.) Friendship as mutual enchantment.

MOUNTAINS

In the mornings, Helen put a wash on. In the afternoons, she draped Rose's clothes, some soft cloth squares, and occasionally her leggings and jeans over the radiators, leaving them to dry there overnight. In this way, mountains formed. She considered them now, mountains formed of condensation, Rose bumping gently in her chair. Perhaps it wasn't just the clothes. It could also be breath – plant-breath and human-breath – or more simply contact; interface. The glass acting as a thin interface between one temperature and another, the season changing, for suddenly it was May; outdoor life touching at life indoors; the indoors pressing out. She watched a big droplet of water run down and cut through one of the largest water formations, leaving an absolutely straight path in its wake: too exact, too direct, to be a plausible mountain trail.

Slowly, over the course of the morning, they'd do this.

A great misted mountain would cut itself in two, then grow patchy, shaggy-edged, its inner paths turning ragged as the droplets found new, zig-zagged routes down.

They'd look pelt-ish for a while, like something completely different. The coat-pattern on a great bear, not mountains at all.

In this way, the window kept time: the view of the street growing clearer as the day moved forward; the water from the glass pooling on the sill.

Sometimes, Helen would run a cloth through it. She'd absorbed this maintenance information from somewhere: her life's education. How, if left, the regular accumulation of condensation could make the paint crack and rot the frame.

But these weren't her window frames.

It was a strange misuse of her energy, arguably, to concern herself with maintaining them.

And yet she lived here.

She and Rose lived here together.

Now it occurred to her: what would be good would be to use it.

Elaborate an indoor watercourse. Find a way of directing the water out of its channel and into the earth surrounding the plant. Helen sighed, rocked her head, to ease the tension in her neck. It was tiredness making her thoughts fixate like this, gathering weight in one spot until they felt too heavy to move. And so she'd stay there, thinking, with the window, with the collected water, the window frames, until there was nothing more to think. A new idea: she could walk back and forth with her cloth. Let it absorb the water until it was heavy, saturated, then carry and squeeze it into the base of the plant.

On the trestle-table, her phone buzzed and moved.

Instantly, the heaviness lifted.

She knew without looking that it was Rebba.

Checking in: MORNING! How are Helen and Rose today? How are Helen and Rose every day?

Helen felt a rush of warm feeling towards the table, the plywood. Towards her phone, the person in the different space it connected her to.

But, in its reflexive rush outward, the warmth ran up against, then eddied around, something else – something blocking and cold. Like a stone, or resentment. Rebba, she imagined, would have slept well. Not even well: she would have slept.

In fact, at this hour, what time was it? Nine-ish, nine-thirtyish . . . most likely, since she'd have been working last night, she would only just be waking up. For a moment, Helen sat in the current of two opposite feelings, a flow and block. She felt the one navigate around the other and compete. Then she gave Rose's chair a little dip; leaned against the sofa to have another go at putting up her hair.

A NEW PROVINCE OF WRITING

With a large hair-knot balancing on the crown of her head, the recent pressure of the elastic band around her wrist, she sunk her attention into the novel:

What was it, actually?

A first; a beginning. Its own startling sort of start.

Herein, the narrator will declare, was a whole "new Province of Writing."

The back-cover copy qualifying this: well . . . among the first.

"*One of the first* and finest English novels."

Here I am, he will claim, marking out the scope, the remit, the borders and horizons of a vast new territory. Its main features, some of its most salient details. The paths tracking through it. For I am in charge; *I* decide.

Like Mr Allworthy's new-built house: it will be generous and roomy. Voluminous. As well as that, it will be venerable; for the first time, properly respectable.

It will be without precedent. Original; inaugural.

And – *with* precedent, altogether conscious of its precedents. Decided and powerfully shaped by an ongoing conversation with its precedents.

With and without: like anyone, like everything.

Like houses (like the way all new-builds function as an indirect response to the utterance of "hut"). In the long passage describing Mr Allworthy's house, the narrator had also said: look. Note how it was all constructed in a style far *nobler* than the Gothic. Note, also, how in its proportions it *rivalled* the beauties of the best Grecian architectures – acknowledging, in these comparative ways, the existence of other structural styles as well as, indirectly, the existence

of certain traditions of long-form fictional prose: the Gothic; the ancient Greek.

Tom Jones: it described itself as a "mental entertainment."

Also – as a "container." That is, a recipient. A sort of folder. A holder.

A CONTAINER CONTAINING:

Helen was more or less reading forwards, having turned back to the start. Or before the start: the novel's great Table of Contents, finding in it a long and comically specific listing of items that, like a stretchy box, it promised to contain.

Listen – she wanted to tell someone. (Rose?)

Among them, BIRTH.

Tom Jones: Part I, Book I: "Containing as much of the birth of the foundling as is necessary or proper to acquaint the reader with in the beginning of this history."

Alright – she smiled at this: a sketchy sketch of birth. Limited to what the novel deems "necessary or proper" for the reader to learn. A containment of BIRTH, both limiting and maintaining its description of it, in the permanently continuous. As if to make clear that the holding function of this particular box, founded in 1749, were still functioning now and could be entrusted to carry on. Long after the life-time of any individual reader. Birthing now, and long, long into the future.

Alright – but listen, she wanted to read aloud to someone: following birth or – possibly? Possibly – initiated by it: TIME.

Book IV: "Containing the time of a year."

Book V: "Containing a portion of time somewhat longer than half a year."

Book VI: "Containing about three weeks."

Book VII: "Containing about three days."

Book IX: "Containing twelve hours."

Book XII: "Containing the same individual time with the former."

It was funny, seeing it set out for her like this: how they didn't match; how clearly there was no way they were ever going to match: the novel's own narrative time and the negotiated durations-to-come of her own individuated reading time. Book IV: "Containing the time of a year" was no longer than – in fact it looked like it was going to be almost identical in length to – Book IX: "Containing twelve hours." For both books contained around ten to twelve short chapters, both went on for around seventy densely printed pages. Each one would take her – how long would reading one of these book-parts take her? Who knew? The novel seemed to anticipate this, and enjoy it. As if it found it funny, too; and, likewise, complicated.

TIME: different portions of imagined time as well as her own future time. But also, SPACE.

TIME *plus* SPACE.

TIME as it plays out in lived-in, occupied spaces. Or, spaces, as they get inhabited and alter over time. Lived spaces (houses, villages, cities, and fields) as well as paper spaces, page-spaces, the way the attention occupies – lives for a while – with a page. Maybe these came first?

Book IV, Chapter I: "Containing five pages of paper."

Book IV, Chapter VII: "Being the shortest chapter in this book."

(Helen checked: it was one short page long.)

Thin paper spaces softened at the edges by someone else's thumbing. Printed spaces acting as the supports for all the invoked places – the impressive house; the varied countryside enclosed by the mountains and the sea; the smaller, packed dwellings in the village; eventually the difference of the city – and the lives they will suggest and support (or fail to).

—

One empty afternoon, when she was still a teenager, Helen read a novel she'd found on her mum's shelf. She read it fast and it had made something clear. It was *The Millstone* by Margaret Drabble: a story of 1960s single-motherhood: a woman taking on the great, grinding weight of a baby, or so the title suggested, even though the baby who was born into the novel was sunny, easy-going, remarkably placid. But it was not the baby who stayed with her, although she had a distinctive presence, as babies do. Even at the teenage time of reading, Helen knew this. She learned it from babysitting, from the evening jobs she would receive passed down from her older next-door neighbour when she was growing up – low-paid, maximum responsibility, casually distributed gigs that the older girl didn't want for whatever reason, or couldn't do herself. Helen turning up at 6 P.M., 7 P.M. to strangers' houses, getting introduced to bigger siblings already pyjama'd, smelling of their own childhoods, ready for the strange and long, oddly intimate evenings ahead, then getting handed an additional six-month-old or five-month-old or even a three-month-old baby, and receiving impressions from those hours spent with them, holding them, sitting awkwardly near them, not of formed people exactly, but of qualities, atmospheres, the complex of energies that each one could bring in and impress upon her, upon the whole room. She had known a bit, then, already, about the characters of babies. What was new and instructive about the novel was the decision the mother-character made. More than that, the basis upon which she made it. If she'd felt enabled to go on with her unplanned pregnancy, it came to this: a setting. The fact that her parents had left her the charge of their central London flat. They were abroad, rich, and ambassadors, not expected to return to the country any time soon. Rather than leaving it unstated, the novel kept on saying this. It insisted on it: if

the central character felt enabled to go ahead and have a baby on her own, her decision must have been somehow bound up with what she wanted from life and how she imagined her own life unfolding, with the illegality of abortion in the UK in 1965, with having an income source (a provision from her parents, supplemented by copywriting work); but ultimately it came down to the flat. A brutal, simplified equation that sounded sharp and true. It made a housing matter into a life or death matter. They support life, and new forms of life, or they don't; they inhibit it or they allow it (to start, to go on, possibly even to flourish). The novel made this clear: the form of co-living its characters could describe together would have been literally unviable – unimaginable, and therefore un-actionable, un-actualizable – had it not been for this life-support system: the straightforward provision of a secure and affordable (or, in the protagonist's case, a rent-free) flat.

The mobile turned and dipped.

Again, Rose kicked.

The aluminium of the hollow chair-frame felt it and replied.

Coming in from the street outside were the sounds of the builders starting work on the scaffolding around the house opposite. Yesterday, they'd constructed a funnel made of buckets leading from the roof to a skip – one big bucket inserted into another, making a long tube – and spent the working day sliding things – roof-tiles? – down it. The falling materials made these irregular smashes, some heavier, some louder and more substantial than the others. All day long: these smashes taking them by surprise, making them feel nervy; at one point, jerking Rose awake.

(Fuckers)

Helen looked down at Rose. Her shock of fine dark hair. Her gaze, which remained fixed even as her body-parts waved, jerked, and fidgeted about it, giving bounce to her chair. Like a centre. Her distinctiveness: Helen received it like an inconstant light-source, in flickers then the occasional unexpected beam. For instance, at the local clinic where she took Rose to be weighed. Looking at her for the first time *alongside* other babies – one squashy, soft and sleepy; another with a bright-red face, its crying sharp and raw. Helen, feeling flustered. Flapped by the effort to get this right. By wanting, badly, to impress the nurse, if not with her competence then at least with her good will and commitment. People-pleasing, making jokes, making jokes at her own expense, feeling a bit cowed as always by any presentation of authority, feeling inwardly a bit irritated as always at how readily she could be cowed by any presentation of authority, and at how deeply – on some deep, hidden level she had no access to – she wanted someone (anyone, the nurse, another parent, acting as a witness in the room) to see her, to register the scale of her efforts and say: Well done! Well done for getting yourselves here. Well done for coping, apparently. Well done, bravo. Rose, meanwhile, showed steadiness. She displayed – the word for it was dignity. There was no coaxing required. She submitted, not with willing but something like cool resignation, and gravitas, to the humiliations of being undressed, lowered onto the scales. But all the while maintaining a clear penetrating stare. It wasn't aggressive, exactly. But it was challenging – and strong. The nurse felt it, too. It took in their faces, the weighing scales, the edges of the room. It seemed to ask questions of them. Like why. While at the same time to stare beyond them. Beyond the small sphere of what they were trying to accomplish in the moment,

toward something larger: a different horizon of action, value, being. Was it fair, or possible, to extrapolate from these first glimpses – the constitution of a person?

The name of the sunny baby in the novel – she remembered it now – was Octavia. Now she remembered something else: a boy of six or so, whom she'd once read a story to and made some gesture of tucking in. There had been star-ships blasting off on his duvet cover, on his pillowcase, very close to his head. She reached for and couldn't retrieve his name. But she remembered bidding him good night. Night-night, stranger. A strange stranger's child. Sweet dreams, etc. Repeating the formulae her own mum used to mark this threshold moment for her – for them both. Then, feeling like it was rude, or too formal, somehow, to leave it at that, she turned at the door, and went rapidly back to the bed. She placed her hand briefly on the boy's arm, leaned in, and kissed his pale cheek. Thinking that this was what she was supposed to do, at fourteen, acting out what she felt the situation most deeply required. She remembered the peculiar way he'd looked at her: surprised. Shocked even, as if she'd crossed a line. He was right. Briefly, they exchanged something: what it is to force intimacy, a sense of trespass. How it was produced by something larger than themselves: the extreme oddity of their situation, normalized by the adults. She'd been shocked, too.

There were NAMES in the novel. Telling names, packed with social information:
Squire Allworthy, replete with benevolence
Partridge
Mr Square, the philosopher
Mr Supple, the curate

Molly Seagrim
Blifil
Thwackum (Thwackum?)
Mrs Honour
Sophia
The hero, plain-named, unremarkably named, Tom Jones

The novel was a folder of NAMES. The telling, repeating, deter-
mining names of its own imagined people, who existed only where
their names were, whether printed closely together, or far, far apart.
NAMES set about each other, in pairs, or in small groups, their positions structured by their relations to and contacts with each other.

And doing what? From the chapter headings, it looked, emphatically,
like nothing special. At least, nothing exceptional, nothing *gothic*
(out of the ordinary or supernatural). Just what it seemed invested in
presenting as the most "common," "natural," matter-of-fact things:

Book I, Chapter V: "Containing a few common matters . . ."

Book V, Chapter VIII: "Containing matter rather natural than
pleasing."

Book XII, Chapter X: "In which Mr Jones and Mr Dowling drink
a bottle together."

Book XII, Chapter X: "Containing several matters, natural enough
perhaps, but LOW."

The most ordinary, not always edifying, MATTERS OF HUMAN
LIFE. In other words: INCIDENTS. Some minor and inconsequential, some looming larger than the others:

Book V, Chapter IV: "A little chapter, in which is contained a little
incident."

Book V, Chapter V: "A very long chapter, containing a very great incident."

The novel taking its own decisions on this. Boldly and unapologetically measuring out – on its own terms, which may also be the general, accepted terms – what *it* counted as a great big incident and what it counted as a little one, a merely incidental one. Taking charge of the distribution of its own attention. And arguably containing this too: its own allocation of ATTENTION as describes incidents prompted by the unpredictability of human behaviour – as well as those directed by the larger, more impersonal forces, such as social circumstance. The social order. Like money. Housing. The novel held these; it narrated the effects of them – even as it was traversed by them. FORCES such as History. Nature and Fortune. For instance, of Mr Allworthy, the narrator will say: here is a man shaped by both. Nature and Fortune. In fact, they seem "to have contended which should bless and enrich him the most." From Nature, "he derived an agreeable person, a sound constitution, a solid understanding, and a benevolent heart." From Fortune, just one gift, but one that played a decisive part in fostering the others (goodness, generosity, health): "the inheritance of one of the largest estates in the country."

Impactful, impersonal FORCES such as geography (the boundary marker of the distant sea, the wild mountains) and the weather.

The weather – producing an atmosphere; changing the mood. A slow dawn: a serene morning of soft clouds and gentle breezes. Later, bright skies, and gustier winds.

The book-box as an open container for a certain quality of ATMOSPHERE inseparable from the telling attitude of the prose itself: its distinctive manner, notable already in the chapter headings – Helen experienced it as a sort of genial taking in hand. As a warmth – not a

chill; a closeness, also a looseness combined with a confidence, that connected in turn with its claims to knowledge. The novel as a repository for its own FORMS OF KNOWLEDGE: what it knew vastly all about and presented as capable of describing – the outdoors, the indoors; sometimes knocking at the doors leading into the more protected spaces of the human heart. What it knew and promised to disclose with regards its own written contents, its incidents, stories and possible people: what they would be doing, where, and with whom, for how long. What it knew about their pasts and suggested about their futures, even as they were prevented from knowing these things about themselves, or each other. At the same time, what it knew or presumed to know about its reader, with whom it proposed to share all this. How its capacity to know could deepen then shallow, or grow patchy – presenting less as a body of information, slowly released, than as an activity, a negotiated process of figuring itself out.

In addition to this, there was everything it passed over. The novel's gaps; its inconsistencies. It contained these, too, if that were possible. The holes in its box; its own lots of opacity.

Book III, Chapter I: "Containing little or nothing."

Helen snorted when she read this, pushing the air out of her nose.

So: she'd read all the way there. Book Three! How many . . . a hundred pages in? And there'd be hardly anything.

Little or nothing: a blank, a vacancy. In what was otherwise a gathering of features: decors and objects, some charged with special meaning, brought in with their own actional properties and lifespans (WET WINDOWS, FLOWERS), some tasked with filling up and making it possible to imagine a room.

A second later, the mobile felt it: the sudden current of air.

It hesitated, chose a direction.

It bobbed and the whole thing turned.

KNOWLEDGE and its unsteady allocations (Who knows this – and how?), like the matter of VOICE and who is speaking (Who or what is seeing, thinking, and saying this when all of it is writing?) – these were the questions the novel also contained. It answered and posed; it posed by the ways it answered them: with KNOWLEDGES, with VOICES, countering and disputing, restating and competing, nuancing and inflecting each other.

From Rose, in her rocky chair, there was reaching. Towards Helen, towards the room, her situation, which was Helen, who for Rose's purposes *was* the environs, her room.

The reach said: I have known your inside sounds. I have been carried by your basic rhythms; I grew up in a space among your organs. I am not yet *not* you. The separation and difference of me is one you bring to bear: with your reductive guessed-at translations, your efforts to fix and limit the open-endedness of myself, my boundary-collapsing sensations.

Helen, feeling suddenly very hungry. Looking up from her page to fathom what she sensed was a communication. She replied in thought: I have known you – sat with you or near you – your whole life. But there are times, in a day, when I'm here and you're just there. We are so close: you low in the room at my elbow, level with my thigh. Yet I can look up and have no idea who you are.

Someone had drawn asterisks here and there in the margins of Helen's copy of the book, as if they'd been studying it, or had been tasked with writing an essay on it.

She might have gone out into town and bought a brand new copy. It was, after all, a classic: a novel being regularly re-edited, constantly in print.

Instead, she had arranged, excessively, for a second-hand edition to be delivered to her door, thereby activating a global system of demand and rapid supply, and precarious, underpaid labour. If she had done this, it was because the bookshop, the public library and the charity bookshop were all a distance away. It was because she had no confidence, yet, in her capacity to calm Rose down without feeding her. Relatedly, it was because she hadn't figured out, yet, how to feed her out of doors (without stripping to the waist). And so, weighing her options, she'd decided that on balance she preferred – that is, she could cope better with – the thought of her money indirectly enriching the richest man in the world, with summoning then swearing at a stranger through her front door, than the prospect of walking two miles with the baby (since the bus was not imaginable, yet) and arriving. Getting there: making it and feeling in a small way triumphant at having made it: to be entering one of those hushed public spaces together (a bookshop, a library). Only for Rose to be disconcerted by the change in soundscape, the sudden switch from sound *on* (the soothing continuity of outdoor traffic) to sound *off*. Only for Rose to wake up soft then bewildered then rigid with distress and cry and cry and cry and cry.

Calculations. Causal predictions: if this, then this. Measurements of energy and capacity, in relation to durations (lengths of walks and sleeps). Helen was making them all the time now.

Before ordering, she'd read some of the readers' reviews online. There were over thirty thousand. And this, only in the past fifteen years or so – since the online reading records and rating sites had begun. Which was a good thing – Helen had taken it for a good sign. She had explicitly wanted a long read. A narrative to cut life with, treating it as a very different place to go to (to go into) regularly, temporarily, a way of leaving, but without ever really leaving, her own life. At the same time, she'd deliberately chosen an old read. A canonical, pre-validated read. Something received as part of her general cultural horizon that she'd never had cause to interact with directly, or establish her own position towards. A pre-rated experience that others – whole generations of others – had been through before her. A novel to offset her own novel experience of living with a baby, which she was now nearly six weeks into doing, as if no one had ever done it before:

Funny! Someone had written.
    Once you get into it: *pacy*.

Also, unexpectedly, in parts, quite touching.

Then again, a note from a different reader: Detestable!
    You know? Just tedium punctuated with banalities.

Someone else: dull as *dishwater*.
    The meat of the plot is surrounded by so much blah, blah, blah, blah, blah!

—

Which was true. From the Table of Contents, the indications of the titles, introducing each new book of narration, there would be chapters unrelated to the plot, interested in doing something else:

Book II, Chapter I: "Showing what kind of history this is; what it is like, and what it is not like."

Book V, Chapter I: "Of the serious in writing, and for what purpose it is introduced."

Book VIII, Chapter I: "A wonderful long chapter concerning the marvellous, being much the longest of all our introductory chapters."

Book IX, Chapter I: "Of those who lawfully may, and of those who may not, write histories such as this."

Tom Jones: it was categorized as a novel. That's what people called it: booksellers, online readers, scholars and historians, even though it called itself "the history" (in fact, "a Heroic, Historical, Prosaic Poem"). It was one of the "first" and most influential English-language examples of the novel-form, presenting itself as an archetype; an inaugurating example. It was a novel celebrated for its narrative architecture, its constructed-ness, the intricacy of its plotting, its satisfying symmetry. (Built from eighteen books, with each of its three phases – country, journey, city – narrated in exactly nine books each.) For the consistency of its pacing, its involving continuation, its fictional *flow*. For all the things "the novel" would be considered to provide, and *do well*. But, in this instance, it was also composed from essay-parts. From "blah, blah, blah": on-the-page speculation as to what its characters were doing, and why, what other writers and forms of writing were doing, and why, also what *it* was doing. The novel-as-container which in this interesting case (also) contained its

own semi-serious, open program for novel-writing, novel-reading, for thinking about itself. A long fictional prose narrative whose compelling course would be diverted, loosened, punctuated – regularly stopped – by these chatty, provocative, digressive surrounds.

Two different kinds of material wrapped around each other, offsetting each other, engaging these two quite different modes of address.

On the one hand, the kind that said: "Look here," or didn't even have to.

It announced: "In that part of the Western division of the kingdom which is commonly called Somersetshire, there lately lived (perhaps lives still) a man . . ." – and in so doing it summoned them forth: Somersetshire, a reality of soft rolling hills, a tour, an ancient chalk horse.

Then, living in it, it proposed a possible man.

It named him Squire Allworthy, and asked the reader to co-imagine him: to suppose him, to say along with its narration that this man lived.

Perhaps he lives still – why not?

A supporting form of agreement which came with no pressure to truly or fully believe *in* him. On the contrary, it worked on the understanding – it kept on making clear, in different ways – that this was a story, in the process of being told.

Even so, built into the terms of engagement: the requirement that the reader at least *allow* him. That is, *permit* him: give him entrance, some form of access to her own imaginative chambers. It counted on this imaginative dispensation – on her willingness – to at least provisionally let him in and (thereby) let him live.

On the other, the kind that put a hand in front of the scenes she was both receiving and projecting and said:

"Dear Reader."

It presumed to address the reader directly – to interrupt her guided imagining:

"Gentle and sagacious Reader."

It said: look: *this* is what I'm doing. What we're doing. This is what it is like, and what it is not like.

This is the experience we – a company of strangers – are involved in together.

"O friendly Reader," the narrator will say in one of the later essay parts: "it is impossible we should know what sort of person thou wilt be."

ROSE

A newcomer. Responsive to her environment. Her existence un-folding from the unique place she occupied in space, time, and the world – configured as living-room (the situated site of a pink, sprung, bouncy chair). The world addressing itself to her in a riot of potential messages: the shift and sideways loom of a great, sometimes familiar, sometimes estranging shape, the inchoate smells and feel of her prox-imity, her mutterings and moods. The immediate overhead canopy of contrasts, patterning themselves, patterning her: pressing down into then drawing out her attention; now blurring, now sharpening her surroundings with light. Her responses were active, productive; small in scale but by no means inconsequential. The work of coming up with them was tense, quickening – and exhausting.

It was a lot. It felt like everything, potentially (contained, whether through presence or suggestion, in the novel in her hands). But there, smoting, sparking in the mix – was also LOVE. The crackle of LOVE.

A further chapter of Fielding's novel titled "Of love."

In what forms?

LOVE: acting not like one among all the other named characters or discrete objects placed in the container but more like a form of knowledge, a condition of knowing, in the way it behaved: a gathering, a focus and a distribution, a connection, an energy of invested interaction.

LOVE: the word could make the floor fall open. Now, in the living room: it could sink a pit.

For Helen, LOVE was a question like a hole she spent a big portion of the day, long sections of the night, edging her way around.

LOVE and its relation to day-to-day happiness. The chance of it, the struggle for it. For who gets a chance at it? The novel's reply: that it depends. It will always depend, surely, on a combination, some planned or contingent composition, of all the above: BIRTH. How and when and into what conditions a person is born. On the big impersonal FORCES: directing lives and forcing the allocation of ATTENTION: what (who) counts, what (who) matters – who is worth paying attention to, worth spending time with, living alongside and getting to know – as well as who gets a chance to live with or nearby whom; who, typically, is primed and positioned to take an interest in and look after whom. It will depend on, or be suggested by, the NAMES people impose on and receive from one other. On their social KNOWLEDGE, or lack thereof, as well as their curiosity: a

revving momentum of wanting to know, wanting to find out more, to get at the distinctiveness of someone else, to receive the living material of their communications and respond adequately. On wealth, whether linked to work or operating independently from it, and to safe and reliable housing (a weather-protected SPACE in which to live; in which or from which to strike out and attend to something or someone else). More basically still, on the capacity to move about and actually *live* in those spaces. And therefore on TIME. ("How much time does love take?" asked E. M. Forster, in his lecture course on the novel). The SPACE and TIME for action, for interaction (for development, for growth, for doing and learning, undoing and unlearning), for the shorter, briefly abundant because inessential pleasures (FLOWERS), as well as for food, for rest, and for sleep. Which is to say on some further idea – some promise, at least – of continuance, connection, and extended duration.

LENGTH – AND ENTERTAINMENT

The practice of folding sheets: an activity for (at least) two people. In this instance, one shorter (Rebba; instructing), one much taller (Helen; towering, following, learning). For indoors or outdoors. In fine weather, depending on access: an activity for a garden, courtyard or field.

The technique: two participants start by facing each other. In fact, they will face each other throughout. They are each holding two corners of a sheet.

The sheet has just been washed, and dried; they pull it out taut between them because it's important to keep it off the ground.

Now, in coordination, they both pass the left-hand corner to their right hand, freeing their left, folding it length-wise. Its centrefold makes a new corner. They reach down to grasp it. Once grasped, they turn the fabric, from vertical back to horizontal.

Now they approach. One of them hands their corners over to the other, who grasps and pinches them firmly together. The other, hands free, bends to catch and lift the middle of the sheet at two corners of its new fold.

They draw apart. Only now, because the sheet has been folded width-wise as well as length-wise, their bodies are closer than they were to begin with.

They are likely to be looking directly, up or down, into each other's eyes, sharing breath and smiling. Possibly laughing, because it's simple, domestic, and very satisfying, this collaborative folding activity. A weekly ritual like a short folk dance. It was only worth performing on Rebba's large, flowery, inherited sheets, not Helen's cheap fitted ones, with the bunchy elasticated corners, that can only be rolled, stuffed, shoved into the back of a cupboard until it's once again time to attach them to a bed.

And repeat. Until the large sheet is folded and the two participants are standing nose to chest, nose to air, with a sheet compacted into thick rectangle between them.

"Entertainment," whether "mental" or physical, defined as an interactive relational activity a bit *like this* – only now with the whole action played in reverse:

In this version, the participants *start out* with a compacted, bundled thing and slowly, collaboratively, spread it, shaking and drawing out the length as well as the width of the sheet, taking up the room, while still taking care to keep the whole thing up off the ground. Now letting it billow, now gather. Noting how it forms a kind of hammock for a potential third person to sleep in – or a means of carrying things: all sorts of things. Things that could either tumble randomly about together or be bounced into finding their separations, as the sheet snaps taut.

Entertainment: the noun comes from the Old French *entretenir*, meaning a holding action, a holding relation, "to hold together, support" from *entre* ("among, between") and *tenir* ("to hold, to stretch out"). In the late fifteenth century it acquired the meaning of "to maintain, to keep (someone) in a certain frame of mind." Later still (1620s), "to gratify, to amuse, offer hospitality." The further meaning of "to allow something, to take it into consideration, take it into the mind" came in 1610, "entertainment" as in the temporary (spatial as well as temporal) hosting of ideas.

LIVING APART

Now they lived apart, Rebba would visit. Often, she'd drop by – pressing the doorbell in a formality they each found bizarre and estranging – to observe and try making sense of Helen's different way of life, also to support her: to hold the baby for a while, in the evenings, to make Helen dinner, give her a break. The surface questions she asked when she came to the flat were: How are you and what is it like? What is it like living with a baby? Not only surface: she did want to know. As she spoke, she'd scoop Rose up with a capable arm and smile broadly over her head with a confidence and near nonchalance that Helen could find extraordinary. But pushing underneath those questions was another one. They both heard it: What is it like to live no longer the two of us? Here in this street, with the same old plant, your baby, your landlady treading over your head? A silent set of questions that also wanted to ask something else:

Not only what is it like.

But also, why did you leave? Why did you dismantle the set-up we had?

They'd look at each other. Look down or away.

Glance back.

Helen seated on the sofa; Rebba standing by the window with Rose in her arms. Rebba's small frame making Rose appear suddenly enormous.

Rose looking up at Rebba, fascinated by the roll of gravel in her voice, this new style of being held, her different and interesting smells.

In an effort to respond, Helen would pull her hands apart.

She'd wait a beat then pull them farther apart.

Then, in confusion, draw them back, a bit closer together, but still maintaining some distance between them. As if she were trying

to measure out something for Rebba in the air. A thing – an involvement, an experience – whose true extent she had no way of describing, or even – for her own purposes – knowing or guessing at.

When her hands were wide apart – as wide as her arms could span – they spoke for her. They said: it's long.

The simple revelation of this would strike Helen afresh each time her hands expressed it for her and she would have to take in a breath.

It's long.

As her hands spoke of this, Rebba waited for Helen to speak.

When eventually she did, she said: I don't know.

I mean.

I don't think it's something that I, or anyone, can just . . . *say.*

MEASURING AND THEORISING IN THE LIVING ROOM

Helen, stilled, her hands spanned and held apart in an attitude of measurement. Trying, spatially, to indicate time ("the amount of time occupied by (or with) something (or someone else)") ("the time during which something continues"); taking her time and using the proportions of her body to, loosely, indicate space. Now making an effort to expand on what she hadn't said. To get at this dimension which felt important, critical. Profoundly un-trivial. What it is to embark on something that won't be (it matters greatly that it should *not* be) over quickly. An undertaking with contours but no evident, already determined end. She was finding it hard.

I mean.

I can't tell you briefly. I mean in like five minutes, or half an hour.

And although (she went on, no longer speaking out loud to Rebba but addressing her silently inside her head): I like it – genuinely, I need it and I appreciate it – when you come around to sit with me, to be with us, to help me out. Truly, I could not do without it. You, here, walking Rose to the window, staying with us for half an hour, for an evening, cooking for me. But you must know, also, and at exactly the same time: it doesn't make the tiniest bit of difference. This dipping in, these small, relatively unpredictable stretches of company and support. It does almost nothing to smooth out the hard angles of our days, the weird loneliness of our wide long nights.

One afternoon, one evening of baby-care. It doesn't scratch the sides.

It doesn't touch the surface.

With this she let her hands together with her face drop. The important thing she was trying to express. Her question: How to give it

the sufficient weight and solidity, so that it had a chance of *landing*? Landing and registering. Landing on a surface sensitive enough to receive it – sitting there for a bit, then actually *sinking in*?

Her answer: rephrase it. Repeat herself. Set stories around it, tell stories about it. Keep saying it in different ways. Ask the narration to help by setting other materials around it – drawing the problem out by setting it on a different plane, or by phrasing it in the language of other projects, developed in other, connected spheres.

Her eyes under her thick eyebrows would defocus and fill, she'd push back her hair, and try saying it again:

I can't tell you in five minutes, half an hour.

It might be that it's not fully *sayable*. (She meant: of the order of the sayable. Also, of the order of the summarizable.)

It would take longer.

It would need a new form. One at least part-defined by length. (By which she meant: Amplitude. Flexibility. A capacity to stretch and make room.)

Helen, speaking to herself from her innermost self: No one understands this but I do.

REBBA

Watching, intently; providing Rose with a thumb to open and close her tiny grasping hand around. Listening, seriously, because she wanted to understand. Whilst also feeling, in a different, tucked away part of her own self, like she probably had a handle on it. Like she'd already gained a reasonable and sufficient sense of the main action. The main actions of feeding, sleeping/not sleeping, walking the baby. Scenes which in any case only confirmed by repeating all the same and already familiar gestures of newborn care. Like everyone else, she'd seen them acted out on TV and in other media: one or two short scenes *standing in for* repetition, for interruption, for responsibility. But now, in the moment, because she loved her friend, she said:

Fine.

She came over to sit near her, Rose in her arms.

She leaned in towards her, and put the back of her open hand on Helen's knee.

She beat on her friend's knee for a while, gently, with the back of her open hand.

Try telling me a bit now and I'll come back tomorrow after work, or over the weekend.

I'll pick it up.

You carry on.

CONTINUATION

I will just go on a bit further with this, Helen thought to herself, since it's arrived.

Since I ordered it – *Tom Jones*. And it's in here with us now – another object in the room.

I'll just try to get going with it – to get into it. Make a little incursion into the great territory of this composition. My novel; see if I do like it.

Rose's concerns lapped at her elbow. Helen leaned into her book.

The ball of hair knotted at the top of her head slumped forward, quivering with its own form of zombie life.

I'll just read the first few sentences of chapter one – the first line:

"An author ought to consider himself, not as a gentleman who gives a private or eleemosynary treat, but one who keeps a public ordinary . . ."

Okay but: "eleemosynary" – is that even a word?

Helen wondered, briefly. Before deciding it didn't matter.

Because – listen, she wanted to tell someone: this container – it's actually a pub!

A "public ordinary": a space to talk and drink and eat and come together; the form making a provision of shelter, refreshment and hospitality; a relaxed open house in which all persons are welcome for their money.

COME IN!

The novel said – with its opening manner, its quickly established informality. (So, who was inviting whom? Who was accommodating and entertaining whom?)

You can.

In principle – in democratic principle – anyone can.

Cost of entry, second-hand: one pound thirty-four.

(Full price, twelve ninety-nine. Once paid, you can stay for as long, or leave and come back as often, as you like . . .).

Helen liked the pub.

She liked how, on dark days, cold, rainy nights, its doors stood open, promising a high stool, a perch at the bar. Or a chair at a table for more than one, or sometimes an armchair or a sofa at a lower coffee table, as if you were in someone's home. The warmth of a real or faked fire, framed paintings on the walls, beer mats set about like coasters on the surfaces, growing softer over the course of the afternoon, into the evening, until they could be pulled apart like bread. Its opening times, its closing times: its last rushed orders. Its occasional animal inhabitant: dogs; cats. A pub with a cat is a good pub.

The pub: Rebba called it one small nation's fantasy of its own best living room.

In principle, Helen embraced the pub: a local space designed for togetherness and conviviality. Public and ordinary. Open and prosaic.

In practice? Helen had strong memories of the beer-gardens of her childhood, the anxious entry-tricks of her later teenage years. The likely pubs, the indifferent pubs. The ones where you'd be actively asking for it (for something you didn't want) if you dared to push on in. The closed-down, emptied out, gutted old pubs. The high-street chains of pubs, their expected décor; the small variations in the patterns of their carpets. The newly refurbished pubs: with bookshelves, board games, candles and expensive, exclusive food. In practice, she recognized, the English-language pub was not what it promised: a hosting space for anyone (everyone) to enter, feel welcomed and easy

in. It came with conditions and assumptions. It achieved its distinctiveness from the ways they could be relied on to reproduce themselves. Like any tradition, it was a matter of who got in there first. Or, who has been recognized as getting in there first. Establishing the horizons of expectation. Claiming and taking up space, spreading themselves out, performing a sense of belonging, their own confident and conspicuous at-home-ness in *this* powerful ideation of a hospitable home. There were pubs with bouncers on the doors:

You look alright.

Come in.

You can.

Yep, you. You, with all your friends.

You can.

But –

Hold on. Not you.

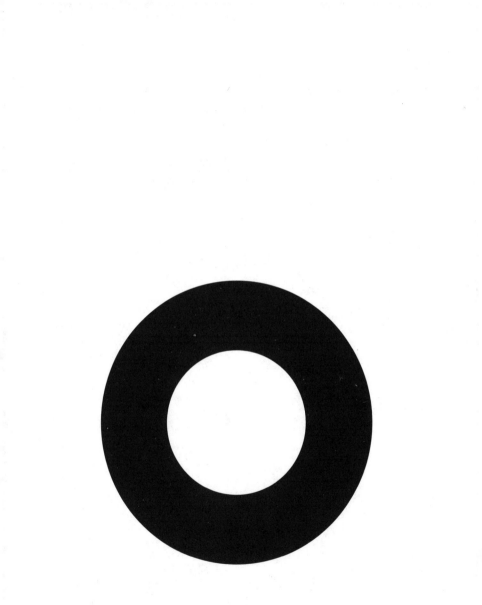

LAYERS; ALTERNATIONS

The view presented by the corner of her desk was of layers. Engineered wood. Its relative strength, its dimensional stability – she'd learned this from Rebba, who could knock up temporary walls singlehandedly, dividing (in the space of half a day) a large, white, indiscriminate cube-like room into smaller volumes, each one proposing its own new world – was achieved by exactly this: layering, alternating. The desk top was a compound made from cheaper, thinner, and more flimsy materials, all of them pressed and glued together – none of which could have managed any kind of support-work on its own. Specifically, by turning each new layer at least ninety degrees before gluing, thereby alternating the direction of the grain. Sideways on, it looked like a sandwich – like her Nanna's sandwich sponge – while in front of it the mobile jogged and turned.

In Henry Fielding's new Province of Writing, his proposition for a novel, it was like this:

It wanted to tell a story.

It wanted to describe itself.

It wanted to open – to unfold – its own fictional world. For this world to hold steady enough for someone else to believe in.

It wanted, also, to think around and *about* it – its world, its project, roaming in the wider vicinity of itself. Bringing in (as well as pointing outward towards) other subjects, other books, and fields of activity: invoking authorities and not necessarily authorities from the broader social world, writing the names Horace, Homer, and Aristotle on pages that faced-touched those recounting the made-up lives of Molly Seagrim, Mrs Deborah Wilkins, and Tom Jones . . .

Why?

It is a question a reader might ask.

Why these mixed materials? The switch and turn, the discontinuous exposition?

Why, when the narrator of *Tom Jones* himself will later draw attention to the essayistic parts, the commentary parts, and call them the boring parts? The skippable, dispensable, "blah blah blah" parts. The send-you-to-sleep, "soporific" parts?

It was a literary-historical question, a category question, a genre question:

In *The Rise of the Novel*, Ian Watt called *Tom Jones* "only *part-novel*."

Lionel Trilling agreed: it was "more literary criticism than anything else."

It was also an aesthetic question, a rhythm question, a technical-compositional question rephrasable as a knowledge-production question, as a social-political question, a co-living and how-to-keep-going, how-to-carry-on question. If Helen could continue reading, give it time, she would find the question not only phrased but addressed, close to two hundred years ago, in the novel she'd only just begun. If it worked, in the sense that if the composition worked for her, managed to activate (to catch then maintain its hold on) her attention, she would find an answer set out – ventured, at least. If she could be left alone to read, to settle into her book, pages would be turned, time would pass, and eventually she'd get there.

BUT ROSE –

Her focus had come unattached. It was roving now – ranging and insecure. She was starting to fret. A leg kicked more vigorously, in jerky agitation, falling out of time with herself. Helen moved to put her right hand across the rise of Rose's belly and waited – for her body to quieten, for her attention to catch at and again be caught by some movement above her, a sharp or shaky basic shape, some rudimentary distinction.

But Rose – she hadn't slept.

She had fed but she hadn't properly slept for hours now.

Helen knew that her interested occupation of that setting – the sort of small-holding she'd made for her within the larger occupancy of the living room – was only ever temporary.

She could prolong their sitting together, like this, for maybe just a few minutes longer. But Rose would need something else soon.

I'm here.

Helen reached over and twisted the top of the mobile, setting it going again.

But Rose was vexed. Vexing, fretting, fussing – such small words for her amplifying, now out-sized agitation. The shapes of the mobile swung against and hit each other. They lost the maintenance of their distance, their respect for inter-space. They jolted and bashed over her – they did nothing for her; having nothing, anymore, to offer her.

For Rose, there had been too much of this for too long now.

Helen dipped the rim of the chair: a last effort to stay their bit of calm, bring her back to the rhythm she'd lost or forgotten:

But Rose – every limb kicked out now.

She was boxing with her whole surroundings, having a local fight with the air. Her fret-fret-fret pitched in volume and urgency.

Helen undid her action; stilled the chair. Would that be enough?

Above their heads, she could hear footsteps: the landlady moving about.

I'm here – surely her adjacency, her presence, spoke for her. Would that be enough?

I'm still here.

And you know what?

HE'D HEARD HER

Through the front door. After he rang the doorbell – pressing hard. Then pressing again, making himself heard in order to get this thing done, one more thing delivered, in order to get on and deliver something else. The street had been empty: all-quiet; deep-set and leafy. A cat under a tree, staring at his legs. There'd been no one else about and he'd heard her shout at him. Through the panelled wood, the bubbled glass of the door's small window pane. Some woman shout-swearing. Then pulling open the front door and aggressing him with the supercharge of her whole body. It didn't matter. He'd made her angry, raging – whatever. It didn't matter. She'd blasted her *angry* out at him and he'd turned, ducked down the steps to get out of the way but still he'd received a bit of it. So what? He could let it go. He was back in his van, temporarily parked in a different nearby street. The spare front seat colourful and crowded with yesterday's wrappers, three empty water bottles. Tunes on. It's not what you need, though, is it? He could let it go. Still, he was aggravated. Because it was seriously not what you – not what any person – needs. Why not just put a note on it, raging lady? Big adult girl. The front door, the bell: you could just put a note on it. If you don't want people *to bring you* the stuff you order, *delivering it directly into your hands*. He pressed his eyelids with the pads of his longer fingers – then glanced down at his phone. He spoke to it for a moment, willing it to light up. He had spent the past few hours speaking quietly to it, coaxing it, waiting: for a message to rise and bloom, thick and lily-like on its surface. Not just anything from anyone but a message addressed to the core of him. Some tender hey babe, how are you, luv u, I love you, a cat-in-love, a bear, a-bear-in-love. It didn't matter what she sent. Only he did need something. Some new confirmation, some each morning renewed confirmation

of shared feeling from the person he'd loved since childhood. Always at a distance, then recently much closer, at first too scared to stand next to her in a room, even, let alone to speak to her, to touch her. It was painful to need it. He felt swollen with it. It was painful to wait. His phone: he called into it silently. It was a magic pond. An ink-black rectangle of wishing-well. If he were to touch it anywhere other than its white and silver rim, it would take his finger-tips. Given half-a-chance, it could swallow a hand. It could sink his arm all the way up to the elbow. Then pull him farther in – he'd lose his torso. He'd be sunk to the neck in its deep liquid power. Within seconds, it could claim and be drowning the whole of his heart.

Now she gathered up Rose, her soft limbs dangling from her different knotted places, her thighs and her lower back a bit damp from her big nappy and the warmed nylon of the chair.

Slowly, ascending in stages, she came to standing.

For Rose, a great whiteness expanded, the world shifted, lifted and tipped. All the sensations were suddenly higher and calming, cool and different.

Helen walked them both down the hall to the narrow length of galley kitchen at the back of the flat.

She leaned her pelvis against the hard edge of the sink.

Rose pulled briefly away from Helen's body. For a second, she held her head apart, straining with every effort of her neck. Then fell back, brow-first, face-first, into Helen's chest. The warmth from that immense body-surface interacting with her own.

Helen's jumper was spongy and ridged: Rose turned her cheek against it. With half of her fingers folded she touched at a section of it: touch, touch, touch.

The kitchen looked out onto a small garden. It could be accessed by an iron staircase that wound down from the landlady's balcony flat above. There was a backdoor next to the sink in Helen's flat, in the kitchen. It, too, led outside: the landlady and her family must have used this to access the garden when they all lived there, when the big house was whole. Helen could open the door, she'd been told. Of course! she'd been told, indulgently. Since it was spring, or later in the year when the days were warmer: in the summer, for air. Whenever necessary: of course! In any case, spelling this out: *obviously* in all seasons, she could walk down the little gravel path to get to the back gate and from there to the alley with the bins. She wouldn't be expected to take the long way around, especially not with the baby.

But the garden itself – the square of hedged-in space, the one stone pot of winter pansies set centre-square to make the paved area look bigger, or grander, but in effect smaller – it was one of the conditions of her tenancy agreement that Helen not "use" it.

Helen looked out the window. So far, the only larger life form she'd seen in the garden was a slow-moving tortoiseshell cat. Each day, several times a day, it jumped down from the fourth step of the balcony stairs to land heavily – front paws, back paws – onto the patio below. Then proceeded to make a new round of its territory, keeping to one side of the path, flattening to push underneath the privet hedge, into the grassier, wilder, barely tended garden next door.

Now she leaned forward to open the tap. Recently, she had improvised a way of clamping Rose's shoulder under her chin as she did this – to prevent her from falling into the sink. With the same right hand, she filled the kettle.

The time the kettle took to boil was very short. It was too short to leave it – to take themselves off and get involved in something else. But long enough for contemplation: for Helen to stand there, holding Rose – Rose looking in the opposite direction, looking over and mouthing her shoulder, her head bobbing warmly at her ear – and feel afterwards like she'd actually looked out of the window.

The kettle, connecting with its base-power, puttered slowly into life.

Helen's thoughts travelled back to the night.

She felt the tight cords of her energy slacken, come loose. The long night. The straight lines and sharp edges of the kitchen drooped, then sagged.

Rose had slept so well to begin with. She'd managed to connect the first of her sleep cycles to the second, to link one of the sequences that Helen had read up about to the next one without a break: to drift

from early, light, muttering sleep down into deep, dreaming sleep, and rise again all the way back up, to just under the surface, but without actually surfacing, without actually breaking the surface – staying under and simply finding her own way back down. It had made a duration of three full hours: a glorious, thick continuity. Helen had woken up feeling new, restored: absolutely astonishingly amazing.

Then she'd checked the time. How was it only 11 P.M.?

Back to sleep.

But, having achieved this once, Rose was incapable of doing it again. She'd slept, but then started, with spacing, to wake. First after about an hour, then after what felt like a good deal less than an hour, and then back to sleep again but only for the smallest portion of an hour. Still, it was nowhere near morning.

And yet, for Rose, the whole enterprise of night-time: it was like it was all over.

She was crying now. Resisting. Resisted being held; resisted being fed. Twisting her small body, turning her hard head powerfully: this way, then that.

In the end, Helen had got them both up and come through to the living room.

The change of setting helped. The temperature of the different room helped. They'd paced around the front room in the dark, every now and then pausing to look out at the street. The houses and flats facing them: looking out for who if anyone was still awake, whose rooms were curtained and dimly lit, who was switching off, who was finally taking themselves off to bed. Upstairs. The landlady: Had she been listening? Had her own sleep been disturbed? Judging, possibly. Was she?

In the end, Helen had switched on the lamp, made tea, pretended for a long time that it was daytime. They simulated a portion of a day together through the deepest, loneliest part of the night. Then, somewhere between six and seven, found another scrap of sleep: a shaving – for Helen a hectic, dream-pulsed snatching of light, unrefreshing sleep.

The kettle kicked off – it started to get noisy in its containment of fast-heating water. Helen reached for the fridge. She considered for a moment the chart taped to the door. The log of Rose: the paper record she was keeping of all their days. Rose's whole life divided into feeding times, awake times, sleeping times. The unpredictable durations recorded in unmatched colours, motley shades of ink and felt tip, as Helen worked her way through the assortment of pens she'd found in the kitchen drawer left behind by the previous tenant, whom the landlady made clear she hadn't liked. She sensed that she hadn't approved of him – did it matter?

Nisha said it didn't. Promised it wouldn't.

She's quite nice really, she'd said.

(She's not, like, a *monster.*)

Helen studied the chart.

She tried hard, as she did each day, to read it: to work out what having one kind of thing for a certain amount of time might lead to, how it might predict what was to come.

Rose felt, not heavy, but heavier, in her left arm.

How was she? Was she sleepy now?

Helen checked: Rose?

Rose was busy with her own experience.

Inside the kettle, a sealed unit, large bubbles were forming, rising; its noise grew louder. Helen had learned about this at school. How a kettle works not through compliance but resistance: the heat

of its central element and – as consequence of the water – rising from the effort to *stop* electricity flowing through it. The metal around the collar had started to sweat. She turned again to the window: there were pansies out there, trembling, hardily, in their pot. Such rich colours: golds and purples. A royal velvety blue. Her thoughts trailed outwards to join up with gardens and she wondered, briefly, if it was true, what the papers said. What did they say?

She shifted Rose a bit higher up her shoulder.

Her mind groped: the lifestyle sections of the newspapers.

The incidental news of the day: how you don't need space, or hardly any. Just a windowsill is enough: it (too!) counts as a garden.

She wondered whether this was real. Real and/or true. Whether she should test it in the coming months: buy a new plant from the supermarket – an easy plant. A spider plant. A good-natured strawberry plant. Put it on the kitchen sill, where it would find the afternoon sun. Discover whether tending to it, watching it grow and produce fruit, throw out its runners and reproduce itself (with the paved-over garden as a backdrop behind it) would give her satisfaction.

Or, on the contrary, make her feel resentful. Feel a great ache of resentment which, once felt, would only grow; it wouldn't ever ease.

Two small birds darted out from the hedge, one after the other.

They bounced back in, clearly conscious of each other.

Then out.

Helen watched them, the water in the kettle sounding close to raucous now.

They flitted around the garden, one leading the other in indirect, zig-zagged pursuit.

Their day: it was out there.

It was out there just ahead of them. Ahead of them both, asking to be imagined, requesting to be composed. And beyond it, the day: there was the evening, and further away, the night. They would come around to all of it. It would come around to meet them, eventually, like the street in front of the house, standing there waiting as they stood here, at the kitchen window, one looking in one direction at the strange surface of a shoulder, the other looking out, into the garden at the back.

It'll be ambitious and beautiful!

This was Helen, addressing the day ahead, addressing and rousing herself. Feeling all of a sudden coursed with energy and purpose.

I decide.

It'll be interesting and new.

She shifted her chest to make a different bit of room for Rose. She modified it: we'll decide.

For what are we doing together – if not world-forming? Engaged in our own practice of social creativity?

We'll find our synchronicity and our prosaic happiness – as a strong pair, a community of at least two.

Or, if not that – she faltered. The quick forward-firings of her brain sputtered, dampened, slowed, started to turn back. Her body remembered again that it was tired. She closed her eyes. She turned her neck to rest her chin on Rose's head. She let herself give in a bit, feel the weight and be for a moment weighted by this.

But so what? She rallied.

Isn't everyone? Everyone is tired; everyone has their own reasons to be tired.

But her body's recollection had marked out limits:

If not interesting, if not ambitious, if *tired* –

If working with tiredness, in the key of tiredness (cut with adrenaline), then –

If no different, in its large strokes, from yesterday, if not exceptional, then – calm.

Let it at least be *calm*.

That is, safe.

A safe day. Surely, the basic grounding for any order of ordinary happy day.

Let nothing happen, in fact.

For who cares if it's boring, as long as it's undramatic?

As long as we get through it (together, intact).

"Three in bed, nobody dead." It was the end-of-the-day rhyme she'd heard Nisha call out – cheerily, cheerfully. Finally reaching the bottom of the stairs after an epic adventure of getting two out of three of her kids to clean their teeth, persuading the big ones into their bunks, putting the little one down in his cot, singing songs, reading stories, declaring lights off. Night night. Then: lights back on. What now?

Sip of water.

What now?

Wee and the existential stuff. (What *is* night?)

What now?

I don't like the way the curtain . . .

Lights OFF and finally down the stairs.

Seriously? Helen had wondered, early on in her pregnancy; she'd been invited for a meal, for a sharing, supportive chat.

It was such a low bar.

Now she held Rose, her head holding itself up effortfully, close to her ear.

She exhaled a long breath.

The truth was: it was the bar.

Like anyone in her situation, near her situation or willing to imagine it, she knew this. She lived with it. She knew it and yet spent a great deal of mental energy investing to the point of almost believing in the fiction that it didn't apply to her, to Rose, to their situation. But it was true, a rare cold fact: how every attention could be paid, every necessary form of care given and still it could be possible, inexplicably, unfathomably, for new life to end.

The birds, it seemed, had made a nest in the hedge.

An idea lit through her: I should put a note on it.

It lit straight through her.

It left.

Now it returned:

I could just put a note on it, she thought. Simple: like a post-it or similar.

She put the milk on the counter, placed a big rubbing hand on Rose's back.

A sticky note above the doorbell saying: hi, hello. In big letters: PLEASE—don't ring.

Just tap on the window. I'd hear you.

The kettle boiled and steamed riotously. Until rising heat-pressure made something inside it trip, flip. So many other worldly processes persevered. Abruptly, this one stopped.

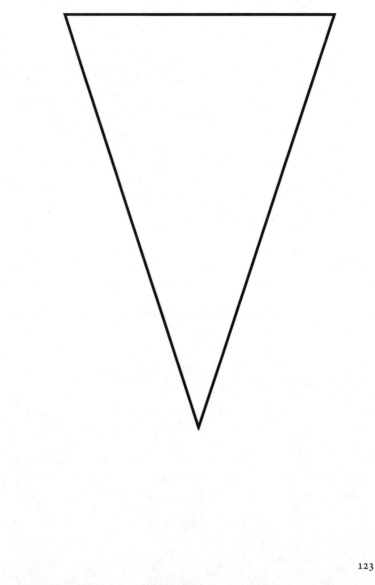

WE WASHED THE NOVEL

A NARRATIVE MAKES ITS OWN TIME

Imagine (just for a short while: the space-time of a page and a half): Helen, seated on the sofa in the same living room, in the future and the sofa is different: a changed fabric pattern as well as larger – the kind that unfolds at night to make a bed. She is working on her laptop.

Rose, nearby, her body transformed by time, food, growth, change and development, working at pushing plastic objects through the holes in the lid of a box. Three-dimensional shapes, two-dimensional holes. Sitting up sturdily with her legs in a V. She fits a cube side-first through a black square and BAM! It disappears.

Now she's distracted by a strange sound.

Helen looks up; she's noted the noise, too.

From the kitchen: a thumping, also a tumbling. Something was getting lifted all the way up, then dropped, regularly dropped: lifted and then let go. The sound has a violence to it. It intensifies. They look at each other, wide-eyed – Helen feeling inwardly a bit concerned. It grows frenzied. It appears to crescendo. They both feel relief when eventually it calms down. It stops. They'll wait. A further thirty seconds. The time it takes for the little red light in the shape of a key that Rose likes to press (LOCK on / LOCK off) on the front of the washing machine to go out. Helen will open the round door, reach into the darkness of the drum, and pull out a new object. It will take her a moment or two to figure out – to recognize – what it is. It feels like a brick. A heavy, wet block. Water having soaked through it, the cheap card of the cover, loosening the colours of its reproduced painting, soaking through every one of its pages. The thin page-paper hadn't dissipated in the machine, covering everything lightly, like a tissue left in a pocket. Rather, the pages have been packed together. They

have soaked into each other, and combined. The wet and the rolling motion of the machine binding them into a density, making a whole. It is a solid now, and ruined. Helen will find this very funny. Look! she'll say, loudly. Laughing at the unlikelihood of the object, of the process – but also a little bit at Rose's expression, which gave away the part she'd played in it: we washed the novel!

Tom Jones.

Then, noting the real consternation in Rose's face. The corners of her mouth turning downwards, her body trembling . . .

Hey, it doesn't matter. *It* won't mind.

Love, love, love! It's alright.

NAMES

A TALE OF FIRST NAMES

When Helen was pregnant she read a story about a girl stealing roses. Helen, who had never stolen anything in her life, at least not directly from a shop or somebody else's garden. Not even when the girls from school would slide eyeliners and lip-pencils up their sleeves, tuck the flatter tubes of foundation and bars of chocolate into the cuffs of their jumpers, their puffed winter coats. Helen would just sort of stand there, slightly apart. Then bundle out of the shop behind them, out into the precinct to marvel at their bounty as though it were also hers. Feeling powerfully excited by the whole adventure but personally cut off from the action of just taking something. Just wanting it and taking it for herself. In the translated story, the narrator describes it as a "glory." Running as a small girl up the long drives and into the well-tended gardens of a city suburb on the other side of the world, breaking the stem of a rose – which can't have been easy to do fast: bending and twisting until it exposed bright green then a hidden column of white and snapped, a ragged snap – escaping with it in her hand, careful to pinch it with her fingers in a space between its thorns, then bringing it home. Putting the rose-head in a bowl – all thick-petalled, lush and heady – to take it in, daydream around it and admire it. Such a short-term, perishable rush was "always a glory that no one could take from me." The choice of Rose's name had something to do with this: the postulate a private inner glory. A splendour that a small person could carry about inside themselves. Perhaps she could give her that (or try to). Let her start out with it, so that later she wouldn't have to take it, snatch it or steal it or require it to be bestowed upon her by someone else. Although there was also a further, more distant story behind Rose's name. Or, if not exactly the story in and of itself, which was old, many-authored and variable, then something closer

to the feeling it produced: a tense fascination for a board book that Helen read over and over when she was a child. On the front cover, she could still see the gigantic woman enlarged further by a massive white fur coat. Each one of the coat's outgrowing hairs traced silver, like the frozen tracks of a fountain, or the arcing spray from a watering can. Snowflakes blasting, in their soft, slow motion, out of the palms of the formidable woman's pale blue hands. All of it under plastic, since the book had come from the library. Helen had once tried telling its story to someone else: conversationally, to a guy she barely knew, some climbing friend of a friend of Rebba's whom she had only just met. They were walking each other on a short trip down the hill to buy booze for a party – their flat favoured for late nights by everyone they knew because of its setting: above a parade of shops, no neighbours close by to complain. They were waiting in the queue for the checkout. Helen had picked up and was planning to pay for a bunch of discounted yellow roses. Ten flowers, sheathed in plastic, dripping at the ends with the water that had been keeping them fresh in a blue plastic bucket: £4.99 reduced to £2. Taped to the side of the bunch was a little sachet of white powder. It promised to keep the flowers alive for longer, once you got them home. Or if not that – because cut flowers are presumably already dying – then at least to help the buds to open. Although, as the guy she was with had just pointed out, by the way they were looking, with the petals already wet, darkening and starting to feather at the edges, the chances were they'd just stay like that: all screwed up and budded. They'd have been forced somewhere far away, draining the water supply there, then flown over here to live and then die like that.

They'd have no scent, probably.

They wouldn't open.

She shouldn't buy them.

But I like them, Helen had said, sensitively.

I always buy roses when I see them. Well, the yellow ones.

Yeah but why?

Well, because I like them. And I can. I have the money – right now, with my job, I have enough money for flowers.

Then, more hesitantly, first a way of skipping over the real inter-activity between her actions here and the water over there, a communication she accepted but had no idea what to do with, and then, not because she wanted to exactly, but more because she sensed an opportunity, a chance to attach a lasting sticker or badge to herself, so that this stranger – who matched her in height but not in volubil-ity – would see that she had attributes and from that point on at least be able to locate her, to fix and distinguish her among the girls and women:

I'll tell you.

I'll tell you what I'll tell you, and the phrasings of the book started to pattern in her voice:

It is the story of two children, a girl and a boy. They live next door to each other, but very high up. Imagine adjacent attic rooms at the top of two tall houses and, between them, a narrow strip of roof. And on that bit of roof: roses; someone has put out two wooden boxes, both of them planted with yellow roses.

Helen began taking the assorted items out of her trolley, and plac-ing them, one by one, heavy packs of beer, wine, spirits, a net bag of lemons, also soap, and butter, and roses, and behind them more things to come, on the conveyor belt. It was her turn. The woman at the checkout must have pressed the pedal at her feet, because almost at once the belt started to move: each item set down in its own chancy sequence, moving at first slowly then faster and faster away.

The two children climb out and meet each other on the roof. Each

day they play up there together. And, in fact, even as a child the idea of this would make Helen feel a bit strange. It seemed so precarious: small children climbing through their windows, stepping out over the gutters, to come together – to play! – at such a height on a narrow strip of roof. Who was not watching so that the kids could play up there? They loved each other: these children who weren't related – who had no family obligation to care for each other, but seemed to anyway. There was also a grandmother, but the story doesn't say whose, the girl's or the boy's. She might also have been a neighbour, some friendly local woman. She sometimes looked after them in the evenings, and would tell them tales. Cautionary, instructive tales. One of the tales was the story of the Snow Queen: how she comes in the dark, always on cold nights, to decorate the windows with ice. Sitting cosily by the fire, when he heard about this, the boy would usually say something like: if she ever comes in here, I'll smash her face. But one day it happens. It's winter, and he goes out to play in the big square. The children are playing at hooking their sledges onto the larger sleighs. The boy hooks his sledge onto the largest, grandest sleigh in the square and it pulls him away. At first just a little bit away, which feels like it's still part of the game, then there's acceleration: the larger sleigh pulling him farther and faster and farther and then a great – immense, unfathomable – distance away. When the sleigh-driver eventually turns around, the boy sees that she has a Queen's face. He looks at her: "he could not imagine a wiser or lovelier face."

That line: "he could not imagine a wiser or lovelier face."

What kind of face do I have? Helen had often wondered as a child, as a teenager, as a grown woman now watching, at a supermarket check-out, a slow parade of drink go by: Is it wise? Do you (will someone, one day) find it lovely?

The Queen says nothing.

She lets the boy climb up into her own sleigh, leans down and kisses his forehead and that's it. His brain freezes. He is gone.

The girl in the great town, meanwhile, in the story, remains.

She stays behind. The story stays with her.

She has no idea where the boy is, or what has become of him. How could she?

She cries.

She cries and she cries. All the way until spring, when the days grow lighter and longer.

Then she sets out alone to find him.

The rivers speak in this story. When the girl reaches the river on the outskirts of the town, she asks it if it has seen the boy. She throws her new red shoes into the moving water in exchange for an answer. The river rolls her shoes around in its mouth and says – *no*.

Running on from its answer, it agrees to carry her in a small boat to a stretch of riverside garden. The garden is tended by a lonely old woman. The woman is kind to the girl. But it's clear that she wants something. She wants her companionship. She wants the girl to forget all about the boy. She wants the girl to stay with her forever – to stop the story here. Knowing that roses – especially yellow roses – will remind her of the boy, their little garden among the rooftops, she touches all the rose bushes in the garden with a magic stick. Instantly they are swallowed up by the ground . . .

And: stop, suspension.

But still, time goes by.

Only more thickly; for the girl, barely perceptibly; like water stilling in a lock.

The girl plays from spring into summer in the old woman's garden, in the grass and among all the other species of flowers that grow

and show themselves: the small sprightly ones; the gaudier, thick-stemmed ones, grown from tubers, shaggy clusters that look like organs, like hearts, whose flowers could grow level with her head.

The girl plays and plays and there are so many games but according to the story nothing happens.

Only there's the low uneasy feeling that something is not right; someone is missing.

Then, one day, for the first time in a long time, an event: she looks closely at the old woman's hat: the old woman had forgotten that her sunhat was painted with all the most common garden flowers.

The girl is stunned. Seeing the painted yellow roses, she's all of a sudden awoken.

I've been here for too long, she calls out – to the river, the roots underground, and all the flowers growing in the grass.

Far too long! The roses hear her: they push up from the earth to hang their heads.

The girl asks them: Where is the boy? Have you seen him?

The girl sets off again, alone and on foot.

Time passes. Adventure time passes. It's no longer still: panicked, it starts racing.

Already, it is autumn.

She heads north, where it is colder. She stops at a palace. A rest-stop.

A crow has told her how two children sleep in a golden bed there, their beds shaped like leaves, and how one of them could be but turns out not to be the boy. The palace children give the girl "clothes of silk and velvet, fur-lined boots" and a warm muff for her hands. She sets off again, now in a horse-drawn carriage made from "pure gold."

She stops.

She is stopped – this time by robbers. The robbers take her carriage and the horses, and little robber girl also wants her for company. Eventually she lets her go, but takes her soft warm muff, swapping it for a reindeer to ride on and a pair of big robber gloves, along with loaves of bread and a ham. The reindeer takes her farther and farther north, where it is extremely cold, and then even colder.

The reindeer leaves the girl at the edge of the grounds of the Snow Queen's palace, vast wastes of cold white snow, and for the last stretch the girl walks on alone.

There, at last, in a palace made of ice, is the boy kneeling on the cold floor.

All that time, he had been playing with a puzzle.

The whole of that time, the boy had been playing, brain frozen solid, with the same cold white puzzle. Fingers numbed; lips blue.

The girl approaches him. She speaks, she makes him remember. She helps him put the pieces of the puzzle back together which means they can leave. They retrace the girl's journey, moving backwards and much faster this time: the reindeer, skipping over the robber girl, the loaves, the ham and the big gloves, the golden palace, the crow, directly to the river.

Winter into spring.

Once again it is spring: all around them the world is greening. They reach home: two high houses leaning into each other, precariously connected by a high strip of roof.

"Everything stood in the same friendly place."

Without anyone noticing, spring turns into early summer.

"The clock ticked comfortably, the roses growing across the roof waved in the open window."

The time of the telling was not the same as the time it took to move through their turn at the checkout. It went over, outpacing and over-

reaching it. Helen had paid the woman. They had left the shop, walked through the carpark, up the steep hill and were at the street-level door to the flat by the time she came to the end of the story. The bags she was carrying were cutting into her shoulder and the palm of one of her hands because, along with the discounted roses and beers, lemons, soap and butter, she'd also bought washing liquid for her clothes and for Rebba's clothes because they washed them together, cans of tomatoes and jam and other heavier goods. It was as if they had never been away: that was the strange and powerful thing. How a great big stretch of time, and, with that, such a great distance, could open up and unfold so expansively, how it could be lived out as protracted and immense – enfolding her too, in the flow, the onflow of narration – but in the end make no difference at all. The story ends how it begins: it loops. In a friendly place, easily knitting itself back together even after everything had been torn apart. How happy this was: the yellow roses still waving at the window, opening their petals and their scent. As a child, the ending would make Helen feel comforted and happy. But on some other, deeper level, also nervous and on edge. The mix of feelings was not wholly unpleasant. (She was conscious that she'd been going on for a while now. Holding forth: going *on*, recounting this story to her audience of one, a listener whose ear she seemed to have but whose inner interest she doubted, truly, she held; a narrative power linked to a persistence that she was able to sustain only for as long as she wasn't interrupted.) The troubling feeling connected to the strip of roof – to the fact of this space between the houses belonging to neither the one child nor the other, with its boxes of planted earth, a tiny shared garden, so dangerously high up off the ground. The pleasure came from the way the children are not related but still they related: they related first through chance and circumstance, the dice-roll of it being him plus her just happening to live next door to each other, and then through familiarity and love. From how even

when one of them was no longer thinking of the other, when his brain had been frozen so solid he could no longer remember the girl, or the roof, or the roses, still they related to each other, because she at least held herself in more or less constant relation to him. This felt important. But then the doubt again: Wasn't it exactly this that was at risk? Here was a benign rooftop world. Here was a place where two little children could play high up and happily, companionably make a life together. But from where they could also, surely – if you took the premise seriously – just as easily – you know: *fall off.* Where, even in this frictionless, steady and re-steadying world, the bottom could fall out from under you. Kids could get snatched. And where even the most loving heart's inner constancy could get switched off – one day simply *stopped* by some external force – like a – here Helen paused to search for an image, something comparable in the real world to drive home her point –

Yeah, but is that not the plot of a Disney film?

He interrupted just as she found it: like a *tap.*

She had paid for the flowers; she was now carrying them up the four flights of indoor-stairs to the front door of the flat she and Rebba used to share. There, in the kitchen, their stems would be cut, the sachet of powder snipped open at the corner then stirred into the water, filling a plastic bottle that had once been sawn in half with a steak knife to serve as a vase. It was true that they'd never really un-furl; they'd never get loose and fully open. He'd be right in the sense that they'd give no scent. They wouldn't be beautiful, especially. The friends, semi-strangers and complete strangers gathering in the space to compose the party, would ignore them. The roses would stand rigid, stock still, petals wrapped around each other, as Rebba turned up the music, asking everyone in the kitchen to spill into the corridor

and then into the living room and pull in a bit more closely if they still wanted to speak into each other's ears. Then, give up on talking. Nod: together in agreement. Finding through instinct or imitation this alternative way of responding outwardly to each other, as well as to other private prompts, seeking and finding within themselves their own small assents, yeses following on from yeses, everyone nodding yes, yes, yes to the same rhythm-questions. Or shaking *no*. Without resentment, there was no risk, here, of disagreement: just gently, benevolently, shaking and smiling no, no, no, to the same rhythm-questions. Hands and elbows at first in hesitancy, then joining in and raising themselves, taking over from heads in the close set of rooms and collaborating with hips and knees to make the shapes of dancing, shapes that would be thrown and collapsed, thrown and collapsed, in the heat, for hours, for hours and hours, until dawn broke distantly over everyone's heads like a great egg, making every one of them feel viscous, tacky, and rich – and *still* this bloke was trying, she felt, to talk her out of buying a bunch of yellow roses.

True, Helen said in reply.

I mean: Yeah. But, I think, you know, only loosely.

She had put the bags down on the landing floor. She ducked her head into her shoulder, groping in her pocket for her key. Then, addressing the rough cloth of her coat, she added: dickhead.

NAME-CALLING

I call you "dickhead": Helen had once said, didn't quite say, to someone she barely knew. It was reflexive. An attribute, like the large
brown moles on her arms, like her hair or the size of her feet: when
flustered or nervous, embarrassed or humiliated, when she felt like
or had been made to feel like she'd said too much, or more exactly
had used too many words to say too little, scarcely anything at all, she
angered inwardly but directed it outwardly and swore.

He didn't hear; he'd soon forget. Say it didn't matter.

Time passed. More life. Different inconsequential days following
other inadvertently consequential, life-changing days, nights. Until *you*.

At first, only panic. Then a cooler, longer feeling of fear. A period
of desperate indecision. A reckoning: what it is to have participated
in the initiation of a possible *you*.

Then, slowly, a determination. The choice to support a still hypo-
thetical *you*. Once the decision was made, the start of an imagined,
each-day-more-plausible *you*.

Did you know that throughout history "yellow" has been closely
associated with the sun? Did you know that yellow roses, unburdened
by the romance of the pinks and the reds, send out a broader message
of appreciation and concern?

The colour, Helen looked it up, represents feelings of warmth, joy,
and delight.

An increasingly more believable, embodied, immanent, immi-
nent *you*.

Hopeful of joy, holding out for delight, for flowers, for new forms
of human appreciation and expanding circles of concern –

I call *you* Rose.

LISTEN

A twelve-year-old girl called Christy is telling her mother a different
story. Her mother has promised to write it down. She'll publish it and
dedicate the children's book to the kids Christy and her siblings grew
up with on their estate. Children called Jane, Moya, Ricky, Michael,
Alice, and Jake. Her mother is the writer Buchi Emecheta, author of
sixteen novels and a memoir, among them, published in 1979: *The
Joys of Motherhood*. The story is quite long, seventy-two pages – a
summary, with some lines directly quoted, and others rephrased, will
be related here. The setting is North London: the housing estate is
called Regent's Park, after the adjacent public park owned by the
Queen. Among stairwells and high walkways, its blocks are named
after places in the Lake District: Windermere; Cartmel; Rydal Water.
It's the summer, the start of the long school holidays. There is a girl,
May, who is nine. There's her little sister June, who is seven, and their
big brother Dan. He is ten, almost eleven. There is the park within
spitting distance: one of London's largest, most beautiful and well-
tended parks. But they are separated from it by "a very wide and busy
road." There's no crossing. The previous summer a neighbourhood
kid died sprinting across it. Once Dan was "knocked down but he was
lucky": he'd only bashed his hip. June "was the luckiest of all": when
she fell over between two cars they all thought she was dead. Until she
suddenly got up and "ran like the devil was chasing her." Since then
their mother had laid down the law: no going over to the park unless
you cross the road with an adult or "somebody responsible."

Christy's story is the story of kids living out the summer holidays on their side of the big divide. The published novel will be titled
Nowhere to Play. The questions asked by each one of its four short
chapters:

Where will they go?

When they get there, what will they do?

Once they have found somewhere to play, how long can their game last?

They go to the green. Their local small-to-medium-sized patch of common grassy ground. Maintained by the council for collective but usually indeterminate use. To start with, the children play a tagging game: Bulldog. The game is a good one, a familiar one, though May doesn't like it: she finds it too fast, too rough. But they all know the rules; they've played it so many times before. And in fact they do play it and it is fast; soon it's thrilling. They are all cheering and jumping and slapping each other on the backs for not getting caught when there's "an angry tap on the window nearest to the green." The kids hear it but ignore it. They know it's the old lady who lives in the flat above the common. But the taps escalate to "angry bangings" and they get fed up with ignoring them: fed up also, eventually, with running about, chasing, tagging, and bulldogging. They decide to do something else. They don't actually say this out loud to each other; they don't need to. They can all feel how the energy has flagged; they drift consensually into doing something else. Little sister June walks a short distance away from the group.

"Where are you going?" someone asks.

"Nowhere," says June.

She stands with her head to one side, looking up at the city's skyline.

Now she turns back; she has had an idea.

She is going to build a tower.

Specifically, she announces it: "I'm going to build the Post Office Tower."

London's Post Office Tower – they all knew what it was. They

could see it. It was a communications tower just a short walk from their estate. The Post Office tower. The GPO tower; later renamed the British Telecom Tower. In the late 1970s, it "was one of the tallest buildings in the world."

But: For June to propose to build it? No, not it. Her own new version of it. It was baffling. It was stupid. It was entertaining.

June finds a milk crate.

The story takes place in the era of wooden milk crates, milk vans, milkmen and gold top, silver top, red top milk, left by written request on your doorstep.

June finds a second empty milk crate.

The other kids watch.

She puts one crate on top of the other: tower-building.

Now they find it intriguing and somehow admirable: in the end, everyone accepts her premise, even the bigger kids, even Ricky, the cool one. They join in.

The setting is the same. No one has gone anywhere, but something has changed. Something is being built, created, ushered in. A new thing constructed partly from what's around, partly from the imagination. June piles one crate on top of another, until eventually the pile grows so high that she can't reach the top to add the next one.

"Here," says Michael. He volunteers: "let me help you." He is taller than June. Soon the tower is towering, taller than any of them.

Now it is finished.

The tower seems stable. It stands. It is leaning slightly to one side, in the middle of the green. It has altered things: perspective, the configuration of the common space (the green has a public sculpture now), the relations between the children (because for once June is in charge).

June steps back. She considers it. It's not a princess tower. A save-me tower. It's her own model-simulation of *that tower* over there.

She says (not with her own words but with her actions, with her project, in this re-description of her project): we've doubled it. We've brought our own scaled-down version of it *in* (to our space of play). Now, if we want to, we can alter it and adjust it. If we want to, we can think around it and decide for ourselves how we see it, what it means to us: this steel symbol (– of what? The innovation, the "success," the imperial expansion of "British communications"?); this feature dominating the skyline of our estate.

She names it. To the crated pillar, all their vertical stacking, she gives the name "Post Office Tower."

NAMING POWER

It was in a hospital bed, a hot room, its temperature charged to blood, the powerful lights embedded in the ceiling making every detail of her nakedness distinct, that Helen was struck, for the first time astounded, by the deep magic of her own naming power. "Rose" was the sound she made, addressing a mottling, light-reactive weight (a blue-grey weight taking on colour, moving, shifting, sounding, slowly finding all her colours). A warmth placed first by someone else's hands on her belly, then shifted up by the same or by different hands – were they blue plastic-gloved or unprotected hands? – to her chest, her own legs trembling a great distance away, one large familiar hand much closer, also her own, likewise trembling, coming down to a cautious thrumming rest on the smallest small of an infant child's still-sticky back. They seemed to be telling her that the warm heaviness was a baby and that this baby was her child – ?

It had been March and now it was spring.

The bulbs in the beds surrounding the hospital, planted in the autumn: if the rains had not rotted and disempowered them, they'd divided, doubled, shooting and pushed – called forth by light and warmth they'd broken surface with the earth. They were tall now: shin-height, knee-height. They'd grown as tall as they could possibly grow, all around the carparks, in concrete planters acting as decorative barriers to the automatic doors: wet daffodils bowed by rain in the middle of the night.

"Rose" was the sound she made.

But there was so much more going on. It was going on everywhere. Birthing. Naming. Live creatures issuing forth. Outside, in the darkness. Animals giving single, multiple births in hollows, amongst wads of sticks and wet leaves. Furred bodies antagonized,

shocked and spasmed by pain. Birds hopping. Women hopping. Foot to foot. The sounds of live birth happening in the next room – so close, through the wall. Energies resisting each other. Large agonies and the strange, absolutely still, absolutely calm spacings in between. Deaths, departures: likewise going on. Out of doors, in the hospital surrounds and in the different spaces leading off from the bright corridors. Now there were different people in the room, chatting across and over her. Indistinct work getting done at a great distance on her lower body, a woozy sense of being stitched up, one hundred percent repaired they said. Laughter. Was she the one laughing? Helen was laughing. Actually, shuddering. She had been high above the room, rising and cresting over it. Then on her knees, crouching and quaking beneath it. Now they were both here.

In sticky contact.

One a moving weight. The other its sloped, supporting surface.

Two hearts beating against each other: quick, quick reciprocations.

Rose, she said.

The vowel long. Her breath elongated.

The bustle around them quietening, thinned.

After an interval, again: Rose.

They lay there together: chest to chest.

Question and answer, call and un-synched, eventual response.

Loose and ductile, like their ligaments, their sockets and their bones.

Rose bobbed her heavy head up, as if searching for something.

Let it fall.

The room shuddered to keep up with the tremor-tempo of her legs.

Then, from nowhere, tucked over them both: a covering.

A light layer. Protective and enclosing.

What was it?

A big white sheet.

Helen. Rose.

The pair of them covered by a pre-warmed hospital sheet.

The last member of the little crowd that had been gathered about them withdrawing.

The name on her name tag: Elvira.

(She who protects everyone. She tries to.)

NAMING POWER: WHAT DOES THIS MEAN?

For Helen, it meant:

I will say the name "Rose" out loud for you because you can't speak, until you can speak.

I will write Rose down for you because you can't write, until you can write.

I will tell the woman whose name I don't know, but whose hands held you first and passed you to me, set you down on my chest, that this is your name.

I will tell Elvira whose job it was to brace me, who let me push my wet open mouth, the flats of my teeth, into her strong round arms, holding me as if she were my mother, that this is your name, and she will use it as a sound to call you by, too.

This is the short noise that other people will make to invoke you for the duration.

"Rose" is the position I put you in.

I realize this. And I take this on, knowing that it is not the same – it is really not the same – as if I were to call you into being, to issue forth your person, with the name of something or someone else.

The power that Helen wielded (that passed through her) wasn't one that she was exempt from. Clearly not. She, too, had been named. A name that located her in her Englishness, a novel-reading social class, an education, a set of expectations. This is what people do to their newly born: they assign a name and with it they suggest a sex, open a path, "bestow a fate." They pull names out from their ancestry and re-use them, disputing their past usages, stamping them with today's date; they lift them from books and songs, celebrity culture and other people's lives.

"Choose names. Have hair. Hold hands," wrote Gertrude Stein in *A Novel of Thank You*. A novel of hello and goodbye, as well as sorry, please, and how are you. A novel of manners interested in how it matters, how it always matters: the ways people (and not only people) address each other, the names they call each other, setting the terms for who they are or who they're in the process of becoming to each other.

A novel that was its own book of thinking about the novel, written in 1926 but not published until 1958, twelve years after her death.

Choose names:

What was her name, his name, their name?

Did they have hair?

Can you describe it? The colour, the texture?

Have there been changes, did they cut it recently, will she lose it?

A name plus hair. It sounds too simple but if a person were to know these things about someone else, real or imagined, what else would they know – what could they surmise or invent?

Possibly enough.

Enough at least to start marking out a space, the contours of a place for a new person to occupy, in which their character might appear.

Now bring in hands:

How small, how big, how soft, how old?

With whom, if anyone, have they ever held – are they right now holding – or might they at some future point find themselves holding – hands?

Choose names: Rose.

Like Helen's, Rose's hair was very dark. She was born with a high thin shock of it plastered to one side. She couldn't, exactly, hold hands. But she could grasp. She was born grasping – flexing her fingers reflexively around whatever was placed in her palm. A relief.

Some of the names that Gertrude Stein let loose in her novel:

Hilda,

Theodosia,

Zenobie and Helen Strong. What's more, she writes: "Florence can be a name."

"Romaine can be a name."

"Finally can be a name."

(May can be a name. June can be the best of months and also a name.)

"Constance can be a name."

Rebba, when asked: it is a nickname but not a common nickname. I guess it is like a nickname that has been made up between friends or family with an insider understanding to it. It is not like calling someone Mia instead of Maria or Pilla instead of Pernilla. It's more like Rob for Robert, kind of . . . But, honestly, I don't know how I got my name.

(Ebba, on the other hand, is a very common Swedish name.)

Naming and learning each other's names, these processes are at the very start of deciding who people are: part of how we all make each other up. A real "Tom Jones" is said to have appeared before Henry Fielding at Bow Street, where Fielding worked as a magistrate, though what this Tom Jones's offence was nobody knows. In the novel, the character named Mr Allworthy will name the foundling

"Tom" because Tom is his own name and it's a good and thoroughly worthy one so why not repeat it? Why not double it, share it, and in this way continue it?

For, it was true: inside the container, interacting with all the other important and more "sundry matters," the forces and ideas, the objects and forms of knowledge, there was also, crucially, a baby. A live breathing vulnerable creature, defined by its need for protection. He will be found in Chapter Three: just two thin pages on from where Helen left off. Ten more minutes of reading time. She'll get there. Later on today; possibly sometime this afternoon. When she does, there'll be no narrated preparation for it: no gestational work, no scenes of birthing labour.

Just a baby, appearing on its own.

Unexplained, unattached.

There it was. There it is.

MR ALLWORTHY

The favoured living man; his lovely house; its incredible, patch-worked view. He is dressed in his nightshirt on an ordinary evening. Bare old feet. Strong calves; creaky knees. He is readying to step into bed. He has said his prayers, is pulling open the covers and there – where he'd been expecting nothing, no one, only a blank space of empty sheets – he'll find an infant child. There – *under* the covers?

Helen will wonder about this when she gets there.

In fact, she'll *worry* about it, her thoughts passing with a jolt from the page to life and back again: the perforations in Rose's small blankets. Regularly, she'd fold one in half and then half again and press it over her own face, re-testing whether it was indeed still possible to breathe through it –

In his own bed, he will behold an infant asleep.

What to do?

Nothing for the moment.

The baby was sleeping.

Allworthy stood there.

Simply stands there. Near it, for a while.

"For some time lost in astonishment at this sight."

But something will have to be done.

Someone new has come.

Who? What kind – what order – of person?

Astonishingly, it's a baby.

Out of nowhere.

A new (nascent) individual.

In a bed; all alone.

But the problem is: "There is no such thing."

This was D. W. Winnicott's claim, based on observation. "There is no such thing as a baby."

For, "a baby alone doesn't exist."

Winnicott is known for a series of broadcasts titled "The Ordinary Devoted Mother." In the published version of the talks, he describes what he intended by this phrase – "ordinary devotion." An ubiquitous form of everyday, closely-focused care. For as long as there are children, alive and hopefully thriving, it's something necessarily going on, everywhere, all the time – the exception is when it fails to be provided, or if abruptly it stops. Setting the two adjectives together, attaching "ordinary" to the scope and depth – the power – of "devotion," tried to get at this. But, he says: "You can imagine that I have been ragged somewhat on account of this phrase, and there are many who assume I am sentimental about mothers and that I idealise them, and that I leave out fathers, and that I can't see that some mothers are pretty awful if not in fact impossible. I have to put up with these small inconveniences because I am not ashamed by what is implied by these words."

A bit farther on in the same talk, he builds in a small story about finding somewhere to live:

> When I was a medical student, I had a friend who was a poet. He was one of several of us who shared some good digs in the slums of North Kensington. This is how we found the digs:
>
>> My friend the poet, who was very tall and indolent and always smoking walked down a terrace til he saw a house that looked friendly. He rang the bell. A woman came to the door and he liked the look of her face. So he said: "I want lodgings here." She said: "I have a vacancy here. When will you be coming?" He said: "I have come." So he went in, and when he was shown the bedroom he said: "It happens that

I am ill, so I will go straight to bed. What time can I have tea?" And he went to bed and stayed in bed for six months.

In the run-up to narrating this, Winnicott had been discussing preparation: the importance of a period of preparation in the lead-up to the arrival of someone new. A period of time, sometimes (but by no means necessarily) the duration of a pregnancy, for a person to ready themselves, mentally, emotionally, materially.

In the context of the talk, the student experience provides a lesson in contrast: the point being, in life, not everyone (surely hardly anyone) finds a home as easily as this. By simply deciding. Boldly, like the poet, stamping out a cigarette, selecting then pressing on a bell, and responding to a face.

When will you be coming?
Look, I've come.
I'm already here.

It's not how it works: babies, like all kinds of others, are not in a position to walk down a street of possible shelter-scenarios, homes housing their chances, their possible futures, until they spot what feels like a good one and *choose*: ". . . babies do not choose their mothers."

But – the first point now getting offset by a counter-point – the story is also an analogy. For they *do* "just turn up."

They turn up a bit like a poet. For however long they have been expected, however extended the period of adult anticipation, imagining and readying, when they do finally arrive, babies, they – turn up. Like strangers. Like newcomers presenting "a new and original" physical fact – an ongoingly present and at the same time radically

different body to deal with – which will always be to some profound degree unexpected. And impossible, in fact, to fully prepare for.

"Look at it imaginatively": this was Winnicott's invitation-instruction (to himself, his listeners and readers). A methodological principle of his work.

Imagine the landlady putting a card up in her window, advertising rooms to rent.

Or not – for there was no mention in the story of a card; a sign.

Imagine she had rooms made up all the time, just in case.

Or, perhaps, it went like this: perhaps the room she offered, readily, when asked, was a vacancy *she didn't know she had* until the very day a poet-stranger presented himself at her door, asking for it, asking her for room – in her house, as well as in her head. (In the course of a few days, Winnicott relates, he and his friends "had all settled in nicely, but the poet would remain the landlady's favourite.") It is conceivable that her accommodation of him only presented as possible (first imaginable, then actionable), at the moment of his solicitation: the landlady's in-the-moment recognition of his need to be accommodated.

In which case, how could she have prepared? Having already agreed to his terms, and ushered him indoors, how could she have known how much he would need her – that he would immediately take to his bed – that he would be ill?

MR ALLWORTHY

Gazing down at the infant asleep, Allworthy was "touched with senti-ments of compassion for the little wretch before him."

But the recognition of vulnerability ("the little wretch") was/is not the same thing as a response to it. It was not yet taking on the responsibility for protecting it.

is one historical name for the category of human (and not only human) work that, for as long as there are children, must be undertaken by *someone*. An individual or partnership or group, taking over from whomever it was that left the baby here, fed and wrapped, seemingly safe and asleep – taking up from where their life-preserving work stopped and *continuing* it. For a baby on its own doesn't exist. It can't. Show me a baby, Winnicott wrote, and I will show you the person (or people) living near it, next to it. There can be no reality of a baby, no proper understanding of what a baby is – as well as, in real terms, no continued life-time of a baby – outside of its relation with/to someone else (the "great responsibility it must be to someone").

But – who will do it? A "mother"? The "mother"?

In this scene of finding and for the first time encountering the novel's foundling, who and where is "she"?

HELEN

Opening and closing the high cupboards in the kitchen, hungry, seeking biscuits or something else straightforward to eat. Helen: she was a gathering, a little group. The self summoned and collected by her name was mobile, tense with types and energies; some bolder, capable and confident, others more nervy and difficult. But among them there was no "mother." The fact of this kept hitting her: first one blow, then another, because even now it still hadn't quite hit home. For the truth was: Helen had been expecting her. All through the slow early swelling and later dragging progression of pregnancy, she had been holding out for her, willing her to come. In the place of her imagination, she would arrive and the group of Helen would be transformed: joined and taken over by her. The mother-character. A person not just physically capable of doing the care-taking work that a baby requires but fully and uncomplicatedly embracing it. Ideally, at every level and influencing every larger-hearted and pettier member of herself. Helen had been counting hard on her arrival. She realized, too late, that she'd been placing every single one of her bets on it: betting on her own emergence from the arrival-event of Rose's birth as someone augmented. Steadier, more coherent, patient and better. Absolutely one hundred percent better. Flooded with easy, selfless, self-generating love. The first new days of life together had gone by in panic and adrenalin, in wonder mixed with pains and exhaustion, and they continued to pass. Still, she hadn't arrived. What was holding her up? The mother she was supposed to have become. Why was she running so late? At times, she felt angry, her core heat rising. She tumbled around inside it, struggled to get out of it: a big tent collapsing hotly about her head. Angry that no one had taken her aside and warned her.

There would be no sudden extension to the space of her character, no instant expansion of patience and tolerance – no. To be clear: there would be no immediate, radical inner change. Instead, there would just be –

THE DOING OF IT

It was her discovery.

Listen – she wanted to tell someone: this was what it involved.

Doing it.

Caring for a baby was an activity, productive of its own relationality, and therefore open to anyone, to everyone. Its meaning came from the day-by-day walking and carrying through of an ancient set of gestures that were new to her, while also keeping on with her own self-care activities – feeding herself, washing herself – and finding original ways of doing them too (now accompanied, often while holding someone else). Undertaking these tasks, thinking about them: also, by necessity, doing the thinking that arose from the doing of them: testing and wondering, querying and revising, inventing and projecting. And it was true that they sometimes gave rise to unexpected, open-ended, unusual sorts of thoughts. Her days with Rose – they were making her look at herself, and the world, from other angles. They were making her do things (and think things) she had never considered doing (or had thought of) before. They were bringing her up against old questions, big questions, strange combinations of questions, hyphenating them and bracketing them and reaccenting them. They forced open the imagination in ways that might one day reveal themselves to have been transformative. For now, though, she just felt stupid. Or was it disappointed. Bouncing Rose around the kitchen, making a piece of toast left-handed, still so much in the style, so clearly in keeping with the familiar limitations and the uneven manner of herself.

He sees this: he knows that the arrival of a baby represents (calls for) work. For somebody's work. An individual or a pair or shared out among an interested group.

The reader knows that he sees it because the next thing he'll do is ring the bell for a servant. He orders "an elderly woman-servant to rise immediately and come to him."

The elderly Mrs Deborah Wilkins arrives forthwith.

And forthwith she is shocked.

Her pure eyes are shocked!

Though not, in the immediate instance, by the presence (in Mr Allworthy's very own bed!) of a baby. More: the appearance of the good man himself.

(For Mr Allworthy had been so deep in contemplation of the sweet child that he'd forgotten he was only wearing a nightshirt and Mrs Deborah Wilkins, "who, though in the fifty-second year of her age, vowed she had never beheld a man without his coat.")

She withdraws; Allworthy dresses.

The baby sleeps on.

When she returns, Allworthy commands her to take good care of the baby; tomorrow, he will send for a nurse.

The old woman splutters, objects. It's not yet clear to her what he means. Surely it was not his intention *to take it in*? But whose child is this? Who laid it here – in your bedroom? In your bed? (As an aside, she exclaims: "Faugh it stinks!")

The woman argues: "If I might be so bold as to give my advice. I would have it put in a basket, and sent out and laid at the church-warden's door."

She says: "It is a good night.

Only a *little bit* windy. And rainy.

And if it was well wrapped up, and put in a warm basket, it is *two to one* but it lives until it is found in the morning . . ."

There are chances, options – this was her point.

Two to one!

Reasonable odds?!

There is no good reason why it *has to be* you.

But nor, come to think of it, why it need not.

By this point, though, Allworthy's mind is somewhere else. He is with someone else, who has been awoken by the commotion, and is emerging from sleep.

Allworthy "had now got one of his fingers in the infant's hand, which by its gentle pressure, seemed to implore his assistance."

The moment lasts.

Now, coming back to himself, he repeats his instructions. He renews his *positive orders* for Mrs Deborah to take the baby to her own bed, after summoning another maid-servant "to provide it pap, and other things, against it waked." Furthermore, "proper clothes" should "be procured for it early in the morning." Specific practical responses to a recognized set of needs. Marking the difference between "I care" –

(I do. Vaguely, theoretically: for the children. That is, for anyone poor and wretched, bareheaded in the rain.)

– and the getting started on it: care-taking.

HELEN

Her life with Rose – the truth was, she'd chosen it. It was something that her own mother, over the phone, also, on occasion, liked to point out. She'd weighed her options, she'd deliberated and actively chosen it: first to gestate then to birth and then to care for "a" baby ("her" baby now, insofar as she had taken on its charge), three distinct phases of work. Exercising her right to choose, she'd chosen (she'd decided) to add a further potential person to the sum/burden of people in the world, making a commitment ahead of time to the work she'd imagined that this would involve. Which was true: it was something that Helen frequently pointed out to herself. She'd ushered Rose into the world and was now trying to show her, in different small ways, what was interesting and good and worthwhile about being involved in it. But, even so, as a truth, it struck her forcibly as a very simple one: violent, even, and crushing in its simplicity. For it was not clear to her exactly when, or with which combined factors of her fertile body, her fantasy-life (the ways she imagined her life unfolding), her setting, her job, her support, the choice had been made. Why there had been an earlier desire, as there must have been, to continue with her pregnancy, which had been unsought and unexpected, how old and how common that desire was, to bear children, and whether, having grown up in the body of a girl, the social inside of her, it had ever been entirely or straightforwardly her own. It was not clear to her when or where any of her desires, inclinations, or curiosities originated – how far back they went and how, by what or by whom, they had been imprinted. Who and what did she like? Who and what was she attached to? Long novels? Hairbands? Rebba? Sleeping – yes. Lush long nights of thick, unbroken sleep. Her big plant that she'd positioned too far from the window. Forcing its leaves to lean forward,

tip forward into the living room – each one so keen for light. It being so vital, to each one, that it maintain a space around itself to be sure of receiving enough light. A slow-motion process of jostling and ducking for position, turning and facing in new directions, the whole plant changing and finding its shape. Beneath: its root-system. Long, white roots coiling tightly around each other, growing ever-thicker and ever-more tightly bound in the limited container space, growing pot-bound in the unrefreshed earth and their too-tight, mock-ceramic pot.

ROSE

Her body folded against Helen's shoulder; her face settled in the dip of her neck and she was breathing it in: wool and skin, sharp-smelling where Helen's hair had hung. Rose: alive with process, responsive to and forever testing her environment. A constant, sometime collaborator, sometime redirector of the intention of every single one of Helen's intentions. Such as putting a wash on, as she was doing now. Squatting between the washing basket and the drum, turning her upper body this way then that as with one hand she pushed handful after handful of their clothes through the round door. Going for a pee. Squashing together into the windowless bathroom which was always too bright then back out into the kitchen which had to wait half the day, the whole morning, for the sun. A narrow galley kitchen full of beautiful, interesting things. Intolerable, unbearable things, humming sounds made by the fridge, the small birds bombing about, in and out of their home in the hedge just outside the window. Now she turned. Rose pushed her forehead against Helen's shoulder; she braced with her knees. With immense effort she made the rest of her body rise up, using Helen as a surface to push against, resurrecting in real time from listless to sharp-angled, from loose-limbed, almost floppy, to purposeful, sturdy, and strong. So, this is the world? This rotating sensation, being low in the room, these sounds and this? Now coming back up to the level above the worktop surfaces, surrounded by the hollowed cupboard spaces, the fridge and the freezer: each one of them its own light-controlled, temperature-controlled little room. These features – these surroundings. They were ground and distance. Surface and space. They burst with potential and confusion. Rose pushed. Helen felt her push and intervened. Can it survive me? This was how Helen received her question – the language she gave

it. This was how she translated the force of it, and silently handed it back: Can it withstand and accommodate *the new inquiring force of me*, coming at it head-first, forehead-first, as well as in the round, from every side? Also, can I survive it?

"Could it be that all the people who worry so much about children – are really worrying about themselves?" It was a question that Helen had asked herself, once, finding it put to her like this, by somebody else, in the pages of a novel: the people who worry so much about the children – could it be that what they are really worried about is "keeping their world together and getting the children to help them do it, getting the children to agree that it is indeed a world."

Now it took on new relevance. For Helen *was* trying to keep the world together. That was one way of describing what she was doing, day-to-day: their own little portion of the world, enclosed as a flat, as a walled, windowed province, enclosed and yet at the same time connected and exposed to the upstairs, traversed by the outdoors, so open to the interference of other people, reality, history, and everything else.

It was true that she wanted Rose to help her. To enlist her in her project. To go along with her: with everything that she was doing, valuing and trying to make happen. To agree to all of it: accept the aspects of the world that Helen herself, as a baby, as child, must have accepted in order to survive and grow up in it.

"Each new generation of children has to be told. 'This is a world, this is what one does, one lives like this.'"

This is a world: it's what she was saying to Rose.

Look: a washing machine. A kitchen. Here is my neck. Here is my body. I'll be your most immediate sensory environment.

This is what one does in it.

Let's look out the window. She shifted Rose's position.

Here is one among so many possibilities.

Look: the sky is good. It changes all the time.

The paving stones are boring. It's sad how she paved over the whole of the garden.

But the birds! Birds and flowers are almost always fantastic.

Helen put one hand on the back of Rose's head. It was warm – always so warm.

But – was it? Was it a world?

And the things they were doing in it together – was this how to live?

They considered the garden.

"Maybe our constant fear is that a generation of children will come along and say: 'This is not a world, this is nothing, there's no way to live at all.'"

ALL-WORTHY

It was alright. Mr Allworthy will not be above misjudging people or certain situations but faced with this "What would you do?" scenario, discovering a newborn in a bed, it'll be alright: a form of improvised mothering will get underway. It will start in Chapter 3 and be continued, undertaken by a man in the latter part of late middle age, with a large heart, a large fortune, no dependents (his own beloved wife, and their children – none of them survived to adulthood; they all died a long time ago). He has no one else to look after other than Bridget, his adult sister, and a workforce whose labour he can activate. Mrs Deborah wants to keep her job. She'll get up when she's called, take the child under her arm, "without any apparent disgust at the illegality of its birth; . . . declaring it was a sweet little infant" and walk off with it into her chamber. She'll be his mother. The next day Mr Allworthy will instruct her to present the baby like a present to Bridget (like a new dress; like an accessory; like a fashionable appendage to her person, like something all women are supposed to want) and she'll be charged with the responsibility for his upbringing as well. In this practical, distributed and outsourced manner, he and his household will take on the fate of the baby. His last instruction, that night, already with a thought for the morning, the continuity of the arrangement is that the baby "be brought to himself as soon as he was stirring."

Though it was not clear – Helen will note this, when she reaches this page, at some point in the future – which "he" the pronoun referred to. Should *the baby* be brought in as soon as he wakes, which, keeping within the bounds of plausibility, could be as soon as thirty minutes or an hour from now? Or should someone else stay with and mind the baby until Mr Allworthy himself has slept a full night, awaking when the sun comes up, at his usual breakfast time?

Either way, for the moment, in the novel: it hasn't stopped being bedtime.

Mr Allworthy has arranged things so, at last, he can betake himself "to those pleasing slumbers which a heart that hungers after goodness is apt to enjoy when thoroughly satisfied."

It is a good arrangement: the baby will be enabled to grow up – to achieve independence of action and decision. To become a protagonist, in fact – the main one.

For now, Mr Allworthy need do nothing further, apart from go to sleep. To find his own peaceful sleep. In the following days, for the following years, accelerating through the baby's babyhood, childhood, youth and into the first phase of his manhood, Mr Allworthy will maintain, for his own part, a steady pace of intermittent engagement.

He will meet with the sweet baby, who in that moment of gentle finger pressure, hand-touching communication, he resolved to "breed . . . up as his own," at the convivial, emphatically manageable frequency of once per day.

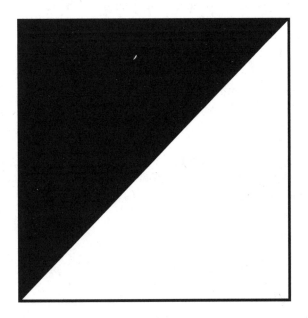

CHOOSE NAMES

for compositions, for practices, for forms of being and living-in-relation.

"Novel" is a name.

It is one English-language name for long-form works of prose fiction. But it was never the only one.

Cheryl L. Nixon: "As they attempted to define the novel, eighteenth-century [writers and] critics relied on pre-existing literary genres and modes, calling the novel a romance, history, biography, epic, fable, story or tale."

The novel was "variously considered to be one of these many forms, a mixture of these forms, or a contrast to these forms."

This rotating, testing, rejecting, and effort to combine the existing names, along with their wholly inconsistent application, spoke of something important. For Nixon, it partook of a certain "experimental energy." For writers as well as readers engaged with eighteenth-century novel-works, there was "a sense of a grasping for a new conceptualization of literary genre while working with terminology that can't quite capture the essential qualities of it."

It is telling that *Tom Jones* doesn't ever call *itself* a novel. It presents, instead, as the "history." But, history without the facts. Hence critic Elizabeth Montagu's proposal of a new named category declaring Henry Fielding a writer of "*imaginary* Histories."

Likewise, in the preface to his earlier *Joseph Andrews* (1742), Henry Fielding defined "this new kind of Writing," with the combinatory logic of a "comic Epic-Poem in Prose." Making use of the existing categories and classifications: it was a comedy (not a tragedy); it was a sort of Epic (sharing with that form publicness, scope, and length); but if it was an Epic it was a comic one, and if it was a kind

of Poem (that is, to some degree *stanzaic*), it was of a peculiar kind, since it was written in unmetered prosaic prose.

This naming process: it was intensively "question-filled." It opened up new territories *with* and *between* existing categories ("history" and "romance"), by setting them alongside each other, enabling them to speculatively, loosely or precisely, redefine each other. It did so with the seeking conviction that names matter. It matters, what things are called.

was one name – the most obvious and appropriate available name? – for Helen's new form of life. For her situation. But the way people used it. Sometimes, often, they made it sound like a bordered place. Like a protected neighbourhood – a gated one. Or, like a mysteriously exclusive, initiated state, a priesthood. The name did the work of inscribing what she was doing within a history of mostly female labour: women supporting the lives of human beginners. And it was true that people she saw, out and about, in the shops, in the park, attending to young children, still presented mostly as women.

But – "motherhood"? Did it get at it?

With its emphasis skewed to the adult player in this interplay – did it do enough to get at it?

It made it sound like a stability, as well as a kind of enclosure. When she experienced it as a facing (outward): facing and being faced with this actual other body, equally present, whose questions ran through her and whose ideas, sometimes, she felt.

It made it sound like something one-note, one-tone, continuous and almost identical with itself. While she experienced it as a countering, a revision, a compensation, a rhyming, a dispute, a pulling outward. In "motherhood," there should (by definition) be more than one live creature involved. But in the usage of this name, she wasn't sure if she could hear it: interchange, exchange, the energy of a relation.

"NOVEL" IS AN AVAILABLE NAME

A name to repurpose, accent again, and work with. In the preface to *Pierre et Jean*, a "petit roman" first published in 1887, Guy de Maupassant insisted on this: "novel" (though the word he used was *roman*) was an available name and it was his freedom as a writer to choose if, when, and how to use it. He wrote, in Clara Bell's translation: "I am not the only writer who finds himself taken to task in the same terms when he brings out a new book. Among many laudatory praises, I invariably meet with this observation, penned by the same critics: 'The greatest fault of this book is that it is not, strictly speaking, a novel.'"

But, he asks, on what basis is the decision taken that "novel" is the wrong name?

"Are there any rules for the making of a novel, which, if we neglect, the tale must be called by another name? If *Don Quixote* is a novel, then is *Le Rouge et le Noir* a novel? If *Monte Cristo* is a novel, is *L'Assommoir*? Can any conclusive comparison be drawn between Goethe's *Elective Affinities*, *The Three Musketeers* by Dumas, Flaubert's *Madame Bovary*, *M. de Camors* by Octave Feuillet, and *Germinal* by Zola? Which of them all is The Novel? What are these famous rules? Where did they originate? Who laid them down? And in virtue of what principle, of whose authority, of what reasoning?"

Henry Fielding, listening in, out of time, answering back with hubris, in semi-seriousness: *me*. I am "in reality, the founder of a new province of writing, so I am at liberty to make what Laws I please therein."

Guy de Maupassant: Well ("Eh bien"), "I know nothing of these famous rules."

is another name, one of the older names. A name for an extremely happy, peaceful, or picturesque period or situation, typically an idealized or unsustainable one. It is a literary situation characterized by a particular relationship to time, where everything is rooted and reliable. The days pass steadily, with actions, songs, the cycles of the seasons repeating in a remarkably frictionless continuity. Together, they render "less distinct all the temporal boundaries between individual lives and between various phases of one and the same life."

Helen and Rebba had been happy, somewhat idyllically. For years, peaceful in their set-up. Their setting-in-common: practical if not picturesque above the shop fronts, the launderette, in a medium-sized city, not too far from the park.

You could stay.

This was Rebba addressing Helen, a charge and a thickness in her voice.

When the baby comes, you could both just stay here.

(She didn't say: we could do it together.)

It had been Helen's compulsion to leave: it was something like a swallowed instruction, received from the outside, from the air, that made the decision for her. She'd tried to explain: it needs a different space for it to happen in. Doesn't it? Living with a baby. A different set-up. To do it plausibly, seriously, realistically. To do it credibly, proving myself, on my own. In the eyes of anyone – everyone – who is watching. She had internalized a lesson based on a fantasy taking the form of an imperative that – since she had the choice (Nisha's husband's mother, with her converted family home, the ground-floor flat providing a new income source) – she really should *progress* from their shared place to some form of more *recognized* independence

and self-sufficiency and, on those terms, *this* high flat, with its mucid bathroom, its glittering skirting boards: it was no setting for a baby.

Now, on her different street: it was true that there were no more stairs. More practical, if you had a pram, which she didn't yet. There was no more hulking the shopping up four flights of stairs. Apparently, so far, on the evidence presented: there were no mice. There was also no Rebba.

Helen missed her – how it hurt.

She missed her all the time.

GUY DE MAUPASSANT, ADDRESSING THE
READING PUBLICS:

"The public as a whole is composed of various groups, whose cry to
us writers is:

> 'Comfort me.'
> 'Amuse me.'
> 'Touch me.'
> 'Make me dream.'
> 'Make me laugh.'
> 'Make me shudder.'
> 'Make me weep.'
> 'Make me think.'

And only a few chosen spirits say to the artist: 'Give me something fine in any form which may suit you best, according to your
own temperament.'

The artist makes the attempt; succeeds or fails."

Gertrude Stein, writing back, anticipating, and responding crossways
from *A Novel of Thank You*, the space-time zone of her own composition: "What is a novel a novel is partly this."

was Helen's full given name. Helen – epic and available, chosen (bor-rowed, lifted) for reasons obscure to her but now attached like a tattoo that it would be painful, complicated, and costly to remove. Strong – a determinism she wore like a challenge, oftentimes like a joke. ("Amuse me.") She had, very recently, acquired a new one. Though the first time someone used it to address her she'd failed to turn around.

It happened at the hospital. At a late pregnancy check-up in a starkly lit room, with a bed like a table covered by a long layer of paper, with one chair for no one to sit on, just a place to tuck your folded underclothes under your small pile of clothes.

For the moment, she was still fully dressed, a hairband in the but-tonhole of her jeans, stretching out the waist band, the elastic stretch-ing almost to breaking point, making her usual jeans wearable for as long she could.

She was waiting, finding it too uncomfortable to stand still.

Shifting her weight from foot to foot, she studied the display of in-formational posters on the wall. The early warning signs of post-natal depression: an incapacity to sleep even when your baby is asleep; an incapacity to relax even when your baby is safe and relaxed. Someone entered the room behind her and said in a brisk voice – not impa-tient, just busy: How's Mum?

Helen didn't think the question could be addressed to her. She was, however, the only other person in the room.

Hey, you there! (Would have been another way of phrasing it.)

Yes, *you*.

See Helen tilt her head uncertainly. See her rotate her body, her protruding belly, forty, then ninety hesitant degrees. See her pushing

back her hair with her hands to show a face slowly coming round to register that it was really *herself* that was being hailed.

Hey!

And not someone else – there was no one else.

"Mum" the preferred informal address of health-care professionals; midwives and nurses dealing with too many names in a day, too many to remember. The more or less willing, unwilling, violent recruitment of subjects, by means of appellation, into new positions, new social and political functions: *Yes*, I mean *you*.

Being addressed, and addressing in turn, Helen now speaking to Rose – a Rose unborn, as yet unnamed: "Mum" is the position you are putting me in – too soon, too soon.

But, like all names bestowed by other people and from the out-side, for all that, not so straightforwardly refused.

Like "Reader" – was it?

Like what happens when a recently bought novel from the past addresses you directly as "Dear Reader." Straight out of the page.

"Kindly Reader."

It was benign – wasn't it?

Sagacious reader. Gentle reader.

Friendly and benign. Just an effort to establish a relationship, set the tone for the form of companionship to come.

Even so, the first time, it felt unearned, affected. Too direct.

Presumptuous – and too soon.

But, then again and for all that: not so easy to refuse.

However doubtful a person might feel about this: the assignation of the position of capitalized Reader, an unspecified addressee imag-ined long ago, by an author who has no idea who they are –

(*What?* Who?

Reader? That can't mean me.

But, then again, since there's no one else around?)

However ill-fitting, loose or imposed that general category might sound, with its accelerations towards intimacy, the fact was:

Yes.

That name – it named her activity for the moment.

It described part of what her body was doing, or could do. (She was an intermittent, interruptive Reader, reading in the living room.)

This was how names got accepted as alright, as bearable or wearable, as more or less fitting: the name a novel gets to call you for the duration:

"Dear Reader."

Why not? Helen would allow it. She had already allowed it. It was part of the pact. A non-conscious decision she'd made because she wanted to keep going – to keep going on with her reading, which meant accepting the novel's terms; picking up, later on today, from where she'd left off.

Of course, at the antenatal appointment, Helen also turned around.

She turned her body fully around after what in the end were only a few short seconds of hesitation. She felt unwieldy, conspicuous and hot. In doing so, she accepted the midwife's intimate, pre-emptive name: "Mum."

Okay, so call me forth.

The sometimes reluctant, sometimes humiliating and painful, sometimes relieved and willing process of arriving at acceptance, at compliance:

Okay, so give me a description that will allow me to describe myself back to myself, and to be recognized, enabled to continue as a person, identifiable in the social world, as well as to myself. Assign

me one of the few identity positions you have available, and persuade me that it was toward *this* form of becoming that my energies were directed all along.

Okay, so make me up, *socialize* me.

Helen's body spoke very loudly for her, ahead of her. To the hail of "Mum," it answered back: Yes, I suppose that could be me.

It was a name that soon other people would start to call her, too. Strangers in the shops, on the street. In shorthand, with reverence, with sentimentality, with incuriosity, with condescension, with disdain, long before Rose's mouth would be capable of forming the mouth-sounds to voice it: neighbours, health-care professionals, nursery workers, teachers, journalists and politicians.

A word meaning, originally, and even now, optionally: be silent.

Also, an *inarticulate close-mouth sound* indicative of an unwillingness or inability to speak. It was only at the start of the twentieth century that it became a common, familiar word for mother in British English. And, at around the same time, an abbreviation of chrysanthemum, in the jargon of gardeners.

The garden: outside the kitchen window, set in a mossy sort of urn, pansies: each one its own rich-coloured, black-eyed thought. They shuddered together. The weather looked breezy and bright. Helen turned down the short hall to the living room, leaving the washing machine running in the kitchen, a knife in the sink.

A SIMPLE THING

Helen carried Rose and hot tea. A re-boiled kettle, a hot cup of tea (its temperature lowered just a few degrees by milk). She carried Rose in the crook of one arm and, in the other hand – tea. Very carefully. So full of care. But still risking carrying them both at the same time: a baby and a cup of scorching water; a domestic danger. She carried them both back to the living room in exactly the way the health visitor had told her not to (explicitly don't do this). How to mitigate it? By walking slowly, very gingerly, holding the cup out sideways, so far apart from them both that her knuckles bumped the wall.

Meanwhile, Rose, her fingers closed over her thick jumper, held Helen.

She held a large part of her attention.

In the time they'd been away, the light in the living room had changed; the sun had risen higher; the room was a shade darker. The mobile looked still – though now it responded to their approach. The fabric meant to cover the sofa had slipped.

Rose held Helen – mentally, also physically. In the sense that she caused Helen to draw close, and to stay there, to remain always within earshot, most of the time within reach.

Their day was the story of their holding arrangements: an ongoing narrative of finding (sometimes planning, sometimes inventing, making up) and holding to (for as long as they lasted: *believing* in), then collapsing little scenes.

Allowing them, stretching them out.

Then causing, sometimes suffering their collapse:

Rose in her sprung chair, entertained by the mobile, with Helen seated on the floor next to her, her face turned away, reading her book.

Rose in Helen's arms, her head handled, standing against the sink in the kitchen.

Helen on the big bed in the bedroom, Rose sleeping flat out alongside her – the evening sun advancing across the sheet toward Rose's face, approaching the thin covers of her eyelids, Helen holding her hand like a parasol over Rose's face to keep her in the shade, to keep the encroaching brightness from waking her. A parasol or a stop sign: a hand gesture intended to temporarily halt the movement of the earth. STOP. Let me prolong this resting moment – Helen holding this pose until her arm ached.

Their day was a cycle, composed from these positions: switching between them, swapping them out. For how many different ways were there, actually, to hold a baby – to be held by a baby?

Seated, like a Madonna, with the baby in the crook of your arm. "The maternal stereotype." Obviously. But beyond that, her babysitting experience over a decade behind her – honestly, Helen hadn't really known.

She'd googled the question on one of the heaviest days before Rose was born, a call-out to the social knowledge of the internet. Instantly, it had replied:

There are eight safe positions.

No, did you know there are seventeen different ways?

Here are some guidelines. Wikihow, with pictures; step by step. Like a rugby ball. (Seriously, a rugby ball?)

She'd found more information in a library book. A library book, a baby-care manual that read, in places, like a literature book, like a philosophy book, offering beautiful calm instruction in the practicalities of composition.

It said: a baby can neither support its own head nor control its own muscles. It's important to remember this. A baby's fundamental fear of being dropped will show up when its head is allowed to droop or its uncontrolled limbs are left to dangle in space. As a result, a baby is only "really relaxed and happy" when someone else does this for them.

It described how the playmat, the cot mattress, or a chair could provide a form of proxy support. How part of living with a baby, making a home-space for a baby, as for anyone, involved identifying or, if necessary, creating, constructing, places of rest: sites where a body can lean or sit or lie down in comfort. It meant, whenever entering a new space, parsing it for the limited number of places where it might be possible to safely put her down.

Even so, it recognized that even when handled with care, for a baby, being picked up or put down – shifted, even when a change is called for – is a form of transition that's always "potentially alarming." (Winnicott wrote poems about these "awful transitions." The flush of hot then cold panic can soak a body when one form of support is removed – like a sudden, unwanted loosening, a collapse, an inner collapse, a breaking apart, an unchecked plummeting, a flailing descent

– before another can be established.)

The technique the book suggested was to give new babies an interval moment during which they could become aware of *both* kinds of support: the old one and the new one. For example, when lifting Rose up

from her low chair, to arrange her hands and arms *underneath* the baby while the chair was still holding her weight. Creating an interval moment.

How she should stay in this interval moment.

She shouldn't even begin to lift Rose from her chair until Rose had had a chance to register "the new security her hands" were providing.

And even then, how it was best to move slowly:

"Keeping to a minimum the distances [the baby] must travel through empty space."

The author ventured to imagine: "Babies who are plucked from their cots without so much as a by-your-leave must feel as though they are being swooped through the air by invisible giants."

"By-your-leave": a form of politeness, or social consideration, was also encouraged. Generally, it was better to ask before abruptly moving someone else, before plucking them up and swooping them into a new situation: Is this all right with you? What I'm doing to you, deciding for you? Is it alright?

Although, to be swooped without warning was its own mode of transition, not without its own powerful, generative effects.

Helen had settled her cup into the earth of the pot plant. She was seated on the sofa with Rose. She lifted her layers, exposed the other breast: it was the right one now that was hot and hard, the skin taut, beating its urgency from the inside out.

Against her, the good ship Rose docked and fed.

Outside, the upstairs cat, having completed its round of the houses, skulked toward the front door, compelled by the memory of an old way in.

There were sparks, stars, but no somnolent bounce of zero-gravity.
There was no drifting into open and quiet.

Helen considered the novel on the floor.
As Rose fed with her eyes open Helen thought about it: what she hoped to get from it. What she imagined it might *do for* her.
Tom Jones, describing itself, variously, as:
A containing container. "A leaf a gourd a shell a net a bag a sling a sack a bottle a pot a box a container. A holder. A recipient."
A public space; an open house. Its door standing permanently open. With its own mood, its charm, its exclusiveness and its exclusions, made for the temporary occupancy of others.
A "mental entertainment." If the box-bag with all its contents and relations were going to spill open and find their positions, it would happen here: in the unbounded space of her own imagination.
A conversation: the situated and private re-activation of a public, ongoing, long-preserved address. Reading, going on with this: it meant putting herself in the position of being spoken to. But also deciding, on her own terms, the pace of her engagement and, in her own way, from the position of her life and concerns, answering back.
Conversation as social involvement: defined by Henry Fielding as the "grand business of our lives, the foundation of everything either useful or pleasant . . ."

How long was it? Helen pondered.
Eight hundred pages?

Nine hundred?

Densely printed, it was massive.

Tiredness dragged through her all over again.

It was a massive long-term commitment.

Loud and very near, booming her soundscape. Rose could hear a heartbeat. Even louder: the burbling sounds of tea being digested.

She twisted her head away from their source and looked up inquiringly: What is this?

Helen noted the look she received as a question and closed her eyes.

There's nothing to see here. This was what Helen said, or tried to express, with her shut-up face: nothing to engage with, nothing of interest.

It's time for sleep now.

I'll hold on to you. She said this with the smallest pressure of her arms:

This time, I won't even try to put you down.

I'll just sit here and I'll hold you while you sleep.

But Rose was not asking; she was craning her head away.

She wanted to release her face to make more sense of the blocked pattern on the under-sofa – she was looking at the sharp line made by the gap where the throw had slipped.

This was not a casual curiosity. (Rose had no casual interests.)

She felt solid, full, and real.

She was tired but – like this, under these conditions – there was no way she was going to go back to sleep.

IT TOOK TIME

Always a little bit of time, sometimes a great deal longer, for Helen to come to terms with what was not going to happen. To accept and adjust her projection of the future from what she foresaw, and what she wanted but couldn't force: her own will met by Rose's counter-field and in the encounter: redirected, modulated. Sometimes thwarted. And then to accept and adjust to the idea of doing what was needed – what, with her grown-up capacity for forward-thinking, she could see now *had to* happen. Drumming up the courage, the energy required of her *to make it* happen, since of the two of them she was the adult with the adult human agency, with the capacity – the freedom – to move and act, to respond to what had come to pass and then plot a way ahead.

The mobile turned over Rose's empty chair.

The condensation on the window had now collected in the dip in the sill; other than one very low, misty hill, the glass was clear.

HELEN STOOD UP

From the hook in the hallway, she took down three metres of stretchy fabric. Briskly, she carried Rose into the little bedroom, a room that was full with her bed, Rose's sleeping basket only just fitting into the narrow space between the bed and the wall. She set Rose down on a towel she kept spread over the duvet for this purpose, and instantly Rose started to cry. Helen responded by removing Rose's all-in-one. Rose cried harder. Helen said something like:

I know, I know, I know.

As if she could remember, as if she were truly in that moment making the effort to imagine (and then know, as if imagining were the basis of knowing, which possibly it is) how this might feel: having, without warning, the protective layers of yourself suddenly stripped away. Rose drew her limbs towards the core of her body, leeching heat, and cried harder. She'd been warm and held and now she was *cold*. Helen changed her nappy.

I know, I know, I know.

She was still saying: I imagine, I imagine, I am trying to imagine.

Among the confusion of contacts, materials, limbs, she managed to dress her in something practical – something with feet.

And then in another layer: a warmer outdoor suit.

With the central heating still working hard, Rose padded in too many clothes for the indoors and already heating up, Helen needed to be quick.

Rose was crying in earnest now, in even louder need, making volume.

Helen began the performance of a technique she'd seen tutorialed on the internet: the same upbeat and deftly competent woman tying expertly, over and over again, a long length of fabric around

her body, forming a soft pouch to contain her calm and compliant baby. The first few times, Helen had paused it at each new step in order to get it right, while Rose, then just a few days old, flailed and wailed on the empty expanse of the bed. Helen had grown agitated and botched it, fucked it up and fumbled about. She felt harried, swore. Then botched it again, whilst trying meanwhile to say reassuring things, to make it clear to Rose that her swearing was never meant for her. But feeling conscious nonetheless that any sound, any emission from her body, must have felt like another address.

This, after all, was how they spoke to each other: Helen's breath in and around Rose's face, the sounds of her telephone chat, her laughter, her swearing, her body's smells and pulses, her handling; Rose's responses to her handling, her holding positions, to how in the moment she was being confidently or inadequately held.

By now, Helen could do without the tutorial: she was faster. Already, after a few weeks' practice, she'd become somewhat expert in this new skill: speed-tying the cloth around her waist, throwing each end over alternate shoulders, drawing them across her back and around, tying another knot; she could be quick.

She lifted Rose, her limbs thickened and reinforced by all her outdoor clothes, and pushed her into the sling.

Rose cried even harder. She hated this: this first stage of a process which was supposed to solve rather than produce a problem. Helen knew, she said I know and this time she felt like, really, she did. Like their sensibilities and sensitivities were wholly inter-connected, beating to the same powerful, accelerating pulse, because Rose's rising desperation – she felt it too. They were both panicked now. Helen could feel it in her lungs, in her pumping heart. It was a bodily response by no means attenuated by the fact that neither of them were in danger, or that it could be predicted: the knowledge

that each day, at some point, the panic would rise up like this and repeat.

She tried telling Rose that they'd be out of it soon. She was putting on her trainers, Rose screaming in the sling. Any minute now, they would both be absolutely out of it, and this would work. Generally, when all else failed: a long sleep-walk in the cooler outdoor air was the tactic most likely to work. Even so, a sense of urgency – of real-time EMERGENCY – inter-animated them both.

Come on, come on, come on.

They could not do this, it was not possible to get through this, fast enough.

Now, in the hallway, with her coat on over the sling and hats on both of their heads, her phone and keys and purse and a cloth bag for shopping in her pockets, along with an apple, Rose rounding out her chest, which was leaping, Helen bent her knees and lunged.

This was the part in the process that she'd not learned but discovered. Copying it, unknowingly, from everyone who'd already mastered it whilst, at the same time, inventing it, out of necessity, for the first time, all by herself. This was how she moved down the hall: in deep, long steps. Dipping her knees. Lunging like the men doing their weekend stretches in the park.

Now they were out the door.

She used the bounce of the short downward flight of steps to jog Rose out of her fiercest protest. Then lunged again until she reached the pavement.

Here, she rose up onto the balls of her feet. She took two high steps then once again she lunged.

She was dancing. In her own way, *prancing*. Dancing like an exercising man, like an ancient horse, with high springy steps.

This was how she made their way out into the mid-morning, the bright day, its high clouds and light wind. This was how she picked up

and responded to its own, distinctive outdoor rhythm, as if the empty street were built not from large, divided houses but from speakers: each flat-fronted house a huge speaker; the street a sound system. It was everyday dancing. Everyday, comical but motivated, full-body dancing for the purpose of getting someone else to sleep, and finding her own rest – claiming back some stretch of at least mental repose. Dancing at first to the upper-most layer of sound: the quick and anxious, skittering syncopations of out, out, out, getting themselves out of the flat, as fast as humanly possible, and a good distance away from the compressed scenes of their mutual distress.

Then, as she continued, ripping that higher layer off. And finding underneath it the beginnings of a slower, steadier relief: a calm that already was synching them together, and synching them both to the outdoors, making a space for all of them in the measures of a deeper, larger, more companionable, more sustainable bass.

This was how she made their way down the smart residential street: with her hands on Rose's rounded back, in bobbing, bouncing, base-level gratitude for its spaciousness, and for the cooler air.

Rose was still crying, wailing and wailing it out, hooded by the fabric of the sling.

But her cries, like Helen's body, had already started to pitch and fall.

Pitch and fall.

Helen eased her dance into an exaggerated walk. Her gait stressing the four-beat fall and lift, lift and fall, in am-bu-la-tion.

Shaking her head, she felt her panic shake off. It was letting her go – thank you. It had released her – thank you. She gave thanks to the breeze. It left in its wake a regulating heartbeat, a strange pinging from her ever-reactive breasts, an underarm wetness of sweat.

She walked on.

Past the parked cars.

The quiet spaces extending between Rose's cries.

Helen walked on – walking into the day. She carried them both on.

There were puddles on the pavement – she bounce-stepped around them.

Rose's cries – rising then falling, then rising a little less and falling a little less. Like her own bright hat, bobbing fluorescent against the many shades of residential spring and dark evergreen.

It was the start of May, but still cold enough for a hat.

She walked on.

The street growing quieter; only the occasional thump and smash of what the builders were doing. Rose was almost quiet now.

Together, they had returned the street very nearly to quiet.

They passed the bench at the end of it: a feeding ground, a bit of shared furniture.

A big cloud moved across the sun.

Helen looked up. Banked and back-lit, it showed its edges: a mass of vapour, looking like a solid with its bright gold edging.

She walked on.

A human envelope. Wrapping fabric, a large coat, holding arms, an apple bulking out her pocket, her high hair-knot bulking up her hat; exhausted, thin-soled trainers.

Until their strange partner dance turned the corner, and all was residual vibration.

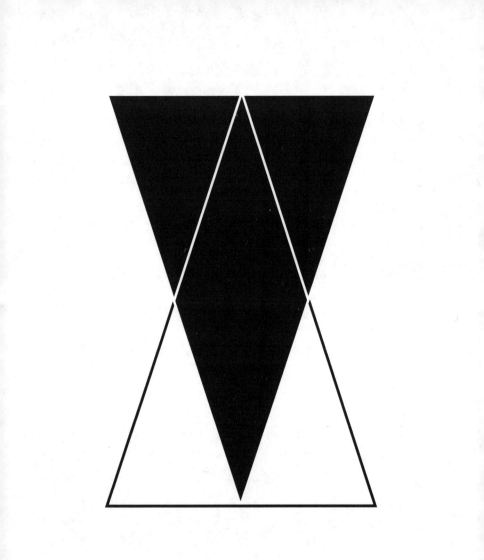

THE LEISURE CENTRE

SWIMMING

Helen, thirty-six weeks pregnant, shifting her weight from foot to foot, rubbing at her ribs; waiting for the bus to take her along the road, up the long hill and around to the other side of the park. She had an appointment at the hospital and it was just starting to rain. The sky like her body held so much water: all the clouds watered dark, watered swollen, a dark, heavy, deep blue-grey. Standing at the stop with a shelter and adverts but no seat, she could feel the full interior weight of the baby, inching through its inner rotations, being tugged ever-downward by the force of gravity. Fat drops fell from the sky. For the moment they were spaced: one individual drop splatting here, then another over there, distracting from the first. Splatting on the roof of the bus shelter, in the gutter. Soon they would bucket. The bus wasn't coming and Helen needed to sit down. Just then, like a miracle, along came a taxi. The morning was still dark and the taxi had its headlamp on. On impulse, Helen put out her hand. In his early sixties or so, the driver was talkative:

Right love, alright love?

That's it. Buckle yourself in.

Where you headed? Ah I see.

Well, lovely. Not so long now then I should imagine.

Sorry love, couldn't hear you. Say again?

He was chatty.

He told her that she'd have to be patient. It was rush hour. It was the school run wasn't it? All the parents driving their one kid to school. He was new to working mornings, to working days. It was not so bad though was it. It was alright. Getting going. Getting the day off to a good early start. He always used to work nights.

He told her about his grandchildren, about when and how they were born.

He told her about his daughter's first time in labour. Escalation – you know.

Nothing doing then it all starts happening so fast and not the way you want it.

She was alright in the end, though. Don't you worry, he said.

They both were. She came out the other side, didn't she? They both did.

Don't *you* worry, he repeated, making a point of catching Helen's eye in the rear-view mirror.

He repeated the name he'd bestowed upon her: love.

He told her that she was his first pick-up of the day.

The traffic was slow. Rain drummed down on the windscreen. Front and back, the wipers were on. Down the passenger window, the largest raindrops ran sluggishly, cautiously, then faster. They ran quick-quick *fast* then unexpectedly settled back into slow. They turned right then left, moving around each other, starting off where others stopped – each of them pursuing its own private route down the glass.

Which did he prefer? Helen asked. Taking the decision to join in the chat. To keep it running, ticking over, like the bright red figures that were turning over – rising, in leaps – on the meter.

Days or nights?

Day-shift now, love. Oh, yeah. No question: day-shift. For the nights: well, you need stamina.

It's not the driving, though there is that. The staying up and the driving. I could do all that. You get used to it. It's the other things.

You know. He paused.

Then continued: all the other things that go beyond, you know. Above and beyond. Lads getting into the cab and they'd be so pissed they'd forgotten where they lived. Their mates lying to you, giving the wrong address for a laugh. Or you'd get them home but then have to get out and bang on a door. Some random door. You know: *I* don't know who lives there. How am I supposed to know? I don't want to wake someone else up to help me get this lad out of my cab and let him in. Find his phone for him, find his keys. But it wasn't just the lads. All kinds. Girls, too. Women. Cleaning up after them. Listening to their nonsense. Worrying after them – did I get the right house?

I'll tell you about one job. Right at the end of the shift, it was. Late. Very late. But – he caught her eye again, and revised his position: early for you my love. About five in the morning. Early, though that'll soon change – and for a little while he seemed to be speaking from a script: Keep you up all hours, don't they? The little ones. When they're tiny.

You enjoy every moment though. Won't you?

You enjoy every moment. They grow up so fast.

Then he resumed his story:

About five-thirty in the morning, it was. It's the worst time for it. You know: just when you're ready to go home, put your feet up, have a cup of tea, switch off. I get a call from the office, and I go round to the address and there's this woman standing outside in her nightie, waiting out in the street. She has a little kid with her. She puts the kid – a little girl – in the back of cab, and tells me to take her to the leisure centre. It was still dark – winter, the sun was nowhere near dawning. Aren't you coming too? I asked her. No, no, she said. She'll be fine. I take it she was her mum. Anyway, so now I have this little girl in the back, sitting just where you are, love, wide awake. It's a weekday. She

must only have been about eight years old. I drive her round to the leisure centre. Wasn't far – only about a ten-minute drive. But when we get there it was closed. Car park empty, those big glass double doors looking all locked up. I say to the little girl: Well, it looks like it's closed, love. Doesn't it? I'll have to take you back home. No, she says – it's the first thing she says to me. I think it was the only thing she said to me – I'm supposed to go in round the back. So I drive her round the back just like she says: it's a dark little road and there are some buildings and there's this alley leading up to a door. And she's right. It was the back entrance. I could see that there was a light on in there, someone was up, someone was home, in the leisure centre – Who was it? I don't know. The cleaner? Staff? But the problem was: there were these men standing about. Round the back. In the alley. Three or four of them, standing about. You know. They were blocking her way in. I don't know what they were doing there. Five-thirty in the morning? Cans in their hands. I don't know what they were up to. At that time? I didn't like it, to be honest. You know. I didn't like it. But what was I supposed to do? I didn't like it. So I said to the little girl: look. I'll not walk in with you. I'll just stay a few feet behind. Alright? I'll just see you in from there. Alright? Alright.

So that's what I did.

He patted his fingers on the steering wheel, now turned it with the heel of his hand.

Yes, but. Helen was confused.

Why was she going to the leisure centre in the first place?

I mean, at that time in the morning?

Helen tried looking out the window, but the rain stopped her gaze from travelling anywhere past the glass.

Swimming club.

    Oh.

They'd started moving again. The taxi was climbing the long hill, up towards the park, close, almost bumper to bumper, with the other cars.

    Well, she ventured. I guess that makes sense?

    She looked forward; again, her eye met the driver's in the rear-view mirror.

    And then what happened?

    Nothing. That was it.

Now and again, especially when lying awake next to Rose, deep in the night, waiting to hear her breathe out from the shallows of her sleep, for the reassurance of a mutter or a sigh, an out- or intake of breath that would cue her into her own sleep – the hall-light on, glowing dimly all the way round the edges of the door-frame – Helen would find herself thinking of the swimming girl. The pre-dawn swimmer. How it might feel to get up in the dark when you're eight or something years old. What it was like to say goodbye to your mum still in her night-dress and be driven by a stranger through the empty streets, feeling yourself to be one among the many awake and purposeful at that time, working, with offices to clean, cold early lengths to swim. It never occurred to her to think any further about the mother, to question if the woman in the night-dress was indeed the girl's mother, or someone else, or to think about the difference that she and the taxi-driver had somehow both decided that made. Instead, she'd play and replay the scene he'd described to her round the back of the leisure centre: the group of men loitering so late, or was it so early into a new day, in the dark passageway between the buildings, blocking the

entrance, drinking together. But she was not interested in the men, either. Or were they still boys. Who they were or why they were there, what company they found in each other. In her head, as in the driver's, they just signalled threat: a hassle, potentially a small, familiar danger to navigate, negotiate. She, too, would have wanted to accompany the girl as she walked past them, or wove her way through them, stepping over their legs. The alleyway was narrow, poorly lit. It smelt bad. She, too, would have stepped out of the car, and walked just a step or so behind her, or to one side of her. Using her height to shield her, but who knew? She'd have been a stranger, too – wouldn't she? Possibly causing more anxiety in the little girl, if she were feeling anxious, more fear, if she were already feeling fearful. In her mind's eye, she saw herself seeing her safely to the back door of the leisure centre. Then pushed through it. Through a door leading directly into a bright corridor, tiled and recently mopped. And then through another door into communal changing rooms. She stayed near the girl, guarding her, as she sat down on the little wooden bench, pulled off her trainers, her soft pink socks, then stood to take off her tracksuit – she was wearing her swimming costume underneath (her pants and vest and school uniform were packed with her towel, to put on afterwards, in her bag). She followed her barefoot walk, the soles of her small feet making prints on the wet tiles, and watched as the girl pulled her swimming cap over her hair, looped her goggles around her wrist. She walked with her through the showers, overstepped the footbath, to the great room housing a still, blue pool. Still and vast. Olympic. The assault of chlorine. The water like a block cut out from something absolutely solid and absolutely blue. One or two other kids would already be there, compact in their strong bodies, yawning and chatting around the edges. It would be surprisingly quiet: the shrieks and shouts that people normally release in swimming pools all on mute.

—

And there Helen would stop. Her waking imagination hit a limit and stopped. But now, always, she dreamed of swimming. She had been sleeping so erratically and so briefly since Rose was born that often-times the only way she could tell whether she'd even been to sleep was if, upon waking, she could catch hold of the fragile tail-end of a dream.

Herself. Swimming. Not in a clean blue chlorinated pool, but in shallower and browner rushing water. And to begin with not swimming at all, just hanging in the water. Her mouth open. Her body, fusiformed, getting lifted and nudged by the current pulling past. The river smelling of minerals and mud. Her mouth downturned, and hanging slightly open. Gently releasing bubbles. Then – prompted by nothing – opening the power in her neck. A jerk. And like that, head-first, she was swimming. It was a propulsion, coming not only from somewhere within herself. But as if the motioned waters once con-spiring to hold her still had all of a sudden decided – why not *now*? – to force her forwards. Directly she plunged into a channel of dark green weeds: it was cool in there. Dark and cold. She nosed through them, her head and her sides stroked by their long flat fingers. Now she was gathering speed: she swam over gravel and out into the more open, middle run of the river, over pebbles and the occasional larger, round-backed, sunken stone. Light danced and bounced all around her. In stipples, in stripes; sometimes in sudden shafts of sandy yel-low, falling through bubbled amber. The river was the colour of beer. On and on she swam, at her own incredible pace, water rushing through her gilled cheeks, her head nudging rhythmically from side to side. She had no shoulders and no arms. Just a thin transparency of fins, suggesting directions. She was all head powered by thick, strong neck – her neck at one with her strong, tapering body, which was

oiled grey and in places spotted with intense colouration. On and on. Past the flash and glint and close shadowy passing of other river-swimmers, under a floating surface of twigs and boatmen and leaves, over the part-buried roots of overhanging, riverbed trees. Carried by riffles and runs, surfacing then re-plunging where the river gathered and rounded into deeper pools. The swimming lasted for a long time – forever, in fact.

Until a pattern of sound came shuddering through the water, slowing her down.

From somewhere farther along the winding channel, far up ahead, there came shaky, irregular sound. A sound patterned, experienced only as vibration: a bell tolling, underwater. Its toll pushed forward to meet her. Now it seemed to churn its way back.

It changed orientation: it grew louder. It summoned her from above. The river began to sink and suck away.

Slowly, Helen surfaced – gasping as her lungs adjusted to the air, and as her elbows were returned to her. They were there: her elbows, her arms. They'd always been there. It was just that for a while they'd been bound against her body, made gloriously useless, in the logic of her dream, by what she now understood had been a rubber suit: a great wetsuit blotched grey and blue over her spine, then paler and speckled with a streak of pink across her distended stomach. It took effort – massive, heaving effort – to pull an arm up and out of that close binding but already she was doing it: using her nearest, most recently rediscovered and loosened limb – at the end of it, a hand – to reach out, anew, in the direction of Rose.

I'm here.

Rose was the bell. She was crying – an inhale and quiet, then one long, ragged exhale. The sound was hot and hard.

I'm here.

Or, Helen was the bell.

Or, the bell was the co-sounding of this refrain: reprimanding and reassuring, summoning and calling. Like a stricture:

I'm still here.

They'd said this.

They had both said it many times before.

Yet here they were: going through the motions of saying it again.

The two of them, calling out their present-ness to each other, re-affirming it, calming with it, sometimes oppressing with it, and in doing so fraying a path for themselves and for their togetherness in the already said.

I'm here.

It was stricture. But it sounded, also, like a structure. Like a basis.

I'm here and you're there.

We'll start again.

A fragile grounding, requiring emphasis and repetition, repeated and emphatic re-grounding, to build two lives upon.

Helen reached out for Rose. She'd hove her out of her little basket into her own bed, push herself up against the headboard. In the crook of her left arm, Rose bashed at then managed to locate with her raw open mouth Helen's breast and make her own crying stop.

Helen took in a big breath of the bedroom's stuffy air.

For how long had Rose been crying?

How long had it taken the noise to reach her, dulled by the cool brown river, in her free-swimming, solitary, freshwater dream?

She must have slept. But for minutes? For hours? For how long?

Helen felt profoundly unrested.

She wanted very much to sleep.

Deeply, deeply, she longed to sleep again, to find her way back to the middle run of the river, to be absorbed in the common stream.

Rose was calming in her arms. She could sense the light changing outside, night-blue fading out, becoming lighter, becoming grey.

And then?

Nothing. That was it.

Rose slept, lightly, intermittently, feeding on and off, dozing on and off, until it was fully morning. Helen, propped up on pillows, recovering the room, recovering herself, stayed on alert. She remembered the propulsive solo-swimming feeling; it was a cool, twisting rush and it was keeping her awake.

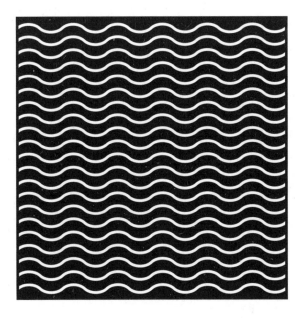

"THE LAWS THEREIN"

"A WONDERFUL LONG CHAPTER CONCERNING THE MARVELLOUS"

I am, "in reality, the Founder of a new Province of Writing, so I am at liberty to make what Laws I please therein." This was the narrator's declaration, the narrator standing in for the author, in one of the essay-parts of Henry Fielding's *Tom Jones*.

For instance: the directive of literary realism.

In a long, essayistic part concerning the "marvellous," the narrator marks out the first boundary: a first, speculative limit to this new, wide-open Province, sketching out the remit of its particular concerns:

"First . . . I think it may very reasonably be required of every writer that he keeps within the bounds of possibility, and still remembers that *what it is not possible* for man to perform, it is scarce possible for man to believe he *did* perform . . . The only supernatural agents which can in any manner be allowed to us moderns are ghosts, but of these I would advise an author to be extremely sparing . . . As for elves and fairies, and other such mummery, I purposely omit the mention of them . . ."

"Possibility" as a sole criterion, though, is soon reconsidered and revised. The bounds of what it might be *possible* for a man to do/to perform – surely, that would have to also include many extra-ordinary, exceptional feats. The field was too wide.

He draws the boundary in. "Possibility," yes, but not on its own: "[W]e must keep likewise within the rules of *probability* . . ."

In other words, within the range of actions both actionable (falling within the range of ordinary human capacity – not superhuman, not supernatural) *and* likely. Which is to say: plausible. For at stake, or in play, for Fielding as well as his contemporaries, was the question-

criterion of credibility. As literary critic Catherine Gallagher points out, unlike Daniel Defoe's *Robinson Crusoe*, published thirty or so years previously, and prefaced by a claim to authenticity, in Henry Fielding's novel it is made repeatedly clear that the work was intended as a fiction. The stories narrated in *Tom Jones* have been made up (they are "*imaginary* Histories"). The account of a foundling found in Mr Allworthy's bed, for instance: it never happened in reality.

But the point is: it could have.

People do this, under duress, in desperation – they leave babies to be found by other people, who hopefully find them and take them on.

Herein lies the territory of the eighteenth-century, English-language, "realistic" novel: a "zone of practice" different from all the other, more self-evidently fictional (incredible) stories of giants and elves, ghosts and miracles. The kinds of stories that the novel, in this setting, explicitly defined itself against: grouping them under the general heading and counter-category of "Romance." Gallagher shows how the novel claimed for its unexplored province the somewhat narrower space of *credible* inventions: made-up stories about believable happenings that – because they were believable – cultivated the risk of being mistaken for real life. In an essay titled "The Rise of Fictionality" she argues that this just *is* fiction: at the start of the eighteenth century, this is what the term "fiction" was brought in to flag. Fiction: a relatively new name used to describe the kinds of stories that don't immediately declare their own fictionality by being so obviously implausible. Stories might actually have happened – that are "life-like" in the sense that they remain in close, deliberate contact with the range of actionable (observable) human activity, and the space-time limitations of a likely (a more or less ordinary) human life.

LIFE-LIKE

But what is life like, really? The necessary, pressing, open question. And for whom? Questions that the novel, through its descriptions, the sharing out of its attention, both answers and asks. What is it like – "ordinary" life? "Common," "plausible," "credible" life? On what scales of action is it to be narrated, how fast should it move? Does it exclude chance, weirdness, transformation – the imagination?

Fielding's instruction to future novel-writers: "in relating actions, great care is to be taken that we do not exceed the capacity of the agent described."

It is important that *great care* be taken to remain always within the recognized capacities of agencies described.

The question this opens and begs, phrased again in the phrasing of the philosophers:

Do we already know (What would it mean to claim to already know? And, therefore, to use the novel as a mechanism never to expand on but merely to confirm and repeatedly reproduce?) what "an agent" (a human agent, a live creature, living out their own intensive version of "ordinary," uniquely situated life) is capable of?

is thinking, hands on waist. Her object of contemplation is the sturdy-shaky tower she'd motivated the other kids to help her build. An unprecedented repetition of an existing structure. With her own potent and fragile resource of naming power, the one she'd called "Post Office Tower."

In Christy's summer story, it is still standing.

But "June was impatient and wanted something to happen very quickly." So it will be June who goes behind it and gives it "a gentle push, at the same time screaming,

'TIMBER!'"

The whole construction comes down with a loud crash.

It's so startling that all the children leap back.

They recover.

Possibly, now, the game can resume.

Now they'd had a chance to explore the potentials of their materials, and found a collaborative stacking method, surely the kids will build something else?

But the adults all around hear the crashing sound too: "It seemed all the windows of the flats opening onto the green abruptly acquired human heads." There are parents shouting, old people "swinging their sticks."

Even the caretaker, normally easy-going, comes after them with a big broom – and chases them away.

The chapter is titled "Chased from the Green."

After that, each one of three further chapters will be its own demonstration of the fact (not the thesis) that there was Nowhere to Play:

The children go exploring beyond their own block of flats, venturing into the zone of a different estate. They find "a kind of bushy

enclosure, full of shrubbery, trees and brambles." "This is the place," says Ricky, whose idea it is to play here. "I used to come here with my friend Roy. Nobody owns it."

"So it can be ours, then?" asks June "uneasily."

"Yeah why not?" asks Michael. "Since no one else owns it, why not!"

But they can't claim it. Partly because June doesn't want to: she finds it spooky, she is scared; she doesn't like playing in dark places. But mainly for the reason that someone does own it: the government.

It is the caretaker from this new estate who spots them. He's been warned about them: the roving collection of kids, knocking about, causing trouble, at a loose end. He shouts at them, chases them, threatens to set the dogs on them next time: they run for it, as fast as they can, through the allotments to get away. The girls feel the residents' vegetables squashing beneath their feet, they feel lettuces under their shoes, and feel remorse.

They try to find somewhere else: they play in the stairwells, the open corridors of their block of flats, outside front doors, below living room windows.

Each time, the exciting start, the opening potential of a game; each time how rapidly it gets closed down. The residents or someone else comes out to shout at them.

For their very last game of the summer, the children spot some scaffolding put up by the builders working on a house next door to a church. Dan goes first: he climbs up the fence, then onto the scaffolding leading to the roof. "The roof seemed a good place to play, we decided." It is high up above the road, but the roof is flat, with only a pointed part in the middle for the clock tower. It is covered with

rubber sheeting. There are no railings. They start playing a game of tag, racing about: "Of course we did know how easily we could fall off ... but as with many such foolish things as we did as children we were enjoying the excitement. Besides, there was no other place for us to play safely anyway." But it's not a good place. They could, one of them really could – very easily – just fall off. An adult recognizes this, too. The children notice a car slowing down below them; a man getting out to shout out them: Oi! Get down from there!

Sheepishly, they head home.

The girls see Michael by the front steps leading to their block of flats:

"Found somewhere nice to play yet?" he asks them, "looking up, rather hopefully." "No, no such luck," says Jane.

"Ah well, that's life," he replies.

That's life.

"I used to hate school before, but I don't think I do now. In fact I'm looking forward to going back."

"Me too," agrees Moya.

"And me," Jane finalized.

Then a voice calls out: "Eh what are you lot doing, writing on the cement?"

The book ends when school restarts: when the children return to the institutionalized structuring (channelling, in the worst case: suppression) of their will to play, which is actually a relief. Because where else can it go? The short novel ends like this: resigned and saddened. It carries the memory of the child who died crossing the road to get to the park – in a second, knocked down by a big fast car; a short clause embedded in a sentence. In each piece of Christy's story, the children had a good go: they were told to play outside and they did. They

put all their energy into it, they improvised with their surroundings. They brought new ideas to them: ideas about how to occupy and make sense of their spaces, how to live in them differently (testing what they could become): finding new corners of potential, cultivating novel ways of inhabiting them together.

But the final lesson of the book is this: on their own, such energy, such imagination, the human impulse to find or make settings for these material acts of the imagination, are not enough. For their experiments to take hold, for their ideas and their own selves to have a future chance of becoming, what is needed is space and time. More of it than the kids in the story are granted (by the powers of who owns what and how things have been decided for them – how life is). A basic support structure: offering space: the provision of a bit more space (protected open space) and time: a bit more time (protected, open-ended time).

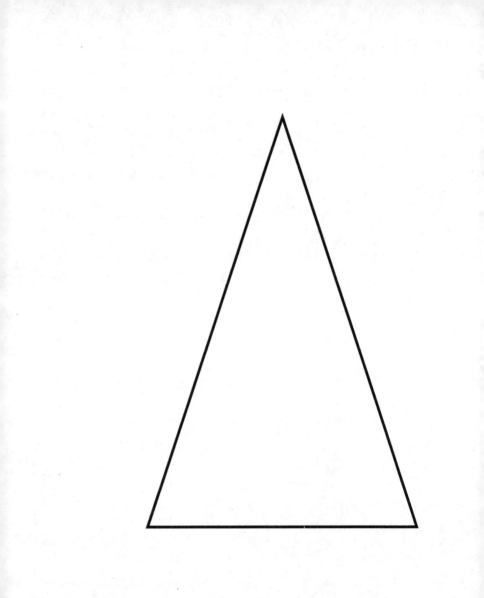

A CHANGE OF ENVIRONMENT

OUTSIDE, WALKING

Helen felt re-energized. Joyous, even. New energy from the reflections in the puddles and the air. From birdsong, her own forward-momentum, the lifting wind and the big arrangements of the slow-moving clouds. It was bracing; she felt stirred up: with this small head against her breast-bone, these legs to either side of her waist; without knowing what this meant, by dint of the fabric sling, Rose had her arms half-wrapped around her. Bracing and embraced.

A LITTLE BRIDGE

Helen walked; she ambulated on. Past front gardens, low-fenced, high-hedged. Some that were carefully planted and tended; others like the landlady's, completely paved over. One housing a tiny sculpture park: a stone rabbit installed beneath a small tree, a concrete frog, a weather-stained permanent duck. At the end of the street she turned another corner. Here was the nearest pub, its big double doors for the moment closed, its outdoor seating – two picnic tables on the pavement – empty, awaiting opening time. Rose's breathing when Helen leaned her ear down and in to listen for it was quiet but steady. Who would know – who could have imagined now – how hard she had recently been crying? Her eyes were closed, her mouth had fallen slightly open, and her head, supported by the fabric of the sling, had tilted upwards. She looked like she could be singing, holding her own silent note. Helen put two fingers against her forehead. It was cool now. She pushed her chin deep into her neck to kiss her, on the brow, kissing her whilst still on the move, since ongoing motion was necessary and she was a bit afraid to stop. Somewhere along this street there was an arrangement she'd look out for whenever she passed (once a day, twice a day). She looked out for it now: a length of wood that someone had extended the short distance from the window of their first-floor flat down to the roof of what looked like a newly built extension below. A plank. Once, a few weeks ago, she saw a young cat make its way, very cautiously, down its steep slope. From the sill of the upstairs half-opened window to the sparkling tar roof of the new structure – it was a distance that, at a stretch, it might have jumped. But it would have been an endangering leap (also at an awkward angle; a fair way down). Recognizing this, responding to it, someone had made their cat an ad hoc ladder. As she neared the flat she looked

out for it – for the cat, mostly, hoping to catch it, as she had done once, in the act of transition. It wasn't there. But she appreciated the ladder: it was a steep but practical and movable bridge. From the sill of a half-open window to the tarmacked roof, it made a connection.

One recent late afternoon, when she and Rose were on their way home from a napping walk, looping and looping the park, accumulating steps and stretching out time, the light from a low sun had struck it at a different angle and with the accent of small shadows she'd seen for the first time that the cat ladder wasn't ad hoc, actually, not at all: the person who'd fashioned it had added little ridges, sort of ruts. What were they called?

These checks to prevent a little cat from losing its footing – on a wet day, sliding?

Ruts.

No. Something else.

Cleats.

THERE WERE OTHER SCENES

A man unlocking his car. They were barely scenes. Small incidents on different days that caught her attention and sometimes expanded before collapsing to make room for new ones, though some she retained. A man lifting his arm.

When? Last week, walking as usual with Rose in the sling – their new, day-shaping habit acquired in just a few weeks – on their way to the park.

A man coming out of his house and lifting his arm to point his keys in the vague direction of all the cars. Circling his arm in the air widely but purposively, like the keys were a wand. They were a wand, effectively. He held them aloft, pointing and pressing, causing a vehicle a bit farther down the street – a truck disguised as a car – to respond.

Just like that, the wand called out: Where are you?

With the same gesture it commanded: OPEN.

Instantly, the car answered. Eager red lights, a responsive three-beat beep: O-VER HERE!

The main occurrence of the scene, though, was not what the man did or the car did.

It was the way their actions caused a large seagull to slowly take flight.

Helen paused her walk to watch it. She could sense the man on the approach pausing too. Between them lay the contents of a split bin bag: all the colours of the peelings, torn packaging, even bones.

And now, at eye-level, the large-headed gull with its hefty wings, lifting into the air – finding its upward trajectory. Only, there was something else: a quick brown movement; a hanging tail. A live creature moving in its beak.

She saw that the man had seen it, too.

For a moment they were complicit, silently conversing: eyebrows raised, sharing out expressions of bewilderment, amusement, mock or real horror.

Really? The man's look said. It was what Helen also wanted to know.

Shudder shudder. Is that what they want? Is that what they do?

COMFORT ME

Part of walking – walking out of doors, joining in with the social life outside, though always remaining more or less within a small district, their postcode of streets – involved a form of asking. Please. Often it was Helen asking on behalf of them both.

Energize us; wear us out.

Interest me, since Rose is asleep.

Shut up or at least attenuate your sudden noises (this was directed to the builders dropping tiles, to seagulls and car alarms, to fire engines . . .).

Help me (to keep going).

Addressing the weather, the sun, the moon, she'd request that it change, lift, or reinforce their mood. Take them by surprise.

It was a form of enlisting: enlisting the environment in their own important projects.

Helen knew that if she behaved like this, acting as if the world had the power to take part and help – it was because the world was not her.

She forgot this sometimes, then remembered it.

For it could feel like it, sometimes: like the world in the form of the specific environments she lived in, and moved through, their climates and forces, were an extension – an expanded province – of her own interiority.

But they were different: roving independently and resistant.

They operated according to their own strange logics, structures, impulses, motivations. They could not be simply co-opted, and incorporated.

Regularly, intermittently, these outdoor scenes gave her cause to remember this.

At times, it felt like she and Rose were co-petitioners, aligned and wanting exactly the same things.

At times, it felt like Rose had asked for and been granted something that Helen didn't want – and would never dream of wanting, because it acted against all reason, all conceivable adult interest.

At times, it was as if Rose were the world, as if she were the locus of all the great forces that Helen was appealing to, with their powers to thwart her, or support her.

Sometimes the world didn't help. It was actively hostile.

Or, it made no response. It just continued: doing its own thing.

But sometimes, though, it really did.

FALLING IN AND FALLING OUT

They were walking in the direction of the park, distancing themselves from their living room, from the play-mat and the plant – from the shelves on which there was a copy of John Dewey's book of social-aesthetic philosophy, facing out. But, in their own manner, they were enacting it. They were their own local demonstration of it: pulsing through the "phases in which the organism falls out of step with the march of surrounding things and then recovers unison with it – either through effort or by some happy chance . . ."

For Dewey, this is what life, most basically, is like.

It is what starts life, gets it going and allows it to continue. People and other live creatures (organisms in the broadest sense), things, materials, settings – interacting. Falling in with and in this way activating or finding some supportive tension in collaboration with each other, calling each other forth – then falling out.

Falling in: a sensation achieved sometimes (only) by chance. The wind lifts a little bit bringing new invigoration and – yes. That's the mood.

Sometimes (only) through intense effort: a concerted adjustment, a willed receptiveness to having one's own strange inner march acted upon: Helen taking the decision to walk faster because the natural pace of the person she was walking with, whom she was talking and listening to – whom she badly wanted *to keep up with* – was a bit too fast. (Rebba's preferred walking pace was naturally extremely fast.) Or, like right now, feeling no longer in any way *at odds* with Rose but in union with her – carrying her as she slept; their different projects happily aligned.

Then falling out.

Getting overtaken, excluded, feeling unaccommodated, frustrated or hurt.

Synching, desynching, stressing, resisting, yielding, resting. These are the rhythmed actions of a live creature responding to its environment, adjusting to it, getting lifted and energized, stimulated and changed or depleted and crushed by it. Also, acting upon it – with the basic human (and not only human) impulse to make their own settings and scaled environments, to elaborate temporary places of shelter, held somewhat apart from the great flux of life, in which to test out alternative ideas and positions, new sets of relations.

They themselves hold for a while, then release.

They hold others: they get attended to, then turned away from, switched off, left or put down.

"[H]uman energy gathers, is released, frustrated and victorious. There are rhythmic beats of want and fulfilment, pulses of doing and being withheld from doing."

Dewey's project, as Nancy Armstrong makes clear, was not to "universalize experience." But to show how the aesthetic impulse is at work across all categories; how it prefigures and is distributed across "the conventionally accepted categories" of "producer, or artist, artwork, and consumer, or audience." If "the actual world, that in which we live," is given like this: as a catching, dropping, but fundamentally involving and aestheticizing rhythm "of movement and culmination, of breaks and re-unions," it follows that "the potential for responding to and making the aesthetic is in everyone." It's not an elevated thing, necessarily, a bettering one; it's not a separate or luxury one. It's a necessary human (and not only human) one; "held in common by the fact of being alive."

THE SKY HAD WHITENED

There were still some high patches of blue. But in one large section of the sky the clouds seemed to be banking. Their lower drifts were loose and grey. Helen's thoughts turned briefly back to the umbrella standing tightly in the hall. She reached under her coat to adjust the pull of the sling, tugging across her shoulder blades. She pressed the heels of her hands briefly into her eyes, and walked one, two steps like this. Then put her hands to rest on the round of Rose's back, blinked hard, and walked on.

THE MAIN ROAD

It was formed of a line of shops, some of them boarded up and closed; the supermarket. There were lights, a crossing and a traffic island, another set of lights and another crossing; four lanes of heavy traffic, a bus lane and a bike lane before the start of the long hill leading up to the gates of the park. Helen hit the button of the first set of lights. Under her hood, Rose's mouth had parted further, making an amazing dark entry into her throat. Helen thought about the quality of the surrounding air: the particles rising from the exhausts of the vehicles bearing past. She cupped her hand over Rose's mouth.

She stood waiting for the lights to change. The traffic moved.

She stood but not still; she shifted her weight from ball to heel and from foot to foot.

She bounced:

      Ball   heel.

              Weight   shift.

      Heel   ball.

              Shift   bounce –

WAIT

Three streets away, at the wheel of the bright yellow van, the boy who'd delivered her novel was still at work. He was a man turned recently eighteen. He was not even half-way through his day. The packages, pouches and boxes packed in the back slid around a bit as, removing them one by one, he made more space for those remaining. He was aware of how many were left, aware of where he was headed next, but his focus was trained on what actually mattered to him. On his phone, many messages had bloomed that morning. Tens, hundreds – it felt like thousands. Nothing from her. He thumbed back to re-read what he'd sent, so early in the morning the trees were singing. The x he'd tapped to sign off looked small now, and scared. Come on, he said – calling to her from underneath his breath. Come on. What was she doing? Sleeping probably. Most likely, she was still sleeping. He saw her naked feet; her hair spreading over, tangling and scenting the pillow; under the soft duvet, her long t-shirt bunched up around her waist. Make me tremble. Something deep inside him quivered, fell off balance. It wasn't even late. He was all incline, leaning, stretching, sliding, and she was the direction. It wasn't even lunchtime. Make me suffer. Make me wait.

Helen crossed. She began walking up the hill in the direction of the park. Rose slept. Her body bundled and rhythmed.

A big bus rushed up too close alongside them; it bowled on past. She walked on.

She took her hand away from Rose's mouth. She was swinging her arms. Her hands were free. Her mind was free. The intention at the start of the day had been to get Rose sleeping in her chair so that she could sleep alongside her but this – the outdoors, this was good too. Say it was better. The world partakes of the attitude it induces and it felt good to walk up a hill.

She took off her hat and her hairband pulled off with it. She unbuttoned the one button of her coat. The incline grew steeper. She could see, now, the tops of the trees that would soon greet her with wide arms and their full proportional height. The wind made her hair lift and fly about. She took a long deep breath, inflating then releasing the cold air from the folds in her lungs.

She checked: Rose was breathing too. She was sound asleep but clearly breathing: Rose was safe and well and as long as she kept walking, moving, bouncing, for the next hour or so, she would stay like this. They both would – alive and well and together. Only now Helen would be free to think her own thoughts, decide her own route, and turn her head with freedom towards whatever appealed to her.

I decide.

She said this out loud. She asserted it chantingly: I decide, I decide, I decide.

Her feet pressed the pavement through the soles of her trainers, layered tarmac and below it pipe-work and sand and mounded earth. She felt the steepening slope level off; the summit reached. The large

wrought iron gates of the park stood there in front of her: wide open. The sky was all white now, a great, covered sky. She found her apple and crunched it. Juice spurted from her mouth. A big drop landed on Rose's cheek, like a tear. It made a picture of sentimentality. Helen laughed with her mouth full. She dabbed it away with the cuff of her coat. They walked in; she walked on.

ROSE

Was she dreaming? Her brow was furrowed. She was for the moment deeply, very privately, asleep. The sling was a fabric bag to gather her sensations and her focus inward.

She liked it. (She liked to sleep in it.) It contained her.

Winnicott once said: "If the baby could talk, he or she would say: Here I [am], enjoying a continuity of being. I had no thought as to the appropriate diagram for myself, but it could have been a circle."

A diagram for Rose, as they walked: it could have been a circle.

The sling, its close environment: it made her into a squashed circle (a sphere, wrapped around Helen's chest). She was a full circle until something happened – until something else, or her awareness of it, broke in.

For instance, a car alarm. Or Helen momentarily forgetting or failing to support Rose's head. Rose's head dropping. The whole world and her very existence in it dropping, cleaving in half. Rose reacting by grasping at it.

In such a scenario, the continuity of her "going on being" would be suddenly broken. In Winnicott's words, instead of one shape, she is being all of a sudden required "to be two parts: a body and a head." He imagines the baby talking: this new diagram "I was *suddenly forced to make of myself* was one of two unconnected circles instead of the one circle that I didn't even have to know about . . ."

The sling worked like a perfect bag because it was stretchy and, if securely tied, undroppable: temporarily, it held all the un-connection in.

The line spoken by an imagined baby could just as well have been spoken by Mr Allworthy, as he prepared to step into bed.

Imagine again: Mr Allworthy at bedtime. His life steady. His interests fixed.

And then, cleave: a baby.

There had been no advance warning: he'd had no idea that a baby could come in like this, unsought, now found. Or, from that point on, how it would interfere with (divide, multiply, and disconnect), shift or expand the purview of his concerns.

Consider the scene as a counter to the way interests are usually channelled. For example, by the algorithms on the website Helen used to order her copy of the book. Making calculations, betting on the stability of what she was like and what she was interested in: in the past you have given time and attention to things like this; *therefore*, in the future, you are most likely to want to give more time and more attention to more things (exactly like or along the same lines as this).

A continuity: your interests are your interests. The circle holds, it gets replenished from the inside. Here is its circumference. Which is to say: here's where it ends.

Now think of Helen receiving her novel: opening the package in the living room and starting to read. She'd chosen it. She must have already been to some degree *open* to reading it. She'd chosen it a little bit at random, mostly because it was old and famous, and long. Still, she was primed to receive it.

Even so, ahead of its arrival, ahead of giving it time and attention – there was no way of knowing how she would respond.

A part-novel, part-book of related thinking about a novel.

Whether it would be *for her*.

Which is something people say about the books they read, sometimes.

It was, or it wasn't, 'for me' (in the end, sadly, unexpectedly, disappointingly).

It didn't speak to me.

(None of the things that matter to the novel matter to or concern me. They've not been presented in such a way to make me feel spoken to, or concerned.)

Her old interesting part-novel. At the place where she'd put it down, so close to the beginning, Helen had been getting into it. It was one of those things: an energy responding to an energy, generating interest. It could be explained up to a point, but never fully. She was into it. She couldn't say (exactly) why.

A low-stakes example of an incursion into the circle of a person's concerns. Low- or no-stakes because it is true that feeling unexpectedly addressed by and wanting to go on with a novel has nothing, practically or materially, to do with being a baby, or the arrival of a baby, nor with the next phase of responding, practically and materially, to the living demands of a baby. It's possible to put a novel down (facedown) on the carpet. To leave it there and forget about it. To attend to all manner of other things and make it wait.

But at a level of abstraction (of diagrams), both present as situations of address.

New demands on a person's time and attention can arrive like this: like unexpected letters, packages or bundles addressed, in this very general way, "to Whom It May Concern."

Which means that it can sometimes be surprising – it is important that it should always remain to some degree *open* and *surprising* – who ends up actually receiving the message, feeling concerned by it and who, therefore, is in a position to respond.

It is what Jacques Rancière calls the non-specific specificity of literature's regime of address: writing addressed to whom it *may* concern – whomever it might have a chance of concerning (with the hope that it might be "someone"). But without those chances ever having been *exhaustively* determined by anything (biology, social training, circumstance, proven spheres of interest) or anyone in advance.

A wide-open remit of address that must itself be contingent upon the writing being intended for "someone" – yes: "a reader."

But the reader defined as "no one in particular."

"No one in particular" – meaning, at least potentially: "anyone."

It is writing (a package, a delivery) prepared to speak to anyone. To call upon and ask for the life-time interest and accommodation of absolutely anyone – "anyone at all."

THE SCENE SAID THIS

It spoke to this, or could be encouraged to. (The discovery of a baby in a bed, it could be read as an argument for the potential *discontinuity* in any person's continuity of being; for the necessity of such interruption and opening; for de-centering centres of interest; for the chance – always holding out for the chance – of a breach in the closed circle of their concerns.)

It also turned, faced in other directions, and spoke of other things.

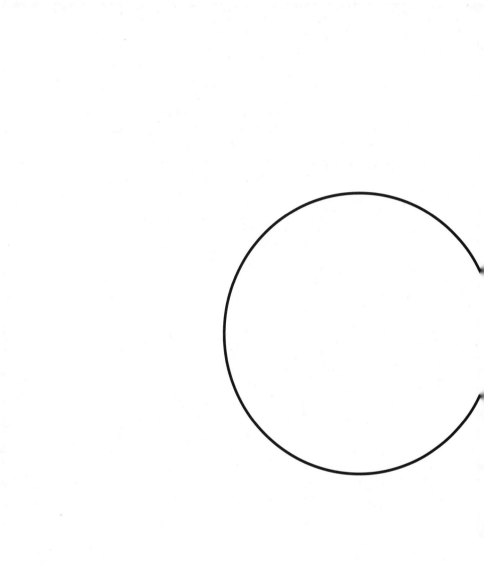

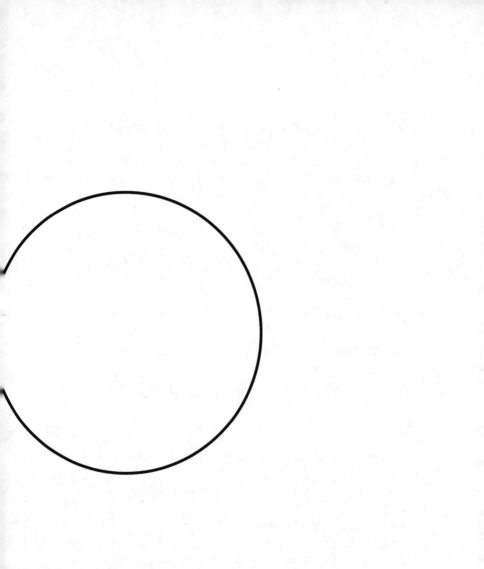

SQUARES (BOXES)

In the kitchen, stuck to the fridge, was the hand-drawn excel-sheet of the days. Helen had taped it up there some weeks ago, and made a project of filling it in. Part of it read:

Monday 5 A.M. start:
    AWAKE (CRYING)
    AWAKE (CALM)
    FEED
    AWAKE (LIVELY & ALERT)
    SLEEP
    AWAKE (CRYING)
    FEED
    AWAKE (CRYING)
    FEED
    AWAKE (sort of TOUCHY – a touchy, sensitive day).

Next to these states and actions: durations. 10 mins. 25 mins. 1 hr. ONE WHOLE HOUR! (Joy and surprise expressed in capitals, exclamation marks.) 3 hrs. 45 mins.

And so on. A twenty-four-hour rolling record, written with an improvised system of pens:
    black marker for the name of the day and its arbitrary "start" time,
    red felt tip for the awake times,
    scratchy green for breastfeeding,
    magenta (a highlighter) for sleep.

There was no logic to this; as the days went by the green pen had grown fainter and fainter, running out of ink, until Helen was just dabbing the vertical page with it, like a dry paintbrush, making no marks. She switched to biro. But the old biro in the kitchen drawer wouldn't always flow, and so then the writing would just be impressions, deep scores in the paper becoming scribbles of blue frustration in an effort to make it work.

The chart of Rose: the way Helen had drawn it was a simplification. In reality, the different actions, or conditions, were a succession of rolling, ragged-edged atmospheric states. Like a weather report: What now?

Delicate sheets of misted water. Now a heavy, heavy lasting rain.

Now a light wind and the clouds dispersing; sunshine, a soft warm light.

Lovely, clear, for a long time.

Now a squally wind.

Now, gathering, now low pressured intensity, now storms.

A weather report as written by someone bareheaded – that is, by a person out in it, experiencing and exposed to it, with perspective on what greater forces might be causing and conditioning it – other than an awareness that she must be among them.

There was no clear plot.

There was no plot to it because there was no subordination: one phase didn't seem to matter any more or less than any other.

One action, one duration, was never the obvious prelude to what would come next. Nor was it the manifest consequence of what came just before.

The book Helen borrowed from the library had tried, gently, to prepare her for this.

It told her: your baby is not yet a child.

Your newborn: she will be unpredictable and demanding, characterized by urgency and unpredictability. For instance, the book warned: "She might cry to be fed every half an hour for six hours and then sleep for one." Or "four." It said: what you may construe as her morning's hunger will be no cue, or clue, no means of predicting what she will need or how she will behave in the afternoon.

For a while, it said, this will just be how it goes.

There will be nothing that can be relied on to last, "nothing that can be relied on to be over and done with in just a minute."

There will be no discernible pattern: she will be unsteady, inconstant, open, and disjunctive. "Erratic": defined as "changing suddenly and unexpectedly." Something that is "not certain, regular or organized in its behaviour."

The reasons it gave for this: Your "baby is brand new."

She is new to you, new to the world, and new to herself.

In this sense, you know nothing about her: "You do not know how she looks and behaves when she is well and happy so it is difficult for you to know when she is ill and miserable. You do not know how much she 'usually' cries because she has not been around long enough for anything to be usual . . ."

What it said, in its own way: Rose is a newcomer.

Meaning both new and different – uniquely placed to be different, to act differently; to initiate change by introducing newness by way of her difference to the world.

She is a beginner. (Hannah Arendt: "It is in the nature of beginning that something new is started which cannot be expected from whatever may have happened before.")

And both of you are unprepared. Whatever your prior experience, knowledge, or understanding, you would always have been unprepared. For, her book said: "However much you know about babies in general, neither you nor anyone else knows anything about this one in particular."

In the midst of all of this, provoked by all of this: LOVE.

The question of love. It will come in: it, too, will present itself. Not as a basis for care, since so much meaningful care-taking gets underway without it. But, nevertheless, it will push you to consider it, wonder about it and doubt it.

Outside, in the air, or readable, at home, on the internet: an essay titled "A Properly Political Concept of Love." In it, Lauren Berlant writes: "Maybe I should say what I always say, which is that I propose love to involve a rhythm of an ambition to stay in sync, which is a lower bar than staying attuned but still hard and awkward enough."

Love proposed as *involving* a rhythm. As an involvement of rhythm. Or a rhythmed involvement. But where the accent falls not on synching – falling into synch and staying there. (For what if the tempos of the other were *constantly* inconstant? What if, due to their age, their vulnerability, their needs, they were defined by *intrinsic* variability?)

But on this ambition – the rhythm not of the other's but *of one's own ambition* – to stay in sync.

(To *stay* in? Or to seek and re-seek? Falling in and falling out. Recognizing that falling in anticipates falling out – and staying is like this.)

It was a low bar, arguably.

Helen felt that it was awkward: to stay with the effort to find a form of living and loving, a common sway, with the beginner she was responsible for.

It was hard.

Awkward. Though that felt like the wrong word.

It was harder than anything she'd ever known.

Her library book of practical childcare accepted this.

It anticipated it and did nothing to downplay it.

It said: it's alright.

It said: try not "to torment yourself with anxiety if you do not feel anything for her [for your baby] that you can recognize as love. Love will come . . ."

Love will come in its own uniquely formulated, interactive forms.

It said: "Love will come but, in contrast to the bolt from the blue sensation of instant bonding, it may take time."

It asked, rhetorically: "And why not?" Why should you not expect it to take time?

"However you define that word 'love,' it must have something to do with two people interacting; getting to know each other, liking what they know and wanting to know more."

Still, it took seriously the particular presentation of the problem: for as long as your baby is brand new "she is neither lovable nor loving. She is not truly lovable because she has not yet got herself into a predictable, knowable shape . . ."

The library book seemed to propose a person as the becoming-pattern of their behaviours. And to make "lovable" into a word for a singular variability calming and regularizing into a recognizable "pattern."

Which sounded – difficult. Possibly true.

For what if it *were* easier to love a pattern when you were a pattern yourself? When social life required that you fall into its established patterns, starting with the basic division of day and night?

What if it were much harder to love what is irregular, interruptive, scattered, and uncontained?

What would this mean?

For who and what "we" (individuals and institutions) are capable of loving – more primed and ready to love?

For "the disclosure" and, crucially, "the welcome" of a force, a potential of newness – what Arendt calls natality? Presenting as *not* yet – possibly not ever – shaped, as unpatterned, as nothing like a discernible rhythm to fall in with.

Helen had no answers to any of this.

Only a clear sense that: love – yes, it takes time, and space. It was going to. It would require a provision of space and time: protected, unmetered, and without prescribed end. The time it takes to learn about someone new. (Who is provided with this? Or enabled to claim it?) The shelter of a reliable space in which to make a place for the difference of someone new, even as they are changing – changing you and changing themselves and already changing the terms of involvement. How, by necessity, this would be a long-term project, a process dependent on having the means to stay with it. In practice, very likely, the means also to regularly leave it. But to keep coming back to it. Making the conditions of love, all forms of longer-term love, contingent upon the large social structures: on living and working situations with the capacity to give this, to provide it and support it: a certain duration and flexibility of space and time. Reliable and unprescribed; to some degree protected, but with a vista – a wide open

view. Allowing for presence and absence, agreement and dispute, for falling in and falling out. A time and space for tolerating, coping with, the phases of falling out. And for repeatedly renewing the effort to improvise a way back in. "Not simply once." Not once and for all. But through the nights and the days. The space-time accommodation to support this happening again and again; many, "many times."

taking off, said the washing machine. Judder judder judder. The wash Helen had put on earlier was reaching its last phase. In their absence, it knocked hard against its MDF frame and was now trying to inch forward and walk of its own volition. A crescendo that would soon peak and pass. For the moment, it filled the kitchen with great shakes of noise.

IN THEIR ABSENCE

Still in the kitchen, behind the chart on the fridge, the ice in the freezer box thickened into clumps.

Here and there, on the chart, the cells sort of collapsed.

In one column, Helen had run a thick permanent marker line through the whole of the day and the subsequent night, printing in large wobbled letters alongside it: WTF??

Now she told herself, in a sort of mantra:

It's alright if you're not sure if you loved her on sight.

It's alright if love feels like a rhythm of reaching and falling short, a reaching out and falling short. Then an unexpected receiving – a sometimes wholly unsought interaction, having nothing whatsoever to do with ambition. A dispossession. Not an achieved steadiness.

It's alright if the feelings you feel are so mixing and mixed. If there can be patches of the day when you feel panic, then nothing – not a thing for anybody, not even for yourself.

It's alright if it's all going to take time, clock time, attention time, mental space, physical space, all the inner-outer spaces that are being constantly traversed by feeling.

The key is to keep going.

It's alright if the whole project can sometimes feel like an unsupported invention, an unprecedented co-production.

It's alright. Say it's alright.

It's okay. It is (going to have to be) alright.

THE PARK

Its entrance was at the top of the hill. Once in, park-space ran all the way down the other side, right down to the river. It was a formal enclosure, partially enclosed.

Also public, also to some degree ordinary, built for leisure and recreation.

Open from sunrise to sunset, its opening times adjusting to the turn of the earth around the sun, the seasons, the more arbitrary changing of the clocks.

Open to everyone; anyone.

Come in.

Look at the flowers: the spring flowers, the daisies in the lawn, the spent daffodils, the still glossy tulips and thick-scented hyacinths in the circular and semi-circular beds. The leaves shaking on the big oak trees. The broad grassy spaces and the way the whole thing slopes. On the condition, though – there was a large sign near the gate spelling out these conditions – that you not:

play with balls in the wrong places,

sleep lengthways on the benches,

drop litter,

pick the flowers,

ride on any kind of wheel (exceptions made for wheelchairs and prams),

light fires,

make a temporary home (pitch a tent or similar) in its small wooded area,

fish the river.

Rebba came here all the time, running.

For Helen, it used to be only occasionally. On a late weekend morning, when everyone else had had the same idea. Now, these days, it was like the rooms of the flat and the broad sweep of the park – together they composed most of the world.

Her feet found the usual path. Always down in the direction of the river.

A crowd of pigeons had gathered with interest around something edible. They were busy, reluctant to move. She skirted around them, stepping onto the grass. Then, back on the path, trailing the one bird she'd frightened into heading in her direction, liking its strut. She became a pigeon herself for a while: her neck shining like spilled petrol, iridescent pinks and greens, her eye cocked and wild. Her chest was domed solid, too, undergirded by a complex of small, new, clicking bones.

She looked around for a place to drop her apple core. She used to think.

Many things.

She used to think, for example, that the park was a place for time off life. A space for life-on-pause (for leisure, for recreation) while the more real and consequential, actual living, went on elsewhere. Now she saw it differently: this vital, practical place.

The park, initially, had been all about its largest shapes: circles (the bandstand set in a round of grass, encircled by a path; the wide curves of the flowerbeds), squares (the sandpit in the playground). Its planes: the verticals (the trees: immense oaks standing well apart from each other, their arms out-stretched, seeming to greet her as she came in); its rises, slopes and moving horizontals (the flow of the

river). She noted its densities (the bushes, the pines, and, crossing the river over a wooden bridge, the patches of briars and nettles in the little wood); its open spaces (high up on the hill, its view over the small city). These were still its most obvious shaping features. They moved and directed her. But as time went on, walking around it on gentle and warm days, on colder, grimmer days, she found other attractions; more details. The strange bulges that pushed out from the inside of the trunks of the oldest trees; how the swings were so often gathered up – why? – their chains twisted around themselves and the seats flung over the top of the frames. The damp woodchip underneath them, and under the taut triangles of the climbing frame, making a cushiony layer where mushrooms grew.

There were people in the park.

Some people working, maintaining the spaces, planting the beds. The park keeper making little journeys around it in his speedy microvan.

Others doing the same things as she was doing; using it as an outdoor space to carry or push someone else, to be carried or pushed by someone else; to hold hands.

Sometimes Helen would seek out their acknowledgement, recognition – a short smile or nod. She knew the park keeper by sight now, and sometimes he recognized her. Sometimes all of these people were the last people she wanted to see.

There were rows of benches. Especially on the crest of the hill, along paths close to the entrance, where the views were. Rows and rows of benches with plaques sharing the names and dates of the people who, in their lifetimes, had also spent time here. Benches marked with special meaning, personal meaning becoming places for anyone, now, to come in and sit down on.

—

There were encounters.

Once, with a large red-faced man who suddenly rounded a corner, his mouth hanging open, a line of spittle loose on his chin. He was half-staggering, eyes popping. He was holding one hand out-stretched towards her, gasping and clutching.

Her first thought was that she was being attacked.

Her second: fuck me, he's dying.

Then she realized: he'd just been working out.

More often, with the person who seemed to live here: she'd see them always at a distance, holding with delicate fingers the rim of their hood, stepping like the path was too hot, far too hot – walking almost on tiptoe, as if it were painful to bear. They carried a few things in a plastic bag in the hook of their arm and seemed to be almost constantly looking up at the sky.

There could be music.

Bird song, the musics of all kinds of birds; small children crying, calling; the harsher sounds of dogs barking about each other.

There was the particular calling music of a man who brought his own tunes in. Of some strange, singular non-age, he made a habit of riding a low chopper bike around and around the circumferential path of the park, which meant standing upright on his pedals, riding up, up one side of the slope, then freewheeling down it on the other side, heading at speed towards the water, even though it was forbidden, even though the park was on a hill and the paths were steep. He kept an open can in his front basket along with a small portable speaker, held in place by something like packing tape. Brown packing tape. She never saw him in the rain but on dry days, windy days,

he carried in the songs he liked and shared them out with everyone. They were seeking songs, aching songs, soliciting songs. Polyrhythmic and monophonic. He could annoy her. His weathered face with a bright lollipop in his mouth. How he'd ride very fast then slow; casually weaving his bike around whomever happened to be in his path – insisting without checking first on their will-to-be-into-this. It could make her nervous; the waking risk of his sudden approach, waking up Rose. More often than not, though, his music involved her. Even ahead of time. It had taken hold of her before she'd spotted or remembered the bike. Its soaring songs, pulling out drawers and opening secret cabinets in her chest, filling them, if only briefly, with jewels. She'd miss it when it pulled out of earshot and look forward to it coming round again.

(Allow me, allow me to participate.)

He was nowhere today.

Helen walked on. Past toddlers getting helped up then assisted or simply let go down the slide. Some of them whacking at the sand in the sandpit, not digging into it, with the flat sides of their bright plastic spades.

Rose shifted and sighed in her sleep.

The path sloped.

Ahead of them was an old man, walking with small frail steps, each one deliberate and hard-earned. A large white bounding dog approached him, encircled him, left him –

It bounded away.

Then it came back to him, in eagerness; asking for this, asking for that.

There was fear and beauty in the park.

Helen plucked leaves as she walked, little snaps of twig, or pine needles. Something to fiddle with. She'd drop them when she was done with them, or put them in her pocket.

The wind rose. Her hair blew, she pulled her hat back on to keep it from blowing into her face. She re-buttoned her coat. The two low buttons that reached their buttonholes and could be fastened with Rose in the sling pushing out from her chest.

Rose was fast asleep.

The old man and his lively white dog turned off in a different direction, disappearing from view. She rounded a grove of trees, and there, a short way ahead, was the fast-flowing river.

There was no one else around.

Helen bent her neck to speak softly into Rose's hair, the pulsing crown of her head.

Look – apart from the swans, it seems that we have the run of the place.

The river-run of the place.

It was nearing midday and the sky was thick with cloud. It was grey, overcast.

She pushed her hair out of her eyes and resettled her hands.

She felt happy. She felt tired.

Adrenalized and knackered.

She walked on.

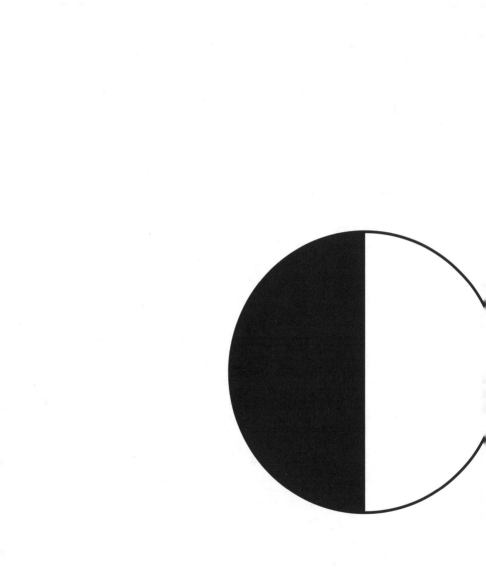

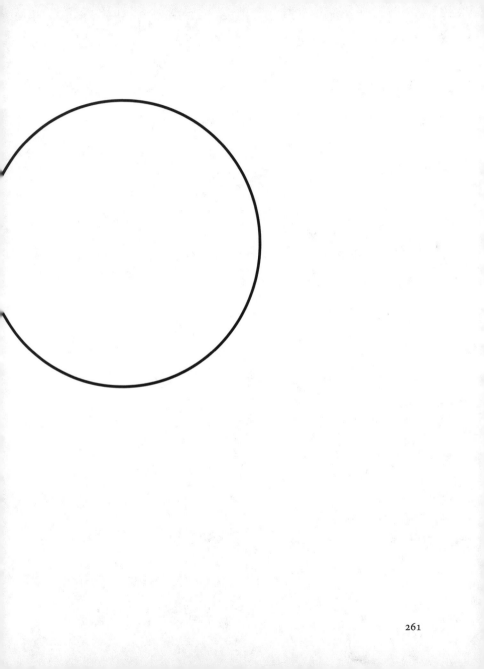

THE TIME ARTS

AND THEN?

In a story she'd once heard – had once been told, or submitted to receiving (in an enclosed space) (a taxi) – a girl gets taken swimming. She is given a lift, then dropped. She is dropped off by a stranger round the back of the leisure centre. Before dawn; first thing on a winter morning.

But then what happened – what, if anything, happened next?

Waiting for something: a further happening – the *next* thing, likely to have been caused by the first (and, therefore, retroactively justifying the narration of it).

Waiting for the larger, unseen consequences of the first event to play out.

"A story is a narrative of events arranged in their time-sequence."

This was E. M. Forster's definition, proposed in a lecture course titled *Aspects of the Novel*, delivered in 1927.

Aspects of the Novel: it is now a "classical critical text," much cited, often taught, still in print, even though it is "systematically disparaged as old-fashioned." Critic Catherine Lanone writes: "Undoubtedly, the book may appear dated, trivial, biased . . ." But, she adds, quoting Daniel R. Schwarz, "one should pay attention [to how] Forster moves away from the doctrine of nineteenth-century realism that novels must be imitations of life and begins to introduce categories that his classically trained audience would have found innovative and exciting, if at times provocatively idiosyncratic, whimsical, and even bizarre." Along with "story," "character," and "plot," categories such as "pattern," "rhythm," and "expansion."

Further terms such as "intensity," "bounce," and "song."

In addition to "time-sequence": the general temporal order of things.

For instance, how "Dinner comes after breakfast, Tuesday after Monday, decay after death," and so on. Time-sense, Forster also called it. Like touch, taste, or smell. A common human sense of time's sequential character, its relentless marching on. Time-boundedness, is another way of putting it. A presumed general understanding if not exactly of what time it is, then of being in-time, living subject to time: a shared feeling of when it's later than it was, or how it feels on a new morning.

"And then?" according to Forster, is the question-motor of "a simple story." The motor and its structure: arranging events in the order in which they were supposed to have occurred.

What happened next?
    Nothing. She swam her lengths.
    That's it.
    Length after length, fast in a cold pool, to warm up.
    She hated it.

Always to begin with. Then, after a little while, finding her power and her pace, her muscle-warmth – she loved it.

We know and live in sequential time. But life is also known by a different measure – this was Forster's proposition. Acting on, complicating, and even modifying time-sequence, there is the value different experiences have, that is accorded them or that they themselves impose: the charge they acquire as we live through and remember them. This is something that cannot be measured by regular units of minutes or hours, days or months, but *intensity*.

THE RIVER

On the approach, it was just the sound of rushing water: a many-channelled rush of undifferentiated sound. First, it was an auditory place. Helen paused her walk here.

She decided – pausing here.

Or, the river decided. It decided for her, with its own authority.

Helen set her hands on the balustrade of the small wooden bridge. Her hands were hot from walking and the wood was damp: she used its dampness to cool her palms.

She stood swaying, looking down into the water, listening to its rushing and its run.

It rushed directly beneath her feet, shallow and fast, clear over pebbles and sandy mud, then darker.

She bent her knees to bounce every now and then, with a mind to prolonging Rose's sleep. But she knew that at any moment the river would give her the confidence to stand still.

Now she stood still and let the river take over.

The work of extending the durations of Rose's sleep: the river – it was her colleague in this, her relief. It was what allowed her to stand still for a while and take a break.

On the internet there were sound files that also proposed this work (this support work). Helen had found a free download of an anonymous woman shushing. It promised to run for eight hours, continuously. The voice would shush then stop – marking an intake of breath. Shush then stop. But the river – it didn't ever need to take a breath. Unlike the sea, it didn't measure, regularly break, or space out its sound. It streamed and gushed. Rushing on: loud and low; aperiodic and unbroken.

Helen responded to its consistency: how it discharged and maintained its noise-intensity, not by cancelling out, but equalising, somehow, all the other surrounding sounds. She listened to how it held. How it held and held *on* (to its one massy note).

Rose heard it, too.

Or, she remembered it. From the deep pocket of her sleep she was reassured by it: this phenomenon called flow. The sound of a continuous (a constant) transfer of energy.

The river wasn't especially wide. It was earthy smells as well as sound. It was the large willow tree weeping over it, its flexible branches getting dragged short distances along with it. It was much deeper in some places than in others.

She felt good here. Would she say this – Helen?

Yes.

The practical actions of this spot, they welled her being. She could see how, in places, the river took on the sky. It collected and carried on its surface tiny cups and scoops of light. There were bubbles on the surface: bubble gatherings, becoming foam. She liked how in others she could see right through it: the wet colours of stone shapes standing out from where they were lodged. The river bore along leaves and sticks and occasionally bits of litter. It carried these things forward very fast, but there were places where they got caught, slowed down, or made to turn back. The river momentum parted itself to allow them their different directions: it moved around them, then once beyond them it regathered and carried on. The river was clearly pushing in one strong general direction, but the more closely and the longer she looked, following it with her attention, she saw how, together with the twigs and leaves on its surface, the river itself was everywhere, also, constantly turning back. Making its own small

about-turns, folding in on itself: pleating back in the wrong direction and in this way making froth, the trails of bubbles that turned and circled around themselves before finding their course and coursing onwards, getting carried lightly away. Flow and counter-flow. In the middle part of the river a central channel opened out the grooves of water, playing at proposing more open liquid shapes, before immediately lapping at their edges, crimping and collapsing them back into channels, furrows and folds.

The river: it filled the long space between its banks and its volume pushed against them, it must have been: pushing outward as well as onward, weakening and widening them. It went on at night-time, rushing through clock-time, while other things paused or stopped.

The bridge made a place to stand and study it and she stood there.

In her stillness she could feel Rose shifting against her chest, moving in the sling.

She dropped things into the water, adding to the scatter on the river-surface. The bits of vegetation she gathered from her pockets: leaf stems, little sticks, and shredded leaves.

She dropped her questions into it; some requests. She asked it to do things for them, for her, for Rose. (Please, why not?) To stop doing other things.

She came here most days to watch her thoughts land on the moving surface, carry forward for a short distance, like boats, then slip under and rush away.

INTENSITIES

Some moments, hours, days last longer than others.

Some moments, hours, days, last longer for some people than for others, depending. Daily life, whatever it may be really, is practically composed of two lives, said Forster: the life in time, ticking, marching by, regular, implacable, and the life by values, slowing or accelerating, shrinking or expanding, condensing or prolonging. The same sixty-second spans experienced as short minutes, as elongated minutes (as thin minutes or thicker minutes). As *separated* minutes: distinctive pockets, or stand-out portions of detached, delimited time.

ONCE IN A LIFETIME

Long ago, over a year ago: a time when Rose was as yet unimagined –
if anyone had predicted her, Helen would have said: Wait. What? No.
She'd have laughed. No no no – unimaginable! (Rose: she was literally unimaginable.) A time, a phase of an ordinary day, when Helen
was seated in the low chair by the window and Rebba had just come
back in, bounding up all the flights of stairs to their high flat, lively
from her run and asking: How was your day, what have you been up
to – what's going on?

Helen saying: *Well.* As a prelude, charged with intention. Preparing her manner, her posture, her tone of voice (and saying with these
preparations: prepare yourself) for the telling of a story. She opened
her hands.

Something happened. She said: I think it was important (worth
telling).

The season was/is important.

Let me tell you: it is a seasonally situated total happening and it is
all about (all about) flowers.

She began: imagine. Me, or you. Sitting by the warm window for
most of the afternoon. No traffic, or barely any, only quiet. Feet up; a
book in your lap, lit by the diffusion of light falling out of the sky. A
bunch of daffodils in a pint glass on the window sill – very green, very
cheap. We bought them – remember? One pound for a closed bunch
in the market. An unpromising bunch of flowers, unless you knew
(But how could you know if you've never seen it for yourself or been
told?) how simply and how fast and how soon – from one minute to
the next – POW! They could bloom.

What happened, Helen said, speaking solemnly.

With a degree of mock solemnity: *what happened* was this.

The flowers we bought. She pointed to them: the daffodils, green like unripe bananas. One of them. She paused (for drama). Opened.

It did just open. Here, in the room, this afternoon.
    On "opened" Helen had made a large expansive gesture.
    She stood there – holding it. Her face full of meaning and intent.

Rebba said: *Okay* . . .
    She was stretching, holding her one arm above her head, clasping it with her other hand behind her back, showing Helen, unselfconsciously, one dark patch of underarm hair and then the other.
    Her attention, which had been willingly given, was now in retreat.

No, said Helen. Shaking her head, shaking her hands out in front of her, as if to wipe out how she'd told it, draw her back and start all over again.
    No, no, no, I don't think you get it.
    She cupped one hand to her ear: *I heard* it open.
    Which is to say: I heard a flower open.
    Helen laughed. *Who on earth gets to hear a flower open?*

Rebba laughed in return. Okay, so now she understood.
    She met Helen's evident delight with her own responsive delight. She wanted Helen to stay up where she was: high and lively in her own wonderment.

It was a little rip.
    Helen continued: it was the sound of tearing. Like paper tearing. I turned towards it, it tore again, and the second time I think I saw it but that might have been because I heard it: a daffodil bursting its *spathe*.

She indicated her phone on the floor by her chair. She'd been using it to look up the word. Or, I don't know: its *bract*. The papery part of the plant that keeps its flower enclosed.

She said: Look, it's open now.

Already, it's opened further. It will be a full trumpet soon. Projecting forward. I say, Helen said, declaring this loudly: I say *within the hour*.

She smiled and stopped talking.

That was it.

Rebba wandered off to have her shower. Helen remembered making daffodils in the first year of primary school: from green card and bright yellow, orange, or white crêpe paper. She remembered cutting out petals from the yellow, rolling small squares of it into cylinders to make the trumpet-parts, frilling the open-end with round-tipped scissors. More than anything, she remembered the texture of the special material: delicate and easily torn from top end to bottom and yet cross-ways almost stretchy – paper with a sturdiness and a good bit of give. Like tissue paper, but definitely stronger (crêpe paper, her teacher had explained, is tissue paper coated with glue).

The story, was it even a story? The one-off occurrence, the incident, falling across and standing out against all the other, more ordinary activities of her afternoon. She could relate it to the material concentrations of childhood but it wasn't about the past. It was all presence. A quiet room; a spring afternoon. It was all co-presence. Her mood and the start of a flower. A more constant state and the brevity of a process. A little rip. It was all general conditions and new fragile presence. But it was also an announcement, extending the quickness of the action into the future. Coming soon: *trumpets*.

THE FUTURE

For the moment, it looked like the river, a complicated folding, enfolding, channelling, and reflecting; it looked like the depths and surfaces of the water: pressing forward, wanting, seeking, if only minimally, to turn back, before pressing-rushing on. It looked like every chance of rain. If you had an umbrella, the prospect of the best kind of rain. Spring rain: a generous, falling shower. It looked like how energetically (with what form of energy), how resourcefully (with what resources), to get through the afternoon. It looked like what to do next, and how to make it happen together: using the mat, the chair, bending over and towards each other, feeding, holding, moving about the front room. It had the anxious quality of how to return to work, when the time came (which would be soon), when her leave expired (who will look after Rose) (what if she still barely sleeps) (could she work partly from home) (should they move). It looked like the flat, mostly, and getting used to the new street (but will she put the rent up) (will she let us stay). It looked like what will the world look like (how will they live in it) (will it be a liveable place, for them, when Rose is older, or grown up). It looked like please (let her grow up) (let me grow old so I can watch her grow up). It looked like getting the shopping in (what's in the fridge), food for the evening and for the morning and possibly even beyond and how to get home without Rose getting wet. It looked like her companion novel: *Tom Jones* (why that old novel, why this one). Its humour and its talking style. Its demands on her time. Her willingness, always provisional, to give it time: the best part of a season, half a year (intercut with reading the news) (intercut with reading the internet) (intercut with home and the park and the rest of life). It looked like Rose as she looked right now, her face asleep and entrusting. Her expression grave and concentrated; her

eyelids, her dark eyebrows, her round cheek protected by the hood of the sling (also, how she might look in a month, or a year, growing into her features, or her features accommodating her). It looked like Rebba (and missing her) (missing her ways) (their ways) (their form of living-together) (what to do about it). It looked for a moment like chance and change: surprise and possibility. It looked like everything had already decided and could only get worse. It opened and contracted, the future: presenting now as a wall, now as an inaccessible garden, whose use-value was to provide access to the bins. Presenting now as the sloping expanse of a grand park, a place of learning and discovery, like a scaled-up version of a zoned playmat, awaiting their return. It flipped like this – alternating between purposefulness and a powerlessness, the longer- and the shorter-term perspectives.

"I ONLY SAW HER FOR FIVE MINUTES, BUT IT WAS WORTH IT"

On the night Rose was born, the time-duration that Helen lay with Rose covered by a warmed sheet was very short, but it was worth it. How much it mattered had something as well as nothing to do with how long the clock said it lasted (twenty-two minutes).

Forster, going on with his lecture, making his point about a certain treatment of time: how, to these two quite different and sometimes competing experiences of time (time sequence and time lived by its intensities), human conduct pays *a double allegiance*.

"I only saw her for five minutes, but it was worth it."

There, said Forster, you have both allegiances paid in a single sentence: to clock time ("I only saw her for five minutes") and how (taken on its own) clock-time says nothing about how those minutes felt, the space-time they opened and held open ("it was worth it").

And it's here, Forster claimed, lecturing at the level of great generality, that we get at the difference between the story *running through* a novel and the novel itself. For, unlike "a simple story," a novel does both: it is interested in how one thing follows another; it is equally (arguably more) interested in what it feels like to live *in time*, in life lived by intensity. As a treatment of time, a novel activates not only curiosity in the reader (and then?) but memory: a form of attention that is accumulative as well as anticipatory, backward-reaching as well as forward-facing, and itself capable of acting *on* time. That is, of repeating or extending the strategies of the narration. By skipping a bit of it. Or staying with it. Thickening it by reading a passage again. Not only folding it and unfolding it but knotting it. Then letting it play out.

As if – imagine: turning back to the ceremony of *un*folding sheets. As if Helen were to take the elastic off her wrist or pull it out of her

hair and use it to scrunch up a great section of the sheet, secure it at the base and in this way make in its centre a large fabric balloon.

Or, if Rebba were to take a pair of sharp scissors out of her pocket and cut into it, then pull one of the corners she was holding through the hole, allowing in this way a small previous moment to push through and hang there in the present, like a cotton tongue.

It would make a contradiction, a kind of temporal impossibility – but one that is not wholly unfamiliar, one that is in fact altogether recognisable, because it's the sort of thing that happens, it's the way time seems to work, not exceptionally, but more or less every day. The novel, by working with the interplay of durations, and inviting the reader to interact with them, has the capacity to pay a double, triple, multiple allegiance to the weird workings of time, to our common-sense idea of its ongoing sequence (what Forster calls "this constant 'and then . . . and then'") *as well as* to what living-in-time can actually feel like, filling it and distorting it. For this reason, said Forster, as a medium, it is the novel, and not the story, that draws closest to the *experience* of life.

And it's true:

"The Snow Queen," for example, told simply, is not very much like life. It's a story that in the telling followed the march of "and then," "and then," "and then" – one thing happening after the other according to their time-sequence.

But even in its structural simplicity the narrative still contains a breach: a splitting, a powerful complication, causing two distinct time-paths to open up. For the boy, frozen and at play, the hours and the days, the seasons, go still. For the girl, the very same duration (can it still be called the very same duration?) is experienced

as crammed, eventful, differentiated. The durations of the girl's days, nights, and weeks are different from the boy's: for her they lengthen; they intensify; they are experienced as waiting, as forgetting, as detour, as acceleration, as *too long*. She is *in* time, paying allegiance to its mobile values, while he isn't, and is prevented from being so – until she arrives. She makes time start up for him again.

But/and then?

It's strange.

The happy setting that the girl returns them to is not so very unlike the Snow Queen's time-stalled hall. The winter palace, the endless idyll of the rooftop garden (with its heavy bower of yellow roses): both present as places where time passes and/or it doesn't. And it doesn't matter, because nothing changes; once there, nothing further need change. The "and-then-ness" (which is also the promise of change, carrying with it the hope of continuation) gets stuck. In both places, the forward-momentum stalls, sticks, and stops.

slept on. By the rushing, flowing, counter-flowing river. All movement and counter-movement, large forward-pulse and microrhythm, hold and collapse.

Helen stood still: looking down at the water from the bridge, at the underneath shapes suggested by the river bed and its fluid surface shapes dimpled with light – at their interplay: the rippling of figures over ground.

Rose slept; Helen started to cry.

"One of the functions of narrative," wrote film critic Christian Metz, "is to invent one time scheme in terms of another time scheme."

Her shoulders shook.

Why crying? Why tears – now?

She wasn't sad. It was just her body deciding. It was just tiredness (deciding for her). Inner water rising in answer to the invitation of river-water. For the fact was she genuinely hadn't slept and there was something about the sobbing rush of the river, its suggestive sort of heave, along with the temporary privacy of her spot on the bridge, and the pair of swans, turning the river's bend, one of them much farther ahead, the other keeping up, keeping to their companionable distance, together but apart – she came here because the river let her stand still and allowed her this release. (Make me weep.)

IN THE MINUTES IMMEDIATELY FOLLOWING
ROSE'S BIRTH

Helen lay with Rose, their bodies sticking together, under a warmed hospital sheet. For how long did those minutes last? That is, before they were moved – because of course they were always going to be moved. There was no question of them or anyone staying there. No one could stay there forever – dwelling long-term in those moments before Rose was lifted away so that Helen could be washed, someone new asking if she felt able to stand up and walk supported to the shower, and rubbed down with a cloth, before being handed back and wheeled together (Helen for the first time holding Rose) in a wheelchair due to shaky legs, due to trembling limbs, to a bed for the night in the open ward.

For Helen – say for Helen: they lasted longer than for anyone else.

Or, for Rose. For Rose who was tasked with breathing on her own for the first time; who was registering the sensation of her skin in contact with the air, with light, with strip lighting, with Helen's body-surface, with the stiffness of a white hospital sheet, all for the very first time.

What was it that made such a duration possible, actually experience-able?

Considering all those involved.

Considering those for whom twenty further minutes were just a part of their ordinary working day, their ordinary working nights, durations in the form of shifts with (at least in theory) a clear start and end-time, broken up with (at least in theory) actually restful breaks, regular snatches of off-time to sit down for a breather, a moment to

reflect, a chat and a cup of coffee from the machine. Those who, in a different room nearby, had been negotiating over the whiteboard that kept a record of the ins and outs, the transfers, the durations of those still in or who'd recently been in labour, all timings nested inside the stretches of their own labour time. Two workers who could see immediately from the board that for once (just this once, occurring like once in a blue moon, once in a busy, overstretched shift) it might actually be possible to give this new pairing, this young woman and her baby, a little while longer together. It was their bit of capacity within the implacable timings of a system, agreed in soft voices, speaking their shared language. Of course, it would be more efficient to wash her right away and move them more or less immediately but. A bit more time – why not?

Ai terminat cafeaua? one low voice asked. Eşti gata să pleci din nou?

Da, the other replied. Standing, pulling at her trousers, taking her turn at the sink, pressing a quantity of bright gel out from the dispenser and vigorously washing her hands.

Why not? Let's. We're in a position to; it might make all the difference. Before moving, wheeling them on.

MOVING ON

The actual duration of E. M. Forster's lecture on the story must have been about an hour (allowing for digressions, elaborations, the expansions that can occur when a prepared speech is delivered live). He was reaching the end now, approaching his summing-up point, which was this: although they may treat it quite differently, neither the storyteller nor the novelist *can do without time* in the official, standardized, clock-time sense.

That might be possible in life, he speculated.

Throwing out the possibility, floating it in the room, the auditorium, just like that.

It might be possible *in life* to do without official time, to deny sequence, all the agreed alignments of the calendar and the ticking over of the big common clock, the framing scheme in relation to which all other durations are measured and plotted – though it is unlikely.

For a person, acting accordingly, the risk would be to become – the word Forster used was "unintelligible."

It was a word intended to bring his sentence to a sliding close, to mark a pause before moving his discourse together with his audience on, leading into his final point, and beyond that to the end of the lecture, or the break.

But there is a woman in the audience.

Before she'd had a chance to think too much about it, she had felt powerfully compelled to come in: to push through the double doors at the back of the lecture hall.

(There were no female undergraduates admitted to Trinity College, Cambridge in 1927; there wouldn't be until 1978.)

But she has been listening – say she has been listening all the while.

She has come in, detouring from her walk – feeling conscious that she has no hood on her coat (she has her hat; she's put it back on), she's forgotten the umbrella, and it is clearly about to rain. Her eyes are tired, reddened, but it was good – it felt important – to cry. She has come in, and before he moves on briskly to his own conclusion she would like the learned man to stop.

E. M. Forster looks up.

From his position behind the lectern, he is too far away to hear exactly what she is saying – the hall itself is too full of other bodies, seated, now distracted by the interruption, and murmuring. But from the way she is opening her coat, from her pointing gesture, he surmises that she's saying something like:

Think of a baby.

There is a baby wrapped to her chest, sleeping in a bundle under her big coat.

Something like:

Consider not a general *idea* of a baby but an actual baby with a weight, and presence, whose needs pitch and fall but don't stop.

Think about how, if there is such a thing as denial – a categorical refusal to recognize and submit to socially organized, collective, "official" time – then here it is.

Here is that denial in a sling, and requiring someone's care.

Rose does not know time. This was what Helen had come in to say.

It's possible that she'd said something like it before, to herself, making a new entry on the chart on the fridge. Regardless, here she was saying it again, in this setting, with a different vocabulary: reckon for a moment with the fact that Rose was born like the rest of us radically oblivious to the common rhythm-consensus that *dinner comes*

after breakfast, Tuesday after Monday, decay after death. Rose is not living her life in accordance with our sequences and grand divisions: daytime as distinct from and following on from night-time.

That was all. That was her point.

Was it?

Forster was looking at her expectantly.

No, he was right, there was more:

For here was a problem – the lived truth of the matter was that Helen, she *was*. She really was – or she was trying to (live in time-sequence).

She was actively trying to find a way back into the structures she had never even really considered, let alone felt attached to. This strange accompaniment of nostalgia for the regularity of the alarm clock, for the oppressive nine-ish to six-ish of her office job sitting opposite Nisha, making her schedule for her, planning, and taking notes in her meetings – the job she'd gone into, straight after her studies, as a way of biding her time while she worked out who and what she wanted to be, a job that now released her with this leave, with this privilege of a period of *months* to spend caring for her own baby – thinking of it, she could easily cry again. For she liked the mornings: she did. All open chance and possibility. The first hot drink of the day which used to be coffee before not exactly progressing but sinking comfortably into tea. She liked bedtime. She loved the calm and the quiet packed into that compound word: its promise of a familiar place, a pillow of softly releasing restful time. A promise of separation, withdrawal, and privacy from the world for a guaranteed duration. She was more indifferent to the length and played-out character

of the afternoons. In her head and across all the entrenched habits of her body Helen was still living, or trying to live, in accordance with collective time, social and official, clock-time.

Hence, the starts to their days, her efforts to start their days, whether they had slept or not. Because she'd read somewhere that this was a good idea, regardless of the night they'd had, Helen would try beginning the day anyway: imposing the morning, trying with each new day to insist on the morning, on wake-up time, on getting-up time, on getting them both up in synch with the timings of everyone else, and the sequence of things, what should happen next, breakfast first, dinner coming much later.

But so far, six weeks in, it hadn't worked.

The instruction, the cultural training of Rose and her quirked tempo, to the big social ways, the larger distinctions of the diurnal, it wasn't working and it hadn't worked. As a result, there had been suffering, and deep, deep disturbance.

Do you know what this is like?

It was a genuine question, not a provocation.

Helen put it to the room, this rarefied space, to students of literature, the novel, and grand ideas, with the expression on her face: Do you know what it is like to live without a pattern, to live a-patterned, subject to the non-rhythm of someone else?

There was fear now: a fear in her face – cold patches of underwater fear. A tugging current of fear that her handle on life –

She was thinking of one particular night. Rose, who'd then been about three weeks old: she'd spent the late afternoon, the whole evening – crying. The crying was of such strength and perseverance it didn't seem to have its source in Rose anymore. There was just cry: crying breaking into them both, shaking them, breaking open the

room, breaking open the afternoon, making great cracks in the continuum. It was sound like the builder's drill. It sounded like persecution. Helen carried Rose around the flat, for hours, around and about the flat, humming to her, singing to her, shifting her into new or alternative holding positions, stopping regularly, to try again, to see if she could feed her. Then, without warning: a full stop.

Something was hit. A limit.

Helen: she couldn't do it any longer (any of it) (anymore).

She went into the bedroom with the intention of putting Rose down in her little basket. She put her down, very fast and abruptly.

A movement on the edge of dumping her down, touching at the hem of throwing her down.

She put the baby down like this: boom.

Then went back into the living room and punched the sofa.

The crying, if anything, increased in volume. Rose was now a room away but the crying was still with her, all around and inside her, right up in her face. Helen was literally beside herself and she had no idea what to do.

She wanted to call Rebba.

But Rebba was at work in the bar and she'd miss the call/not hear her phone.

She wanted to call her mum.

And her mum would have come. Helen knew this. She would have got up and got in her car. Helen's deep knowledge that this was true (it was something she could count on) was what made her own life, her own risks, her own loves, plausible, possible.

But her mum was sleeping, and three hours' drive away.

She thought of the police? But that was a nonsense thought.

The neighbours?

As a wild last resort she considered going outside to ring the bell of the flat upstairs and begging her landlady: please.

Could just you hold the baby for a minute. Maybe for five to ten minutes. Fifteen minutes max (max max max).

She punched and repunched the sofa.

Then she stood up.

She put her trainers on. No socks.

She put her coat over the long t-shirt she wore as nightie. Then took it off, went into the bedroom where Rose was still crying in her basket, pulled on a jumper and leggings, then put her coat back on over the top. She searched and found her keys in her pocket.

She went to the toilet.

Rose was still crying.

She went and stood by the front door.

She leaned her forehead against the small pane of bubbled glass. At certain times of the day, for instance on sunny mornings, it could throw a soft golden light onto the hall floor, marking out a square where the letters, pamphlets, and thin packages fell in.

She rested her forehead against the glass: hot on cool.

Now she bounced it: at first gently and then with more daring and power, bouncing it against the glass in the way Rose bumped her own hard head against Helen's breast bone, or her breast when it was solid, not soft, because she hadn't fed for a while.

She considered tilting her head all the way back then bringing it suddenly forward, with force. Wondered what it would be like to inter-

rupt the sound of a baby crying with the crack of her own forehead smacking against this section of bubbled glass.

She wanted very badly to provoke something.

A catastrophe bigger than a baby crying.

Far bigger than the small circumstance of a newborn baby who, for a while, an afternoon and an evening, wouldn't stop crying. Which wasn't a catastrophe – it was a banality. Wasn't it? A banality. One of the most common, everyday happenings, going on in the surrounding houses and concerning people, all the time. She wanted to do something major enough to provoke these strangers, the neighbours, all the independent adults acting independently in the world, to recognize the scale of epic drama within this banality: rush in, witness her helplessness and help.

Outside, the night was cold.

The strange thing was: it wasn't even late. The pubs had just closed; people were wending their way home.

Alright love?

She walked past them: a group of blokes sensing her distress – you alright love?

She walked with great speed and determination: at a trot, at a clip.

She walked at this fast animal pace all the way up the hill to the entrance of the park, and because it was closed she walked around it. Around and around its perimeter fence. Its tall railings, pointy and sharp at the tops. Circling the big circle of the park from the outside; its circle on a tilt.

There was a full moon in the sky: perfectly white and bright.

Rose had stopped crying almost the moment Helen had managed to get her into her sling, from the moment she bent her knees and

bounced. She'd been asleep by the end of the street. But still Helen had needed to walk – all the way to the locked park. Then around and around its perimeter fence. Clouds passing over the moon, then making it reappear. She walked and walked until the sky started to pale and she finally felt safe enough to go home.

Come, said Forster, mildly, beginning to formulate a reply, a response that would both take into account and contain the force of what she was saying.

But the woman – Helen – she was worked up now, her mouth was trembling; she hadn't finished:

Rose SMASHES time! She fucking *smashes* it.

She wanted to shout this. But she couldn't shout – Rose asleep on her chest, lying directly over her lungs. But that, she realized, without realizing it until she'd said it, was what she'd actually come in to say.

The young men in the lecture hall were aware of her now, her presence, her interruption. Some curious, some bewildered, some irritated: they'd prefer it if she went away. They muttered to each other: Do we really need to hear this?

Their take on her giving her a new read on her own position, her intervention, on everything she'd just said, Helen calmed. She was suddenly aware of the comedy in it. She smiled, and continued: there's this idea that "the novel produces a specific kind of temporal knowledge, that the novel" – the subject of your lecture course – "allows us to 'know' time in a way that no other mode of thinking can."

She asked, rhetorically: really? "*no other* mode of thinking?"

She said: the point is, I know time. I know time differently now. I

know it because I am unlearning it. It's not a knowledge particular to me. I know it because the baby is teaching me that the rhythms of the clock and the calendar, and even the most elemental diurnal patterns – they *don't go without saying*: they are acquired, if not violently imposed. It is a lived and not an abstract form of knowledge that comes from living alongside a beginner – the way the days can all of a sudden feel like they're undivided, divided by nothing, only water . . .

Come, said Forster. I see the baby.
Helen paused, swallowed.

Come, said Forster. I take your point.

But there's one more thing – and this really was the last and final thing. She wanted to say it, though now she was saying it mostly to herself: I can see what Rose is proposing.

I can. I can see how she brings in *the chance* of inventing a whole new time scheme, a radically new way of living in and acting on time. I recognize her invitation: to question and query before simply reproducing and continuing on with these habits of living, these rhythms to living, this commonsense imposition of how to live in the world: this is when we all get up, go to school, go to work, go to sleep, this (by some forgotten logic or habit or sense of necessity) is what follows on from that. I can hear her asking: Why? Why should this count as a day? Why should this be how we measure, pace, and time ourselves?

But the problem, Helen went on – my problem, is this: her offering, Rose's provocation, I can't take it up. She raised her voice slightly, making an effort to speak to the whole public. Seriously: What great reservoir of resources, courage, and imagination might a person need to take her proposal up? To go along with, support, and extend her

powerful denial of the most basic and structuring principles of a human life – of a human social life?

She paused, considering. Maybe others can – maybe Rebba. Maybe she could.

But for Helen: the very well-being of her mind and her body were at stake – and she couldn't. Not without – she was preparing to leave now; she was already pushing her shoulder into the double-doors. Not without *risk*. Not without what could feel like colossal, life-or-death risk to her own – she reached back for the word Forster used, because it was the right one – *intelligibility*.

She was mostly out of the door now, her hat glowing fluorescent against the panels of dark wood. She paused to rebutton her coat.

I can't. She shook her head.

But, she re-stated her point: the original time-signature offered by a baby, her wild a-rhythmia synched only to the rise and fall of tensions, the gathering and dissipating of intensities – it could be an alternative. I can see how it might represent, for others, if not for myself – a new structure, a new intelligence, an emancipation, a sort of freedom.

She was through the doors; she left.

The energy in the room ruffled, smoothed itself down.

E.M. Forster took a breath and refocused his attention on his true audience.

He started again: Well!

He moved his papers. Then picked up from where he'd left off: "I am only trying to explain that as I lecture now I hear that clock ticking or I do not hear it ticking, I retain or lose the time sense; whereas in a novel there is always a clock."

For the sake of "intelligibility"; "there is always a clock."

Henry Fielding famously consulted an almanac in the composition of *Tom Jones*: "to check phases of the moon and journey times, respecting objective time."

The author *may dislike* their clock, Forster said. "Emily Brontë in *Wuthering Heights* tried to hide hers. Sterne, in *Tristram Shandy*, turned his upside down. Marcel Proust, still more ingenious, kept altering the hands, so that his hero was at the same period entertaining a mistress to supper and playing ball with his nurse in the park. All these devices are legitimate, but none of them contravene our thesis: it is never possible for a novelist *to deny* time . . ."

At this, Forster paused.

He coughed and again shuffled his notes. Then went on:

Well . . . "there is *one* novelist who has tried to abolish time, and her failure is instructive: Gertrude Stein. Going much further than Emily Brontë, Sterne or Proust, Gertrude Stein has smashed up and pulverized her clock and scattered its fragments over the world [. . .] She has hoped to *emancipate* fiction from *the tyranny of time* and express in it the life *by intensity only*. She fails, because as soon as fiction is completely delivered from time it cannot express anything at all, and in her later writing we can see the slope down which she is slipping. She wants to abolish this whole aspect of the story, this sequence in chronology, and *my heart goes out to her*. She cannot do it without abolishing the sequence between the sentences. But this is not effective unless the order of the words in the sentences is also abolished, which in turn entails the abolition of the order of the letters or sounds in the words. And now she is over the precipice."

"Not through naughtiness!" exclaimed Forster. "But –"

STOP

Stop Forster talking now. See Gertrude Stein – her large head, bending over her work. Her sentences in their continuous, persistently active, unsubordinated present. Drafting a chapter from *A Novel of Thank You* titled "COMPOSITION" which describes the process she was engaged in:

"Preparing a novel."

"Preparing a novel and preparing away."

"Preparing a novel prepared to stay."

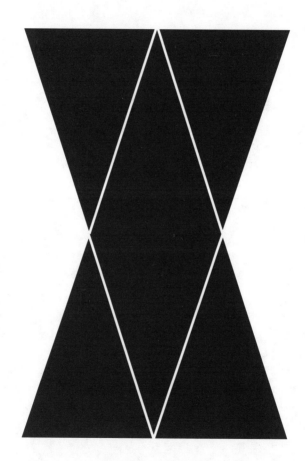

PREPARATIONS

THE NIGHT BEFORE; THE DAY AHEAD

In those years living with Rebba, every now and then, Helen would leave. She would take herself off to visit her grandmother, getting on the train on a Friday after work, returning on a Sunday afternoon. After the train, her journey would continue on a slow countryside bus, the kind that marked every single stop, riding all around the houses, winding down long narrow lanes, tree branches scraping the top-deck windows, pushing through if the windows were gapped open, as if the branches wanted to get on the bus and come too, to the stop in her grandmother's village. She'd stay for two nights in the one-bed bungalow because her grandfather had died and for the first time in her long life (eighty-three years) her Nan, or Nana (the names Helen called her), was living alone. It was new for Helen to do this as an adult: visit an aged relative of her own volition. Feeling like she probably should; also, like she wanted to. Simply, was how their weekends passed. The days were always very precisely timed: in the morning, the papers would fall with a whump on the doormat and Helen would retrieve them, pulling out the magazines and spending an hour concentrating on the celebrities. At eleven, her Nana would make them both a strong instant coffee, served in a saucer and a cup, a chocolate biscuit resting and melting on the side. They'd read a bit more. Some of their own books; the ones Nana borrowed from the library which Helen liked too: the thick romances. After lunch they'd go for a walk, circumnavigating the village to the stretch where the pavement turned into lane and ran for a while alongside the fields before looping round and turning back into pavement and re-joining her Nana's road. They took a bit of apple, sometimes, or a carrot, because Nan liked to say hello to the horse. From 5 P.M. onwards, they'd watch TV. Nana seated formally in her high-backed chair, printed with swirls

and giant feathers; Helen sitting, then slouching, then stretching all out, her arms folded behind her head, her feet up on the plush sofa, as soft and as large as a ship. Nan always took charge of the controls, setting the volume very high, but regularly turning it down during the ad breaks, so they could comment on what they'd watched: the programmes she'd been watching for decades now, one following immediately after the other, the casts changing but some of the key players remaining the same, only growing older. Nana would catch Helen up on the long arcs; they'd talk about the little stand-alone stories that started and ended, their episode-by-episode resolutions. Before bed, when they were both in their dressing gowns, Helen borrowing one – a fleecy funnel-necked gown, which on her Nana came down almost to the floor, though she too was a tall woman – they'd move, two tall figures, back and forth from the kitchen to the tiny dining room, padding in bare feet, brushing past each other in the doorframe, fleece creating static, laying the table for breakfast. It was something her Nana did whether Helen was visiting or not: set out her cereal bowl and her cup, her saucer, spoon, her sugar bowl, her cornflakes, her toast rack, her butter dish, her jam. Ending each day (rounding it off) by preparing for the first thing to happen on the next. Creating the conditions for coming through in the morning gloom, or, depending on the season, to a chorus of birdsong and in the light, thinking – or Helen, at least, would always think this, no matter how many times she took part in the preparations, no matter how often she herself went through motions of setting the table just before bed – Oh! Who did this? It was like the elves, the breakfast fairies had been. This was how Helen described it – it was a bit like that. There was a sort of a miracle to it. They'd prepared the ground, but then forgotten, and so had enabled their own surprise. And Rebba, knocking about in the flat while Helen was away – if she were pressed to describe what

it was (about Helen) she missed: she might have gestured towards something like this. She might have pointed to the things which were not exactly things that Helen did for her: small miracle-types of things, continuing this life-habit (or was it a life-skill, a life-tactic or life-technique) that Helen had inherited from her Nan. Not the end-of-the-day laying out of the breakfast materials but a more general investment in domestic rituals which might have felt oppressive, or sad, or limited, if it weren't for the fact that there was never any pressure to take part – more a sense of: this is how I do things. This is how I am doing things in any case, and you can join in (participate, benefit) if you want, but only if you want. It was what Helen's Nana always did: set out her teapot in the evening to save time in the mornings, although she had all her time to herself. To trick herself into forgetting that she lived alone, or as a way of finding her own, new pleasures in it. It was the sort of thing Helen did too. Announcing, all of a sudden (announcing and inviting): hey, let's drink *this*, out of *these* cups, around this regular time because why not? It's a good thing and a good time and makes an ordinary drink into an event we can both look forward to. It was something Helen was good at: not only at structure but ceremony: buying flowers at the market because it's a Saturday (and this week, I think we can afford flowers?), because doing so was a way of drawing out the distinctive moods, the different colours of the days. (Make Saturdays daffodil-coloured, tulip-coloured, rose-coloured, with all the possible through-the-year, market colours that implies.) For some reason, Rebba had been unused to it; she'd not been brought up to expect anything like it. For a long time, she'd been in a daily way astonished by it: how a basic action like making something to drink, a sandwich to eat, or getting up in the morning could be elevated. How someone could elevate it for you, with care and this order of simple surprise. She'd come

home from a late shift in winter and there'd be a hot water bottle in her bed. Not always, but often enough to experience it as a reliability, as a grounding – a grounding she was slow to realize she needed. As if she, Rebba, were not a person but a sheet that could easily billow and buffet – come loose. Get trodden in the dirt or just fly off. Fly off out of the morning. Fly off from her work, the bar, her existence in this small city, this weird country. Fly off the planet. It was how she felt sometimes (formless). It was how she might have felt more often, if it weren't for Helen very lightly, here and there, pegging her days, and not just her days but her very being, to a tentative kind of line, making a framework for her looseness to fall around, to find a shape in relation to – and making it from all these small but mostly pleasurable, prosaically ceremonious things.

In her novel, the stories came in their own sequence.

Pushing forwards, sometimes turning back, it – the novel containing them, the title of which was *Tom Jones* – continued.

The foundling baby goes on with growing up, becoming child, becoming youth in the accelerated way infants tend to in novels.

This was another of Forster's observations, something he said in a lecture on the kinds of made-up people (and in what phases of their lives) a novel is most likely to pay attention to. Which is to say: adults. He noted: "When a baby appears in a novel it usually has the air of being posted. It is delivered 'off'; one of the elder characters goes and picks it up and shows it to the reader, after which it is usually laid in cold storage until it can talk or otherwise assist in the action." What is implied by this criterion of "talking" or "otherwise" assisting in the events of the novel, who and what it excludes from the spheres of meaningful and consequential (which is to say, political) action: the value that the novel (at least in its English-language presentation) typically places on the fantasy of the self-determining individual. Its foregrounding (or, it's been argued, its invention) of the particular kind of subject whose interest and worth is directly linked to their capacity to speak, act, and decide for themselves – in other words, independently.

This, for Ian Watt, was the whole story – a set of ideas inextricable from the emergence and "the rise" of the novel in its most popular, recognisable (dominant) form.

The novel: defined in Watt's terms by its "serious concern with the daily lives of ordinary people." Ordinary, credible people, and their daily lives. For Fielding and his contemporaries, this, Watt argues, was a *new* concern. It provided the subject-matter of a whole new

province of writing. But it is a provision dependent "on two important general conditions":

First, a "society must value every individual highly enough to consider him the proper subject of its serious literature."

Second, "there must be enough variety of belief and action among ordinary people for a detailed account of them to be of interest to other ordinary people, the readers of novels." Both depend on "a society characterized by that vast complex of interdependent factors denoted by the term 'individualism.'"

Individualism.

"Even the word," Watt notes, is relatively recent, "dating only from the middle of the nineteenth century." Individualism: meaning not egocentrism, nor originality of opinion or way of life – traits long identifiable in certain individuals, in all ages, across all societies. But something else: "It posits a whole society mainly governed by the idea of *every individual's intrinsic independence* . . . from other individuals" as well as from "past modes of thought and action denoted by the word 'tradition.'" For such a society to exist, a special type of "economic and political organisation" is required, along with its own matching ideology: specifically, one which "allows its members a very wide range of choices in their actions, and on an ideology primarily based, not on the tradition of the past, but on *the autonomy of the individual* . . ." Which is to say, capitalism, and its attendant promise: that whatever mesh of conditions a person may have been born into, to whatever extent they were formed, acted upon, their lives supported and limited by other people, by circumstance, by tradition, they can separate themselves (distinguish themselves). They can act autonomously, on their own account. They can and, really, they

should – after all, they have (everyone does, according to this worldview) *a very wide range of choices* in their actions. In this story of the British, English-language novel, people are "interesting" to imagine and to closely describe if and when they are capable of standing upright, "on their own two feet"; if and when they are capable of speaking, thinking, and deciding for themselves (rather than being spoken for, sharing thoughts, being decided for, or speaking or acting on someone else's behalf); capable of leaving (the home, for example), rather than staying, and in this way of progressing, changing (*breaking with* past modes of action and thought rather than perpetuating them) – in other words, in Judith Butler's words, the point at which they release themselves from the human conditions of "beholdenness" and "dependence."

By Book IV of *Tom Jones*, baby Tom, along with his half-brother Blifil, the son of Mr Allworthy's sister Bridget, and Sophia, the daughter of Mr Western (who owns the neighbouring estate), have all reached the age of eighteen. Now (on the basis of this equation of agency with adulthood, or at least with the more autonomous stage of late childhood) they can do things, make the interesting things happen.

But, before the narration proceeds any further, pushing into a scene of the first-charged-because-adult encounter between Tom and Sophia, it stalls. It folds and turns back:

Book IV, Chapter III: "Wherein the history goes back to commemorate a trifling incident that happened some years since; but which, trifling as it was, had some future consequences."

Trifling; unimportant. Trivial, but nevertheless somehow consequential.

THE INCIDENT OF THE BIRD

When Tom Jones was still a boy, he'd presented Sophia with the gift of a little bird.

A bird taken from the nest, that he'd nursed up, and taught (or encouraged?) to sing.

Of this bird, Sophia had grown extremely fond: she'd made it her chief business to feed and tend to it, and her chief pleasure to play with it. She named it "Tommy."

The bird became so tame that it would feed out of her hand, perch upon her finger, and lie contented in her bosom, where it seemed almost sensible of its own happiness (though she always kept a small string about its leg, nor would she ever trust it with the liberty of flying away).

Now, with this history established, the narration moves a step forward, starting again from where it had wanted to start – at the trivial incident, which had occurred two years before the present of the novel. On this day, the families, along with the boys' tutors, Thwackum and Square, are dining all together at Mr Western's.

The young people are keeping their own company out in the garden.

Master Blifil, observing the extreme fondness that Sophia is showing for her little bird, desires her to entrust it for a moment in his hands.

She hands it to him with caution: her caught, tamed, much-petted bird.

And indeed: no sooner is Blifil in possession of it than he slips the string from its leg and *tosses it* into the air.

Why? Because – jealousy. The narrator points us to the obvious conclusion: Sophia prefers Tom. Tom's general temper has been established (since babyhood) as easy-going, fun-loving, impulsive. Master Blifil's, on the other hand, is presented as glum, severe, sober. Sophia's clear preference for Tom over Blifil "would often appear so plainly that a lad of a more passionate turn might have shown some displeasure at it." But – he didn't. The narrator directs us towards the most obvious explanation for Blifil's action then says something else – in his outward manner, Blifil never did show signs of such feelings: jealousy, or dismay, or disgust. So why not take him on face value, the narrator suggests, and probe no further. Indeed, "it would be an ill office in us to pay a visit to the inmost recesses of his mind, as some scandalous people search into the most secret affairs of their friends, and often pry into their closets and cupboards, only to discover their poverty and meanness to the world."

The bird, of course, flies away.

It comes to perch on the bough of a nearby tree.

Sophia, upon seeing her bird gone, screams so loudly that Tom Jones runs to her assistance.

He is no sooner informed of what has happened than he curses Blifil for being a pitiful, malicious rascal. Then, stripping off his coat, immediately applies himself to climbing the tree to which the bird escaped. He has almost recovered his little namesake – when the branch on which it is perched, and that hung over a canal, breaks. And the poor lad plumbs "over head and ears into the water."

Hearing this commotion, the adults come forth.

Just as they reach the canal, Tom (for the water was luckily pretty shallow in that part) arrives safely on shore.

Thwackum falls violently on Tom, who stands dripping and shivering before him.

Allworthy asks for patience, and Blifil for an account of what happened.

Mr Blifil answers: "Indeed, uncle, I am very sorry for what I have done; I have been unhappily the occasion of it all. I had Miss Sophia's bird in my hand, and thinking the poor creature languished for liberty, I own I could not forbear giving it what it desired: for I always thought there was something very cruel in confining anything."

He pauses, then goes on: ". . . but if I had imagined Miss Sophia would have been so much concerned at it, I am sure I never would have done it; nay, if I had known what would have happened to the bird itself . . ."

(What happened to the bird itself was this: when Tom Jones, having climbed up the tree after it, fell into the water, "the bird took a second flight, and presently a nasty hawk carried it away . . .")

Poor Sophia. She's crying her heart out. Concentrating on Tom, she hadn't witnessed the final fate of her bird; she sheds a new shower of tears.

Her father, Mr Western, chides her for crying, but cannot help telling young Blifil, if he were a son of his, that his backside should be well flayed.

Sophia retreats to her chamber; the two boys get sent home.

The rest of the company returns "to their bottle, where a conversation ensued on the subject of the bird, so curious that we think it deserves a chapter by itself."

So the chapter ends: with a rounding off, "a minor conclusion" which serves also as an announcement of what is to come. Like preparing

for bed by readying the table for breakfast, it is both a closing gesture and a clear invitation to continue (to wake up, to get up, to carry on). It allows for pause, for rest, for a new or regathering of anticipation. It puts a stop (to this phase of narration) but, in critic Philip Stevick's words, "does not end the work."

THE NEXT CHAPTER

"Containing such very deep and grave matters that some readers, perhaps, may not relish it" will be a collective talking over – a general reflection and sharing of views on the incident of the bird. What to make of it? How to *appraise* it?

Throughout the long work, the impulse and narrative strategy of Fielding's novel will be this: to present an action from one perspective, then to look at it a bit differently; to show a given character doing something, then doing something else, possibly something contradictory and somewhat *out of character*, thus presenting them in a new light; to think about each one of its scenarios from at least one alternative angle.

It is a provision of view and counter-view.

Mr Square's take on the release of the bird: clearly, what was *most wrong* about the whole debacle was the trapping of the little bird in the first place (the cruelty of taking it from its nest, keeping it captive; a pet for a rich girl). To Mr Allworthy: "Sir, I cannot help congratulating you on your nephew [Mr Blifil], who, at an age when few lads have any ideas but of sensible objects, is arrived at a capacity of distinguishing right from wrong. To confine anything seems to me against the law of nature, by which everything hath a right to liberty . . ."

Mr Western (who, later in the novel, will lock his daughter Sophia in her bedroom, keeping her a human captive for disobeying his wishes): "*Pox* on your laws of nature." I don't know what you mean: right and wrong. "To take away my girl's bird was wrong, in my opinion, and my neighbour Allworthy may do as he pleases; but to encourage boys in such practices, is to breed them up to the gallows."

Mr Allworthy's calmer line: "He was sorry for what his nephew had done, but could not consent to punish him, as he had acted

rather from a generous than unworthy motive." Elaborating: "If the boy had *stolen* the bird, none would be more ready to vote for a severe chastisement than himself; but it was plain that was not his design." (Soon, Tom will get into deep trouble for stealing – poaching – ducks and other birds.) As to that malicious purpose which Sophia seemed to have suspected – that Master Blifil could have been jealous, or angry over her preference for Tom – it never once entered Mr Allworthy's head.

The action, said Mr Allworthy in sum, was inconsiderate, yes, but pardonable – though, he added, perhaps "pardonable only in a child."

Mr Western: Pox! What of Tom? The poor lad! Does he not deserve to be commended? "To venture breaking his neck to oblige my girl was a generous-spirited action; I have learning enough to see that. D--n me, here's to Tom's health, I shall love the boy for it the longest day I have to live . . ." At this point the debate gets interrupted. "But it would probably have been soon resumed had not Mr Allworthy presently called for his coach . . ."

The minor incident raises major questions, ongoing and timely ones, that no single discussion was ever going to straightforwardly resolve. Questions about animal rights, property, the priority or otherwise of human-to-human consideration, forms of freedom, the age of responsibility (what should be considered pardonable in whom and under what circumstances (at what age)). It does so, more generally, with a view to showing how "circumstances alter cases"; a practice of "casuistry" which is built into Fielding's novel, proposing scene after scene in which general rules or maxims are announced only to be immediately tested, the limits of their applicability exposed. This happens with the larger questions of ethics (how to live well alongside

other people; the importance of thinking basically well of them – the principles of open-mindedness, open-heartedness; how to minimize the harm a person might deliberately or inadvertently do to other living things, making space for their own impulses, pleasures and projects) as well as with the principles of "good" writing: as Robert L. Chibka observes, countering every grand proclamation (for example, the blanket ban on ghosts) there is a "case narrative" exploring how these theories might get practiced in a complex living situation. The result is a novel which continuously points up the need for flexibility, for adjustment, sometimes even for exemption to a given law (there *is* a ghost in *Tom Jones* – but just one, and caught sight of only very briefly). The chapter ends on another widening of perspective: a small step *up* into survey position from which to look back over the ground covered as well as forwards, onwards – anticipating the great stretch of what's still to come: "Such was the conclusion of this adventure of the bird, and of the dialogue occasioned by it, which we could not help recounting to our reader, though it happened some years before that stage, or period of time, at which our history is now arrived."

STOPS, BREAKS

The sky hanging low and grey. Helen crying on the bridge. Rose sleeping; the river, meanwhile, saying shush. The swans – now they were out of view.

New phases were starting.

They kept on starting, and going on – playing out their own co-existent but unsynched durations, before being stopped or enabled to draw towards their own necessary but temporary conclusions – endings which may close the phase but do not (must not) end the work. This is what length (continuance; life) is made from (falling in and falling out). It is what staying-with (a question; a theme; a live, vulnerable creature) over time actually involves: starting and stopping, beginning again, likely from somewhere else, on a new basis, because the whole thing has not yet ended and it is important that it should carry on. It is a description of the unsteady, disjunctive tempos of care: the point being, as philosopher and psychotherapist Lisa Baraister observes, that although "the need for care" may appear to "*go on and on*," care itself is "not *a continuous flow* that moves from" the caregiver "*out* towards children, the sick, and elderly people." It is, in practice, more like an on-off provision, a presence or set of gestures that are called forth when the demand for them is formulated (irregularly, unpredictably) and when the capacity to respond is restated (here I am / I'm here). It also raises a literary-historical question, a novel question (a different take on the planetary history of the novel), whose scope extends far beyond the remit of a day with Rose: when, why, in what circumstances (under what conditions) did it become interesting (artistically interesting, materially necessary or urgent), for writers of narrative prose fiction to start working at length? Length redefined: conceived in these terms not as a trivial,

more or less contingent because external feature of the novel (even if the threshold for what counts as long will always be arbitrary; E.M. Forster set it at 50,000 words), but a constitutive (material and experiential) dimension of the medium. As a way of thinking, especially about durational (which means interruptive) forms of being-in-relation, especially about its own form of being-in-relation (the order of extended, discontinuously continuous entertainment it seeks to provide). It is the work still to come that critic Alexander Beecroft sketches out in an essay titled the "Rises of the Novel, Ancient and Modern": a different history of the novel that would consider the achievement of length (in prose) as its own distinctive project, one that suggested itself anciently, then faded from view, before re-emerging, in different languages and contexts, according to actual paths of interest and influence uncontained by historical periods or national boundaries. It is a history not yet written, but whose purpose would be to remove the pressuring criterion of "realism" as the defining feature of the novel, a distinction between "ordinary," "credible" life and the wilder, stranger concerns of the romance that scholars such as Margaret Doody have long contended was not only exclusionary but, in novelistic practice, clearly unsustained; it would shift the scholarly emphasis from "a too-ready insistence on the Anglo-French realist novel as the paradigmatic form of narrative fiction" and locate "the most meaningful invention of the novel" not in its content – its sudden interest in particular, separate, and separable lives – but in the more open-source, repurpose-able domain of the formal-technical. For, unlike the great lengths of the epic poems (sixteen thousand lines; over a hundred thousand couplets), the earliest documented works of prose fiction (written in Ancient Egypt, in Ancient Greece, Tang China) were short – "only a few pages long."

HENRY FIELDING: THEORIST OF CHAPTER DIVISION

Henry Fielding was one of the first English novelists to theorize the formal achievement of length. He did so by drawing the reader's attention to the techniques of linking, sequencing, transitioning between and piecing together smaller narrative units. It made for a formal inquiry into the practice of continuity. But approached from the opposite (related) direction of interruption.

It is interesting – it is perhaps even "especially paradoxical" – to note, argues Philip Stevick in a book titled *The Chapter in Fiction*, that the novel, a form "which most consistently displays an awareness of time in its minutely ordinary passage should be so frequently interrupted." This is Stevick's starting observation: "Thirty-seven times in *The Wings of the Dove* white space interrupts its richly detailed continuity, in *Vanity Fair* sixty-seven times, and in *Don Quixote* one hundred and twenty-six." Two hundred eight short chapters make up the length of *Tom Jones*.

Stevick: "Although continuity must have meant something vastly different to the author of *Lazarillo de Tormes*, to Fielding, to Sterne, to Galsworthy, and to the Joyce of *Finnegans Wake*, yet for each, to make a continuous prose fiction was to make it out of partly discrete, partly enclosed units." Indeed, "nearly every work of any length proceeds from beginning to end by route of its subordinate beginnings and endings . . ." This, for Stevick, counts as true even for "typographically continuous works." For instance, one-sentence novels whose presentation on the page is never once interrupted by "white space." For there, too, continuity is generated by "subordinate" beginnings and endings, discrete arcs or phases modulating what is presented as unbroken prose, a rhythm of minor openings and movements and closings, landings which land somewhere with a view to taking off again.

Henry Fielding's thoughts on the chapter present less as a grand unified theory than a loose set of semi-serious, sometimes contradictory propositions, first formulated in the earlier novel *Joseph Andrews*, then developed (ventured again and put into practice) in *Tom Jones*. "Upon first consideration," he wrote, the reader might be forgiven for thinking that the chapter divisions, and the white spaces accumulating between them, are there only "to swell our Works to a much larger Bulk than they would otherwise be extended to." But be assured, this is not the case, not exactly or solely the case. They have other functions, too.

For instance, they are there to help. Chapter breaks are "of great Help" to both author and reader. In the first place because – a practical consideration – they discourage readers from dog-earing or otherwise damaging the pages of their books. They serve to mark progress:

Where are you at, with this object you're reading, this experience you're going through?

Well, from memory: Chapter One. Chapter Two. Book Four, Chapter Three.

(Orient me.)

But clearly that's not all: what the novel borrowed (what it learned about the techniques for achieving length) from epic poetry was the necessary provision of rest. Homer and Virgil also saw fit to divide and rhythm their work. The breaks make a breathing space. Fielding explicitly figures "those little Spaces between our Chapters" as "an Inn or Resting-Place, where he [the reader] may stop and take a Glass, or any other Refreshment, as it pleases him." In the context of his own work on the history of the chapter, critic Nicholas Dames writes: "What the chapter did for the novel was to aerate it: by encouraging us to pause, stop, and put the book down – chapter before bed, say

– the chapter-break helps to root novels in the routines of everyday life. The chapter openly permitted a reading oriented around pauses – for reflection or rumination, perhaps, but also for refreshment or diversion. Laurence Sterne's *Tristram Shandy* insisted that 'chapters relieve the mind,' encouraging our immersion by letting us know that we will soon be allowed to exit and return to other tasks or demands. Coming and going – an attention paid out rhythmically – would become part of how novelists imagined their books would be read."

(Coming and going. Falling in with the knowledge there will be an opportunity to fall out. A work without such spacings, Fielding's narrator suggests, would be like "the Opening of the Wilds or Seas which tires the Eye and fatigues the Spirit when entered upon.")

Rest links to the matter of attention. In his analysis, Stevick shows how Fielding's chapters often appear as "arbitrarily ended units." Smaller parts whose lengths were decided less by the internal necessity of an interaction or a scene than by the fact or the feeling that its narration has "simply gone on long enough." Fielding acting on a sense that they should end or at least break *now* – "before the reader has a chance to become fatigued" and dip out – before they have a chance to pause the narration themselves by putting the book down. The chapter conceived as its own attention span, an attention unit, limited by the lengths of reading time Fielding felt he could "legitimately ask of his readers." (In *Tom Jones*: these never last longer than two to three small-scale but densely printed pages; five 'pages of paper' maximum.)

But then, disputing this, there are chapters in Fielding's novels which, like the "Incident of the Bird," seem to work on the basis of their own internal beginnings, middles, and endings – the chapter

makes a micro-site for the small-scale simulation of the larger movement of the work, which begins, goes on, and likewise will eventually end. (Prepare me.) For Stevick, the chapters provide rehearsals for the novel's final ending, and therefore for all of life's endings. They begin this almost from the start, offering what Dames calls "a modest, provisional kind of closure" and they do it throughout: again and again and again – "a pause that promises more of the same later, like the fall of night."

(Move me.)

The chapter break can mark a movement. Or a change. Movement as a form of work that depends on change. They mark it and again help to prepare for it, making it easier both for the author to effect and for the reader to accept a skip, a jolt – for example, the leap in the form of a collapse of what Fielding calls "irrelevant periods of time" (Tom's babyhood, the long years of it; childhood, most of his youth), making it possible to end a given sequence in one time-place, and start the next one days or years later. Chromatic transitions, in Dames's phrase. But also other kinds of modulation: the sharp shifts and changes in tone within *Tom Jones*. For example, the abrupt switches from the fictional portions to the essay parts: "[t]hese adjustments and modulations *are made considerably easier* by the presence of chapters," Stevick suggests. The break signals and in its own minutely stalling way readies itself, its reader, for a change of mood, setting, material. A swap in company or style; an alternative mode of address.

OUT OF DOORS, THE PARK WAS OPEN
AND STILL THEIRS –

only now – *now*:

Here were the first tiny, soft-falling drops of rain.

A downy refreshment of light spring rain. It mixed the greens and the grey-blue-browns of river. It brought down a change: its own strange, dove-grey light. It landed, gently, on the bridge and inter-acted with the river. It picked out colours: every distinctive shade of green. In the distance, it beaded the waterproof hood of the woman with the tiny brown dog who'd called Helen sweetie, once. Hello sweetie, she'd said, as they passed one another, each on their own way through their respective days.

A misting, cucumber-scented rain. It altered the sensorium, mak-ing Helen feel briefly heady with the smells of refreshing earth, the now stronger river-notes (muddy, mineral).

Rain landing on the backs of Helen's hands.

It felt like nothing.

Like vapour – slightly weighted vapour.

She adjusted the tug of the sling over her shoulders and crossed the bridge to join the path into the woods. It was a little end-zone of the park: a wood-chipped path, covered by densely growing trees. A place whose shelter she'd embrace if it were not for the fact that it always felt a bit reckless to be walking here, in the loneliest part of the common space. On her own (with a baby).

She pushed on.

The woods formed the last part of her loop. It gave a satisfying round shape to her walk.

Even so, a socialized sense of precaution pushed back. Frustration. The exercise of her walking freedom would always come up against and feel its way around this limit.

For there were clumps of bluebells in the wood, though almost over now. She wanted to see their low-to-the-ground colour. When massed as blue: it was heart-lifting.

The interdiction resisted: it was too dark and too quiet.

It is stupid to walk in there (on your own) (with a baby).

But: beauty. She quarrelled with it. Clumps of bare bluebell beauty. Freedom.

She walked on (in). Her compromise, the same one arrived at each day, though for some reason each day it had to be newly reached: she'd walk on. She wouldn't linger.

Rounding the little path through the woods, she walked fast. Even lower to the ground, there were strawberry plants: wild ones, throwing out networks of horizontal connecting stems. Stems taking root, producing new plants; here and there, already: the tiny and hard, white starts of fruit. There were the large discs of elderflower, the nubs not yet in bloom. There were bright green nettles. There was one good den: an ever-complexifying arrangement of branches and sticks that the different kids would come here, unafraid (so why was she afraid, her fingers in her pocket, folding around her keys) to work on, taking over from each other, pursuing or actively destroying what must have been someone's original project, but forgetting whose it was – it no longer mattered. What mattered was the ongoing renewal of the den-building idea.

It was a quick-quick circuit.

A simple walk, under the trees, into the lonelier, shadier part of the park. Gloom and overhead vegetation. Still, an everyday sense – a

pulsing, physical sense – of putting herself and her child at unnecessary risk. How weird, she thought, that she should be so accustomed to this. Habituated to it. The same patch of park offering both (shelter and risk).

RAIN

Lines and slanting cords of steady, purposeful rain, now intending puddles, intending wetness, making her hat (which she'd pulled back over her hair) and shoulders wet.

It hit circles into the stiller parts of the on-flowing river. Concentric, expanding circles with, at their centres, a spray, a bounce. Having looped the short path through the woods and now crossing back over the bridge, Helen stopped, briefly, to look. Mini-fountains. Suggestions of flowers. But Helen's feet were growing cold in her trainers. She was hungry again and needed to pee.

On a different day, she might have tried prolonging Rose's sleep even further, doubling her park-loop, but now – coming down upon her, there was all this rain. It decided. Helen unbuttoned her coat and lifted it like a wing. She held it over Rose and started with great strides back up the long slope, trying to keep underneath the branches of overhanging trees. A man ran narrowly past them, powered by downward momentum, his bright trainers hitting the path hard and plashing out a rhythm of wet prints.

A PURVIEW OF RAIN

The path under the trees offered some protection, but the uncovered grass and playground met the full force of the weather. Here, there: everywhere was reaction, causing the projects of the moment to alter or redirect. The few visible figures quickened their pace, pushing ahead with buggies. Some with their hoods up, some holding onto their hoods. Shelters appeared. People found them, for the rain pointed them out. Under here, it said: the little roof-edge of the block of public toilets.

Rain gathering in the flower cups (tulips, mostly tulips); dampening the seats of the benches.

The sand in the sandpit absorbing it, and darkening (saturating) in response.

The slide rejecting it, throwing it off. Its metal slope sounding a metallic scatter: a sharp pitter-patter.

Drops hung down from the triangular cordings of the climbing frame.

Now it paused its falling for a moment.

As if it had exhausted itself. As if, already, it had let everything fall and had nothing left. In the space the pause made, Helen darted out from the path under the trees and cut up and across the sopping grass to the exit.

Someone was calling to their child, high-up in the register of a young female voice: Come here!

Now lower, adding emphasis. *Come* here!

Now deeper still, and resonant, vibrating through the silence, swapping the landing place of the emphasis:

Come. HERE.

A child under a cape of pink plastic raging something back.

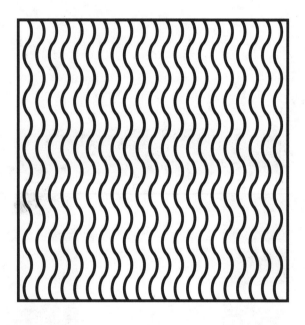

But the rain was not spent. It or the clouds were just breathing in, taking a breath. And now, with new resolve, it fell down again. It had been a powerful falling wetness and now it redoubled its weight and its wet.

The water droplets falling around Rose's face, falling through and thickening the air she was breathing – from under Helen's arm, they entered her dreams. For she was dreaming now, her eyelids flickering, her lips parting, her whole being setting itself apart from her environment as she entered the most private, deepest, and distant phase of her sleep. She dreamt of contrasts and bounces, small pinpricks of light. There was a word for this strange, maximal knowledge. Ahead of them, it rained on the private back gardens: the paving stones that refused to absorb it. It rained into the stone pot of pansies; it was accepted by and over-brimmed the small provision of potted earth. The land-lady stood at her window, looking out. She touched at her necklace and lifted her chin. It was raining everywhere, indiscriminately, on everyone who happened to be outdoors. Raining into the privet hedge. Part-sheltered underneath it, among the thick roots: the landlady's large, elderly tabby cat – raindrops glistening on the fur of its ears, its tail – longing to be indoors. It entered everyone's lives not in exactly the same ways but at more or less exactly the same time: all those in the vicinity of the weather-system, a big spread of shower. It fell against the living room window: throwing great dotted lines across it. Wetting it afresh only this time from the outside. Onto every responsive surface in her walking remit, the rain brought down a change. It concerned everyone, changing them in minor ways, in important ways. Rain, impartially, on and for everyone. Rain drumming on the roof of a yellow van, wetting cardboard, decorating it with dark splashes and spots. Even

indoors, it made a subtle difference to the room-temperatures, blowing in a cool which made the mobile wobble, then nudge, then turn. There was a word for this: implausible, limitless, maximal knowledge. Its source wasn't in Helen. It seemed to suggest the big eye of the now hidden moon, or the great spread and vantage-point of the sky. There was a word for it and when eventually it surfaced it would lead them somewhere else.

OMNISCIENCE

ON HER FIRST NIGHT AS A MANIFESTLY
SEPARATE BODY

Rose simply slept. Remarkably, she slept. On and on, quietly, in a special, newly arrived form of stillness. Her limbs weighted down and held close by the wrappings of a pale green shawl. A gift from Rebba: not knitted by her own hand but obscurely inherited: Was it a grandmother's hand, some aunt's hand? In any case, Rose needed to be wrapped and it wrapped her. As if she were already old. As if this were what Rose was planning to do for the rest of her life: just sleep, in stillness, and with depth. Sleep in a plastic lidless box, embedded in a trolley, the box raised to the height of the single hospital bed, a roll-around-able storage solution to keeping her within reach.

Helen, in contrast, put her head on her arm.

Her cheek in her palm. Turned to lie flat on her back.

She could not keep her eyes closed.

She was flat-out, on high alert.

She buzzed with it: with exhaustion, triumph, wonder, fear, hormones and adrenaline.

There was a tremble running through her body – she couldn't make it subside. It was the throb of preparedness: to whatever the question, whenever it came. She needed to be ready.

And so, rather than sleep, she kept watch.

Rose, who was no longer a moving shape or set of angles inside her, doming her from the inside out. But right here next to her, in adjacency, making alongsided-ness their new condition, contained in an open box.

The box and the bed they'd been allocated were divided from the rest of the ward by a peach-coloured curtain.

Helen kept watch: watching over Rose, wondering at how this novelty, who had so recently arrived, whom she'd only just met, could so soon absent herself.

She wanted to wake her up and ask her.

Let her sleep.

Her baby seemed to know far more than she did about what was supposed to happen – about how their first night together should unfold – and Helen submitted to her authority.

She let Rose decide.

Let her sleep.

Beyond their curtained zone, there was a sensing of the other bodies in the room. Every now and then, a new pair would be wheeled in, allocated their own portion of the ward with a bed, a plastic box-on-wheels for the baby, and settled. A ward for up to ten people, ten or more newborns. Helen tried imagining them. Exhausted, elated; relieved, grateful, ecstatic, knocked out, in pain and wrecked – these strangers and their babies, all with their own range of feelings and complicated thoughts, passing their first nights together.

The ward felt full. The collective lights had long ago been dimmed; the baby in the next berth woke up crying. Helen listened to a woman's voice murmuring something soft: gentle sounds that were comforting; they sounded rhythmed and true. Helen heard her gather up the crying baby into what must have been practiced arms. For in the next moment the baby was quiet. Helen considered them. She thought towards them through the peach-coloured curtain – cross-

ing the distance of their metre, metre and a half, apart. She wondered whether the woman could sense her, too: if she could tell that she, too, was awake.

She wondered whether it had been the tremble in her own legs, her nerves, twitching at the curtain between them and agitating the air, that had disturbed the woman's baby, making it cry, waking them both up.

Behind the curtain, everything was quiet.
Minutes, clusters of minutes went by.

Still, Helen kept watch.
Rose: her eyelids, long eye-lashes, her pursed mouth. Surrounded by shawl. Her nostrils, her nose.

There was a nurse seated at a desk in the far corner of the room, dimly lit by a low sort of reading lamp, as if the room were a study-space, a library, a learning-place.

It was impossible to understand how exactly they all came to be here: this loose group, sleeping, trying to get to sleep in such proximity to each other.

These people who, all being well, would be discharged from the ward tomorrow or the next day, without ever looking directly into each other's faces. And, therefore, would not know, if in the future they passed one another in the street, or sat side by side around the concrete edges of the sandpit in the park, that they had shared the long hours of their beginner's night together.

Rose slept on, unstirring.

Helen tried slowing her own breath; she focused on relaxing her toes.

From somewhere on the other side of the room, a different baby: suddenly it cried out. Its cry pierced the room. This was a different order of cry. Very sharp; a shriek. Bodies all around the ward muttered and shifted in response. Now it lengthened into something like a scream. It was the sound not of general discomfort, of bearable distress but – anguish. Helen heard someone moving her body around, trying to soothe the baby. The screaming broke, then went on; she could hear the mother stressing, standing up, tugging at the curtain.

The whole ward seemed to rouse. It turned its collective ear toward this one pair. It reached its attention out to them, distressed. While at the same time remaining allocated, staying sub-divided, each to their own allotted space, their curtained zones.

Inaudible words were exchanged; the woman was asking for help.

A nurse came, whispered suggestions, moved things – limbs, positions, coverings – around. Eventually, she took the baby in her own arms and started walking with it. Walking it with sturdy legs, in presumably practical shoes, out of the ward, up the corridor, pulling the sound farther away.

Up.

Then down the corridor.

Drawing it closer.

For a long time: the cry was weaker.

Then stronger.

Farther away.

Then closer. But ongoing, and so eventually ignorable.

It became part of the soundtrack to the room.

People fell back asleep to it. The ward resettled itself.

Still (restless) Helen lay awake.

Buzzing, fretting through the whole duration of Rose's long sleep about the prospect of her waking up. It was wasteful: a great waste of what would become the most precious resource of a chance to sleep. But also, wanting her to wake up. Willing her to wake up, so that she could hold her, talk to her, rediscover and confirm that she was actually present, here and real.

Helen lay there, her mind pumping, scrabbling, ranging.

Now it took direction. It groped sideways. She imagined parting the curtain separating her from the woman next to her. Just to see what a real mother looked like.

She thought about breaching that enclosure to gaze for a moment at the stranger's face, their hair, their hands, their sleeping position, their baby. Then doing the same around the ward: making a little gap in the curtains, peering through to contemplate each pair of persons in turn. All of them feeling strange, surely, in their hospital beds, their baby storage units, a different bag of things for each pair somewhere on the floor. Noting how each woman, with the same furniture elements – a bed, a box, a small bedside table with an open cupboard section and drawer in it, a lamp, a plastic-covered chair near the bed – deliberately or in the spread chaos of moving in, would have already made it somewhat their own: a water bottle within reach, a thermos, breast pads stored here, maybe makeup; everyone had phones, stained clothing at the bottom of the bed in a plastic bag, slippers or not. An everyday thought experiment.

But what would it be to do this? What orders of creeping intrusion would it involve, and what strange new knowledge might it produce?

If she were to see their hair, their hands, consider the colours and textures of their skins. If she were to make reasonable guesses at their ages, note the fabric-quality of their night-dresses, the labels in the tiny clothes they'd brought to the hospital with them in the basic hope – the basic necessary hope – of dressing their newborns, bringing them home.

These exterior markers would disclose something – not nothing. They would tell her which of them had been more likely to die in the childbirth they'd all just hours ago survived, which of the babies in the room were more likely to thrive. They'd predict whose children were most likely to do well in school, most likely to feel safe, to grow up in the assumption that the world was a reasonably safe place, at least for them, that it would make a space for them, pay attention to them, address them humanly with interest and respect. This roam around the room: nine pairings, more or less asleep, plus the night nurses, swapping out shifts, in a ward that could cope with ten – it would yield a quantity of social information.

It might also say, in a cursory gesture of expansion and inclusion, look: these different pairs are *also* at the start of their stories together, and how they do this, how they live together, from this night on, will matter to them. They, too, are invested in figuring their dynamic out. The ward making a one-off setting where the habitual social distances contract – all these different people, from different walks of life, in the same sleeping space together. They, too, will find this preoccupying, difficult, transformative, overwhelming, boring, interesting. It will be as consequential to them as it will be for Helen and for Rose.

But what if the imagining then went further? Parting not only the peach curtains but the hair, venturing into the moving intimacies of interior spaces: minds, hearts, stomachs, bowels.

The young girl on the opposite side of the room, a large baby boy sleeping alongside her, a pale blue helium balloon, secured by a long ribbon to the handle of her bedside drawer – she will wake up elated.

The woman sleeping fretfully in the corner space: older and richer, her heavily ringed fingers curling around the lip of the box holding her child – she will wake up to a weird inside fluttering, like a cold trapped bird, and recognize that she's afraid.

Helen not imagining but presuming, claiming to know all this.

Helen becoming-narrator. Becoming all-knowing narrator, the God of the maternity ward, her probing consciousness gaining access – unrestricted access – and with that the right to appraisal, to commentary weighted with judgement, and prediction, not only of herself (and the quiet sleeping mystery of Rose) but the inner life of every other – any other – passing stranger.

What to make of this exercise? What to say back to it?

One response: *No.*

They had their reserve and so did she.

So did Rose.

So did Helen – and so did they all, and so did she.

No to this unwarranted intrusion.

Henry Fielding part-refused it. Openly critical of Samuel Richardson, author of *Pamela*, of *Clarissa*, suspicious of the innovation he gets credited with, "of slip[ping] into the domestic privacy of the

characters" and, in this way, pushing "inside their minds as well as inside their houses." Feeling like "there was something ungentlemanly, un-magnanimous and snooping" in what Richardson was doing. He pointedly mocked these breathy "scrutinies of inner consciousness" in his own novel-in-response – the funny, angry, *Shamela*.

Again: *No.*

But this time phrasing the objection differently.

Pointing to Rose as an example.

Rose, who on her first night alive outside Helen's body was put into an unlidded box.

Helen, who had wanted to keep on holding her. But the nurse had advised her to put her down, put her nearby (so that she too could get some sleep).

Rose, who after this first night would be taken home to the new flat; who in the weeks and months to come will learn things.

She'll learn almost everything.

She will learn that the world is not all rising and falling heat, looming and retreating presence, warmth and shallows – not only emptying and filling, jiggery patterns of light. A world composed of complex pulses and beats, vectors of vitality, extension and continuity. But not only. Also of barriers and separation. Interesting as well as maddening, profoundly frustrating *barriers* made from plastic, metal, skin, and other less touchable and physically manifest materials but still very real in the sense that they keep people apart.

She will learn that she is separable: not-Helen.

Helen is not-her.

There are limits to the extension of her body, the extension of how far her thinking-feeling-imagining mind can push into and collaborate with the world, making it up, making whatever she needs

more or less instantly appear – calling forth and thereby *inventing* her own mother, in limbs and in parts: her breasts, her arms, as and when she needs them.

Within months, she will reach these limits, test them, rap at them, set her open mouth against them and be required by life, by everyone, Helen included, to start coming to terms with them. It will be a long, drawn-out education: painful and bewildering, but construed by the discourse as a development. A progress. A leap into the cruel but basic reality that novels – all art forms – should not shirk from acknowledging.

On the contrary, they should start out from here. This basic truth: we are not each other. None of us are. If we are born into believing we are, we shall soon grow out of it.

We do not know what it is like to be each other.

Therefore, the most genuinely life-like solution to made-up narration is "the limited first person." Single-consciousness narration. Rose was born out of Helen's body and within hours was set apart like a limited first person – like the one she was destined to grow up to be: self-contained with an individual name-tag (bearing her institutionally recognized name) securely fastened around the miniscule circumference of her newborn wrist.

In the ward, there was a low glow around the edges of the room. The nurse's lamp. Also, the luminous green of the emergency exits.

But is it like this – really? In literature, in life, are the options *all* (knowing everything) or its opposite: (knowing and sharing) *nothing*?

E. M. Forster: when it comes to other people, "We are stupider at some times than at others."

People are closer to each other at some times than at others.

Sometimes they know more – feel more – about, have more access to, each other.

A pair can be sensitive to each other, picking up on each other, reading each other well and getting a new read on themselves through the fact of being addressed by the other.

They put thoughts into each other's heads.

Here's an idea.

Helen sharing out her ideas.

But more importantly: discovering (regularly rediscovering) that the ideas that pertained most directly to her seemed always to come from somewhere (someone) else.

Sharing her ideas with Rose. Handing them to her so that she might make use of them, in her own manner. Offering out the commonplace, general ideas of sleepiness, of hunger, of warmth, of happiness, frustration or pain as descriptors – no doubt inadequate descriptors – for the range and nuance and total novelty of what she actually felt.

Then, the channel gets broken. For a time, no one involved knows anything. They can only guess at each other, from behind a closing, thickening curtain, offering up misdescriptions, misrecognitions.

Forster: "We are stupider at some times than at others, and this intermittence lends variety and colour to the experiences we receive." ("Nothing to make a fuss over here."). "[T]his right to intermittent knowledge – I find it one of the great advantages of the novel-form."

Perhaps it is a question (for some invested novel readers, it has long been a question) whether OMNISCIENCE is the right word for very different forms of "involved narration"; why some degree of "unusual

knowledge" about one or more fictional minds should necessarily be scaled up to a position of total knowledge/all-knowingness; why knowing some things, sometimes, about a character's inner life, or more than one, or about the landscape as it falls around the back of a person's house, or the weather approaching, should necessarily be conflated with a comprehensive knowing and also with an appraising, judging, therefore controlling form of knowledge of everyone, all the time, and everything; whether, in any fictional work narrated in the third person, this is ever actually (manifestly) the case.

The so-called "GOD-LIKE" third-person narrator of *Tom Jones* – a self-described pub landlord, running the whole shop, lording (in a generally genial and friendly way) over his public and ordinary domain – he knows a good deal about his characters. It is true.

He knows where they are, what they are doing when his attention is with them, what they have to say to each other.

He knows what they ate, how much they boozed, who they slept with and if they slept well. He knows the temperaments of their horses.

Helen fell asleep. Finally, in the ward, her exhausted body decided: all tremble, breast-song and bruise. It took over, seeming to switch her conscious vigilance off.

But weirdly, even underneath the blanket of sleep, she was still on alert. Some sensing capacity was still reaching out towards and sensing Rose. In the weeks to come, this would develop further. She would find herself waking just seconds before Rose had a chance to wake her: anticipating from her own unconsciousness that Rose was rousing.

Helen slept. And "[a]s to the present situation of her mind I shall adhere to the rule of Horace, by not attempting to describe it, from despair of success."

Henry Fielding's knowledge of his characters is mobile and inconstant.

At times, the narrator *will* describe the situation of his characters' minds, if only fleetingly. Fleetingly and cursorily (especially compared to Samuel Richardson's constant inside view). Sometimes, he'll know what they are thinking and feeling, privately.

But more often, he'll hold back.

Sometimes further knowledge is hinted at and deliberately withheld for comic effect, or in the service of the plot. At others, the narrator claims really not to know. Or – more often and more delicately – not to want to presume to know.

The novel's shifting attitude is in itself a position. It chooses intermittence by refusing to choose between renouncing all knowledge of the other's inner life (beyond what they might want to or feel capable of telling someone else about it, beyond what, despite themselves, their outer behaviour, their phrasings, their utterances, might disclose about it, in the name of our condition of separateness) and presuming to climb in and live in their brain, make a living inventory of their sensations.

It is a consciously uncommitted (free-ranging) position that recognizes when the curtains between thinking and feeling minds *do* part, letting something pass through. Interchange. Mutual understanding.

It is at other times protective of privacy – knowing when to draw back, to leave even an imagined person alone, and allow them their basic right to opacity.

It is frank, finally, about its own not knowing. Blank spaces in the narration pushing against the fantasy of total command, comprehensive imagining, and, from there, partial selection: this image of a novelist-narrator knowing *everything* about their book, the past and future lives of its characters, and selecting from there (from that *complete* understanding) what, partially, strategically, to disclose. On the contrary, what these patches say is this: that what the novel narrates (what it writes) is precisely *all* it knows.

This – gapped and roving – it is the fullness of what it knows.

A form of knowledge not assignable to a given subject (for example – "the narrator"), because it is contingent upon, which is to say it is produced by, the interplay of the whole composition.

Its intention may always be to intend more than its own limit-views. But that expansion will happen with the reader, the other mind in the different environment it was written for, with whom it is intended to interact.

Helen got woken up and ticked off. Ticked off: told off. Reprimanded by a friendly nurse who tugged her curtain open without warning, noted Rose asleep in her shawl, calculated with Helen how many hours she'd gone without feeding – five! – and told Helen off for not waking Rose up to feed her in the night. Then she said: if Helen was hungry and alright with walking she should go *now* to fetch herself some breakfast from the breakfast room off the corridor because clearly it was important for her to eat.

Helen felt returned to childhood.

She felt ashamed: she'd got it wrong, this first thing (how long to let Rose sleep).

She watched the nurse continue her round of the ward, opening up curtains, throwing light on the different pairs, giving everyone more or less the same instruction.

Helen considered. Yes, she was hungry. When had she last eaten, in fact? Yes, she thought she could probably walk. A padded and tender, hollow-legged walk. But the problem, now occurring to her, was: the nurse hadn't told her what she should do with Rose. In her instructions, she'd left this bit out.

Rose was still asleep. Was Helen supposed to wake her up right now, and try and get the knack of the painful rigmarole of feeding her, for what would be only the second time in their lives? Or feed herself first?

There was likely to be a protocol, a mandate, she felt sure.

But what was it and how was she supposed to know?

Would it be unsafe, and already neglectful, if she were to leave her

baby for a short while – sleeping on an open ward? For what would have been the point, then, of keeping vigil all the way through the night only to wake up first thing and leave her?

But there were the nurses keeping watch now, surely.

And it wasn't far: Helen could see, from her bed, looking down the corridor, how short the walk was to the room the nurse had indicated.

Not unsafe, then. Not especially neglectful. Possibly practical to go and feed herself first. But would it be – the word bounced toward her like a hard, round ball – *rude*?

The unlikely question of manners now felt like the most critical question. The chance of a new relation and ongoing social involvement question. Like the most potentially consequential decision of her entire life.

None of the other women on the ward were making any signs of getting up. There was no one more experienced to take a cue from.

She thought of Rebba, who would be there as soon as there were visiting times. As soon as she possibly, possibly could. To take Helen's hand. Find and press Rose's feet. To gasp and wonder at her. But she didn't yet know when that was.

She was hungry.

So hungry now that she threw her legs over the side of the bed.

She stood up, slowly. A dizziness. A self-steadying.

Then, edging sideways. Keeping one eye on Rose, one eye on where she was going, like she was a bird with eyes on either side of

her head. She edged past the next bed and out to the corridor. Across blue rubber hospital flooring, it was about eleven adult steps. She stood at the doorframe of the room the nurse had indicated, one eye on Rose.

She glanced into it. Rapidly, she scoped it. She saw that it was a narrow sort of kitchen, with a worktop laid out with tea-making things, bowls, single boxed servings of cereal, bread, butter, and a toaster.

She stood, at the door-frame, her eyes on Rose, on the hump of pale green shawl she made in her plastic box. Taking her in, believing in her, willing her to stay there, to stay asleep for just one moment longer.

Then – she dashed.

Post-partum *dashing* into the breakfast room. It was a raid. Toast? Out of the question. She grabbed a hard bread roll, a plastic knife, and a blister pack of jam. Grab-grab-grab and within seconds she was back *out*, panting, in the corridor.

Rose. Still and once again in sight. Relief – the soaping sweetness of relief.

Helen walked towards her barefoot. She felt newly conscious of her body, where it was numb, where it hurt, its weird lightness, a slackness in her womb, a space inside which yesterday had been packed-full to the absolute brim. She felt rather than saw Rose stirring.

Was this what it was going to be like? Helen asked herself the question, as she touched the plastic rim of Rose's surrounds. Trial after

trial. Local test with no immediately obvious answers. Trying to get the simple matter of fetching herself breakfast *right* in the eyes of anyone watching, including her own. Knowing that there were expected behaviours: to leave your baby, to carry your baby, to *wheel* your baby (of course, the boxes were on wheels). But not already knowing – not instantly and spontaneously knowing – what they were. Nevertheless, learning them, or trying to, trying first to make sense of them, then trying to make them apply to this case, their own case – all the general rules that were written long before either Helen or Rose came on the scene. And yet, within that impersonal regulating framework, having to act – having no choice but to act. In accordance with the usual lines or differently, idiosyncratically (creatively) – but then having to take responsibility for the ways her actions deviated from expectations, from the norm. The future would be like this: it would involve it. The effort of one person in her own uniquely implicated situation making small-scale and large-scale decisions – impactful decisions, and doing this repeatedly, with and without guidance, after very little or a great deal of inner debate.

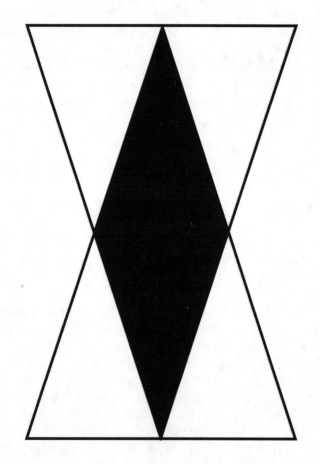

STANDING STONE

Should she run? Helen considered. She was at the top of the park. The path had flattened out at its highest point. They were near the gates, on the windy crest of the hill. She could. But the insides contained by her pelvis felt profoundly insecure. The soles of her trainers might cause her to slip on the pavement on the way back down. What if she fell on Rose? Also, she hated running.

But the *largesse* of the rain: heavy, heavy generosity. Her coat was a protective cape but her crooked arm was aching. What had been a change, a welcome new atmosphere – it was now starting to feel like an unnecessary, hard-falling, unwarranted stress.

Come on (she addressed it, calling it names). It was a drenching source of *stress.*

Rain drops bounced around her feet, fell down her neck and soaked her shoulders, her upper back. Her hat dripped sky-water into her eyes. It was no longer important that Rose continue sleeping because by Helen's reckoning she'd slept long enough, but what was relevant was they were getting wet and still some distance from home. She put her spare hand over Rose's ear, cupping her cheek, holding her to her chest. She turned out of the park, and was for a moment stalled – not by a person exactly, but a shape. A large boulder set down – no, arisen – by the gates, in the middle of the open area, the park's forecourt, which was slightly set back from the busy road. A standing stone formed from the dome of a grey umbrella, the curve of a bent back in a dark raincoat, both bending and holding themselves over the hood of a dark grey, almost black pram. It made a bulk and an outline. It was solemn and imposing. A solid lith that was also a tent. She rounded her own steps around it, keeping to the respectful distance that its sudden presence seemed to command, and as she did so she noticed its inner motion. It was rocking, infinitesimally.

The boulder-shape, it was nudging one way then the other, as the rain drove down upon it in thick lines, hitting and leaping away from the compound curves of the inclined back, the rounded shoulders, the umbrella, the hood and the wheels of the pram. The standing stone might have sought its placement somewhere else: somewhere more likely, inside the park, sheltered to one side, under the trees. Instead, it had arisen and grounded itself exactly here: erected like a great permanency in the middle of everyone's path. Helen walked around it and paid tribute to the mystery of its being-there, on its own, un-compromising logic. She felt she understood it: For why move, if it was calm in there? In this downpour. Why not *abide*, exactly on that spot, if for now it was calm and happy in there, drumming and pro-tected and temporally enclosed?

She passed the sign that marked the entrance to the park. Its lengthy list of interdictions – regulations for use which seemed to leave the most important ones unstated:

Don't intimidate anyone.

Come on, come in (you can – and you. All of you). But do not deliberately encroach on anyone's space of thought or play, making them feel unnecessarily cramped, or afraid.

Let other people be quietly or loudly and boldly themselves in the park. Whether alone, or holding themselves open (open despite themselves) to the possibility of meetings, unexpected conversations, new alliances, fleeting interactions.

Think of it as an infrastructure made from a great range of out-door materials. Surfaces and smaller settings on which the rhythms and inclinations of very different kinds of people have been invited to act (on which they have a renewable invitation to act).

Use the place as a sleeping route. A dreaming route. A thinking place or crying place (standing over the river, dropping sticks). (Or,

seated on a bench in remembrance of a stranger's life, imagining how they were loved, contemplating the view they were said to have enjoyed, and thinking how life is short.)

Observe how different bodies adjust to a park's enclosures, its play spaces, its seating suggestions, and its shelters. Take note of where the awareness lands; slides, lifts, lands . . . how it fixes on details.

Bluebells. But also swings.

Admire the ongoing reinvention of the den.

Consider how often and where, supported by what resources, in a city, a town: a body is given the opportunity to replenish its energy, to shift its moods.

Look, flower beds. Publicly maintained.

Open flowers in the flower beds. Rose bushes, holding aloft their fat buds of potential colour.

These familiar "natural" things – gardened and contained – they don't work on everyone. They won't work reliably on anyone.

They do make a setting.

An ordinary, accessible setting for everyone/anyone to come in and respond to.

A changing setting, responsive to and releasing its effects depending on the season, the time of day, and evidently the weather.

The sign dripped with rain. It hammered down. Rose stirred then jerked then seemed to resettle. Helen put her hands under the base of the sling.

And now, for the speculative sake of it, imagine: instead of no ball games, no littering, no fires, no fishing – a sign at the entrance to the park that read:

IT IS FORBIDDEN / TO ENTER THE PARK / CARRYING FLOWERS

THERE WAS SUCH A SIGN

In real life, according to Jean Paulhan, writer, editor, critic, and translator. He claimed to have seen it at the entrance of a public park in the southern French town of Tarbes in the 1940s. On it was printed:

> IL EST DÉFENDU
> D'ENTRER DANS LE JARDIN
> AVEC DES FLEURS À LA MAIN

Paulhan transcribed the wording in a book titled *The Flowers of Tarbes or, Terror in Literature*, published in 1941, translated by Michael Syrotinski, described as a complex statement on literary aesthetics, a part-defence of rhetoric. Paulhan's provocation: "the same sign can be found these days at the entrance of literature." Envisaging literature, the open field of literary production, as a kind of park. A tended, semi-regulated space, for public use, for recreation. For exactly that: for re-creational activities indebted to and drawing unreservedly and unapologetically on how things have been done in the past.

Except – this was Paulhan's contention: writers have stopped doing this; they have become afraid of doing this. In Paulhan's diagnosis, young writers have been terrorized (back?) into an ambition of unprecedented invention, feeling the pressures of "originality."

The "flowers" that Paulhan saw young writers forbidden from carrying (from bringing *with them* into the park) were the "flowers of rhetoric": common, in England, like roses, like daffodils, like bluebells; in the south of France: like cornflowers, like blood-red roadside poppies. Flowers: an image for the much-tested devices; the established conventions; the commonplaces; the figures and formulas of

which literary language is composed – the small tools and mechanisms that get it going and have been proven to set it to work.

With editors and writers so invested in *novelty*, in originality, new writers are feeling like they have been forbidden, or should be actively forbidding themselves, from drawing on these resources – for fear of cliché.

Resources in the form of phrases like "they grow up so fast."

Or, "life is short" (a platitude). "They grow up so fast!"

Like the sound of the rain ("pitter-patter").

Saying of eyes, for example, that they sparkled. Her eyes sparkled.

Such common "flowers" are now considered worn out, overused – they have become fixed, frozen, stripped of their mobility and capacity to move (thought, feeling, the imagination). They are a bit embarrassing. But the problem, as Paulhan saw it:

What if someone's eyes do sparkle? Or they did?

What if the rain does make a pitter-pattering sound, especially when it bounces off the metal slope of a slide?

A heart pinches.

It lifts. It sinks. It can open. It's what it feels like, sometimes.

Or, it's what familiarity with these phrasings (their patterns and their pictures) allows us collectively to feel: let's meet in the commonplace. Say it this way and there's a chance I'll know how you feel.

Sometimes life hits with a brutal, hammer-blow reminder that it's short.

I'm not saying, wrote Paulhan, that the valuing of the newly coined and the personally stamped (a given writer's "original" writing) is all

wrong. I have no idea, he writes, whether it is or not. It's just that there is something humiliating, a bit saddening and depleting about seeing words, sayings, formulations that have *charmed* for so long being abruptly withdrawn from use. This action of taking things away (don't write like that anymore, don't say things or think things like that anymore – they're dull on the account of overuse; predictable, trite), without being given back anything in return. Without suggesting an alternative, a way forward. As if the ambition were to make writing *stop*.

But these formulations, or some of them, at least: it's possible they still have a going value. After all, they are the phrasings inherited, translated, repurposed from literatures of the past; they are the figures, the shaping gestures and postures in language that are most commonly recognisable, and grasp-able, which is to say inhabitable, assumable, personally quotable, not only in books, but in life. Phrasings like "luv u."

Like: "I love you."

Among the most powerful and transformative of all communications, its old-hat three-beat intonation still working exactly like a charm, like an ancient spell, its everyday repetition doing nothing to diminish its capacity to release the lover from waiting. From a place of stasis. A stuck morning duration of stagnant waiting that was at the same time over-full with demands, activities, labour: lifting and driving, stopping and starting, pressing and belling – small and large package-delivery.

Noting it. Feeling it – because it was falling into his day too. Bouncing on the bonnet of his van: a mini-shower, even heavier, caused by the branches of the tree he was parked underneath accumulating, accumulating and bending under the weight, then all of a sudden springing back and shaking off a quantity of water. His thoughts now overtaken by memory:

It had been his idea to get out of the rain. Rain like this. Chucking itself down from a dark grey sky. They'd been walking slowly, elbowing and shouldering and finding reasons to touch each other, and were somewhere in the neighbourhood of home. It was the first time she'd ever come round to his house. They set their damp rucksacks down on the living room carpet and sat next to each other on the sofa – he'd not dared ask her up to his room, the one he shared with his brother, even if his brother was likely to be out. She'd leaned against him, let her breath fall across him, as together they watched – tried to concentrate on watching – something on her phone. His mum had put her head round the door, startling them apart: he'd had no idea she was in. Oh hello – sounding embarrassed and embarrassing them both. He remembered how he'd wanted her to leave – immediately, his mum. Get out and leave them completely alone; never dare set a foot in her own living room again. But also, unexpectedly, how he'd wanted her to stay: stay and bear witness because he was so proud of who was actually here: the person he loved, sitting so closely next to him in his actual house it was frightening (Mum, he'd said, silently calling her back from inside his head: it's petrifying – wanting to call her back but also wanting more violently to send her away: because it was also private, so private, this being-together on the sofa, and thrilling). He'd kept his trainers on, even though he was supposed

to take them off at the front door, out of a self-consciousness for his socks, and as they turned back towards each other, then down at what they were supposed to be watching, he remembered she'd put a finger, just one finger then her full hand on his knee. Her amazing fingernails. Each one its own miniature painting. A micro-burst of colours: dots, swirls and glitter. He wanted to forget the phone, bend his head over her nails and study them. These tiny paintings she'd made herself. Designing stencils, cutting them out with a sharp knife in her bedroom, watching tutorials, she said, all by herself. They were so detailed and strange and beautiful and she was so detailed and strange and beautiful it was like his whole body had no sides anymore, no edges, it was opening towards her and yet the only words he had for the power and scale – the immensity – of this feeling were the small ones everyone else used. The words everyone is likely to say at some point in a life-time – meaning them, not meaning them, throwing them away. Only now here he was, trainers muddying the carpet, holding them ready in his own mouth, a mouth drawing closer to hers, exchanging breath, readying himself to quote them – to address them – direct them this way, in her direction, for the very first time. To thicken and soften them, weight them and intone them with all the intonational materials of his own intention, in this sofa-setting, two zipped school bags wet and watching, his mouth or was it her mouth alive with colour, shape, glitter, and fear.

LUV U x

This was the sum total of what he'd written – everything he'd sent to her so far today.

Restarting their communication, as he did each morning, because he was up earlier for work, adding to a now long-standing, lengthening thread of stickers and content, their small exchanges nested between them.

A message, it was true, that did not ask – at least not explicitly – for a reply.

She might have received it like a single statement, a declaration self-completed, asking for nothing in turn.

But – normally she answered. Faster than this.

To his mind, the statement was always a sort of question. An open half that would remain raw and restless until it was replied to, and closed.

Waiting, waiting.

A different memory stole in: a bedtime ritual he had started with his brother, two years older. What felt like long ago in childhood. They'd be put to bed at the same time and his Mum would kiss them both good night and say her habitual "night night, sleep tight" at the door.

She'd leave it there – rounding off her day of looking after them, probably hoping to – letting them go.

But for him, the day, or the sequence, wasn't quite finished. The ending she'd proposed wasn't enough: for some reason, he needed to repeat it.

So he'd say a quiet one beat "night" to his older brother.

It was a ritual, or the first part of one, intended as a prompt for his brother to come back with the same word, returning the "night" back to him. (Call and response.)

The order mattered: it was his role to say it first.

Night then night; me then you.

It was the magic formula that, to his ear, could finally close the day and give him entry to the relaxations of sleep.

But his brother being his brother had soon figured this out – that it mattered to him – and so he would mess with it.

He'd call out NIGHT loudly and pre-emptively.

And if he did this he'd have to reply, wouldn't he? He had no choice. But then he'd be responding when his role was caller and nothing would have been closed. It would make the world feel wrong and the only chance of making it right would be to start a fake conversation – to chat about something for long enough till he'd produced the opportunity of saying it again, saying the first quiet "night" in the right way: performing the ritual again, only this time, please, in the right way – my opening followed by your closure, my venturing followed by your big-brother, confirming, reassuring return. And if his brother was feeling magnanimous he'd get it and be alright with it and after messing around for a bit he'd let him do it this way – and why not? Why not just go along with it – and let him have what he needed? That's what he felt. Like it was not as if he was asking for a lot, and now as the space between his message and her non-response gaped wider, he felt like she should do this, too. The quality of his waiting changed: it became edgy, piqued. She should know this, surely, by now: know what he needed and offer him a reply. She'd not even read it. The space opened even wider. Could she not just wake up now – and reply?

SCARCITY, ABUNDANCE

Jean Paulhan: the problem is this. If it is forbidden to bring in what for centuries was considered a resource, readily available; if the new turns of phrase, when they are coined, are not put into public circulation but held back, preciously, because they have been signed-stamped by the "original" coiner; if not only phrasings but whole gestures and situations cannot not be redescribed, out of a concern for repetition, for banality, for re-treading over too-common and overly familiar ground, then the writer will be afraid (terrified).

And there will be less.

We will all have less.

According to Paulhan, the "ancients" took proverbs, clichés, phrasings, common formulations from all over the place. They welcomed this abundance, they used it and gave back in kind: proffering ways of saying intended for recirculation. Their literatures were a well to be drawn on and replenished. Like Henry Fielding who, for all his large claims to formal innovation, worked, at the level of the sentence, in this way, too: putting familiar figures of speech back into written use without fear or embarrassment. Not seeing the need or feeling the pressure to modify well-used phrasings but showing interest, instead, in their recognisability, their efficiency. A novel like an open house. Like a meal, like a feast of many courses. A novel like a container. Like an ancient carrying device: a bundle, a sling, a net bag. These images did not start (or end) with Fielding. He will make Tom enact the same, time-worn gestures of the Greek heroes: like tear his hair. Tom Jones like Agamemnon, tearing at his hair as a way of signalling grief and distress.

—

"How nice it would be," Paulhan mused, to see the young girls of Tarbes (all the writers imagined as young girls) "carrying a rose, a poppy, a little bunch of poppies."

"For it is indeed a question of flowers!"

What was on the sign again?

> IT IS FORBIDDEN
> TO ENTER THE PARK
> CARRYING FLOWERS

Did that seem obscure by the way? Paulhan asked.

The sign, the phrasing of it? Strange? Unlikely?

It was a real sign.

Here is what happened. Here is the backstory to the rule, he wrote (at least, I think. Let's imagine it went like this):

A woman is walking in a park; she's carrying a bunch of flowers, recently picked. (Possibly she's a young girl from the story, with a reckless habit of stealing roses from rich people's gardens. Or, she's older. Walking fast past the exit sign of the park in the rain.)

Someone shouts out: Hey! You there!

Then louder: Oi!

Eh, what do you think you're doing?

It's the park-keeper: You know very well you're not supposed to *pick* the flowers.

These flowers? The flowers in her hands? The girl/woman is confused.

But she didn't pick them in the park!

She was carrying them with her when she came in.

How, though, can the keeper be sure?
Who is (ever) in a position to tell, for sure, who owns the flowers?
Who has property rights over the flowers?

The park keeper – wanting to be clear.
He wanted to be *absolutely* sure, in this story, where the creation was, where the re-creation was – who was taking what from whom and where. Hence the new rule, invented on the spot: from this point on, *no one* will be permitted to enter the park *carrying* flowers.

But, wrote Paulhan, it's a bad rule, clearly an impoverishing rule. At the end of his book he proposed to rewrite it. Like this:

IT IS FORBIDDEN
TO ENTER THE PARK
<u>WITHOUT</u> FLOWERS IN YOUR HANDS

without flowers and *without* precedents, which is another way of saying: it is forbidden to enter the park unaccompanied, unsupported; *without* bringing in (with you) who or what you live with, shaping the gestures of your body, the curves of your sensibility and imagination; *without* the distanced or close-up patterns, the callings or suggestions of someone else's tunes, pumping through a speaker taped to the handlebars, or was it the basket, of a low and unlikely chopper bike . . .

ALLOW FLOWERS

In principle. Pickable, portable, plentiful flowers. There were flowers for sale in the supermarket. Carnations, generally – which could look plastic, faked, from a distance, beautiful if you paid them some attention. Different individuated flowers.

Now an arrangement.

THE SHOP

The traffic splashed down past them in a spraying water rush. Helen re-crossed the big road, ducking out of the gloom of the heavy rain into the small format supermarket. For a moment, she was dazzled by the brightly lit indoors. She lowered her arm. There were wet patches all over the floor.

Against her chest: a small hard head bumped.

It jerked backwards, pulling outwards, and met the resistance of the fabric of the sling.

It fell back in, solid, skull-hard.

It turned itself one way, then the other: setting cheek to chest, setting the opposite cheek to chest. Helen felt the angles of elbows and knees, bracing against her, a sharp shoulder-jut.

Causes: it was the way her arm had fallen to her side, swapping out the dark covering of a heavy coat for the strip-lighting of the shop, as if she'd pulled the night away and made it – summer.

It was the sudden change in atmosphere, dry and artificially warm instead of rain, and, from within the protection of the sling, the sensing of wet.

It was the soundscape: the new buzz of refrigerated cabinets.

It was stillness. In the entrance area of the shop Helen had, for a short moment, stood still: removing and squeezing the rain water from her hat. Stillness acting as its own intervention – a waking force.

Or, it was a different, unknown, deeply internal prompt simply saying it was time: this process has gone on for too long. Whatever the explanation, retroactively proposed, the fact of it was, turning into the first aisle of the little shop – Rose was awake.

She'd started into the world again, confused. Helen's face looming down into hers like a welcome mat. Tugging the fabric away from her face so that she could greet her. Hello baby. A mat to cry on, to cry directly into, because the re-start was always startling. A surprise and at some level a fright: to reinitiate the raw process of existing, suddenly in a shop. With limbs bundled, a limited capacity for stretching, and the stark white lights of the supermarket appearing, disappearing, overhead.

Rose twisted and struggled within the confines of the sling.

Moving quickly, into her basket, Helen grabbed and dropped a variety of things: more tea, more biscuits, more apples, more bread, more nappies, more absorbent paddings for her own body, filled pasta – something easy to cook and eat one-handed.

What else? Batteries – where were they kept?

The layout of the shop proposed a sequence and a path and she did her own dash around it, but at the self-service checkouts there was a long, long queue.

Clearly it was break time, the tail end of lunchtime. For there was a great line of kids from the nearby secondary school, choosing this moment to buy not a lot with their own money, their parents' money. Not kids. Not yet adults – co-existing at different points on the vulnerable plane of transformation, bewildered by and in thrall to the new inhabitations of their bodies. Loving them and sometimes hating them, wishing their needs and complications away. They took up so much space. They wanted to, and they really didn't want to, draw attention to themselves. A security guard hovered near them as (one by one) they took their sweet-sweet time to pay for their

ONE
              sausage roll. Their

ONE

packet of biscuits. Their

ONE

can (of soft fizzy drink).

Helen was tired again, feeling it again. She willed them to get a move on. She'd given Rose her knuckle to suck on but soon she would need that hand and Rose would start, inevitably, to cry. She bobbed her deep bob, bending her knees, bouncing and bobbing, shifting her weight from foot to foot as (in slow motion) the young people paid for their

ONE

chocolate bar. Their

ONE

big bag
(the world's biggest bag)
of paprika-flavoured crisps.

Hungry – Helen was hungry again too. Rose was wailing. In response, two of the girls ahead of them turned their heads: they took in Helen, took in the moving shape of Rose pushing through the gap in Helen's coat, the shapes of her limbs working inside the fabric container like some alien thing, not yet born. Then turned back and blinked at each other: wild colours painted on their lids, making them look hooded and heavy; their lashes clotted, ponderous, magnificent.

When eventually their turn came, Helen took the cloth bag from her pocket and paid for a new plastic bag to tear open and hold over

Rose's head while carrying the cloth bag on her shoulder because outside, on the busy road, into the traffic, the crossing, the forks made by the branchings of the trees, it was still raining.

THOUGH EASING

It was easing off a little bit – and the fresh air helped. Helen could tell, without looking down, that Rose was calmer. She'd found an interest, her quiet sucking on the near edge of the sling. She was registering her own impressions of the raining presentation of the world as they turned back into the residential streets, bobbed past the pub on the corner, the spaced placing of the trees, gates and small front gardens. Past the wet ledge-to-roof ladder for a cat. From a weighted force falling down upon her, working against her, the rain once again altered its mode of relating: now making a gentle vapoured environment to move through. The ends of her hair fell around her shoulders in thick lines. Maybe the extra bag was unnecessary – who needed it after all.

IT STOPPED

A change. The cars were shining. Every surface was wet and they all glistened. Suddenly, in volume, there was bird song. On their street, falling in slant-wise, washing the houses opposite with unexpected colour, the light was a curious lemon-yellow.

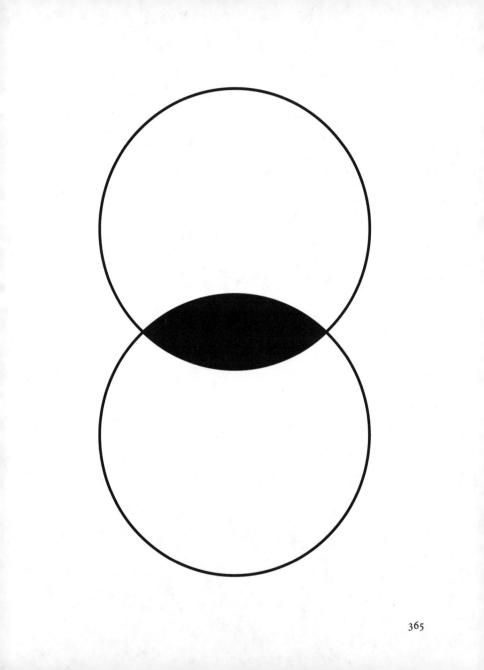

BRINGING THE ENERGY HOME

HALLWAY; SEPARATION

Two trainers treaded off at the heels. A big wet coat dropped; a cloth bag of shopping dumped damply in the kitchen. A quick pee. Rose straining and turning, crying loudly. Helen nipping into the kitchen for a shoving of biscuits into her mouth. Then, with her mouth full, spilling crumbs over Rose's head, landing them in her dark hair, untying the knot of the sling at her waist. Standing over the sofa, her hands behind her back to undo the crisscross of fabric. Feeling the whole tight environment holding Rose (in place, in sleep, in proximity) suddenly loosen – undo. Helen using her arms to take on the weight of Rose that the fabric, its pouch returned to a length, was now fully prepared to let drop. She tugged at it, unwrapping them both – there was a stickiness, then the return of an almost forgotten spaciousness, a weight being literally lifted from her chest. She sat them both down on the hard sofa with a feeling of great freedom and relief.

It was interesting: they'd been so close, pressed body to body, front to front, for the whole duration of their walk. Yet it was only with this new sense of separation – this rediscovery of physical distance – that they had a sense of returning to each other.

Helen smiled at Rose, greeting her again (again and all over again), saying hello with her eyes, her large teeth. They sat for a while and looked at each other.

Now with amazing co-ordination, with unrushed but perfect inter-understanding, they found a good feeding position.

Now it was quiet. Rose feeding slowly, calmly, studying the darker spaces animating Helen's face, their contrast with the whites of her eyes.

More gladness. Rose feeling it, taking it on in her own manner, which was seriously. It was a relief to have made it back to this living

room within their set of inhabitable rooms and for it all to still be here, waiting and the same. The mobile hanging about: turning casually, its structure open like a tree. There was the soft fact of the playmat. The cup of tea Helen had left in the soil of the plant pot had stayed placidly within reach. It had cooled to cold. But it was not, by her standards, undrinkable. The situation proposed by the room was wholly familiar, yet while they were out clouds had gathered and now they had re-parted; the sun had moved over the roof of the house; the earth had tilted and turned on its axis. It fell into the kitchen now, onto the countertops, into the sink. Dimming, softening. On their return they had found a new way of taking up the offer of the room, and it felt surprisingly simple: just these actions, in this setting, doing them together. The sofa didn't matter, the environment, the window, the desk and the shelves. These strange solid things – they held no tension. Rebba's postcard: it was a thought-form, made from colour and vibration, extruding into the room. There was her novel waiting on the floor.

Later, it might feel difficult again.

On a scale that could slide without warning from easy to a bit awkward to challenging to hard to difficult to touching at the very limit-edge of the humanly possible.

But for now it felt simple and they were both profoundly glad.

MR ALLWORTHY FALLS ILL

The forward-momentum of the novel – for Helen, it had stalled. She'd stalled it. It lay on the carpet: all latent energy, potential motion, ever-ready to be restarted. For others, it continued. Tom was no longer the rattling rascal impulsed to climb a tree, recapture a bird, and fall headfirst into the canal. Two years have passed. He has grown older. Mr Allworthy has aged, too. The consequence of Tom's maturity, for Allworthy, was his own older age. By now, he will have loved the foundling baby (bringing him up as his "own") for a long time.

Twenty years? A good long time.

Loving him at a formal distance, with none of the intimate inter-actions of day-to-day handling and care, but in his own intermittent manner: their meetings constantly spaced, steadily spaced.

Tom loving him back. He might be inconstant in romance, but this man, Mr Allworthy, has been his one, longest love.

Only now Mr Allworthy is unwell.

Mr Allworthy has for some days been indisposed with a cold. A common cold attended with a little fever. He pays scant attention.

The fever increases.

The doctor is summoned.

The doctor at his first arrival will shake his head and express his strong wish that he had been sent for sooner.

With remarkable calm and collection, Mr Allworthy will prepare to die.

He will gather his household around his bed.

He will address them, saying: "If the wisest of men hath com-pared life to a span, surely we must be allowed to consider it a day. It is my fate to leave it in the evening . . ."

—

Such luck, such good fortune to have seen the whole day through!

To leave one's life in the evening, when in any case the sun is going down.

He will say: "One of the Roman poets, I remember, likens our leaving life to our departure from a feast – a thought which hath often occurred to me when I have seen men struggling to protract an entertainment and to enjoy the company of their friends a few moments longer. Alas! How short is the most protracted of such enjoyments!"

He will say, more or less, that life is short.

It's a short day. Then night falls.

And death? Death is gigantic and terrible. But here it is.

(Even the longest day can only go on for so long.)

There is a gravity, an urgency to the moment; all the practical arrangements – the apportioning out of his fortune – will be made. His nephew Blifil will inherit the whole of the estate. Tom is much-loved. But, in fairness, he's not, and has never been, his "real" son. He will receive five hundred pounds a year.

AND THEN?

Miraculously, he recovers. Marvellously to the point of implausibility. The narrative was clearly heading one way. Only now – *now*:

There's a whole new direction.

Mr Allworthy recovers absolutely, all the way back to full health.

(It's possible he was never really all that ill in the first place; could it have been in the medical man's interest to build it up, dramatize, in order to stage-manage this relief?)

Mr Allworthy will live on, stay on, protracting his hold on life, or life's hold on him, his time at the table, as well as his time in the novel, for a good while yet.

His sister, however – will leave. People die in and out of order. She will step out / drop out / fall out of the novel, dying unexpectedly in London while, at home in Somerset, Mr Allworthy makes the unnecessary preparations for his own departure.

The two pieces of news come almost together in the novel; they sit in relation to each other and ask to be offset, or compared.

For Tom, there's no contest. No need even to weigh it up: it is clear which of the two events (the one event and the non-event) is the more consequential. When he'd thought Mr Allworthy was dying, Tom had crept back into his room, just to sit near him. He had flung himself onto the floor beneath his bed and taken hold of his large old hand, crying out "O my friend!" when he thought the moment of departure was close.

Tom has no real thought for his somewhat peculiar aunt. Mr Allworthy is alive and he is overjoyed. Because his heart is of the kind that pumps with big feeling, tending towards immoderation, he will be overcome with an immoderation of rapture. He will be "drunk with joy" – "an intoxication which greatly forwards the effects of wine." He

will inflame joy with booze: drinking many bumpers to the doctor's health as well as other toasts. He will "kiss the doctor, and embrace him with the most passionate endearments, swearing that next to Mr Allworthy himself, he loved him of all men living." (Like Helen floating high over the labouring room, tethered only by the anchor of Elvira's rough hand, Rose alive on her chest, the ever-intensifying crescendo of contractions suddenly, unexpectedly, *over*, declaring:

I love you!

I love you!

Thank you! I love you! Let me kiss that hand!)

Drunk on chance and happiness, Tom will celebrate.

To life! To the start and *continuance* of life!

For Blifil, however, the feelings are different. Mr Allworthy may have survived, but his own dear mother has just died. What's more, he'd just come very close to being the sole beneficiary of a great fortune, only to have that prospect snatched away. It is unseemly, he thinks. This celebration.

They will quarrel, harsh words: heat and temper.

Tom will go out for a walk in the cool open air. He will think ardently of Sophia, with whom he considers himself to be profoundly in love, in heart and in mind. But as chance would have it, he will encounter someone else: Molly Seagrim, his actual, very recent lover, to whom his body speaks. He will go with her into the woods, because he is intoxicated and happy, because they are both persuadable and horny, their youthful bodies pinging out messages to each other, exchanging communications on the mulchy, twiggy forest floor.

Blifil and his tutor Thwackum will surprise them by chance, or more likely not really by chance, in the thickest part of the grove.

There will be a fight.

Later in the novel, in a pub, two minor characters will report the whole episode:

Tom Jones? The first, louder one will say. Heard of him?

What, that little baby who got "dropt at Squire Allworthy's door?"

I heard, the quieter one will reply. But: a pause, a doubt. What did you hear?

Well (the "well" making preparations, saying prepare yourselves, again, for a story).

What *I heard*. Was this: one of the servants found him in a box *so full of rain-water*, that he would certainly have been drowned, had he not been reserved for another fate.

Is that so? the quieter one will ask, his role being to interject; to act as a motor-function encouraging the story, discouraging the story. Is it though?

It is. It was: "The squire ordered him to be taken in, for he is a *timbersome* man as everybody knows, and was afraid of drawing himself into a scrape; and there the bastard was bred up, and fed, and cloathified all to the world like any gentleman; and there he got one of the servant-maids with child, and persuaded her to swear it to the squire himself; and afterwards *he broke the arm* of one Mr Thwackum a clergyman, only because he reprimanded him for following whores; and afterwards *he snapt a pistol* at Mr Blifil behind his back; and once, when Squire Allworthy was sick, he got *a drum*, and *beat it all over the house* to prevent him from sleeping; and twenty other pranks he hath played, for all which, about four or five days ago, just before I left the country, the squire *stripped him stark naked*, and turned him

out of doors." Which was true: the last part, at least, will come true. Mr Allworthy will find that he cannot forgive Tom for drinking and cavorting and *celebrating* on the non-day of his death, the actual day of his sister's death (which is how Blifil will tell it; the slant he'll put on it; compounding it with many other smaller misdeeds and misadventures). Tom won't be stripped naked but he will be cast out of the house he grew up in – his home. The promise of reliability, made implicitly when Mr Allworthy took on the fate of the foundling, offering a provision of care like a foundation, a flexible and accommodating ground that Tom could test and test and trust that it would withstand his testing –

Now, all of a sudden, it was conditional.

That basis, the durability of that foundation, was re-presented as condition.

Not fully real or reliable.

It had started: this accommodation of a newcomer.

Then, one day, on this day, it was made clear that it could stop. It did stop.

THE ACTIVITIES OF THE AFTERNOON

The day continued. Helen spread out the mat. She considered it again: the large sunken garden, its suggestion of a green field, and its other, unmatched colours. She set Rose down in the dotty part of it, the slow actions of the mobile in her peripheral vision. Rose palpated the parts of the mat that were under her hands: patting, clutching, scrunching the material. She kicked her legs.

Helen collected the cup from the plant pot and quietly left the room.

Now she came back.

She'd put the kettle on in the kitchen.

She left (to make herself a fresh cup of tea, a fast sandwich).

She came back.

She ate and drank sitting on the mat alongside Rose.

She stood up again and left, returning her plate and cup to the kitchen, pulling the wet washing out of the drum.

She came back.

She carried with her the laundry basket, a soft blue cloth.

Rose was conscious of all of this. Her sited awareness sensed movement, sensed a rhythm of presence, absence, a large body-shape pulsing about her; approaching, retreating, changing the light-fall, but also staying with her, staying with her taking the form of leaving but returning to her, not forgetting about her, bearing her always somewhere in mind, and in this way holding her in place.

Helen swapped out the small dry clothes with small wet clothes all along the run of the radiator. With the blue cloth, she dusted, somewhat cursorily, the plant's broadest, dustiest dark-green leaves.

Now she drew close, settling herself on the mat, her back against the base of the sofa.

She put a hand on Rose.

The mobile jigged and dipped over the empty chair.

With the other, she picked up her novel and stretched out her legs.

She picked it up in the place where she'd left off. There was the familiar effort of reorientation: having to re-find her footing in this expanse of imagined ground. (Where was I? Where was it? Where were they, Helen and this other narration, in relation to each other?)

She concentrated. The printed words on the page concentrated her.

At her hip, sheltered by her thigh, Rose's attention gathered and dispersed, gathered and lifted, spotted and dispersed. There was a relation between the rise of Helen's leg and the furred surface that her hand was patting, involuntarily.

Helen read quietly at her own pace.

In the slower progress of her own private reading, Tom had not yet been exiled from Mr Allworthy's commodious house. In fact, he'd not yet even been discovered – she knew nothing, yet, of this dependent baby, later to become a separated individual, who was now making his own adult way in the world, exiled from his protected childhood, now making his own bareheaded, indirect way to London.

Tom: he felt injustice as he walked. Also, shame. For his drunkenness, his recklessness: there was no denying these charges. He had no defence. Every faculty of speech and motion had deserted him. Because of this, it had taken some time for him to leave. At their parting, Tom had kissed his mother-father-benefactor's hands. He'd done so with a passion difficult to be affected and as difficult to be described.

His heart was almost broken. His spirits were so profoundly sunk.

He did leave, in the end.

A flood of tears gushing from his eyes.

He sets out and walks for about a mile.

He comes upon a little brook, obstructing his passage.

He throws himself down by the side of it. And there, his feelings shift: he cannot help but mutter some indignation. He was still on Mr Allworthy's property, after all, in the grounds he'd been ordered never to set foot on. "Surely my father will not deny me this place to rest in?" Despair giving way, briefly, to pride, to pique: "Surely . . . ? He would not . . . ?"

Then closing over his head: a new, more powerful and even more devastating wave of despair. By the brook, on the ground, he gives in to it: to violent agonies, tearing the hair from his head "and using most other actions which generally accompany fits of madness, rage and despair." External indicators of a disturbed inner state: the sorts of signs we read people by. Let him feel it. Let him be.

(Why go in any further, the narrator will ask, when there is already so much information here: in actions, in gestures, in language, in looks? Why penetrate any further, when we are all, still, so capable of reading these legible indications – and imagining the rest?

Also, when what is most essential about Tom in this moment may not be what he himself is feeling, raging and despairing on the inside,

but how it connects with, or indeed, how it contrasts with and off-sets what *else* is going on: what is going on all around. For instance: the bright blue sky, making a backdrop to his suffering. This surplus view – what *he* can't see, but another could, or can? The sky: hidden from him, because his face is in the turf. It was bright and blue: full of sunshine.)

Helen negotiated the movement of the prose at her own pace, some-times lifting her head, thinking a way off from it, sometimes adjusting the position of her legs, and resettling her attention on the page.

Why not like this, she thought: let the afternoon unfold.

Then a practical thought came in.

A LITTLE CHAPTER, IN WHICH IS CONTAINED
A VERY GREAT INCIDENT

Helen carried Rose into the bedroom. She laid her down carefully on a big pink towel spread out more or less permanently on the bed for this purpose. She removed her footed tights, her heavy nappy, wiped her clean, and released her bottom half to the cool open air.

Rose lifted her legs to the ceiling; gave a great kick; the happy sounds of freedom.

Helen hovered over her, her face close but not too close.

Hey, she said, smiling. Hi baby. Hello.

So many greetings in a day: here we are, they said to each other. Re-introducing ourselves.

She bounced the palms of her large hands against the soles of Rose's bare feet.

She noted and welcomed Rose's pleasure.

She played the keyboard lightly on her toes.

Helen frowned. For a moment, her face – all the animation in her face – went still.

It was alright. It was just that in that moment she was thinking about something else – her mind had moved out of the moment and out of the room as she re-tied her hair.

But Rose had no way of knowing this and wished her back. From the blankness of her expression, she urgently required Helen to come back.

Helen shook her head and returned.

Taking hold of one little foot she slowly, with deliberation, starting with the biggest, proposed a different name for each small toe.

It was a familiar game. Familiar and renewable.

They played it multiple times a day:

Larry,

She gave the big toe a waggle as she bestowed its name. Like a knight. Like Helen was the Queen and Rose's toes were the Knights. She went on.

Barry,

Harry,

Gary and –

reaching the tiniest toe, barely a toe at all, she hesitated. The waiting beat had to do with her own efforts at comic timing; it was solely for the purposes of her own entertainment.

I don't know, Helen said. What do *you* reckon, Rose?

She tickled the arch of that impressively wrinkled sole.

Colin?

She reached for the other foot. Now she wondered out loud: But why these names? On the other set of toes, she started the process again:

Diamond! (the big one)

Let the names loose . . . ! Constance! Eugenia! Finally!

The little one she named April-May-June!

She nodded, smiling widely at Rose.

Rose, whose eyes were alive with attention, following her so closely, bobbed her head.

Helen took back ahold of the first little foot. She recited from novel-memory:

Mr Aggs

Mr Baggs

Mr Caggs

Mr Daggs
Mr Faggs
Mr Graggs
And – Mr Boffin.

Helen laughed, let go of Rose's foot and leaned over Rose. There were more names than toes, but who was counting?

Rose caught her eye, lost her eye, caught her eye.

They looked directly at each other, resuming and deepening their study of each other. They looked fully and directly. Interchange, interchange: with rising reciprocation.

Helen nodding, laughing – Rose, trembling. Her gaze holding, her interest mounting.

Helen, with a strong sense of Rose's interest mounting.

She could sense it: a tension, growing, intensifying.

An abundance of interest – about to spill over. Something important was about to happen.

And then?

Rose scanned her eyes down to Helen's mouth. It was a wide mouth, a dark hole. She fixed on the opening and closing mouth as Helen made encouraging laughing sounds.

She travelled her gaze back up to Helen's eyes and back down again to her mouth.

Her eyes glittered. Both pairs of eyes were glittering.

Helen felt something contract in her chest.

It contracted with what was almost a pain and then there was a lift.

It was her heart lifting.

Her heart which felt like it could fall right out of her open mouth.

Something was about to happen. She was a part of it.

She was playing a major contributing part in producing the conditions for the chance of it.

They were both there – teetering on/in the brink.

Really Rose? she said, her smile widening, her eyes bright and wide, showing all the enamel of her big adult teeth.

Her face encouraging, encouraging.

A connection was being made: contact between the one face and the other, one bright site of animation faced with the other: each amassing the other's energy, engaging in the electric transfer of energy; the relay of potential and responsive imitation.

Between them the space was almost and now fully charged, and something fizzed.

Helen laughed again, with nerves, with anticipation, with her own excitement.

Now Rose?

Now?

Leaning directly over Rose she was all prompt, all encouragement, all incitation.

Now?

The interactional knot they made together: it knotted and it knotted and now at last and all at once it untied: Rose's face bloomed open – transformation!

It opened wide, wide, wide and she held it: this unprecedented expression.

She smiled.

For the very first time, Rose was smiling.

With her eyes, her cheeks, all her gums, her habitual gravity for the moment completely out the window. Her face offering unprecedented open-access to a loose and gamesome inner light.

It looked like LOVE.

Rose smiled and Helen smiled back even wider and Rose smiled back even wider and in this circuit of social interaction, the energy moved back and forth, around and around. It bounced between them. It pinged and it flowed.

It looked like LOVE – even if it wasn't that.

Even if it was reaction, inheritance, mimesis.

Helen felt like she'd won.

She felt like: CONGRATULATIONS!

She'd been singled out for an everyday display of extraordinary virtuosity. Rose had superseded herself. She was born unfinalized and now she had shown (with this new form of abundance) how unfinal, undecided, and surprising she was. Possibly, Helen had too. Everything was superseding itself: the bedroom, their relation, the future, the afternoon.

It was a gift.

What must it be like, Helen wondered, to be capable of bestowing something like this, making such a donation to someone else, without even knowing you were giving it – to be so unconscious of your own luminosity?

THE SIMULTANEOUS RECEPTION OF LIGHT

He felt it before he looked. His phone jumping on the dashboard. A tiny, almost imperceptible jump: movement, making buzz as well as light. What was it?

The sudden *delivery* (into the sensitized space of his own character zone) of two words in return.

It closed the door that had been hanging open – that had been left hanging, gaping, half-way off its hinges.

He smiled, too: a small, inward-facing smile. He ran his long fingers across his cheeks, his chin. The outward changes in response to this release (release from waiting) were infinitesimal. The feeling, though, was immense.

HELEN AND ROSE

Do it again! This is what Helen was asking – hanging over Rose . . .
  Where was her phone? She should take a photo.
  Do it again, Rose!
  Come on – do it again?

BUT ROSE

She wouldn't immediately, not *on command*, do it again.

Helen found her phone and composed a message for Rebba.

But how to put it? What word was MAXIMAL enough to contain it . . . ?

She typed something: enthusiasm + eventhood.

Exclamation marks + smiley face smiley face smiley face.

THE ONE WHO WAITS

The next delivery was a large rectangular box. It contained something shaky, as if it were all broken inside. But it wasn't heavy at all. Little separate pieces whose rattling sounds he recognized from his own birthdays, from Christmas. Parts to be put together according to instruction and then dropped or deliberately broken down and rebuilt into something else. Something possibly better – worked on and reworked. The muscles behind his knees were tight, painful. He rang a stranger's bell, went through the motions of an interaction all the while thinking (turning over in his mind) what she'd given him – what, on his phone, he'd just received. It was enough. For sure, for now.

It would last the day, carry him through to the start of the night.

But, already, there was this slow, creeping, emptying-out feeling: Was it enough?

Already, the question: What if it was never enough? What if the structure of this relation, what revved it as momentum, was not the completion, the rounding off, but the dismantling, the collapse, with a view to starting it off again?

These were not his own words. But they helped to phrase his inner question. What if what he loved most about loving her was this rhythm – the charged delay between question and answer, call and response? What if he loved the full-up feeling, the temporary sating, only as a prelude to the way it would inevitably hollow out, renewing the chance of waiting?

But so what. That was the thought he used to close down this set of thoughts.

For now, it felt good. It felt light – buoyant and a bit shaky like the box. It felt really good. More than alright.

WHOOP!

Rebba's reply: WHAT?!!!! Then, in the seconds it takes to type:
    Have to see this. Working now.
    Soon as I can.

Pacing back around the living room, there was an afterglow of excitement, achievement.

Helen and Rose, they were still intermittently buzzing at each other. A shared sense of something having shifted. The knight's move of a developmental leap: not an incremental trackable progress, never a simple step-up or on, but an awkward L-shape. Nothing doing then all of a sudden – hop, hop: Ta-dah! – Rose was over there. Over here.

Helen knelt over the shopper bag to re-examine Nisha's present of a plastic star. It needed a tiny screwdriver to open the casing as well as new batteries; you couldn't just pry it open. Helen had neither. The sleep solution the object contained, the one whose efficiency Nisha had promised: a little night-sky movie projected on the ceiling accompanied by tunes, a play of light and shadow that would simply go on, uninterrupted and unassisted as long as the batteries held out – it would have to wait.

Would it work, even? When she did manage to get it going? Would the focus it offered – the immersion provided by a darkened room, lit only by the projection, no distractions – replace her own arms and movement and bounce, and *really* help Rose to get to sleep?

It was hard to believe.

Helen put Rose in her chair and turned this promise over in her hands. It was smooth, moulded, and enclosed.

She set it down and took up her novel.

She put that down, too. The figure on the bookshelf lay with his back to them: his body still a perch for the water birds. They'd find out that it didn't (it wouldn't) work (for them) (it might work for others) (but not) (instantly, with the alacrity Helen wanted it to) (stupid fucking thing) on a new day (tomorrow).

ANTICIPATION

Outside, there was a late-in-the-day energy: a lower, yellower, angled light. There was a van returned emptied to the depot; a handheld record of as many tiny social interactions or missed ones as there had been unmemorable boxes and packages. Putting his key into and pushing open his own front door, he could hear his mum laughing in the kitchen, his brother gaming in the living room. He'd join one or the other of them in a minute. He'd eat his dinner. He'd rest up, relax. His body was tired. His brain. He'd do some stretches.

Later, he'd start getting ready.

The night ahead: it was cavernous, lit with laser-colours, soft and pulsing possibility. It beckoned. She'd messaged again. They'd made a plan.

Imagining it, anticipation pulled like a long thin thread. There was never anything steady, steadying, about being near her, ever. The thread tugged at him (a sharp inside twist); something tweaked. Later: clubbing. On a Tuesday night. He'd have to get up early the next morning. Even so, they were going out.

PREPARATIONS FOR LATE AFTERNOON

Now Helen took off all her clothes. Rose was in a new nappy, a new suit. She had been clipped into her chair and positioned in the doorway of the bathroom. Helen stepped into the shower, leaving the curtain open, to keep her eye on Rose. The warm water wetted then re-soaked her hair – it was still damp from the rain.

Rose angled her head, listening. (Let Rose enjoy the gush of water.)

Helen closed her eyes. She allowed herself to get, just briefly, tugged somewhere else.

There was a river.

Possibly, it was the river-source of her swimming dreams.

They weren't expecting to find it but it was a proper swimming spot so they'd just plunged in: Rebba's insistence. It was a hot day; it was a cool, shaded portion of river. There were kids swimming there – they'd heard them shouting, calling out to each other, on the approach. They were taking turns to swing out over the widest run of it on a bit of rope tied to an overhanging tree, soaring for a short second then splash-landing from high in mid-air. To get to the deeper, swimming parts, they walked a little way out over sharp stones; they held hands to keep balance. They went in up to their ankles, wobbling, finding and losing their footholds, then their knees, a bit farther and from that point on they could wade, then lift their feet and swim.

There was a spot in the middle of the river where the current was stronger. It made its own faster channel. They'd watched how the kids did it – the idea was to tread water nearby and then sort of launch yourself into the faster-running channel. It could whoosh a buoyant body around in a fast, short curve and deliver you back to the shallows under the trees.

—

Rebba went first.

Then Helen.

Then Rebba.

Then Helen. Now together.

Again and again. Come on? Just one more time.

Back over the small sharp stones that were painful but bearable under cold bare feet, especially if it was possible to hold on to someone's hand.

The rush and momentum of the current.

It wasn't even especially fast.

But there it was: a provision of great pleasure. A natural acceleration.

A force among living forces, a faster flow of an already rushing river, waiting and wanting to knock you gently off your feet.

"The live being constantly loses and re-establishes equilibrium with [their] surroundings." This is its base rhythm, its bare rhythm, wrote John Dewey. But possibly, it's the tipping. The risk of necessary transition. "*The moment of passage* from disturbance into harmony is that of intensest life."

Helen felt it in the shower: the moment of passage from one state of feeling to the next, ordinary, banal concerns (washing her hair) to the most essential, carried forward by the memory of river-swimming. I'm alive, she said out loud. Washing her body very fast. Opening her eyes now to check on Rose, who had turned her face towards the u-bend under the sink. Washing her body parts for their own sake but also for the purposes of keeping this other small body alive – since they would keep on touching. Since they were always touching each other, then coming apart. Her tall, recovering, wrecked and healing

body, tender in places, solid in places, receiving comfort from the warm running water, little splashes of water leaping out onto the floor, around the base of Rose's chair, because the curtain was open. But not too many splashes – she kept an eye on this too. Not enough to make it dangerous. She couldn't risk slipping and smacking her head.

I'm alive. She said it again.

She was thinking of her Nana, the only person she'd observed in her life so far in the process of dying. If aliveness was quick, darting and unpredictable, powerful and slippery like a fish, then death was a noisy horse. Her breathing was so laboured in her final days: snorting, whinnying, nickering. The planes of her face so pronounced. Her eyes and her teeth outsized because her face had grown smaller, thinner. Helen had held her hand. There was strength and great warmth in her grip. In this way, they communicated, because by that stage Nan was finding it hard to speak. In fact, she'd stopped speaking altogether. She was predominantly teeth, which sometimes she'd have to show, despite herself, folding her lips around them, as if to make room for them, gritting them, as she coped with her pain. She was predominantly eyes – a new intensity to her gaze. The sound of laboured breathing. She was predominantly warm, gripping, communicating hand. Helen hadn't known what to say, so she'd just held her hand for the duration of the last visit. Amidst the bustle of checks and in-and-out care going on all around them she worked on keeping her voice steady enough to say, with some degree of conviction: It's alright, Nan. It's alright.

Now she rinsed her long hair. When her body was dry and in her sleeping clothes, which were more or less her day clothes, although it was still officially the afternoon, it was the baby's turn:

A slower, more formal ceremony.

All the fast, get-this-done gestures radically slowed down.

Rose's bathing spot was a shallow turquoise tub. Helen filled it with warm water from the tap, adding a few drops of special oil, then placed it at the centre of the pink towel in the middle of the bed. Pink and turquoise.

Carrying the full tubful through first.

Then returning to the bathroom to carry Rose through in her chair.

Receiving but pushing through her protests as she got her undressed (again).

Trusting that when her limbs found the water, she'd fall silent.

As she did. She did in the warm water.

Rose. Her expression softened. It turned inward.

Now she was absorbed, set off on her own thinking, dreaming paths – looking like she'd been put in touch with something important.

Helen gave her time.

She tried to: managing her own impatience. She tried very hard to open out and provide Rose with as much time as she needed. As well as the space to float. Rose floated, bumping her foot against the rim of the bowl, almost too small for her.

Her arms lifted and from underneath they made shapes on the surface of the water.

With the fingers of one hand, Helen flicked droplets onto her stomach, taking care (with the other) to support her neck.

READING

With them both dressed, Helen bounced Rose to and fro from the bedroom to the kitchen to the living room. Making a little set up: a sort of nest for the early evening on the floor near the chair, within the remit of the mobile. Bringing in what she thought they were likely to need: a big glass of water; something to snack on – was she hungry? Later, she'd eat properly. A blanket and a pillow from her bed. She moved her laptop, her phone, set them down within reach. She set the mobile turning: bobbing black and bobbing white. She balanced her novel on the sofa's arm. She moved the lamp from the table, plugged it in near them on the floor.

She switched it on: outdoors, it was early evening; indoors, the lighting changed.

With Rose in her chair, the mobile entertaining her, the lamp providing its gentle lamp-light, Helen read her novel. Her progress was paced by the movements of the composition: the sentences, the short paragraphs, the short chapters and their breaks. Also, by the forward-dart and backward-skip of her own travelling eyes. They ranged all over the place, all over the page, in great forward-flights, back-tracks, and brief, brief perchings, though the impression was of a steady linear progression. At semiregular intervals, Helen shifted. She turned a page using only the fingers of the hand that were also holding the book, sometimes with her chin, or her nose. At her own, directed-undirected pace of receptive engagement she read, in full:

  "The introduction to the work, or a bill of fare to the feast." (essay-part)
  "A short description of Squire Allworthy and a fuller account of Miss Bridget Allworthy, his sister." (narrative-part)

"An odd accident which befell Mr Allworthy at his return home. The decent behaviour of Mrs Deborah Wilkins, with some proper animadversions on bastards." (narrative-part) She read the chapter in which Mr Allworthy finds the baby. Stands very still. Is speechless in his night shirt. Then finds his finger being worked upon, his feelings summoned and pressed by the involuntary grasp of Tom's small hand.

THE MOBILE COMPOSITION

As it happened, Rebba had been with Helen – keeping her company, helping her – on that recent pregnant afternoon: the day when all the separate bits and pieces of the mobile had been delivered (in a flat package) to her home.

Let me come round, Rebba had said, when she'd learned how Helen was planning to spend the afternoon: let me help. And it was true, Rebba was good (generally much better than Helen) at practical things, at aesthetic things, and so likely also kinetic things.

The mobile was a close descendent – a popular and available sort of rip off – of the sculptures of Bruno Munari.

Munari, writing in 1933 about how his first mobile sculptures came to be made: "I cut out the shapes, gave them harmonic relationships to one another, calculated the distances between them and painted their backs (the part one never sees in a picture) in a different way so that they would form a variety of combinations. I made them very light and used thread so as to keep them moving as much as possible."

They were sculptures made "of cardboard, painted in plain colours, and sometimes a glass bubble [. . .] the whole thing [. . .] held together with the frailest of wooden rods so as to turn with the slightest movement of air . . ."

Other artists at the time, in the same decade, were making similar discoveries. For instance, Alexander Calder. But, notes Munari: "his things were made of iron and painted black or some stunning colour." Munari's materials, on the hand, were deliberately cheap and light, generally monochrome. "Calder triumphed in our circle, and I came to be thought of as his imitator." Munari relates: my friends laughed at me. "This was the time when the movement

called '*novecentro italiano*' ruled the roost, with its High-Court of super-serious masters, and all the art magazines spoke of nothing else but their granitic artistic productions . . . everyone laughed at me and my useless machines."

His friends laughed but they all wanted one. Not for their galleries, but for their homes. They displayed his sculptures in their children's bedrooms.

By the time Rebba arrived, Helen had already pressed or cut out the different parts. She'd made an arrangement of tools and materials on the carpet: the lengths of dowel. Fishing line. The plastic arm. G-clamp. Scissors. She was considering the different shapes. She had strong ideas about sequence, progression. She was feeling sensitive: anxious about her baby, counting her kicks, conscious of how long it had been since she had last rolled over, since she'd last felt her kick. Anxious about birth, about living in the new flat. Nervous and touchy about her ideas. She said, her voice firm with intention: it should tell a story.

This was her plan: to start the thing with DOTS.

It would tell a story about the origins of the universe. Very good. It would narrate the emergence of form!

Starting with DOTS it should move on to – what? To waves? She appreciated the distractions provided by this inner debate: whether waves came before spirals or, it could be argued: no, no, no, the other way around.

In any case, she was clear: it should *end on* a SQUARE.

But only for a moment. Before turning, dissipating, dissolving and returning itself to DOTS . . .

Helen was pleased with this conception – with herself for having come up with it. She thought it was clever. She deepened her voice

as she described it. She smiled and laced her fingers together around the back of her head.

Rebba listened to her account of her project. She thought about it.

She took the matter seriously.

She respected Helen's approach: there were great pleasures in being told something, from start to end (and then around again). But the thing is, she said.

We will hang it. Won't we?

And once we hang it.

Once it is up a little bit off the floor. Suspended like that from the edge of the table.

She paused, tapping on her mouth.

She tilted her head. Took her own time. Resumed her discourse.

We will hang it. And it will move.

It will make an open – she reached for the words she wanted: *spaced out* thing. Multi-directional.

She added: the shapes – it's very cool that the baby will see their backs. But it won't exactly make – she walked her fingers forward in the air: a *procession*.

Munari's idea: to conceive a new kind of object. One which took the static nature of a picture and spaced its composite elements out, attaching them very delicately to one another, conceiving them as aesthetic things that might actually live with people in their surroundings, sensitive to the atmospheres of real life, breathing its air, and changing. He wrote: "Whether or not Calder started from the same idea, the fact is that we were together in affirming that figurative art had passed from two or at most three dimensions to acquire a fourth: that of time."

—

Helen watched and listened, responsive to Rebba's authority.

She watched her take over the shifting of shapes about on the floor, finding and changing combinations; how she made one describe an arc around the other.

Rebba continued: for the baby, there won't be, like, a – "through-line," "a thread." I don't think there'll be "a story," exactly.

Helen twisted her mouth to one side.

Even so, Rebba went on, speaking encouragingly: I think she'll enjoy it.

She lowered her chin to address the baby: the live creature, unmet, but already attending to the sounds of their conversation, taking up every inch of available space in the great pocket of Helen's womb. It won't be a story.

But it'll still be good, Rebba insisted – saying it louder, so the baby could hear. It'll be a different kind of pleasure, she said.

But, you know, just as meaningful – just as real.

Rose – gazing up into the spaces made by the mobile. If the black DOTS seemed to burst out towards her it was because they were set against white; if the pointed tips of the TRIANGLES presented as pointed and sharp it was because they were offsetting the curves of the UNDULATION, the roundness of the CIRCLE, the perfect full moon; if the nearer shapes showed strong edges, it was because they described the fuzziness of those that were hanging higher and farther away . . .

The project of a baby's mobile: to entertain her. To stimulate her. But also, more specifically, to lengthen her attention span. Rose could look at the mobile for longer – for longer than almost anything else – because it kept changing. Because it was composed of smaller and larger, more subtle and more striking differences. Continuation, which is to say duration (longing), supported (made possible) by contrast.

Eventually, in Fielding's novel, there will be an explanation for the essay-parts. It comes at the beginning of Book V, a small quarter of the long way through.

The title of the piece: "Of the serious in writing and for what purpose it might be introduced."

The subtitle: *In which we shall . . . proceed to lay before the reader the reasons which have induced us to intersperse these several digressive essays in the course of the work . . .*

It begins (humorously):

"Peradventure there may be no parts in this prodigious work which will give the reader *less* pleasure in the perusing than those

which have given the author the greatest pains in composing [the essay-parts, the novel-theory parts]. Among these probably may be reckoned those initial essays which we have prefixed to the historical matter contained in every book; and which we have determined to be *essentially necessary* to this kind of writing, of which we have set ourselves at the head."

Essentially necessary to this novel-kind of writing. But why? (Why if it's predicted that readers might find them the least pleasurable to read?) The narrator goes on:

"For this our determination we do not hold ourselves strictly bound to assign any reason, it being abundantly sufficient that we have laid it down as a rule necessary to be observed in all prosaic-comi-epic-writing."

I decide, says the narrator, acting as a proxy for the author.

It should be sufficient that I – or is it more accurate to say *this* (the composition) – decides. (For once set down, and juxtaposed, once set in motion, there are suggestions and effects produced by the force of these hyphenations of which the narrator-author will never be wholly in charge.)

Even so, he recognizes a risk.

Should he withhold from explaining altogether, their function might be misunderstood – so, to explain, after all: "to lay before the reader the reasons" for the essay-parts:

If they have been interspersed, if the novel has been composed on the principle of this regular interruption, it is because the essays partake of – they open and activate – "a new vein of knowledge." A vein which "if it hath not been discovered, hath not, to our remembrance, been wrought on by any ancient or modern *writer*." A grand claim which the narrator immediately undercuts by listing all the ways its potentials have been recognized by the other art forms, and

are constitutive of everyday experience. "This vein is none other than that of contrast . . ."

Wolfgang Iser: "it is the basic principle that gives shape to the whole novel."

Contrast: it runs through all "the works of creation, and may probably have a large share in constituting in us the idea of all beauty, as well natural as artificial," the narrator declares.

Consider, he invites: how "the beauty of day, and that of summer, is set off by the horrors of night and winter. And I believe, if it was possible for a man to have seen *only the two former*, he would have a very imperfect idea of their beauty."

Contrast: John Dewey phrases it explicitly as a matter of rhythm. Night and day, tension and release, rain and sunshine – in their alternation, these are large rhythms of the world which directly *concern* human beings. They have always been a part of life, shaping life, starting life – for newcomers as well as for our ancestors. In Dewey's account, summarized by Vincent Barletti: it was "precisely the decisive moment when these ancestors unmoored themselves just a bit from nature's 'universal' rhythms and began to apply the logic of these to new domains" – to their own smaller-scale repetitions, simulating their contrastive logics in dances, paintings, and song – that it became possible "to speak of artistic rhythm" and – in Dewey's terms – *therefore* "aesthetic form."

EVERYONE IS AN AUTHORITY

It is a matter of seeing what the counter-term can do: the perspective it brings in; the light it sheds; the relation it produces. It is a distribution of authority. Everyone and everything is its own authority, supporting, nuancing, or actively countering the authorities of everyone and everything else. What this initiates is a whole dynamic process.

Reading Fielding's essay on contrast, Robert L. Chibka shows how the composite form repeatedly rephrases and unsettles the question: Which is the more authoritative? Which is the more essential – the most powerful and important? Which of the parts, really, can be skipped over, and dismissed?

Background or foreground?

Day or night?

Essay (thesis) or narration (fiction)?

Large general statements or the smaller situated actions?

Supporter or supported – Helen or Rose?

When the point is: they are all *so sensitive* to each other. They have been conceived and set in relation to each other. They have been made to turn about each other. To think about and redescribe each other. When they live in such proximity to each other. In the same living space, if not always in exactly the same rooms.

NOVELNESS

was the name Mikhail Bakhtin gave "to a form of knowledge that can most powerfully put different orders of experience" – competing orders of experience that might ordinarily overwhelm or seek to cancel each other out – "into dialogue with each other."

The part-novel, the novel-essay, its compound form based on the conviction that: "There is never any problem, ever, which can be confined within a single framework."

PACING IT OUT

The curious thing about reading a canonical novel, so cheaply and readily available, so frequently re-edited, is the thought of someone, somewhere else, possibly even a large group of dispersed readers, making their way through the same territory at the same time. Reading for study or pleasure, for entertainment, for their own private purposes. All of whom are likely to be at different stages. Helen, who had just started, with the whole thing stretching out ahead of her. Others drawing closer to the end.

Book XVIII, Chapter I: A Farewell to the Reader

The last essay-part of Tom Jones is a farewell to the reader. A goodbye which will feel meaningful – which has a chance of being experienced as poignant and meaningful – if and only if the extended passage of time provided by the novel has indeed been undergone; if and only if the reader and the narrator have spent the novel's length of time together, in each other's company: if and only if the novel has been given time, accommodated within a person's time: over days, weeks, a process sometimes spaced over months, years.

It will be a direct address: an honest farewell, heading up a book composed of twelve further chapters. It will turn out to be a comically protracted goodbye.

The next chapter: "In which the history is continued."

Mr Allworthy will repeal his banishment of Tom. He will revise his harsh judgement in the light of new knowledge, new circumstances, and try to repair it. The loving relation he caused to break off – from his side, to end – will start up again.

—

The next chapter: "In which the history is farther continued."

He'll remember, with a poignancy that depends on – it cannot do without – the distance of many, many pages (more than eight hundred pages), on the accompanying and unskipped stretch of reading time (of life-time) as well as narrative time having gone by, on everyone having had the chance to grow up, fall ill, recover, and grow older, the moment he first set eyes on the baby. Length providing the materials as well as the means for distanced recall: the sudden collapse of all the page-spaces, all the countless events, in between.

A further chapter, titled: "Continuation of the history."

As if the whole purpose of the project were to see if it could keep going. To see if, even in the process of ending, it could still keep going – open up the outer edges and write beyond its own conclusion.

A further chapter, titled: "Further continuation."

John Dewey: "There are ideas [scenes] that would be destroyed if they were spaced differently."

Yet another short chapter, likewise titled: "Further continuation."

Mr Allworthy will say out loud, thinking of Tom, the great grown man, remembering who he was, how he arrived in the world. The newcomer: "I still remember the innocent, the helpless situation in which I found him. I feel the tender of his little hands *at this moment.*" The recollection will make him cry.

A further chapter titled "A further continuation."

"O my child!" will be his exclamation of regret. Tears standing in his eyes.

Again, a chapter: "Wherein the history begins to draw towards a conclusion."

Working towards its ending, which involves a turning back.

The next chapter: "The history draws nearer to a conclusion."

It's a tension, a productive hesitancy. The impulse to continue. Working counter to; with and against the impulse to end.

The next chapter: "Approaching still nearer the end."

"Such impulses are only possible in a world with an open future and in a world where everything important is not already over." Nothing here, no one here is *already over*. Finished, complete. Finalized and decided. Until:

"Chapter the last."

Even this will not be, exactly, how the novel concludes. But at some stage in the final sequence of explicitly drawn-out chapters, mixing humour and pathos, riffing on the whole project of length, the constitutive ambition of the long forms, Mr Allworthy will say of Tom:
   "He was my darling, indeed he was."
   In the novel, he will be again. Living still: he still is.

HOLD; HOLDING

A CHANGE OF INPUT

It was hard to read *at length* with Rose growing restless.

The first part of the evening: it was always a potentially agitated time. A drowsy but tetchy, sensitive time. It was nowhere near a prescribed adult bedtime but Helen, too, was getting ready, almost, to call it a day.

She let go of her big novel and reached over to open her laptop. A change of input: D. W. Winnicott's radio broadcasts to "all the mothers" – it was possible to listen to them online.

She set a talk running.

She liked listening to him, especially at the end of the day.

It was comforting: this feeling of being directly spoken to. Winnicott calling her (as well as anyone else listening, so long after the fact) "you."

His voice was quite high and surprisingly thin. Plummy, but also fragile, through laptop speakers. She lifted Rose out of her chair and put her to her breast.

KNOWING AND LEARNING

The talk was titled "Knowing and Learning."

It began: "There is much for a young mother to learn."

For example, "useful things" received from experts about "the introduction of solids into the diet, about vitamins, and about the use of
the weight chart." This accumulation of knowledge, Winnicott called
it "learning": important general things to learn about, to get told (off)
about. For example, there are vitamins to prevent rickets, and it's important to know this, when you're tasked with feeding a child.

But then there's knowledge of a different kind. A knowing that
comes from doing.

Winnicott: "It seems to me important for you to be quite clear
about the difference between these two types of knowledge." What
"you do and know, simply by virtue of the fact that you are the mother
of an infant, is as apart from what you know by learning as is the east
from the west coast of England."

Helen bristled a bit at this. She went – she felt like she could go
along with the general distinction. But on the condition that "mother
of an infant" included other people, anyone else stepping in, or the
different person who had been there from the beginning. And on
the further condition that the "naturally" in the sentence that came
next – "Just as the professor who found out about the vitamins that
prevent rickets really has something to teach you, so you really have
something to teach him about the other kind of knowledge, that
which comes to you naturally" – translated as – what? she wanted a
word suggestive of everything that also felt *unnatural*, strange, effort-
ful and forced. Prosthetic and contrived.

Winnicott talked on: "I want you to be able to feel confident about
your capacity . . . and not feel that because you could not know about

vitamins, you also could not know about, for instance, how to hold your infant."

The discourse might have sounded patronizing, very paternalistic, if it weren't for the quality of feeling and intention in the high speaking voice: its strange fragility. An "emotional-volitional *tone*" which seemed to release the locked-in content of the thought, allowing it to attach itself to her – making it sound actually interested in her own situation.

Also, the surprising-seeking placement of the verbs: "I want you to be able to feel . . ." / "and not feel that because you could not know . . ." / "you could not know about, for instance, how to hold . . ."

HOLDING

"How to hold your infant; that would be a good example for me to follow up."

The talk about the differences between "learning and knowing" had become a talk about holding.

Let me tell you, it said, about what, basically, you already know.

Or, about what, basically, you're already doing – what you've already had experience of, whether it's a baby you're holding, or another species of live creature, or something else that you're actively trying to keep alive.

Let me describe it all back to you – and offer you a different vocabulary, new terms with which to draw out the interest of what you're doing – its real-world relevance. Doing this for my own purposes – but also for your own self-recognition.

This is what holding means:

Helen eased both Rose and herself up from the floor to settle on the sofa, the pillow at her back. She stretched out her legs, resting her calves on the farthest sofa arm, letting her feet push in and settle on the earth among the low stems of the big plant. It made the broad leaves shudder. She pulled the blanket over them both. Rose seemed to be dozing now. It was very likely that she would need to feed again. But there was no urgency. Sensing what was available, reassured by Helen's availability, Rose had sunk slightly but not entirely – she was just skimming the surface of a doze. Her folded hand patted, touch-touch-touched at Helen who was now thinking about how it would have been better to have closed the curtains before finding this position, and how it was too disturbing to get up and do it now. But

maybe it didn't matter. In any case, it was so light outside: only about six o'clock – was it? Possibly half past. The room was dark and cool but the sun around the back of the house had more hours to go before it sank. Now and then, a figure walked past the window. If they happened to have glanced in from the street, they'd have seen a loose circle of light thrown by the lamp. Inside it, the tiny scene: its circumference marked by a mobile hanging (twitching, turning), a laptop, a glass of water, overhung by a plant, the detail of a phone. They'd have seen an adult head in a posture of inclination. What was she doing? Thinking? Resting? Working? Something about the angle: she was concentrating. For some reason, she was clearly involved with what was going on in her arms.

The voice, cracking slightly, said: "Let me start from the place that you are very likely to already know":

Holding: the word itself "remembered its earlier contexts" – it carried in with it, to every new situation, all the ways it had been spoken about in the past.

Winnicott said: as you know, the "phrase holding the baby has a definite meaning in the English language; someone was cooperating with you over something, and then waltzed off, and you were left 'holding the baby.'"

It said: "By this we can see that holding is to take responsibility, if a person has a baby in their arms they are involved in a special way."

Rose shifted and pulled away, suddenly a bit too hot. Helen got rid of the blanket; they both looked up at the ceiling.

"Of course, some women get left holding the baby literally, in the sense that the father is unable to enjoy the part he has to play, and unable to share with the mother the great responsibility which a baby must always be to someone."

There was a pause.

The high voice said: "Or perhaps there is no father."

Helen leant forward to pick up her glass from the floor. Rose was squashed, momentarily, packed in. Helen took a long sip of water.

She lay back and Rose was released.

The voice resumed:

"You don't let people hold your baby if you feel it means nothing to them."

"A mother will not just take for granted that someone else is safe with the baby in her arms."

Again, the oddity of the phrasing, the redistribution of emphasis: taking the worry away from the baby, locating it in "that someone else" – whether or not *they* would be safe (whether she would be safe) with her baby in their arms (her own baby in her own arms).

"This would be to deny the meaning of it all."

The meaning of holding: to maintain, to sustain, to support. To stop and stay. To keep to and persist in. A situation involving an intentionality as well as the promise of a certain duration.

She sank back into the sofa – Rose's head in the crook of her arm. Rose cuffed her. She kicked with her leg and muttered out sounds. Getting squashed had roused her, now she needed to find her way back down into her settlement – into drifting.

In the best case, which is also the most ordinary case scenario, Winnicott said: "You are not anxious and so are not gripping too tight."

"You": it was an address intended for Helen.

It meant her: clearly, it intended her commonplace activity.

Looking after a baby.

Now it expanded to include other actions and situations, provisions of support.

Or, listening, she made it expand: she made it mean environment. Environments. It meant the room. The flat. Social situations. It intended the structures and participants that made co-living possible; viable and actually liveable.

"Lack of room is denial of life, and openness of space is affirmation of its potentiality," wrote John Dewey, in his lectures on the bookshelf.

"The very word 'breathing-space' suggests the choking, the oppression that results when things are constricted. Anger appears to be a reaction in protest against fixed limitation of movement."

"Room is roominess and a chance to be, live and move."

The limit-edge of the nest Helen made was proportional to her reach. The temperature of this zone within the room was warm for the moment, not too hot. The throw protected them from the true pattern of the sofa. It was a setting. A semi-bounded world possessed of details and volume, both gathered (composed) and gapped – sharing its roof with the ceiling. This small setting within the larger setting: it mattered a great deal how it was arranged.

"Overcrowding, even when it does not impede life, is irritating."

The feelings of being "cribbed and cabined." These were aesthetic feelings. But now there was a confusion, or interchange, between the aesthetic and social. Cabined and cribbed – this could feel, sometimes, like the predominant aesthetic of her days. It was part of her

carework (for herself and for Rose) to embrace it. To translate it when necessary into something like "cosiness," like "nestedness." Also, to push against it, to offset it with spaciousness, opening the back door in the kitchen to let the air in; regularly, regularly, summoning the energy to head back outside.

"What is true of space is true of time." A provision of room requires also a provision of time.

About them were just the ordinary house sounds. The living sounds, not too loud: hums and murmurs. For now, there was no treading from upstairs; a temporary reprieve from Helen's self-consciousness of that presence and power.

There were street sounds falling in from the outside.

Cars again. A throaty singing bird.

No builders. It was quiet; the builders had finished for the day.

People parking their cars, snatches of songs from their car radios, slamming car doors closed, coming home from work. The boy next door was sitting on the high back of the bench at the end of the street, chatting, interacting, laughing loudly (smoking discreetly) with a few of his friends.

Dewey: "we all need 'a space of time' in which to accomplish anything significant." Our life's projects. Tower-building, tower-collapsing, playing at anything, testing the possibilities of anything: collaboration, friendship, art-making, love.

But "space and time in experience are also" – "occupancy." And without "the third property, spacing," another word for *contrast*, "occupancy would be a jumble."

Place and position.

How we stand in relation to each other, and how these relations, by necessity, adjust, accommodate and, even in their apparent permanency, will always need to move. They matter, and are "determined by distribution of intervals through spacing . . ."

By proportions: proximities and distances. By rhythms: rest-breaks and changes.

Helen drew the blanket up again, this time arranging it over her knees.

"The feeling of energy and especially not just of energy in general but *of this or that power in the concrete* is connected to the rightness in placing."

"Things may be too far apart, too near together, or disposed at the wrong angle in relation to one another to allow for energy of action."

Helen shifted the pillow at her back, then adjusted her arm underneath Rose.

"Too much distance or too undefined an interval in a novel," for example, as likewise in a room, "sets attention wandering or puts it to sleep." Meanwhile, "incidents . . . treading on each other's heels detract from the force of them all."

Helen swallowed and looked in the direction of the window.

"Pauses are holes when they do not accentuate masses and define figures."

"Extension sprawls if it does not interact with place."

The principles of aesthetic composition extending and repeating – or were they prefiguring and re-grounding – the principles of social composition. The layout of a room. The form of a book. A novel: a source of suggestion (detailed speculation) as to how – in what kinds of real or invented spaces, and under what rhythmic conditions – it

might be possible for live creatures, with their ages and energies and competing authorities, their interests and their needs, to co-exist, to live together.

The glass was clear, which meant her view was stopped by the tree.

Winnicott resumed his lecture.

In the best-case, most ordinary holding scenario: "You are not afraid to throw the baby onto the floor." It was true: the point was, Helen herself felt supported. Which meant that, in the moment, she wasn't afraid.

"You adapt the pressure of your arms to the baby's needs, and you move slightly, and you perhaps make some sounds."

Helen shifted Rose from her breast to the place where her shoulder met her neck.

"There is warmth that comes from your breath and your skin, and the baby finds your holding to be good."

Rose relaxed. It was a good position. It meant I'm here.

The little phrase – there were times in the day when it meant everything. There were times when it meant nothing: just a banality of ongoing presence. Where else would either one of them be?

The high voice said: "Look at it imaginatively."

It said: "Here is the infant right at the beginning." A newcomer.

The baby is "a live creature."

Unexpectedly, here was Winnicott using John Dewey's phrase. Unexpectedly, or unsurprisingly: drawing a line between the laptop and the book on the shelf, a dotted line of connection between the two bodies of work.

She is apparently contained, "yet surrounded by space."

She doesn't know anything yet about that space surrounding her. She doesn't know that space around her is being maintained by you.

Consider: "The infant moves an elbow, a knee, or straightens out a little."

What happens? "The space has been crossed." "The infant has surprised the environment."

Now consider: "You who are holding the infant jump a little, because the door-bell rang, or the kettle boiled over, and again the space has been crossed. This time the environment has surprised the infant."

Such small events: a baby reaching out from their immediate surrounding space, making a tiny incursion into the larger space, touching at it and discovering a part of the wider world. Acting on it, meeting it: bringing to it their own newness and resistance. The world, making an incursion back into that intimate surrounding space, pressing into and opening it up, unsteadying it, before the compositional forces of holding adjust, and steady it again. The work of accommodation: providing steadiness and openness, ground and surprise.

The lecture asked: Who has taken the time to describe them?

Rose, Helen could sense, was breathing with soft regularity: she was falling. She was almost asleep. Helen's arms said: I'm still here.

"It is because the infant is being held that the baby in the space becomes ready, in the course of time, for the movement that surprises the world."

"And the infant who has found the world in this way becomes, in time, ready to welcome the surprises that the world has in store."

The world is surprising. It has undiscovered stores. It is not yet wholly given. There will be new gestures, new questions, new forms of life. The capacity to welcome them, to make room for them (to accommodate without crushing them), to learn from and be transformed by them depends on the provision of this "quiet yet live holding" – in this form. Then in all its further expected and unexpected, tested, and as yet unimagined forms.

The voice exclaimed: "How careful you are that the world shall not impinge before the infant has found it!"

The outburst caused anxiety to flood back in. Is this what careful is? Helen's eyes smarted. Was this careful enough?

If there was no one around to tell her, how was she supposed to know?

The short lecture was coming to an end:

"It might be thought that I have been trying to teach you now how to hold your baby. This seems to me far from the truth. I am trying to describe the various aspects of what you do . . . in order that you might recognize what you do."

The voice stopped talking.

HELEN LAY QUIETLY FOR A WHILE

On the sofa, waiting for Rose to fall deeply enough asleep, waiting a few more beats for it to feel safe to move, and their situation could present as sweet and easy, over-earnestly described and basically sentimental only to an eye determined not to see how it might figure and repeat other formal holding situations: social, environmental, architectural, pedagogical, institutional. How it might pertain to them without standing in for them, or claiming precedence over them, while also asking questions of them. Sweet and easy – "falsely harmonious." But possibly only to a sensibility determined to gloss over the stamina and creativity that all forms of "live" holding likewise involve: the struggle to maintain them, the effort to keep going on with them. Tolerating the collapses and the breaks, committed to reestablishing the sorts of environments that hold steady enough and prove flexible enough to accommodate someone else's discoveries: the provision of a mutually invested setting to imagine out from.

Stay a moment, said Rose's sleeping body. Don't move yet. Helen rounded her shoulders, put her mouth to the place where Rose's hairline met her brow. "The way a body holds itself, the many ways it holds itself, on many different scales of action, and the way it holds the world is cumulative. All the holding you have experienced, all the holding of you and by you, moves within and through your holding of yourself and has a part in your holding onto something," wrote the collaborative energies of Madeline Gins and Arakawa quoting Winnicott and Margaret A. Ribble, author of *The Rights of Infants,* in their book of architectural-life philosophy. Helen held onto Rose as well as her own, different thought.

ROSE WAS FULLY, DEEPLY ASLEEP

Now she was able to come up to standing. Helen bounced-walked from the living to the bedroom with Rose against her chest, one hand behind her neck, one hand under her bum. The floor, the carpet, was thin and resistant, but in places (in odd patches) it was softer, it seemed to sink with her steps. She pulled down the blackout blinds in the bedroom, designed to simulate the dead of night. She returned to the hall to put on the hall light, to offset the darkness with a fainter glow. Over the basket where Rose slept, she bent, using the lever of her own body to bring Rose's down into gentle contact with the micro-territory of the mattress. The timing of this could not be planned ahead. It depended on a local impulse – knowing, or feeling, when the right interval was reached. She lowered, tentatively, bending at the knees, hinging at the waist, while, in the living room, the mobile reacted to the small current of air they'd left in their wake.

LATER: EXPANSION

Rose will wake up. Almost to the dot, she will connect two sleep cycles, making one magnificent three-hour continuity with no breaks. And then, after those hours of restorative sleeping together, she will wake, wake Helen, starting up their co-presence again. With beautiful timing Rebba will arrive just as Helen and Rose are stirring: 9 P.M. or so . . . texting ahead and tapping on the window, not ringing the bell. Rebba will make filled pasta. So much pasta! She will hold Rose and talk to Rose, show her things, allowing Helen to eat on the sofa, at her own pace, with both hands free. Helen and Rebba will talk, narrating their days, passing Rose between them. They'll lie out, all three of them, on the mat, contemplate the ceiling.

Rose will smile for Helen. Then for Rebba. Then for the mobile, then for Helen all over again. It will be like this: luminosity succeeding luminosity. Event, event, event, event.

Towards midnight, Rebba will take out the bins. The lights will have switched off upstairs so she'll deliberately, provocatively, walk the full circumference of the garden, holding the bulging bin-bag aloft like a flag. Making Helen laugh, also whisper furiously. She'll do a star-jump, bin-bag in hand, it threatening to split. They'll stand together, Helen leaning in the doorframe, holding Rose, Rebba a little way out in the garden, which will be dark and green, still holding all the moisture from the rain, using her weight to tilt and wobble at one of the paving stones as they continue, in quieter voices, to converse. First without thinking, then realising what she is doing, she'll point it out to Helen: potentially, these stones, or at least one or two of them, could be lifted. Look, she'll declare, then restate in a stage whisper, they're *asking* to be lifted. Immediately underneath there'll be sand. But presumably deeper than that, there'll be earth. They'll

make plans. Open, imaginative, loose kinds of plans along with more concrete, to be actioned-in-the-coming-days kinds of plans. Rose will sleep again, this time against Rebba, her face in her neck – with Helen sharing all the tricks they'll use together to carefully put her down. They'll talk further – further and further: And why not let the day end like this? On conversation. In continued conversation, with what they meant to each other expanding and deepening, allowing for Rose.

and for now Rose was asleep in it. Helen thought: I'll just lie down next to her. She considered going back through to the living room – to go on with her novel; Rebba was coming later and had not yet arrived. But the desire to lie down was stronger.

She lay down next to Rose.

She listened out for her. Her breathing.

She folded her hand around the plaited rim of the sturdy wicker basket.

Rose's breath – or was it her own: it made a steady noise.

She thought and felt a number of things. But these feeling-thoughts were very private.

She thought about the night to come, the days to come. About lengthening and how to. About carrying on; about contrast as the only chance of continuance; about adjustment, interference, capacity, and tolerance. "Disturbing the medium so that it may travel differently."

Her eyelids grew heavy.

She felt the room shift, keel ever so slightly, and turn.

She lifted her hand to reach in towards Rose. Her reach was a SPIRAL, pushing forward whilst also turning back on itself, going on, around and around, though always on a different trajectory, which meant that she never reached in quite the same way, nor landed her hand in quite the same place.

She let go of the basket and rolled over, turning towards the open vistas of her own protected mental space, scrunching her eyes, relaxing her mouth.

Her body dropped.

Then it jerked as it remembered the bed-support.

A soft blankness opened its arms.

She was dispersing.

The blankness was what allowed her to open. She yielded to it and gave in to becoming dispersed. For a moment, she was DOTS.

She was rising, falling. Heaving, and rolling. Becoming-UNDU-LATION.

The blankness gathered all the angles and circles, the different shapes of her up. It composed her. She shifted position and it recom-posed her. It took her in its arms and carried her forward, in its own mysterious directions.

Rose twitched, muttered. But managed to stay low, somewhere just beneath the thin sheet of her slumbers.

Helen sank under it too.

Now, separately, they were both fast asleep.

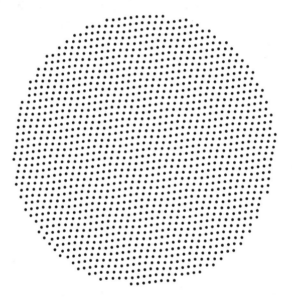

SOURCES

Hans Christian Andersen: the edition of *The Snow Queen* recalled in the section titled NAMES is "a new adapted version" by Naomi Lewis, illustrated by Errol Le Cain (Middlesex: Kestrel Books, 1979).

Mikhail Bakhtin: the description of the dynamic between Helen and Rose makes use of Bakhtin's vocabulary with a view to (re)activating, in this living-room setting, a number of his key ideas as they are quoted and contextualised in *Mikhail Bakhtin: Creation of a Prosaics* by Gary Saul Morson and Caryl Emerson (Stanford University Press, 1990), and *Dialogism: Bakhtin and his World* by Michael Holquist (London: Routledge, 1990). Specifically: ideas of constitutive responsivity, addressivity, and "existence as dialogue"; the "illusion of closed-off bodies"; the idyll; getting "a read on oneself" via the other's response; Helen's discovery that the ideas that pertained most directly to her seemed always to come from somewhere (someone) else; ethical decision-making; the "surplus view" – how what Tom is unable to observe about himself (since he has his face in the turf) can only be provided by someone else (the sky is blue); the way words carry with them, into every new situation, all the ways they have been spoken about in the past; on "novelness" (the name Bakhtin gave "to *a form of knowledge* that can most powerfully put different orders of experience – each of which claims authority on the basis of its ability to exclude others – into dialogue with each other") and surprisingness ("such impulses are only possible in a world with an open future and in a world where everything important is not already over") – both are quotations from Holquist's book. The line "the world addressing itself to her in a riot of potential messages" (in a section titled ROSE) repurposes Holquist's summary of Bakhtin's "dialogism" (the original line reads: "Existence is addressed to me as a riot of inchoate potential messages, which at this level of abstraction may be said to come to individual persons much as stimuli from the natural environment come to individual organisms.") The line "There is never any problem, ever, which can be confined within a single framework" is from Fernand Braudel, an influence on Bakhtin, quoted in *Mikhail Bakhtin: Creation of a Prosaics*.

Roland Barthes: the title of this book, *The Long Form*, quotes directly from Barthes's *The Preparation of the Novel*, translated by Kate Briggs (New York: Columbia University Press, 2011), where throughout the phrase works as a synonym for the novel. In the same lecture course, Barthes conflates the question of length in writing with the question of continuation in life (how to piece things together, how to negotiate or invent transitions between apparently disparate parts; in other words, how to carry on). The section titled

ONCE IN A LIFETIME engages with Barthes's thinking on the shortest form (for him, the haiku) and whether it can ever be expanded. The definitions of the verb "to hold" in the section titled LENGTH – AND ENTERTAINMENT indirectly refer to Barthes's listing of all the possible definitions of "tenir" in the seminar titled "Comment tenir un discours?" (How to Hold Forth?) in Barthes's *How to Live Together*, translated by Kate Briggs (New York: Columbia University Press, 2013), as does the idea of "a narrative power linked to a persistence that she was able to sustain only for as long as she wasn't interrupted" and the image of a narration rising in increments (like a meter ticking up in a taxi). The section title THE ONE WHO WAITS is a quotation from *A Lover's Discourse*, translated by Richard Howard (London: Vintage, 2010).

John Dewey: quotations of the lectures titled "The Live Creature," "The Natural History of Form," "The Organization of Energies," and "The Common Substance of the Arts" are from the Perigree paperback edition of *Art as Experience* (New York and London: Penguin, 2005).

Buchi Emecheta: *Nowhere to Play*, a children's book "based on a story by her twelve-year-old daughter Christy," with illustrations by Peter Archer (London and New York: Allison & Busby, 1980). Also, *The Joys of Motherhood* (London: Heinemann, 2008); *Second-Class Citizen* (London: Heinemann, 1994); *Head Above Water: An Autobiography* (London and Nigeria: Omenala Press, 2018).

Henry Fielding: quotations of *The History of Tom Jones, A Foundling* are from the 1996 Oxford World's Classics Edition, edited by John Bender and Simon Stern (Oxford University Press, 1998). The description of Fielding's feeling that there "was something ungentlemanly, unmagnanimous and snooping about [Samuel] Richardson's scrutinies of inner consciousness" is from Doreen Roberts's introduction to the Wordsworth Classics Edition (1999). Fielding's "An Essay on Conversation" is downloadable from public-library.uk

E. M. Forster: quotations of *Aspects of the Novel* are from the Penguin Classics edition, edited by Oliver Stallybrass (London and New York: Penguin, 2000).

Madeline Gins: the section titles GUESSING AND MOVEMENT IN THE LIVING ROOM and AN ENVIRONMENT WITH ITS OWN SUGGESTIONS are lines from Gins's *WORD RAIN (or A Discursive Introduction to the Intimate Philosophical Investigations of G,R,E,T,A G,A,R,B,O, It Says)*, a facsimile of which is reproduced in *The Saddest Thing Is That I Have Had to Use Words: A Madeline Gins Reader*, edited by Lucy Ives (New York: Siglio Press, 2020). The floor-plan which appears in this book directly references the floor-plan

that opens *WORD RAIN*. The notion of a "landing-site," the phrase "parsing the room for a landing-site," the understanding of housing as a "life or death matter," the thinking of the park as "an infrastructure made from a great range of outdoor materials. Surfaces and smaller settings on which the rhythms and inclinations of very different kinds of people have been invited to act (on which they have a renewable invitation to act)," and the passage on holding are all direct or indirect quotations from *Architectural Body*, Gin's collaborative work with Arakawa (Tuscaloosa: The University of Alabama Press, 2002).

Russell Hoban: the novel quoted in the section titled ROSE ("Could it be that all the people who worry so much about children – are really worrying about themselves?") is *Turtle Diary* (London: Penguin Classics, 2021).

Ursula Le Guin: the section titled BRINGING THE ENERGY HOME is a line from Le Guin's *The Carrier Bag Theory of Fiction* (London: Ignota Press, 2020), as is "A leaf a gourd a shell a net a bag a sling a sack a bottle a pot a box a container. A holder. A recipient."

Penelope Leach: the baby-care book Helen borrows from the library is the fourth edition of Leach's *Your Baby & Child* (London: Dorling Kindersley Ltd, 2003). The phrase "the baby can't see your face but she can hear your heart," the advice on how to hold a new-born, and the thinking on love in the sections titled A SIMPLE THING and SQUARES (BOXES) respectively all quote from Leach's deeply philosophical work.

Bruno Munari: the shapes that appear throughout *The Long Form* were drawn by Ray O'Meara and reference Munari's mobiles from the 1930s. The section titled THE MOBILE COMPOSITION quotes from "The Useless Machines" in his *Design as Art*, translated by Patrick Creagh (London: Penguin Classics, 2008).

Jean Paulhan: *The Flowers of Tarbes, or Terror in Literature*, translated by Michael Syrotinski (Champaign: University of Illinois Press, 2006).

Gertrude Stein: attributed quotations, the name "Helen Strong" together with the phrasings "No one understands this but I do," "All about all about flowers," "Allow me, allow me to participate," "Now an arrangement," "People die and in and out of order," and the section titles ALLOW FLOWERS and EVERYONE IS AN AUTHORITY are phrasings drawn from *A Novel of Thank You*, with an introduction by Steven Meyer (Normal: Dalkey Archive Press, 2004).

Rosmarie Waldrop: in the 2019 introduction to the reissue of Waldrop's *The Hanky of Pippin's Daughter,* Ben Lerner describes Waldrop's "formal strategy" of "destabilizing section headings" as producing "a standoff between flow and fragmentation." This titling strategy has been repurposed in *The Long Form* with the hope of achieving a similar effect: I wanted to make "the novel stutter" (as Lerner puts it), while exploring how these stallings and breaks could also be what "allow it to go on" (St Louis: Dorothy, a publishing project, 2019).

D. W. Winnicott: the explanation of the phrase "ordinary devotion" ("I am not ashamed by what is implied by these words") is from a talk titled "The Ordinary Devoted Mother," as is the story of finding digs as a medical student. The baby thinking of itself as a circle ("A diagram of myself could have been a circle") is from "The Newborn and its Mother." These original broadcasts are all published, along with the talk titled "Knowing and Learning" quoted in HOLD; HOLDING in *Babies and Their Mothers* (Cambridge, MA: Perseus Publishing, 1987). They can be listened to online here: "Index of Available Audio Recordings" in Robert Adès (ed.) *The Collected Works of D. W. Winnicott: Volume 12, Appendices and Bibliographies* (New York, 2016; online edn, Oxford Academic, 1 Dec 2016), https://doi.org/10.1093/med:psych/9780190271442.00 3.0011, accessed 8 Feb. 2023. The phrasings "There is no such thing as a baby" and "a baby alone doesn't exist" are drawn from "There is no such thing as a baby. The mother-child couple at the centre of Winnicott's Practice" by Jean-Pierre Lehmann in *Journal de la psychanalyse de l'enfant* (Vol. 5, Issue 2, 2015). The idea that the baby invents her mother, or the mother-parts she needs, is also explored in Nuar Alsadir's *Animal Joy* (London: Fitzcarraldo, 2022).

OTHER WORKS INFORMING THIS WORK:

Hannah Arendt: "Action" (excerpt) from *The Human Condition,* republished in *Revolution: A Reader,* selected and annotated by Lisa Robertson and Matthew Stadler (Publication Studio Bordeaux, 2015) and *Arendt, Natality and Biopolitics: Toward Democratic Plurality and Reproductive Justice* by Rosalyn Diprose and Ewa Plonowska Ziarek (Edinburgh University Press, 2018).

Henry Andersen and Laura Herman (eds): *The Floor Is Uneven. Does It Slope?* (Milan: Mousse Publishing, 2021).

Isobel Armstrong: the line "the potential for responding to and making the aesthetic is in everyone" is a quotation from Armstrong's discussion of Dewey in *The Radical Aesthetic* (Oxford: Blackwell, 2000). The phrase "social

creativity" is from her *Novel Politics: Democratic Imaginations in Nineteenth-Century Fiction* (Oxford University Press, 2016).

Nancy Armstrong: *How Novels Think: The Limits of Individualism from 1719–1900* (New York: Columbia University Press, 2005). The section titled HELEN STRONG draws on Armstrong's discussion of Louis Althusser's mechanism of "hailing" or "interpellation" ("Hey, you there!").

Sheridan Baker: "Henry Fielding and the Cliché," *Criticism*, Vol. 1, No. 4 (Fall 1959).

Vincent Barletta: *Rhythm: Form and Dispossession* (Chicago and London: University of Chicago Press, 2020).

Lisa Baraitser: attributed quotations as well as the play on "start" (starting something new and being startled) and the wondering at how a newborn baby, so recently encountered, could so soon absent herself (via sleep) are drawn from *Maternal Encounters: The Ethics of Interruption* (London: Routledge, 2009).

Andrea Brady: "The Determination of Love" (Journal of the British Academy, 2018).

Alexander Beecroft: "Rises of The Novel, Ancient and Modern" in *The Cambridge Companion to the Novel*, edited by Eric Bulson (Cambridge and New York: Cambridge University Press, 2018).

Andrew Bennett and Nicholas Royle: the idea of creating a world and holding it steady enough for someone else to believe in, along with the phrase "unusual knowledge" (as a description of the magic of third-person narration) are drawn from *This Thing Called Literature: Reading, Thinking, Writing* (London: Routledge, 2015).

Jane Bennett: *Vibrant Matter: A Political Ecology of Things* (Durham and London: Duke University Press, 2010).

Lauren Berlant: "A Properly Political Concept of Love: Three Approaches in Ten Pages," *Cultural Anthropology*, Vol. 26. Issue. 4 (November 2011).

Barbara Bolt: the notion of "co-creating the conditions" for art to appear (in the section titled LECTURE ONE: THE LIVE CREATURE) is drawn from Bolt's

"Material Thinking and the Agency of Matter" in *Studies in Material Thinking*, Vol. 1, No. 1 (April 2007), which I read thanks to Linus Bonduelle.

Wilfred Bion: the proposition that Helen is translating Rose, allowing her thoughts entry into her own mental space and offering "out the commonplace, general ideas of sleepiness, of hunger, of warmth, of happiness, frustration or pain as descriptors – no doubt inadequate descriptors – for the range and nuance and total novelty of what she actually felt" draws on Bion's description of a formative interpersonal process he called "maternal reverie."

Wayne C. Booth: *The Rhetoric of Fiction*, second edition (Chicago and London: University of Chicago Press, 1983).

Rachel Bowlby: *A Child of One's Own: Parental Stories* (Oxford University Press, 2013).

Peter Boxall: the section titled MOVING ON is in close conversation with the "Making Time Matter" chapter in *The Value of the Novel* (Cambridge University Press, 2015); the proposition that the novel "allows us to 'know' time in a way that no other mode of thinking can" quotes Boxall quoting from Mark Currie's *About Time: Narrative, Fiction and the Philosophy of Time* (Edinburgh University Press, 2006).

Brigid Brophy: the section title ENTER SELF-CONSCIOUSNESS is a quotation from Brophy's *Prancing Novelist: A Defence of Fiction in the Form of a Critical Biography in Praise of Ronald Firbank* (London: Macmillan, 1973).

Judith Butler: love figured as a kind of slope (in the section titled WAIT: "He was all incline, leaning, stretching, sliding and she was the direction") and the phrase "falsely harmonious" (in the section titled HELEN LAY QUIETLY FOR A WHILE) are informed by "Leaning Out, Caught in the Fall: Interdependency and Ethics in Cavarero" in *Toward a Feminist Ethics of Nonviolence* edited by Timothy J. Huzar and Clare Woodford (New York: Fordham University Press, 2021).

Adriana Cavarero: *Inclinations: A Critique of Rectitude* (Stanford University Press, 2016).

Helen Charman: "Tenancy" and "Tenancy Project'" https://mapmagazine.co.uk/tenancy

Robert L. Chibka: "Taking the 'Serious' Seriously: The Introductory Chapters of *Tom Jones*," *The Eighteenth Century*, Spring 1990, Vol. 31, No. 1.

Céline Condorelli: *Support Structures* (London: Sternberg Press, 2009): the discussion of a discovery of a baby discovered in a bed and its production of the capacity to care is in conversation with Jan Verwoert's contribution to this volume, titled "Personal Support: *How to Care*."

Jonathan Culler: "Omniscience," *Narrative*, Vol. 12, no. 1 (January 2004). On how poets "From the Greeks to the moderns . . . call upon a universe they hope will prove responsive," like Helen asking things of the river, see *Theory of the Lyric* (Cambridge, MA and London: Harvard University Press, 2015).

Rachel Cusk: "How to Write Fiction: On Point of View," *The Guardian*, October 17, 2011.

Nicholas Dames: "The Chapter: A History," *The New Yorker* (October, 2014) and "The History of the Chapter (with Nicholas Dames)" https://www.how-toreadpodcast.com/nicholas-dames-the-history-of-the-chapter/

Craig David: *Magic* ft. Yxng Bane (2018)

Moyra Davey, ed. *Mother Reader: Essential Writings on Motherhood* (New York: Seven Stories Press, 2001).

Gilles Deleuze: the section titled REBBA ("What is the word for this protected, enlarging existence with someone you really like?") draws on Deleuze's description of his friendship with Michel Foucault in *Dialogues II*, written with Clare Parnet, translated by H. Tomlinson and B. Habberjam: "But what precisely is an encounter with someone you like? Is it an encounter with someone, or with the animals that come to populate you, or with the ideas that take you over, the movements which move you, the sounds which run through you? And how do you separate these things?" (London and New York: Continuum, 2002); the description of Helen as a gang or a little group is likewise inspired by Deleuze; the question "What would it mean to claim *to already know* what a human agent is capable of?" in the section LIFE-LIKE references Spinoza's claim that "We do not even know what a body is capable of . . ." which Deleuze discusses at length in *Expressionism in Philosophy: Spinoza*, translated by Martin Joughin (New York: Zone Books, 1990).

Charles Dickens: *Our Mutual Friend* (1864–65); when naming Rose's toes, Helen has in mind the chapter titled "Mr. Boffin at the Temple."

Josephine Donovan: *Women and the Rise of the Novel, 1405–1726* (New York: St Martin's Press, 1999).

Margaret Anne Doody: *The True Story of the Novel* (London: HarperCollins, 1997).

Margaret Drabble: *The Millstone* (London: Penguin, 2017).

Rivka Galchen: *Little Labors* (New York: New Directions, 2016).

Catherine Gallagher: "The Rise of Fictionality," *The Novel, Vol 1*, edited by Franco Moretti (Princeton and Oxford: Princeton University Press, 2006).

John Gardner: *The Art of Fiction: Notes on Craft for Young Writers* (London: Vintage Books, 1991); it is his proposition that fiction is like a "vivid and continuous dream," which works for as long as the illusion remains unbroken.

William H. Gass: *Fiction and the Figures of Life* (Boston: David R. Godine, 1978). On naming and characters, he writes: "to create a character is to give meaning to an unknown X; it is *absolutely* to *define*; and since nothing in life corresponds to these Xs, their reality is borne by their name. They *are*, where it *is*."

Édouard Glissant: *Poetics of Relation*, translated by Betsy Wing (Ann Arbor: University of Michigan Press, 1997); "the right to opacity" is Glissant's phrase.

Erving Goffman: *Interaction Ritual: Essays on Face-to-Face Behavior* (New York: Pantheon, 1982); the phrase "conversation as social involvement" is Goffman's.

Robert Hass: *A Little Book on Form: An Exploration into the Formal Imagination of Poetry* (New York: HarperCollins, 2017); Hass's opening paragraph to the chapter titled "Two" has been essential to the thinking in this book: "One line is a form in the sense that any gesture is a form. Two lines introduce the idea of form as the energy of relation."

Roman Ingarden: *The Literary Work of Art*, translated by George G. Grabowicz (Evanston: Northwestern University Press, 1973); the descriptions of the

mobile as "held in readiness" with "spots of indeterminacy" speak back to this work.

Wolfgang Iser: "The Role of the Reader in Fielding's *Joseph Andrews* and *Tom Jones*," *The Implied Reader: Patterns of Communication in Prose Fiction from Bunyan to Beckett* (Baltimore: Johns Hopkins University Press, 1974).

Mary Jane Jacob: *Dewey for Artists* (Chicago and London: The University of Chicago Press, 2018).

F. Kaplan: "Fielding's Novel about Novels: the 'Prefaces' and the 'Plot' of *Tom Jones*," *Studies in English Literature 1500–1900*, Vol. 13, No. 3 (Summer 1973).

Sarah Knott: *Mother: An Unconventional History* (New York: Picador, 2020).

Catherine Lanone: "*Aspects of the Novel*, or E. M. Forster's (In)formal Criticism," *Études britanniques contemporaines*, 33 (2008). The line "Disturbing the medium so that it may travel differently [with sensitivity and responsiveness]" is from Lanone's expansive reading of Forster.

Sophie Lewis: *Full Surrogacy Now: Feminism Against Family* (London and New York: Verso, 2019).

Clarice Lispector: "One Hundred Years of Forgiveness" (this is the story about a little girl stealing roses) from *The Complete Short Stories of Clarice Lispector*, translated by Katrina Dodson and edited by Benjamin Moser (New York: New Directions, 2015).

Marielle Macé: *Le Genre littéraire*, an introduction to genre theory which opens with Paulhan's sign at the entrance to the park (Paris: Flammarion, 2013). In the section titled JUNE, the sentence which begins, "They brought new ideas to them: ideas about how to occupy and make sense of their spaces . . ." translates some of the propositions in Macé's book on den-making, *Nos cabanes* (Lagrasse: Éditions Verdier, 2019).

Carole Maso: *Break Every Rule: Essays on Language, Longing, and Moments of Desire* (Washington, D.C: Counterpoint, 2000). The essay "Notes of a Lyric Artist Working in Prose: A Lifelong Conversation with Myself Entered Midway" shares many preoccupations with *The Long Form*, especially its concep-

tion of the novel as "a certain spaciousness. There would be room and time for it all." She writes: "The novel is something, even when stopped, that is continuous." Maso is also a reader of *A Novel of Thank You* (a different essay in her collection shares its title and is built from lines drawn from Stein's work).

Guy de Maupassant: "Le Roman" ("The Novel") first published as a preface to *Pierre et Jean* (1887), translated by Clara Bell as "Of the Novel" (1902) and accessible online at: https://en.wikisource.org/wiki/Pierre_and_Jean_ (Bell,_1902)

Maurice Merleau-Ponty: *Phenomenology of Perception*, translated by Colin Smith (London and New York: Routledge, 2000). The descriptions of the world from the viewpoint of Rose were especially informed by the chapter "Sense Experience."

Lukas Meßner: "midland," a poem published in *Short Pieces That Move* by students of the MFA in Fine Art at the Piet Zwart Institute, Rotterdam (2020). The section titled ONCE IN A LIFETIME borrows the last two lines of this poem, swapping "drums" for "trumpets."

Christian Metz: "Notes toward a Phenomenology of the Narrative," *The Narrative Reader*, edited by Martin McQuillan (London and New York: Routledge, 2000).

Cheryl L. Nixon: *Novel Definitions: An Anthology of Commentary on the Novel, 1688–1815* (Toronto: Broadview Press, 2009).

Alice Oswald and Paul Keegan: *Gigantic Cinema: A Weather Anthology* (London: Jonathan Cape, 2020). The description of the fridge chart as a weather report "written by someone bareheaded" with "no clear plot" draws on Oswald's preface to this volume.

Lola Olufemi: *Experiments in Imagining Otherwise* (London: Hajar Press, 2021). Olufemi's endnote "on the child" is one of the most powerful, eloquent, and persuasive interventions in the debates over children – who "has" them, what it means to "have" them or to want them or not, what kind of world we are collectively providing for the children who are born, nevertheless – that I have read.

Holly Pester: *Eclogues for Idle Workers* (London: Distance No Object, 2019). "*Tell the universe it must be fucking kidding me*" recollects a line from this brilliant sequence of poems.

Jacques Rancière: *The Politics of Literature*, translated by Julie Rose (London: Polity, 2011).

Denise Riley: *Impersonal Passion: Language as Affect* (Durham and London: Duke University Press, 2005). The section titled NAMES is in conversation with "Your Name Which Isn't Yours"; the line "bestow a fate" is a direct quotation from Riley's essay.

Sara Ruddick: *Maternal Thinking: Towards a Politics of Peace* (London: The Women's Press, Ltd, 1990). The point that a recognition of vulnerability is not the same thing as a response to it (it is not yet taking on the responsibility for protecting it) is Ruddick's, as is the description of mothering as "one historical name" for the work that, for as long as there are children, must be undertaken by *someone*. It is also Ruddick who separates out the three phases to this work: pregnancy, labour, and child-care; at each stage the work is different and could in principle (and in practice) be undertaken by someone else.

Michael Schmidt: *The Novel: A Biography* (Cambridge, MA and London: The Belknap Press of Harvard University Press, 2014). The story that Henry Fielding once met a real Tom Jones is from this book.

Daniel N. Stern: *Diary of a Baby: What Your Child Sees, Feels, and Experiences* (New York: Basic Books, 1990). One of the rhythm-descriptions of breast-feeding ("the initial sharp and short, rapid tugs giving way to an easier, calmer feeding rhythm") and what happens for Rose when Helen's face goes momentarily blank are informed by passages in this book.

Philip Stevick: *The Chapter in Fiction: Theories of Narrative Division* (Syracuse University Press, 1970) and "On Fielding Talking," *College Literature* Vol. 1, No. 1 (Winter 1974).

Preti Taneja: *Aftermath* (Oakland: Transit, 2021). Of all the essential ideas, questions, provocations, and laments composing this book, this passage (which to my mind resonates with and renews the politics of John Dewey): "Now she starts dreaming of different possibilities and worlds; a way not to have the question of what 'art' be consistently considered answered as *a good, a luxury*, but instead consider it an essential part of human development; and of an equal society [. . .]."

Lionel Trilling: *The Liberal Imagination* (New York: New York Review Books, 2008).

Isabel Waidner: "The British novel reproduces white middle-class values and aesthetics" (an interview in *The New Statesman*, UK edition, November 3, 2021). The question "Do we already know (What would it mean to claim to already know? And, therefore, to use the novel as a mechanism never to expand on but merely to confirm and repeatedly reproduce?) what 'an agent' (a human agent, a live creature, living out their own intensive version of 'ordinary,' uniquely situated life) is capable of?" in the section titled LIFE-LIKE references this comment from Waidner: "I have come to think of the British novel as a – if not *the* – technology for the reproduction of white middle-class values, aesthetics and a certain type of 'acceptable' nationalism."

Ian Watt: *The Rise of the Novel: Studies in Defoe, Richardson and Fielding* (London: Bodley Head, 2015).

T. H. White: *The Sword in the Stone* (London: HarperCollins, 2008). The section titled SWIMMING, especially the neck-technique and the colour of the river (like beer), draws from the scene in which Wart is transformed into a perch.

James Wood: *How Fiction Works* (New York: Picador, 2009). The use of "possible person" as a synonym for "a fictional character" comes from Wood's book.

Virginia Woolf: in *The Years* it rains, impartially, everywhere and on everyone: "Women in childbirth heard the doctor say to the midwife, 'It's raining.'" The character named North says: "Contrast [. . .] remembering something he had read. 'The only form of continuity . . .'" (London: Penguin Books, 1998). In *The Voyage Out* Rachel says: "'Does it ever seem to you [. . .] that the world is composed of great blocks of matter, and that we're nothing but patches of light' – she looked at the soft spots of sun wavering over the carpet and up the wall – 'like that?'" (London: Penguin Books, 2019). Also, *The Pargiters: The Novel-Essay Portion of The Years*, edited by Mitchell A. Leaska (New York and London: Harvest, 1978).

FIGURES

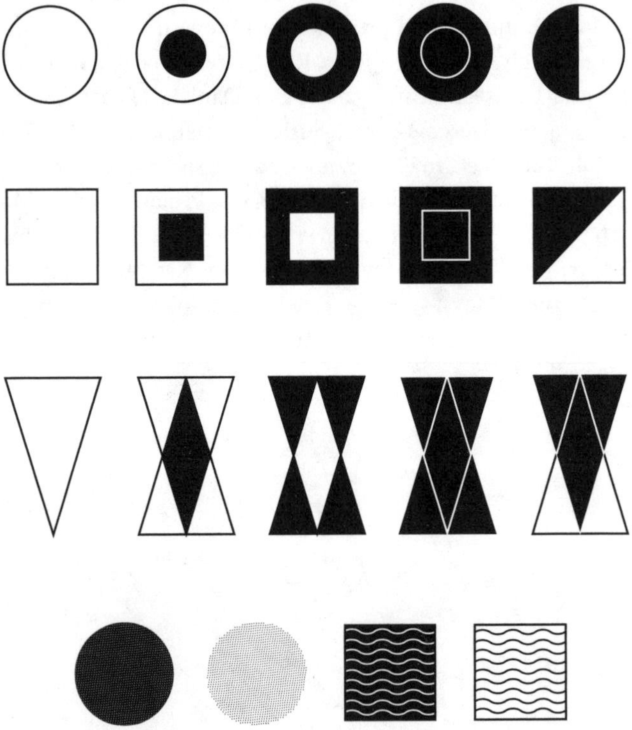

ACKNOWLEDGEMENTS

The main intention of this novel is to say thank you, wrote Gertrude Stein. Likewise, immense gratitude to the Windham-Campbell Prizes for the unexpected provision of time and space. Thank you, also, unendingly, to Jacques, Joely, Ray, Clare, Rosie, Danielle, Marty, Lucy, Anna-Louise, Moosje, Daisy, Peter, Daniela, Natasha, Katarina, Sarah, Paul, Francesco, Annie, Susie, Emmeline, Nienke, Raluca, Clara, Lili, Tom, Jack, my Mum, my Dad, my sister Chloe and my sisters Erica and Hannah. In loving memory of Professor Laura Marcus (March 7, 1956–September 22, 2021), whose beautiful mind this was always written toward. In loving memory of Kev "BB" Banks (September 5, 1981–May 15, 2022), forever grateful for your time, your timing, your grace, and your cool. This book is dedicated to Anthony, Arthur, and Sam.

ABOUT THE AUTHOR

Kate Briggs grew up in Somerset, UK, and lives and works in Rotterdam, NL, where she founded and co-runs the writing and publishing project "Short Pieces That Move." She is the translator of two volumes of Roland Barthes's lecture and seminar notes at the Collège de France: *The Preparation of the Novel* and *How to Live Together*, both published by Columbia University Press. *The Long Form* follows *This Little Art*, a narrative essay on the practice of translation. In 2021, Briggs was awarded a Windham-Campbell Prize.

1. Renee Gladman *Event Factory*
2. Barbara Comyns *Who Was Changed and Who Was Dead*
3. Renee Gladman *The Ravickians*
4. Manuela Draeger *In the Time of the Blue Ball* (tr. Brian Evenson)
5. Azareen Van der Vliet Oloomi *Fra Keeler*
6. Suzanne Scanlon *Promising Young Women*
7. Renee Gladman *Ana Patova Crosses a Bridge*
8. Amina Cain *Creature*
9. Joanna Ruocco *Dan*
10. Nell Zink *The Wallcreeper*
11. Marianne Fritz *The Weight of Things* (tr. Adrian Nathan West)
12. Joanna Walsh *Vertigo*
13. Nathalie Léger *Suite for Barbara Loden* (tr. Natasha Lehrer & Cécile Menon)
14. Jen George *The Babysitter at Rest*
15. Leonora Carrington *The Complete Stories*
16. Renee Gladman *Houses of Ravicka*
17. Cristina Rivera Garza *The Taiga Syndrome* (tr. Aviva Kana & Suzanne Jill Levine)
18. Sabrina Orah Mark *Wild Milk*
19. Rosmarie Waldrop *The Hanky of Pippin's Daughter*
20. Marguerite Duras *Me & Other Writing* (tr. Olivia Baes & Emma Ramadan)
21. Nathalie Léger *Exposition* (tr. Amanda DeMarco)
22. Nathalie Léger *The White Dress* (tr. Natasha Lehrer)
23. Cristina Rivera Garza *New and Selected Stories* (tr. Sarah Booker, et al)
24. Caren Beilin *Revenge of the Scapegoat*
25. Amina Cain *A Horse at Night: On Writing*
26. Giada Scodellaro *Some of Them Will Carry Me*
27. Pip Adam *The New Animals*
28. Kate Briggs *The Long Form*